26

STORIES OF RISK AND ABANDON FROM **ECOTONE**'S FIRST DECADE

ASTORIA TO ZION

Foreword by BEN FOUNTAIN

LOOKOUT BOOKS
University of North Carolina Wilmington

First printing, March 2014

Cover design by Stitch Design Co.
Interior design by Becky Eades, Heather Hammerbeck, Kathleen Jones, John McShea, and Katie Prince for The Publishing Laboratory

LIBRARY OF CONGRESS CATALOGING-IN-PUBLICATION DATA

Astoria to Zion : 26 stories of risk and abandon from Ecotone's first decade / foreword by Ben Fountain.
pages cm
Selected short stories originally published in the periodical, Ecotone.
Includes bibliographical references and index.
ISBN 978-0-9849000-9-1 (pbk. original : alk. paper) — ISBN 978-1-940596-00-6 (e-book)
1. Short stories, American. 2. American fiction—21st century.
I. Fountain, Ben. II. Ecotone (Wilmington, N.C.)
PS659.2.A88 2014
813'.010806—dc23
2013039328

Lookout Books gratefully acknowledges support from the University of North Carolina Wilmington and the National Endowment for the Arts.

Printed in Michigan by McNaughton & Gunn, an FSC Certified company

Lookout Books | Department of Creative Writing
University of North Carolina Wilmington
601 South College Road
Wilmington, NC 28403
lookout.org

CONTENTS

FOREWORD: IN FAVOR OF PLACE

Ben Fountain

SOME YEARS AGO I MET an American who'd lived in Senegal for a time, a woman who told me in passing of a traditional Senegalese greeting that's stayed with me ever since. *Nanga def?* Are you here? *Manga fi rek*. I am here only. In other words, my person is here and my full attention too, flesh and spirit, body and soul, the whole package. *I am here only*. For years I've carried those loaded, seemingly simple words in my mind, years that have happened to coincide with the rise of the Internet, smart phones, laptops, downloadable music and movies, Twitter, Bluetooth, Google glasses, and all the rest of it, the avalanching culture of technology that makes it easier than ever—makes it, in fact, the default human condition—to be anywhere but *here only*, at the particular point in space where one's body is located.

How about this for a salutation suited to our time, more of a warning than a greeting: I am here vaguely, barely, sort of. I'm hardly here at all. One of the great boons of technology is the ability it's given us to push awareness beyond the limitations of place; and it's one of the great dangers of technology that awareness can be so easily severed from the tangibility of place. When I was growing up in North Carolina in the sixties and seventies, the world was that thing we entered when we rolled out of bed in the morning, the flow of people, events, and settings that occurred as we moved through space. The only screen we encountered was the one in the television set, but that was mostly after darkness had driven us indoors. With only three channels to choose from and a daytime schedule of soaps and talk shows, TV simply wasn't interesting enough to dominate us. The world out there, that's where all the interesting stuff was, the raw material with which you made your life.

Television, radio, the telephone, the record player, these were part of the world, objects and phenomena that existed within the larger landscape. Technology occurred in the context of the place where you happened to be, a relation that's been neatly flipped in the past twenty years—now technology is the world, delivered via the ubiquitous and increasingly supple screen. Our physical location is largely irrelevant, as long as we're within cord's length of a power source and in range of the necessary Wi-Fi waves.

Am I here only? On the contrary, I'm scattered all over creation. This freedom is truly something new under the sun, this almost effortless liberation of awareness from place. It will be interesting to see how the human animal fares in this uncharted territory, especially considering that we are, in essence, sensory creatures. Sight, hearing, touch, taste, smell—so much of our humanity resides in our senses, as shown by how completely we fall apart in their absence. Put someone in solitary confinement 24/7 and he quickly loses his mind. Subjects in sensory deprivation experiments start to hallucinate within hours. A solitary cell, a sensory deprivation chamber, these may be as near as we get to being no place in this life without leaving it completely, and one wonders how close the digital world is to this neighborhood of no place.

Without our senses to anchor us, might everywhere start to thin at some point into a fog that feels very much like nowhere?

The digital world is great for visuals, wonderful for its delivery of glorious sounds, but a wasteland when it comes to our other senses. Cut off from sensory information, we're apt to find ourselves unmoored, floating in limbo. Susceptible to being, literally and figuratively, lost. For an example, look no further than Steve Almond's exquisitely eerie "Hagar's Sons," in which Cohen finds himself whisked by private jet to "the New Emirate," a gleaming, frictionless world of black truffle omelets, silk bathrobes, and $11,000-a-night hotel suites half a mile above the earth. A world, we begin to suspect, made possible by vast corruption, where Cohen's sole psychological and moral anchors lie back home, in his real life. Not that these anchors are particularly appetizing—a colicky baby, a beautiful but cranky malcontent of a wife, a cramped apartment that reeks of baby poop. In the Emirate his senses aren't so much deprived as lulled, sedated, and seduced. He begins to wonder if he's in a dream, or dangling outside of time, and hangs onto thoughts of his fraught, chaotic home like his soul and sanity depend on it.

The hotel convention center of Robert Olen Butler's "At the Cultural Ephemera Association National Conference" offers a more downscale version of the New Emirate's ethereal nowhereness. Naugahyde chairs, hungover scholars, an untouched pitcher of ice water. Here, the sensory barrens are salvaged by touch: a man and a woman shake hands, and, later, a hand is placed on an arm, then a hand laid on top of that. Human contact. Eyes on eyes. Heat rising from a woman's face. Stephanie Soileau's "The Ranger Queen of Sulphur" gives us Deana LaFleur, a lumbering, pot-addled, computer-addicted woman-child who would love nothing better than to escape into nowheresville, and who could blame her? Her hometown of Sulphur, Louisiana, is hell's own armpit, its complex of petrochemical plants belching poison like a Southern-fried version of Tolkien's Mordor. Her father is dying from that poison; her brother is morbidly obese; Deana, no lightweight herself, has a suck job at Payday Loan and small prospect of doing better. Compared to all this, the digital world looks pretty good, and she devotes more time to her computer games than to work and school combined, but reality, the real world, keeps dragging her back into her own life. Deana's vision of Sulphur and her place within it is worth quoting at length:

> It was the plants and the heat and the ruthless mosquitoes, the price of gas, the addictive games, the crappy jobs, the hostile rednecks, hopeless brothers, delinquent cousins, complacent mothers, jobless fathers, spiteful uncles, polluted waters, the stifling reek of sulfur and fast food and tanker-truck exhaust... It was all of this and it was none of this. And if it wasn't this, what was it? It was her. It was in her. It was something awful in her.

So convincing and terrible is Sulphur's grip on Deana LaFleur that the reader feels the nudge of an idea. Maybe place isn't where the human condition happens; maybe place *is* the human condition. "It was her. It was in her." Place shapes personality just as relentlessly as climate shapes place. Flaubert dreamed of writing a novel comprised entirely of style, a novel, as he envisioned it, in which nothing happens. Some hundred and fifty years later, a novel of nothing happening doesn't seem so much of a stretch; Samuel Beckett took us a long way down that road. Much harder to imagine is a novel in which all the nonhappenings have nowhere to happen.

As these stories show time and again, place is the means by which we locate ourselves in our own lives. For better or worse, one might add; human experience being what it is, the comforts of "closure," "healing," and "redemption" rarely result. In Lauren Groff's "Abundance"—a standout story in a book full of standouts—the terminally ill Oscar approaches the house where he's lived his whole life: "Every inch was haunted by himself at various ages. Here at twenty, one arm thrown around Henry's shoulders, staggering drunk. Here at fifty, tall and strong, his lascivious, goaty years. Here at four, the small watchful son of parents who loved their venom more than their child." The elegant old house provides a structure for his sense of self, and his ambivalence is such that he thinks it's too bad he won't be around to watch it fall into the sea. The returning warriors portrayed by Brock Clarke in "Our Pointy Boots" and Miha Mazzini in "That Winter" are traumatized by their homecomings, whipsawed between past and present, home as it was and is now, the gap between their former and present selves. In George Makana Clark's "The Wreckers," Roland's love for Ezadurah—a slave owned by another man—becomes his only fixed point amid the chaos of a slaving voyage, his thoughts of her framed sharply with particulars of place and time. The recently widowed Marcie's rural and emotional isolation leave her vulnerable in Ron Rash's "Burning Bright," and Bradshaw's suburban house in "Winter Elders" by Shawn Vestal makes him an easy-access target for the Mormon missionaries who won't leave him alone. Is it heaven they come bearing, or an earthly incarnation of hell?

Heaven and hell, those warring city-states of our interior lives, take more than a semblance of earthly shape in Ben Stroud's "The Traitor of Zion." Port Hebron, Michigan, is God's chosen "holy city," a town founded and nurtured by the Hebronite revelator Josiah Kershaw as "a place where men would live in harmony under new laws and seek pleasure in labor, purity in distance from all the corruptions of the East." In Kershaw's conception, it's no less than ground zero for the Second Coming. Aspiration has a spot on the American map, and at least for a while paradise seems possible, the human condition coexisting with divine intention. In the deliciously mindbending "Falling" by Andrew Tonkovich, the portal to heaven takes form as an actual, physical hole in the ground, a perfect circle with the radius of a human torso. Smooth-sided, utterly vertical, and apparently bottomless, and into it—think of the Rapture as a vacuum cleaner set on low hum—disappear an atheistic geology professor, Jo-Jo the search dog, the professor's former student mistress, a few hundred disciples, and, finally, our intrepid narrator. A long, strange trip ensues.

Ecotone defines itself as the magazine for reimagining place, a claim that deserves to be applauded as a rare instance of truth in contemporary advertising. In an age where place has never seemed more tenuous and abstract, it's hard to conceive of a more relevant mission for a literary magazine. The screen, the ubiquitous, miraculous, infernal screen, keeps taking us farther and faster from ourselves. Cyberspace can be wonderful, but in the end we have to return to our bodies, to the not-virtual and non-digital, to the funk, gunk, and friction of the natural world. More than ever, we need an understanding of place, because we're wandering so far. For that we need the proper language—malleable yet precise, to the point but still capable of doubt and ambiguity—and the imaginative will to grapple with questions whose answers are rarely settled. Knowledge that seems fixed and solid today dissolves in a muddle tomorrow. We try, but the search never really ends. The narrator of Brad Watson's masterful "Alamo Plaza" is engaged in such a search, sifting and resifting the memory of a childhood vacation to the Gulf Coast. His parents, his brother, his dreamy eight- or nine-year-old self, an unremarkable family at the unremarkable Alamo Plaza Motel Court, a few days at the beach where nothing especially remarkable happens (although there is the small matter of a misplaced toe). And yet, in retrospect, those few days in that ordinary place seem to contain everything. "Memory is reductive," Watson's narrator reflects at one point, a statement belied by the richness and mystery of his own recollections. Returning home from that trip, seeing his family's brick ranch-style house come into view, he can barely contain "the inexplicable everyday, the oddness of being, the senseless belonging to this and not that." It's almost too much for the boy—close enough to too much that he finds himself wishing it blown to pieces.

Short stories fix us in place, in experience, as few things can. With their insistence on the particular and the specific, they're a corrective to the digital world's propensity for blasting awareness into a thousand scattered fragments. Our humanity is being tested in ways that our ancestors never dreamed of. We need *Ecotone*, and we need these stories, the twenty-six beauties collected within these covers. Read on, and find your place.

Ben Fountain
Dallas, Texas
August 2013

ASTORIA TO ZION

BURNING BRIGHT

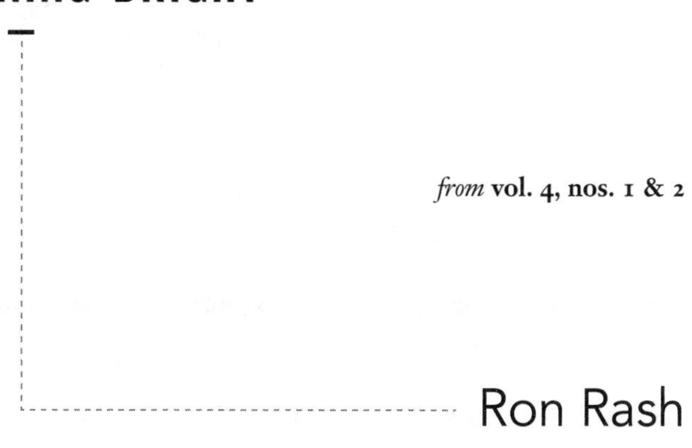

from **vol. 4, nos. 1 & 2**

Ron Rash

AFTER THE THIRD FIRE IN TWO WEEKS, the talk on TV and radio was no longer about careless campers. Not *three* fires. Nothing short of a miracle that only a few acres had been burned, the park superintendent said, a miracle less likely to occur again with each additional rainless day.

Marcie listened to the noon weather forecast, then turned off the TV and went out on the porch. She looked at the sky and nothing belied the prediction of more hot dry weather. The worst drought in a decade, the weatherman had said, showing a ten-year chart of August rainfalls. As if Marcie needed a chart when all she had to do was look at her tomatoes shriveled on the vines, the corn shucks gray and papery as a hornet's nest. She stepped off the porch and dragged a length of hose into the garden, its rubber the sole bright green among the rows. Marcie turned on the water and watched it splatter against the dust. Hopeless, but she slowly walked the rows, grasping the hose just below the metal mouth, as if it were a snake that could bite her. When she finished she cut off the spigot and looked at the sky a last time. She thought of Carl, wondering if he'd be late again. She thought about the cigarette lighter he carried in his front pocket, a wedding gift she'd bought him in Gatlinburg.

WHEN HER FIRST HUSBAND, Arthur, had died two falls earlier of a heart attack, the men in the church had come the following week and felled a white oak on the ridge. They'd cut it into firewood and stacked it on her porch. Their doing so had been more an act of homage to Arthur than of concern for her, or so Marcie realized the following September when the men did not come, making it clear that the church and the community it represented believed others needed their help more than a woman whose husband had left behind fifty acres of land, a paid-off house, and money in the bank.

Carl showed up instead. "Heard you might need some firewood cut," he told her, but she did not unlatch the screen door when he stepped onto the porch, even after he explained that Preacher Carter had suggested he come. He stepped back to the porch edge, his deep-blue eyes lowered so as not to meet hers. Trying to set her at ease, she was sure, appear less threatening to a woman living alone. It was something a lot of other men wouldn't have done, wouldn't even have thought to do. Marcie asked for a phone number and Carl gave her one. "I'll call you tomorrow if I need you," she said, and watched him drive off in his battered black pickup, a chain saw and red five-gallon gas can rattling in the truck bed. She phoned Preacher Carter after Carl left.

"He's new in the area, from down near the coast," the minister told Marcie. "He came by the church one afternoon, claimed he'd do good work for fair wages."

"So you sent him up here not knowing hardly anything about him?" Marcie asked. "With me living alone."

"Ozell Harper wanted some trees cut and I sent him out there," Preacher Carter replied. "He also cut some trees for Andy West.

They both said he did a crackerjack job." The minister paused. "I think the fact he came by the church to ask about work speaks in his favor. He's got a good demeanor about him too. Serious and soft spoken, lets his work do his talking for him."

She called Carl that night and told him he was hired.

MARCIE WENT INSIDE and made her shopping list. As she drove down the half-mile dirt road, red dust rose in the car's wake. She passed the two other houses on the road, both owned by Floridians who came every year in June and left in September. When they'd moved in, she'd walked down the road with a homemade pie. The newcomers had stood in their doorways. They accepted the welcoming gift with a seeming reluctance, and did not invite her in.

Marcie turned left onto the blacktop, the radio on the local station. She went by several fields of corn and tobacco every bit as singed as her own garden. Before long she passed Johnny Ramsey's farm and saw several of the cows that had been in her pasture until Arthur died. The road forked and as Marcie passed Holcombe Pruitt's place she saw a black snake draped over a barbed-wire fence, put there because the older farmers believed it would bring rain. Her father had called it a silly superstition when she was a child, but during a drought nearly as bad as this one, her father had killed a black snake himself and placed it on a fence, then fallen to his knees in his scorched cornfield, imploring whatever entity would listen to make it rain.

Marcie hadn't been listening to the radio, but now a psychology teacher from the community college was being interviewed on a call-in show. The man said the person setting the fires was, according to the statistics, a male and a loner. Sometimes there's a sexual gratification in the act, he explained, or an inability to communicate with others except in actions, in this case destructive actions, or just a love of watching fire itself, an almost aesthetic response. But arsonists are always obsessive, the teacher concluded, so he won't stop until he's caught or the rain comes.

The thought came to her then, like something held underwater that had finally slipped free and surfaced. The only reason you're thinking it could be him, Marcie told herself, is because people have made you believe you don't deserve him, don't deserve a little happiness. There's no reason to think such a thing. But just as quickly her mind grasped for one.

Marcie thought of the one-night honeymoon in Gatlinburg back in April. She and Carl had stayed in a hotel room so close to a stream that they could hear the water rushing past. The next morning they'd eaten at a pancake house and then walked around the town, looking in the shops, Marcie holding Carl's hand. Foolish, maybe, for a woman of almost sixty, but Carl hadn't seemed to mind. Marcie told him she wanted to buy him something, and when they came to a shop called Country Gents, she led him into its log-cabin interior. "You pick," she told Carl, and he gazed into glass cases holding all manner of belt buckles and pocketknives and cuff links, but it was a tray of cigarette lighters where he lingered. He asked the clerk to see several, opening and closing their hinged lids, flicking the thumbwheel to summon the flame, finally settling on one whose metal bore the image of a cloisonné tiger.

AT THE GROCERY STORE, Marcie took out her list and an ink pen, moving down the rows. Monday afternoon was a good time to shop, most of the women she knew coming later in the week. Her shopping cart filled, Marcie came to the front. Only one line was open and it was Barbara Hardison's, a woman Marcie's age and the biggest gossip in Sylva.

"How are your girls?" Barbara asked as she scanned a can of beans and placed it on the conveyor belt. Done slowly, Marcie knew, giving Barbara more time.

"Fine," Marcie said, though she'd spoken to neither in over a month.

"Must be hard to have them living so far away, not hardly see them or your grandkids. I'd not know what to do if I didn't see mine at least once a week."

"We talk every Saturday, so I keep up with them," Marcie lied.

Barbara scanned more cans and bottles, all the while talking about how she believed the person responsible for the fires was one of the Mexicans working at the poultry plant.

"No one who grew up around here would do such a thing," Barbara said.

Marcie nodded, barely listening as Barbara prattled on. Instead, her mind replayed what the psychology teacher had said. She thought about how there were days when Carl spoke no more than a handful of words to her, to anyone, as far as she knew, and how he'd sit alone on the porch until bedtime while she watched TV, and how, though he'd smoked his after-supper cigarette, she'd look out the front window and sometimes see a flicker of light rise out of his cupped hand, held before his face like a guiding candle.

The cart was almost empty when Barbara pressed a bottle of hair dye against the scanner.

"Must be worrisome sometimes to have a husband strong and strapping as Carl," Barbara said, loud enough so the bag boy heard. "My boy Ethan sees him over at Burrell's after work sometimes. Ethan says that girl who works the bar tries to flirt with Carl something awful. Of course Ethan says Carl never flirts back, just sits there by himself and drinks his one beer and leaves soon as his bottle's empty." Barbara finally set the hair dye on the conveyor. "Never pays that girl the least bit of mind," she added, and paused. "At least when Ethan's been in there."

Barbara rang up the total and placed Marcie's check in the register.

"You have a good afternoon," Barbara said.

On the way back home, Marcie remembered how after the wood had been cut and stacked she'd hired Carl to do other jobs—repairing the sagging porch, then building a small garage—things Arthur would have done if still alive. She'd peek out the window and watch him, admiring the way he worked with such a fixed attentiveness. Carl never seemed bored or distracted. He didn't bring a radio to help pass the time and he smoked only after a meal, hand-rolling his cigarette with the same meticulous patience as when he measured a cut or stacked a cord of firewood. She'd envied how comfortable he was in his solitude.

Their courtship had begun with cups of coffee, then offers and acceptances of home-cooked meals. Carl didn't reveal much about himself, but as the days and then weeks passed Marcie learned he'd grown up in Whiteville, in the far east of the state. A carpenter who'd gotten laid off when the housing market went bad, he'd heard there was more work in the mountains so had come west, all he cared to bring with him in the back of his pickup. When Marcie asked if he had children, Carl told her he'd never been married.

"Never found a woman who would have me," he said. "Too quiet, I reckon."

"Not for me," she told him, and smiled. "Too bad I'm nearly old enough to be your mother."

"You're not too old," he replied, in a matter-of-fact way, his blue eyes looking at her as he spoke, not smiling.

She expected him to be a shy, awkward lover, but he wasn't. The same attentiveness he showed in his work was in his kisses and touches, in the way he matched the rhythms of his movements to hers. It was as though his long silences made him better able to communicate in other ways. Nothing like Arthur, who'd been brief and concerned mainly with satisfying himself. Carl had lived in a run-down motel outside Sylva that rented by the hour or the week, but they never went there. They always made love in Marcie's bed. Sometimes he'd stay the whole night. At the grocery store and church there were asides and stares. Preacher Carter, who'd sent Carl to her in the first place, spoke to Marcie of "proper appearances." By then her daughters had found out as well. From three states away they spoke to Marcie of being humiliated, insisting they'd be too embarrassed to visit, as if their coming home was a common occurrence. Marcie quit going to church and went into town as little as possible. Carl finished his work on the garage but his reputation as a handyman was such that he had all the work he wanted, including an offer to join a construction crew working out of Sylva. Carl told the crew boss he preferred to work alone.

What people said to Carl about his and Marcie's relationship, she didn't know, but the night she brought it up he told her they should get married. No formal proposal or candlelight dinner at a restaurant, just a flat statement. But good enough for her. When Marcie told her daughters, they were, predictably, outraged. The younger one cried. Why couldn't she act her age, her older daughter asked, her voice scalding as a hot iron.

A justice of the peace married them and then they drove over the mountains to Gatlinburg for the weekend. Carl moved in what little he had and they began a life together. She thought that the more comfortable they became around each other the more they would talk, but that didn't happen. Evenings Carl sat by himself on the porch, or found some small chore to do, something best done alone. He didn't like to watch TV or rent movies. At supper he'd always say it was a good meal, and thank her for making it. She might tell him something about her day, and he'd listen politely, make a brief remark to show that though he said little at least he was listening. But at night as she readied herself for bed, he'd always come in. They'd lie down together and he'd turn to kiss her good night, always on the mouth. Three, four nights a week that kiss would linger and then quilts and sheets would be pulled back. Afterward, Marcie would not put her nightgown back on. Instead, she'd press her back into his chest and stomach, bend her knees, and fold herself inside him, his arms holding her close, his body's heat enclosing her.

ONCE BACK HOME, Marcie put up groceries and placed a chuck roast on the stove to simmer. She did a load of laundry and swept off the front porch, her eyes glancing down the road for Carl's pickup. At six o'clock she turned on the news. Another fire had been set, no more than thirty minutes earlier. Fortunately, a hiker was close by and saw the smoke, even glimpsed a pickup through the trees. No tag number or make. All the hiker knew for sure was that the pickup was black.

Carl did not get home until almost seven. Marcie heard the truck coming up the road and began setting the table. Carl took off his boots on the porch and came inside, his face grimy with sweat, bits of sawdust in his hair and on his clothes. He nodded at her and went into the bathroom. As he showered, Marcie went out to the pickup. In the truck bed was the chain saw, beside it plastic bottles of twenty-weight engine oil and the red five-gallon gasoline can. When she lifted the can, it was empty.

They ate in silence but for Carl's usual compliment on the meal. Marcie watched him, waiting for a sign of something different in his demeanor, some glimpse of anxiety or satisfaction.

"There was another fire today," she finally said.

"I know," Carl answered, not looking up from his plate.

She didn't ask how he knew, when the radio in his truck didn't work. But he could have heard it at Burrell's as well.

"They say whoever set it drove a black pickup."

Carl looked at her then, his blue eyes clear and depthless.

"I know that too," he said.

After supper Carl went out to the porch while Marcie switched on the TV. She kept turning away from the movie she watched to look through the window. Carl sat in the wooden deck chair, only the back of his head and shoulders visible, less so as the minutes passed and his body merged with the gathering dusk. He stared toward the high mountains of the Smokies, and Marcie had no idea what, if anything, he was thinking about. He'd already smoked his cigarette, but she waited to see if he would take the lighter from his pocket, flick it, and stare at the flame a few moments. But he didn't. Not this night. When she cut off the TV and went to the back room, the deck chair scraped as Carl pushed himself out of it. Then the click of metal as he locked the door.

When he settled into bed beside her, Marcie continued to lie with her back to him. He moved closer, placed his hand between her head and pillow, and slowly, gently, turned her head so he could kiss her. As soon as his lips brushed hers, she turned away, moved so his body didn't touch hers. She fell asleep but woke a few hours later. Sometime in the night she had resettled in the bed's center, and Carl's arm now lay around her, his knees tucked behind her knees, his chest pressed against her back.

As she lay awake, Marcie remembered the day her younger daughter left for Cincinnati, joining her sister there. I guess it's just us now, Arthur had said glumly. She'd resented those words, as if Marcie were some grudgingly accepted consolation prize. She'd also resented how the words acknowledged that their daughters had always been closer to Arthur, even as children. In their teens, the girls had unleashed their rancor, the shouting and tears and grievances, on Marcie. The inevitable conflicts between mothers and daughters, and Arthur's being the only male in the house—that was surely part of it, but Marcie also believed there'd been some difference in temperament as innate as different blood types.

Arthur had hoped that one day the novelty of city life would pale and the girls would come back to North Carolina. But they stayed up north and married and began their own families. Their visits and phone calls became less and less frequent. Arthur was hurt by that, hurt deep, though never saying so. It seemed he aged more quickly, especially after he'd had a stent placed in an artery. After that Arthur did less around the farm, until finally he no longer grew tobacco or cabbage, just raised a few cattle. Then one day he didn't come back for lunch. She found him in the barn, slumped beside a stall, a hay hook in his hand.

The girls came home for the funeral and stayed three days. After they left, there was a month-long flurry of phone calls and visits and casseroles from people in the community and then days when the only vehicle that came was the mail truck. Marcie learned then what true loneliness was. Five miles from town on a dead-end dirt road, with not even the Floridians' houses in sight. She bought extra locks for the doors because at night she sometimes grew afraid, though what she feared was as much inside the house as outside it. Because she knew what was expected of her—to stay in this place, alone, waiting for the years, perhaps decades, to pass until she herself died.

IT WAS MIDMORNING the following day when Sheriff Beasley came. Marcie met him on the porch. The sheriff had been a close friend of Arthur's, and as he got out of the patrol car he looked not at her but at the sagging barn and empty pasture, seeming to ignore the house's new garage and freshly shingled roof. He did not take off his hat as he crossed the yard, or when he stepped onto the porch.

"I knew you'd sold some of Arthur's cows, but I didn't know it was all of them." The sheriff spoke as if it were intended only as an observation.

"Maybe I wouldn't have if there'd been some men to help me with them after Arthur died," Marcie said. "I couldn't do it by myself."

"I guess not," Sheriff Beasley replied, letting a few moments pass before he spoke again, his eyes on her now. "I need to speak to Carl. You know where he's working today?"

"Talk to him about what?" Marcie asked.

"Whoever's setting these fires drives a black pickup."

"There's lots of black pickups in this county."

"Yes there are," Sheriff Beasley said, "and I'm checking out everybody who drives one, checking out where they were yesterday around six o'clock as well. I figure that to narrow it some."

"You don't need to ask Carl," Marcie said. "He was here eating supper."

"At six o'clock?"

"Around six, but he was here by five thirty."

"How are you so sure of that?"

"The five-thirty news had just come on when he pulled up."

The sheriff said nothing.

"You need me to sign something I will," Marcie said.

"No, Marcie. That's not needed. I'm just checking off folks with black pickups. It's a long list."

"I bet you came here first, though, didn't you," Marcie said. "Because Carl's not from around here."

"I came here first, but I had cause," Sheriff Beasley said. "When you and Carl started getting involved, Preacher Carter asked me to check up on him, just to make sure he was on the up and up. I called the sheriff down there. Turns out that when Carl was fifteen he and another boy got arrested for burning some woods behind a ball field. They claimed it an accident, but the judge didn't buy that. They almost got sent to juvenile detention."

"There've been boys do that kind of thing around here."

"Yes, there have," the sheriff said. "And that was the only thing in Carl's file, not even a speeding ticket. Still, his being here last evening when it happened, that's a good thing for him."

Marcie waited for the sheriff to leave, but he lingered. He took out a soiled handkerchief and wiped his brow. Probably wanting a glass of iced tea, she suspected, but she wasn't going to offer him one. The sheriff put up his handkerchief and glanced at the sky.

"You'd think we'd at least get an afternoon thunderstorm."

"I've got things to do," she said, and reached for the screen door handle.

"Marcie," the sheriff said, his voice so soft that she turned. He raised his right hand, palm open as if to offer her something, then let it fall. "You're right. We should have done more for you after Arthur died. I regret that."

Marcie opened the screen door and went inside.

When Carl got home she said nothing about the sheriff's visit, and that night in bed when Carl turned and kissed her, Marcie met his lips and raised her hand to his cheek. She pressed her free hand against the small of his back, guiding his body as it shifted, settled over her. Afterward, she lay awake, feeling Carl's breath on the back of her neck, his arm cinched around her ribs and stomach. She listened for a first far-off rumble, but there was only the dry raspy sound of insects striking the window screen. Marcie had not been to church in months, had not prayed for even longer than that. But she did now. She shut her closed eyes tighter, trying to open a space inside herself that might offer up all of what she feared and hoped for, brought forth with such fervor it could not help but be heard. She prayed for rain.

WHAT THE AX FORGETS THE TREE REMEMBERS

from **vol. 8, no. 1**

Edith Pearlman

I.

THE FIRST HINT OF TROUBLE CAME EARLY in the morning. The telephone rang on Gabrielle's desk in the lobby—her glass-topped, strategically placed desk: she could see everyone, anyone could see her.

"It's Selene," lisping through buckteeth. "I have flu."

"Oh my dear...you've called the clinic?"

"The doctor forbids me to leave my home." Home indeed: a heap of brown shingles in an alley in a town forty miles north of Godolphin. Three children and a once-in-a-while man..."My friend Minata will give testimony in my place. From Somalia too, and now she lives on the next avenue. She knows the fee, and that she will stay overnight in the inn. She agrees to come, and tell."

"And she has...things to tell?" Gabrielle softened her voice. "Was her experience like yours?"

"Ah, worse. Thorns were applied. And only palm oil for the mending. She will take the same bus..."

Thorns and palm oil and two fullback matriarchs, each with the heels of her hands on the young girl's shoulders as if kneading recalcitrant dough. Someone forces the knees apart. Horrifying tales; Gabrielle knew plenty of them. But would this Minata touch the heart like Selene? *I am happy to be in this town Godolphin, in this state Massachusetts, in this country USA*, Selene always concluded with humble sibilance. *I am happy to be here this night.*

Would the unknown Minata also be happy to be here this night, testifying to the Society Against Female Mutilation, local chapter? Would she walk from podium to chair in a gingerly fashion, remembered thorns pricking her vulva like cloves in a ham?

GABRIELLE HAD FIRST HEARD SELENE three years earlier, at the invitation of a Dutch physician whose significant protruding bosom looked like an outsized wedge of cheese. Gabrielle privately called her Dr. Gouda. Dr. Gouda was staying at Devlin's Hotel where Gabrielle was Concierge Extraordinary—Mr. Devlin's own words. Gabrielle said yes to guests whenever she could. She'd said yes to Dr. Gouda. She'd accompanied the solid woman to an empty basement room in a nearby church. After a while twelve people straggled in. Then photographs were shown—there was an old-fashioned projector, and a screen, and slides that stuttered forward on a carousel. A voice issued from the darkness beside the projector—the doctor's accented narration. The slide show—the Follies, Dr. Henry Ellison would later name it—featured terrified twelve-year-olds in a hut. Behind the girls was a shelf of handmade dolls.

The brutality practiced in the photographs—shamefully it made Gabrielle feel desirable. She was glad that she and her stylist had at last found a rich oxblood shade for her hair; and glad that her hair's silky straightness conformed to her head in such a Parisian way, complementing the Parisian name that her Pittsburgh parents had snatched from the newspaper the day she was born. She knew that at fifty-two she was still pretty, even if her nose was a millimeter too long and there was a gap between a bicuspid and a molar due to extraction: how foolish not to repair that, and now it was too late, the teeth on either side had already made half-hearted journeys toward each other. Still, the gap was not disfiguring. And her body was as narrow and supple as a pubescent boy's. She was five feet tall without her high-heeled shoes, but she was without her high-heeled shoes only in the bath—even her satin bed slippers provided an extra three inches.

In the basement room of the church there was no podium, just a makeshift platform. After the slide show a white-haired gentleman unfolded a card table onto the platform and fanned laminated newspaper articles across it. Dr. Gouda then stationed herself in front of the screen now cleansed of enormities. She wore a navy skirt and a pale blouse and she had removed her jacket, idly revealing her commanding bosom. The width of her hips was apparent to all. In ancient China child-buyers sometimes constricted an infant's body so that the lower half far outgrew the upper. Gabrielle had read about it: they used a sort of straitjacket. The children thus warped into human pawns often became pets at court.

But the Dutch doctor's shape was nature's doing, not man's. "This is Selene," she said, and surrendered her place to a mahogany woman.

My mother was kind to me, Selene began that night, begins every year, would begin tonight if it weren't for her flu. *My mother was kind to me. Yes, she brought me to the hut, as her mother had brought her, as her mother her, on and on backward through time, you understand.*

When she bears witness Selene wraps herself in native costume—a colorful ankle-length dress and turban. Her face is long and plain. The thick glasses, the large teeth with their goofy malocclusion, the raw knuckles—all somehow suggest the initial maiming.

My mother loved me.

The thing was done for my good and for my future husband. This was believed. I believed it too. I was held down, yes, the body fights back, that is its nature, no one scolded me for struggling. But they had to restrain me. My . . . area was swabbed with something cold and wet. The cutting was swift. Painful. A small curved knife cuts away a portion of your flesh, it could happen by accident in the garden or while preparing food, that tiny slice I mean, though not in that . . . area. The wound was salved. There was no shame. All the women in the hut had gone through the cutting.

My mother was kind to me. She was kind to me throughout her life. She procured for me a fine husband, one who would not have taken me whole, as someone might say that piano lessons had broadened her marriage opportunities. *I was sorry to leave my husband when I took our children and ran away.*

"Your experience of intimacy?" Dr. Gouda usually asks from some dark place.

The lids behind the glasses close, open. "My husband was not at fault."

"And childbirth?"

"I wished myself dead."

The listeners are still.

But I love my children, she continues. *I have a new husband*, not an entirely accurate statement, Gabrielle would learn; but the fellow was as good as a husband, or as bad. *It is the same excruciation with him. He understands.* No one asks if he spares her. *I think of my mother and I do not scream. But the cutting should stop. I hope you can make it stop. I am happy to be in this country. I am happy to be here tonight.*

THAT FIRST TIME, the Dutch doctor stood at the table and waited until the silence turned into murmuring. Then she said that regrets were unproductive. The challenge was to save today's victims, tomorrow's. To that end... She went on to speak of the work of the World Health Organization, of associations in Europe, of the Society Against Female Mutilation she represented, which hoped to form a chapter tonight here in Godolphin, Massachusetts. Dr. Henry Ellison the noted gynecologist would serve on the advisory committee. "And we are looking for more help," said the Dutch doctor tonelessly.

Many attendees signed up, and several took out checkbooks. Two were elderly women who looked alike as old friends often do. A pale, emaciated college girl clasped and reclasped her hands; perhaps she felt personally threatened by mutilation. There was a thuggish dark fellow. He probably had a taste for porn. The man who had unfolded the bridge table now folded it up again. That handsome ruddy face, that crest of white hair—he must be Dr. Henry Ellison the noted gynecologist.

At last Gabrielle approached the Dutch doctor. "I'd like to sign up," Gabrielle said.

"Of course!"

II.

THERE WAS NO OF COURSE ABOUT IT. For half a century Gabrielle had avoided Good Causes as if they might defile her. Efficiency and orderliness were what she cared about, and her own lively good looks. She cared about Devlin's Hotel too, a double brownstone on the border of Godolphin and Boston. Mr. Devlin had transformed it into a European-style inn, Gabrielle its Concierge Extraordinary, Gabrielle with her clever wardrobe and her ability to say two or three sentences in half a dozen languages... Gabrielle was made for the job, Mr. Devlin had sighed, more than once.

Really the job was made for her. It left her time to read, to tend her window boxes, to give an occasional dinner party, to go to an afternoon concert. She lived alone. She wasn't burdened with an automobile—she biked to and from the hotel in all but the worst weather, her confident high heels gripping the pedals, two *guiches* of hair pointing forward beyond the helmet. She wasn't burdened with family either, unless you counted the half-crippled aunt back in Pittsburgh. The old woman loped along on a single crutch, the filthy adhesive that wrapped its hand bar replaced only on her niece's annual visit.

Until that night in the church basement, this game relative had been Gabrielle's only responsibility. And yet now Gabrielle was writing her name on a clipboard and undertaking to work on behalf of females unrelated to her, unknown to her, half a planet away.

Something had stirred within her. She supposed that a psychologist would have a name for this feeling. But Gabrielle would as soon discuss emotions with a psychologist as with a veterinarian—in fact, she'd prefer a veterinarian, she thought, biking home with a packet of information in her saddlebag. It was as if the kinship she felt to those pathetic girls was that of mammal to mammal, house pet to feral cat. The jungle creatures had been cruelly treated by other beasts, attacked with needles and knives as sharp as flame; whereas she, a domestic feline, had in her two brief marriages only been left cold. Free of sex, at last she was disburdened of her monthly nuisance too. The loss had been hastened by a gynecologist—not the distinguished Henry Ellison, rather a Jewish woman with unpleasant breath who advised Gabrielle to rid herself of the bag of fibroids beginning to distend her abdomen. The hysterectomy was without complications. And now, flat as a book below her waist, dry as linen between her legs, she felt pity for the Africans' dripping wounds... well, curiosity, at any rate.

III.

GABRIELLE'S CHIEF RESPONSIBILITY within the new chapter was arranging its semiannual meeting—the visit of Dr. Gouda, the visit of Victim Selene. The first thing she did was to thank the church for the use of its chilly basement; then, in its stead, she commandeered the function room of the hotel, a small cocoa-colored space with three elongated windows looking out onto the boulevard. She wheedled a promise of wine and coffee and cheese from Mr. Devlin, and convinced him to charge his lowest rates to the chapter for the overnight stay of doctor and witness. She did other work too. She and the two elderly women—who were in fact sisters, and hated each other—designed a fund-raising brochure. She helped the emaciated girl, who had volunteered to be a liaison with the local university, withdraw without shame. "Suffering affects me too strongly," the goose said, her hand on her meager chest.

"Of course, dear," said Gabrielle, flashing her compassionate smile with its friendly missing tooth.

And she listened to the boring conversation of the man with white hair. He turned out to be not Dr. Henry Ellison, as his dignity suggested, but a retired salesman with time on his hands. He was good for running the Follies, though he sometimes got the slides upside down. And she answered e-mails for Dr. Gouda, who hated the computer, and she wrote letters on behalf of Dr. Henry Ellison.

Henry Ellison was the man who looked like a thug. On closer inspection he was merely unwholesome. He had pockmarked skin, teeth like cubes of cheddar. His children were grown and his wife suffered from some malady. He wasn't on the prowl, though. He seemed to welcome Gabrielle's indifference to romance just as she welcomed his pleasure in quiet evenings and good wine and the sound of his own voice. He liked to answer questions. "Is the Dutch doctor gay?" she asked him one night when they were sorting new slides in her living room.

"Doubt it. She's got a muscular husband and five children." A well-trained surgeon, she could have had a splendid practice in the Hague. Instead she was now running a fistula repair hospital. She drove a van around the African countryside, performed procedures under primitive conditions, sterilized her own instruments.

Henry held a slide up to the light. "Oh, Lord, too graphic. Our folks want terrified damsels. They want stories of eternal dysphoria. This..." He kept looking.

"What is it, Henry?" And she did an eager jig on her high heels.

He didn't relinquish the little square. "It's an excellent photograph of the separation of the labia with a speculum, a wooden one for heaven's sake—the thing ought to be in a museum." At last he handed the slide to Gabrielle.

What a strange mystery lay between a woman's legs. The skin of thigh and pubis was the same grainy brown as the old instrument, but within the opening all was garnet and ruby. "Yes, too... graphic."

Henry adjusted the carousel on her coffee table. He held another slide to the light.

"What's that, Henry?"

"A trachelectomy... a sort of D and C. I hope they used some analgesic, something more than the leaves from the stinging nettle."

"Why is she sending slides we can't show?"

"She wants to remind us that despite our efforts, despite our money, the practice continues." He switched off the lights. They sat in the dark, and Henry clicked, and the wall above Gabrielle's couch—she had removed her Dufy print—became a screen. Gabrielle and Henry watched unseen hands manipulating visible instruments.

"Surgery is thrilling," he mused. "Do you mind if I smoke? These village witches probably get a kick out of it. You divorce yourself from everything except the task at hand. Your gestures are swift, like a bird's beak plucking a worm. The flesh responds as you expect. Someone else takes care of the mess."

Gabrielle imagined herself collecting blood in a cloche.

Click. "An excellent example of splitting the clitoral hood. Sometimes they excise the external genitalia, too, and then stitch the vaginal opening closed. This is known as..."

"Infibulation," supplied Gabrielle, who was growing knowledgeable. She too was enjoying a rare cigarette.

Click. "Here's a procedure not yet legal here." An instrument was attacking something within a vagina; there was a glimpse of a pregnant abdomen. "They are destroying the infant's cranium," said Henry.

IV.

WITH HER USUAL THOROUGHNESS Gabrielle went beyond her official chapter assignments. Often on one of her days off, Wednesday or Thursday, she visited Selene in her town, once thriving with factories, now supported, Henry said, by the Welfare Industry.

There were houses in Pittsburgh too that had been home to factory hands—little brick two-stories, near the river. But there they had been rehabilitated and now belonged to young academic gentry. Here they belonged to the wretched. Here immigrants and their children and a stream of relatives packed themselves into the structures and their uneasy porches. The railroad station was a mile away. Gabrielle walked from the train along a broad and miserable street, never wobbling in her high heels though she was always carrying two bulging paper bags. She took a right and a left and fetched up at Selene's shanty. She distributed toys and clothing to the children and delicacies to Selene—it would have been insulting, she knew, to bring grocery items, and anyway there were food stamps for those. She played with the kids, she talked to Selene, she learned songs, she admired the proverbs that Selene had embroidered on cloth and nailed to the walls. *A cow must graze where she is tied. Men fall in order to rise.* Some were less explicit, riddles, really. *A bird does not fly into the arrow.* "A woman does not seek a man," interpreted Selene.

At nine o'clock on those occasions Selene's consort drove Gabrielle to the last train in his pickup truck. He had a spade-shaped face as if his jaw had been elongated by force. One Wednesday he returned to the house too late to drive her—as it turned out, he didn't return at all.

"Stay with me," shrugged Selene.

The children were asleep. It had been a mild wet spring, and Gabrielle's raincoat and scarf were hanging on a hook in Selene's bedroom. She took off her little dress and hung it on another hook, and took off her strapped high-heeled shoes that exactly matched the pewter of that dress, and in her silk underwear climbed into Selene's bed. A light blanket was all they needed. They fell asleep back to back. But during the night the weather turned cool. They awoke in each other's arms... or, rather, Gabrielle awoke in Selene's arms, her head between warm breasts, Selene's fingers caressing her area.

V.

"MINATA WILL TAKE THE SAME bus I take," Selene had said.

Gabrielle met the bus. She had no way to recognize the new witness—so many dark-skinned people were disembarking. Perhaps Selene had told her friend Minata to look for a *petite femme, stylish, nice face*. Walking toward Gabrielle was a rare beauty. She wore a chartreuse raincoat made of tiny scales. Long brown hair combed back from a broad brow. Wide eyes above a simple nose. "Ms. Gabrielle?"

"Ms. Minata?"

They shook hands. *Short skinny white woman with dyed hair and ridiculous shoes*, maybe that's what Selene had said to Minata. *Brilliant blackie in a coat of fake lizard*, she might have said to Gabrielle. Minata wore golden sandals. Her toenails were golden too. She carried a leather hatbox with brass fittings. "We take the subway from here, yes?"

"Tonight, a taxi," said Gabrielle. *Goddesses don't hang from subway straps.* She explained that the Dutch doctor and an American doctor and an American lady in pink would join them for dinner in the hotel. In the cab Minata turned her head toward the city lights. "Have you been to Boston before?" Gabrielle wondered.

"Oh, yes, it's not the moon. It's the Cradle of Liberty. My children learn that in school."

"You have borne children?" Did you wish yourself dead?

"Five."

Gabrielle was quiet during dinner. She was thinking of Selene, her spectacles, her teeth, her martyred air. She was remembering Wednesdays. She was feeling the probe of Selene's strong hand, the fingers then spreading like wings. Her own fingers always fluttered in a hesitant way, fearful of causing pain. Sometimes Selene guided them further inwards...Minata too said little, was no doubt conserving her energy for the testimony. Dr. Gouda, just arrived from New York—she was on her stateside fund-raising tour—spoke in low tones to Henry. Doctor talk: the gabble of baboons.

After coffee the little group moved to the function room. There they were greeted by a group smaller than the previous one. "Female circumcision fatigue," Henry whispered. She shook her earrings at him. To her relief a few more chapter members wandered in. Perhaps they wanted to hear the progress of the fistula hospital and of the opening of a new clinic. Perhaps they wanted to see the Follies. Perhaps they wanted to listen to the witness. Perhaps they had nothing else to do.

The evening followed the usual pattern.

Dr. Gouda made some introductory remarks.

The white-haired man showed the slides. Some were new, some were old, none were from the batch that Henry and Gabrielle had judged too gory.

Minata's presentation resembled Selene's, though her voice had no sad lisp but instead a kind of lilt. She talked of the cutting, of the women's belief in its necessity, of the children's bewildered compliance. She provided a few extra details. "My cousin—they left her genitals on a rock. Animals ate them." Gabrielle attended, her high heels hooked around the rung of the folding chair as if around the pedals of her bicycle. Her black crepe knees were raised slightly by this pose; her white satin elbows rested on those knees, her fingers were laced under her little French chin.

"It causes immediate pain," sang Minata. "Recovery also is painful." She bowed her head.

"And the sequelae—the aftereffects," urged the accented voice of Dr. Gouda.

Minata raised her head. "Ma'am?"

"You must have suffered further...when touched by your husband," said the doctor in a kinder tone.

The head rose further. "I have never had a husband."

"When touched by a man..." the voice softer yet.

"I do not usually talk about these things..."

"Of course."

"...to strangers. But you are perhaps like friends. To me, being touched by a man is a happiness. Perhaps the cutting made it more so. I also enjoy amusement parks."

"Me too!" from the projector, heartily.

"But childbirth," moaned the barren Gabrielle.

"Oh, one of my sons was a breech: awful. The other four children...pushing and straining, yes, you know what it's like. Pain?—no." The listeners were silent. "It is a matter of...choice," said Minata. "You can choose to like, to not like. 'Wisdom does not live in only one home.'"

Gabrielle's aunt too had been childless. She had lived as a scorned spinster with Gabrielle and her parents, part of the dry severity of the family. In Gabrielle's room there had been a few books, a few records, curtains with embroidered butterflies, their wings trapped within the gauzy folds. She thought of this squeezed girlhood, her careless husbands, the restrained Henry. She remembered the slides, the jeweled vagina.

What had she chosen?—divorce, self-sufficiency, an enameled piquancy: the phrase remembered from some novel. She had achieved it all, hadn't she. But she felt weak. (Later Henry would tell her that her blood pressure had dropped.) She grew dizzy. (He would tell her that she began helplessly to swoon.) The heels of her shoes clawed the bar of the folding chair. She toppled sideways, her shoes still clinging to life. The chair toppled too, but in a delayed manner, as if only reluctantly following its occupant.

"USUALLY AN ANKLE BREAKS from a fall because of the sudden weight that is exerted on it. But in your case it was the twist itself that did the work. You managed to wrench your left fibula right out of its hinge. And break a few other things, like the ankle joint, very important, a gliding joint, supports the tibia, which..."

"My left fistula?" she said, turning toward him from her hospital bed.

"Fibula. A bone. Poor Gabrielle."

"What pain I was in."

"You had every right to be in pain, the nerves in the foot..."

"A different kind of pain," she muttered.

"...you'd be in pain now if it weren't for that lovely drip. You won't be able to walk without assistance for a while, old girl."

"Minata," she said. Now she turned her head away from him.

"Minata had several drinks afterward with the doctor and the projectionist."

"Minata betrayed the chapter."

"Dear Gabrielle, we surgeons can never confidently predict the outcome of our work. The midwives of Somalia... likewise."

She leaned forward, and some dismayed tubes shook. He slipped a pillow behind her back. She hissed at him. "You can't say mutilation may enhance sex."

"Minata said it for me."

"'Choice,' she said," Gabrielle bitterly remembered.

"'Luck,' she meant," soothed Henry. "Probably rare."

GABRIELLE'S RECOVERY WAS AWFUL. One of the little bones failed to heal properly. "We have to go in again," her surgeon admitted. Back to the hospital, back to rehab, back to her apartment at last. Her hairdresser couldn't make a home visit. Her coiffure acquired a wartime negligence. Wherever she parted it a white stripe appeared.

Still: "I have a darling device to get around the house," she told her friends. It was like a child's four-wheeled scooter. Rising from its running board was a post, and atop that post, at knee level, was a soft-curved resting place. Gabrielle could bend her affected leg at the knee and lay her plastered shin on that resting place and then grasp the scooter's handles and propel herself by means of her good leg. In this circus manner she went from room to room, from chair to chair, from bed to bathroom. With it as support she could water her flowers, even make an omelet.

She received many get-well cards—from friends and coworkers, from Minata, from her aunt. "I wish you a speedy recovery," wrote Selene in penmanship that resembled her samplers. Men and mannish women sent flowers—the white-haired projectionist, Dr. Gouda, Mr. Devlin of course. Henry brought books. "I could go back to work now, my surgeon says," she told Mr. Devlin on the telephone. "With the scooter. Perhaps the guests will be amused..."

"Come back whenever you're equal to it," he said, sounding harried. "Not a minute earlier. But not a minute later."

Another week went by and the surgeon took off her immobilizing plaster and replaced it with a fat walking cast and a crutch. The cast was white fiberglass with wide blue straps. The monstrosity reached almost to her knee. Within its unyielding embrace her bones and tendons would continue to heal. But of course she couldn't bike. And she was to throw her high heels into the trash, the doctor said, and never buy another pair.

Mr. Devlin sent the hotel handyman to pick her up every morning. At the end of the working day sometimes the handyman drove her home, sometimes Mr. Devlin himself, sometimes she took a cab, sometimes even Henry showed up. At least she hadn't gained weight. But her hairdresser had rented a house in Antigua for a month.

"Why don't you just go gray," said thoughtless Henry.

She waited a minute or two, then asked, "What's happening with the chapter?"

"Oh, still high on the list of do-good causes," he told her. "Contributions are up, in fact."

"Minata..."

"Didn't hurt us. May have helped us. People adjust to contradictions, you know. And she's prettier than that horseface."

"She gave the lie to what we believe," said Gabrielle, furious again.

"Anything we believe may be disproven. Think about it, Gabby. The Salem women were possessed by the devil. Homosexuality was a sickness. Cancer was God's punishment. False beliefs, every one."

"The earth still circles the sun!"

"Today," he admitted. "Don't count on tomorrow."

VI.

GABRIELLE WAS WORKING LATE one evening, sitting at her glass-topped desk, reviewing tomorrow's tasks. She looked up, as was her habit: to see what was going on in the little lobby, to smile at guests in a welcoming but not forward manner. She could not avoid the glimpse of herself in the mirror beside the clerk's desk—head striped like a skunk's fur, leg awkwardly outstretched within the disfiguring cast, crutch waiting against a pillar like a hired escort.

A woman stood at the elevator, her back to Gabrielle. Though she was wearing an orange jacket, not a green raincoat, and though her hair was flicked sideways into a toothed barrette, not hanging loose, Gabrielle knew who it was. The hatbox was a sort of hint. But beauty like Minata's once seen is recognizable even from the rear—beauty originating in a place where skin is brown and teeth white and nymphectomies the local sport. Gabrielle identified also the white-pompadoured man pushing the elevator's button.

This is not a love hotel... She kept staring until Minata turned. Minata flashed a happy grin, and Gabrielle gave her the professional grimace with the gap where a tooth once resided.

Minata walked across the lobby toward Gabrielle. Her eyes traveled downward and stopped at the boot. Her smile collapsed. "You must wear that thing? For healing? They tell you that?"

"Yes. I can hobble now. When they remove it I'll be able to walk."

"Do not wait. Go to Selene."

Gabrielle felt her face redden. Shame? No, desire: desire that had eluded her for fifty-two years until Selene, maimed Selene...

"Hobble to her from the train station," Minata suggested. "Or take a cab," revealing a practical streak, perhaps the very quality that enabled her to make the best of things.

Gabrielle frowned at her own enlarged and stiffened leg.

"Ugly but only a nuisance," said Minata. "'The tortoise knows how to embrace its mate.'"

HAGAR'S SONS

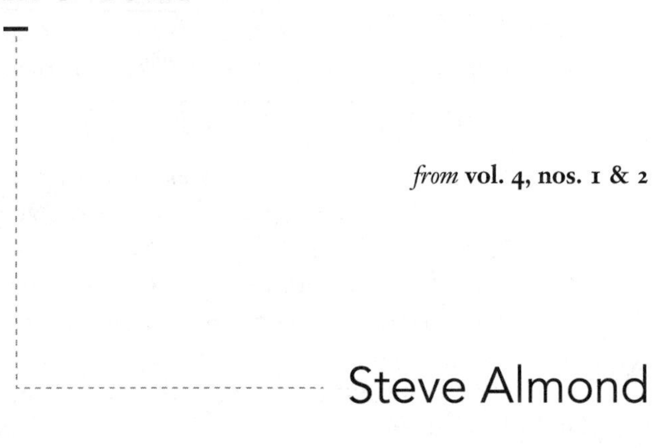

from **vol. 4, nos. 1 & 2**

Steve Almond

COHEN (AT WORK)

The call startled him. Cohen rarely received calls at work. The voice—silky, vaguely hostile—belonged to Mr. Vanderweghe's assistant.

"Mr. Vanderweghe will need to see you," she said.

"Of course," Cohen said. "I'll just, let me look—" He glanced at his desk calendar. It was blank, aside from a note in the lower right-hand corner, which read DIAPERS, RUBYLICIOUS (HUGGIES): REMEMBER!

"Now, Mr. Cohen."

Cohen wanted to ask whether he should bring the preliminary results from his currency project, but the line went dead. He carefully redacted the Huggies note and hurried to the bathroom to brush his teeth.

MISSION

Vanderweghe was dressed in the dark wool of a minor Dickens villain; the suit collar bit into his jowls. Cohen had seen him only once before, on the day of his arrival.

"Cohen."

"Sir."

Vanderweghe nodded for him to sit.

"The sheik has asked to meet with you."

Cohen nodded reflexively. He had never heard of any sheik and, in fact, knew next to nothing about the firm for which he worked. Four months ago, he had been plucked from the research division at Salomon Smith Barney at the behest of someone, he assumed, much more powerful than himself, and installed in a small office and told to study yen mode differentials until further notice. He was happy to have escaped Wall Street, the vulgar, caffeinated masculinity of the place, the bellowing traders with their sirloin tongues. Cohen had a high-strung wife, a colicky newborn, significant debt. He did not, as such, sleep.

"The sheik is a valued client, as you know."

"Of course," Cohen said.

"*Valued.*"

There was a pause. "What might the sheik want with me?"

"If I knew that—" Vanderweghe's face twisted into an abrupt silence. "Get your suit pressed," he murmured, and handed Cohen a file. Inside was a glossary of Arabic terms, cultural customs, and a history of the New Emirate. The only itinerary was a handwritten note informing him that he would be picked up at eight the next morning.

COHEN (AT HOME)

"I don't unnerstand," Chantal said. "They say you go, you just go? No plane ticket? No return date? It's the year 2000, not medieval times. You are not a slave on a galley ship."

Chantal was the Wife. She was French Tunisian. Fine bones. Black hair. A quick temper that blotched her cheeks.

"It's my job," Cohen said.

"Your job!" Chantal dug her spoon into a pint of gelato.

The baby was wailing.

Cohen had met Chantal at a Salomon Brothers function. They had gotten drunk and done what young couples do. A few weeks later she was pregnant and Cohen, wanting to do right, married her. His father was dead, his mother was thrilled. His younger sister, floating somewhere outside Santa Cruz in an irritable lesbian phase, said, "Do yourself a favor and get a paternity test."

Now they lived in a one-bedroom in Queens. Chantal was an aspiring model, but the pregnancy had ruined her skin. She blamed Cohen. Ruby was a pork chop, a doll face, she maybe had his mouth, he thought so, and a little Mohawk, but she cried so much.

Cohen unstrapped her from the high chair and stared at her face. It was rutted with distress, a red pecan. "What's the matter, baby?" Cohen said. "It's okay, baby."

Chantal made a fart noise with her cheek. "That's right. Reason with the baby. And what if you never come back? You go to this Arab place with your Jew name and your nose—"

"He's a major client. This is an *honor*." He rubbed Ruby's back and felt her begin to subside. "It could lead to things."

"And if you never come back?"

Cohen sighed. His apartment smelled of baby shit and artificial lavender. All the lamps were broken. "Stop being dramatic."

Chantal thwacked her spoon against the wall. The baby tensed. He felt her engine knock, then catch—the inexorable ascent to a tantrum.

"Americans! So naive. So sure of yourselves. Did you get the fucking uggies? The *uggies*! I thought no."

TRIP OVER

The plane looked like a shark, long and sleek. It was unmarked beyond the call letters, and Cohen was the only passenger on it. A pair of young women served him shirred eggs and dispatched him to a couchette, where he fell into a profound sleep. He woke over a blue expanse decorated with islands in the shape of Arabic characters. These were the Suras, the Emirate's latest project, 114 luxury islands.

"All dredged from the Gulf," one of the beauties explained. "That one is the Thunder. The Moon is there. The Spoils of War. Oh, and that one is Repentance. Repentance is new!"

The articulation of the letters was astounding, but Cohen wondered aloud who, aside from plane passengers fluent in Arabic, would be able to appreciate the project.

"God will see them," the girl said softly, "and smile."

WHAT COHEN NOTICED

1. Everything was clean.

Immaculate. It was as if a giant vacuum had sucked up all unwanted matter and left behind fresh carnations. This was moving to Cohen, whose floors at home were scattered with half-chewed mini-waffles, who was himself sheathed in a thin, chemically detectable layer of poop. He soaked in the tub for an hour.

2. It was like being in a casino.

There were no clocks anywhere. The surfaces sparkled. The air was richly oxygenated. Cohen was staying on the top floor of the Haj. From his window he counted 143 cranes. There were hotels in the shapes of a crescent, a scimitar, an oyster shell. Directly across from him a row of workers sat in slings half a mile above the earth, squeegeeing the windows of a building whose summit Cohen could not see.

3. The Emirate was exploding.

This is what his tour guide said, over and over. He pronounced the word "ixploding." The new civic projects included an underground aviary with more than eighteen thousand species of birds, a library of antiquated books larger than Alexandria's, a facsimile of the Temple Mount rendered in electrum. His guide had a fascist's passion for statistics and the feline smile of a pharaoh. Did Cohen know how many tons of marble had been quarried to create the Jubilation Pavilion?

Cohen called home three times. Chantal refused to answer.

*

BLADE NIGHT

He dreamed of his father, hunched in his recliner, lecturing the world on its failings. His father who had flunked out of college and fought in the Korean War, then flunked out of college again and sold insurance to widows. Death: his first and only ally. That was the joke.

"Dad?" Cohen said.

His father made no indication of having heard him.

The baby started wailing.

"That's Ruby," Cohen said. "That's your granddaughter."

His father drew a knife from his coat pocket and calmly punched it into his own stomach. Cohen woke with his ribs pounding. It took him a full minute to remember where he was.

HIGH ABOVE THE EARTH, AN OMELET

In the morning, a butler led Cohen to a private elevator, which opened onto a helipad atop his hotel. He was whizzed to a second helipad and driven along a narrow path to an egg-shaped platform whose means of suspension was unclear. At the center of the platform a table set for two awaited. The sheik wore a crisp dishdasha and sunglasses. To his left, a chef stood at attention behind an omelet station.

"Mr. Cohen," the sheik said.

"Good morning," Cohen said. He wasn't sure whether he should shake hands or bow.

The sheik made a sweeping gesture. The breeze rippled his headdress. The distant cranes were toys. Cohen suffered a wave of vertigo.

"You like eating outside? The prophets felt the same way. They did their best thinking on mountains." The sheik was younger than Cohen had expected. His accent sounded Southern Californian. "Everything good so far?"

"Very nice," Cohen said. "Spectacular." Some miles away, the glittering girdle of the Emirate gave way to a drab yellow.

"You know how much that suite runs? Eleven thou a night. Seriously, right? No worries." He lifted his glasses and rubbed his eyes, then let them drop back into place. A Bloody Mary appeared in his hand. "Agassi and Sampras played tennis right where we're sitting. You seen either of those guys play?" The sheik drained his Bloody Mary. "What sort of omelet you want? This man here, Bernard, makes the finest omelet on the planet. He's Belgian. Flemish. Name an ingredient. Any ingredient." The sheik waited for him.

"Tomatoes?" Cohen said. "Goat cheese?"

"Come *on*," the sheik said. He ordered shaved black truffle and foie gras.

The sheik began to discuss an actress he admired. She had starred in a cable television program about female astronauts. He had flown her over for a special screening sponsored by the Ministry of Culture. A parade had been held. The sheik wanted it known that he had not slept with this actress, despite the opportunity. Their relationship was professional. The Emirate would soon initiate a space program.

The omelets arrived. They were impeccable, diaphanous, the sort of omelets that deserved their own television show.

The sheik picked up a knife. "So you wanna know why you're here."

"It has been a little mysterious," Cohen said.

"Yeah, Arab customs. Here's the deal: the sheik needs your advice."

"The sheik? I thought—aren't you the sheik?"

The man across from him laughed. "No, man. I'm his nephew."

Cohen knocked his forehead with the heel of his palm and laughed and took a huge, relieved bite of omelet. "Of course I'll offer advice. That's what we, the firm, get paid—"

"The sheik asks this of *you*, Mr. Cohen." The nephew removed his sunglasses and narrowed his red eyes. "You understand?"

"Not really," Cohen said.

The nephew smiled without much warmth. He produced an envelope, upon which Cohen's full name was embossed in gold. "It's all good," he said.

WHO ARE YOU?

Inside was an invitation to the royal track. Cohen didn't know what to do. It was Saturday, the office was closed. He called home.

Chantal answered on the first ring. "Dan'el! Is it you? Where have you been?"

"Here," he said. "I'm here."

"Why you don't call? I thought something terrible—"

"I *did* call," Cohen said. "Three times. The machine didn't pick up."

"The fucking machine!" Chantal cursed in French. "You know how I hate the fucking machine!"

"Calm down," Cohen said.

"You travel to this place, like you're some kind of James Bonds."

"It's a business trip," Cohen said.

"So why there's no number to call? Which kind of business is that?"

Cohen moved the receiver away from his ear and waited. Chantal's mother had been an aspiring opera singer. She appeared at their wedding, unannounced, drunk, with a man younger than Cohen and too much rouge. Chantal wore hers the same way, glamorously bruised. Cohen told her she didn't need that stuff, she was beautiful, never mind the pimples. The makeup made him nervous to touch her face when they made love, which wasn't a lot these days but it did happen. It was something they could still give each other. Cohen wanted to be able to touch her face, to undo some of the worry there. She was stuck; they both were. He closed his eyes and felt a stab of pity, the unpleasant sensation of love draining from his sympathies.

"How's Ruby?" he said.

Chantal yelled something in French. She began to cry. Then Ruby began to cry.

"Let me talk to her," Cohen said. "Let me say hello to the baby."

The line went dead.

SHIPS OF THE DESERT

The royal track was a dirt strip flanked by highways. Cohen sat beside the sheik's nephew in a canary-yellow Hummer and gazed at the far end of the strip. The winner's circle, a patch of lawn, glowed against the sand.

"Kentucky blue," the nephew whispered to Cohen. His breath

smelled of limoncello. "The real shit. They flew these guys in from Louisville, sod specialists. Like five of them, all named Bob. They thought they were going to stay in tents."

Cohen wanted to ask the sheik's nephew what his name was, but events seemed to have progressed beyond that point. "Is the sheik here?" he said.

"Somewhere."

A metallic siren sounded above them. The nephew pointed to a small corrugated compound. A procession of camels lumbered forth, each with a tiny rider in colorful silks.

"They look like kids," Cohen said.

"They are! Pakistanis, a few from Sudan. The Pakis are stronger with the whip." The nephew bellowed across the track at a young sheik, who grabbed his crotch and spit over his shoulder. They both laughed. "Fucking Al Fayeed."

"The jockeys are really kids?" Cohen said.

"Yeah, we buy them from their parents." The nephew shook his head and giggled. "Come on, man. Don't be so gullible."

The windows of the Hummer scrolled down and the heat socked Cohen in the face. A bell sounded. The camels took off. The caravan of SUVs lurched after them. None of the drivers were watching the other drivers, because they were watching the camels and yelling into walkie-talkies and smoking.

The nephew was rammed from behind. He laughed and snatched an energy drink from a refrigerated tank built into the dashboard. "Ships of the fucking desert, man. I just made forty-five thousand dollars. Nice fucking work."

Cohen asked if he might visit the clubhouse.

"You're gonna miss the second race. There's only three. You got to drop a deuce or what?"

WHIRLIGIG

Inside the cinder-block clubhouse were a bartender and an old man nibbling at an ice-cream bar. Cohen asked the sbartender for a soda water and got tonic instead.

The trip had been a mistake. He was not someone who did well in unstable situations. His father had told him this long ago, at an amusement park, after he threw up on the whirligig. "So rides aren't for you. So stay off them." The tonic was flat.

Cohen closed his eyes and saw Ruby on her changing table, the puddles of rosy fat. He wanted to take a bite out of her thigh, just a little one, but she was busy weeping. And then Cohen himself was choked up, thinking about how much he loved her and how perhaps useless his love was.

Outside, the race bell sounded.

"Beware the prerogatives of wealth."

Cohen looked up.

The old man smiled at him. He looked like an Arab Santa Claus: twinkly, animated. Bits of chocolate were affixed to his beard. "Galloping camels. A foolish pleasure. But perhaps you're a fan."

"Not really," Cohen said.

"You look sad."

Cohen shook his head.

"You are far from home, I presume. What brings you here?"

"Business," Cohen said.

"Of what sort?"

"I don't mean to be rude." Cohen smiled in apology. "I really don't. But I'm thinking it might be best if I just had some quiet time."

The old man tapped his chin.

A few minutes later the sheik's nephew appeared. He glanced at the old man. "I see you've met the sheik," he said to Cohen.

THE SHEIK (AT LAST)

The sheik apologized to Cohen. He'd intended no deception. It was tradition, to see how a man behaves without the cloak of duty. This was at dinner, on the outskirts of the Emirate. They sat in an open courtyard, under torches, partaking from a large common bowl. The air was scented with cloves.

Cohen ate, miserably.

"You are unhappy," the sheik said.

"I'd just like to know—I realize you have customs, but I've been here for two days. It's been very nice. But I have a family at home, a young daughter, and I'd like to know, with all due respect." Cohen cleared his throat. "How can I help you?"

"Yes. Caution can descend into obscurity." The sheik scooped some rice into his mouth and chewed thoughtfully. "Tell me what investments you would advise in the event of an airborne disaster."

Cohen wasn't quite sure what he'd heard. Was it *urban*? "A disaster?" he said.

"A hijacking. Perhaps several. An attack on civilians initiated by airplanes."

Cohen took a moment to gather himself. "That's not really my specialty," he said. "I work mostly with currency issues. Differentials. Perhaps there's been a misunderstanding."

The sheik continued to chew.

"We have an entire risk-assessment *division*," Cohen insisted.

"I know who you are," the sheik said. "And I am asking what *you* would advise."

Cohen gazed at the faint outline of a crane. "I'm not sure I feel comfortable answering that question."

The sheik regarded him with a warm smile. He was one of those men who exuded fatherly benevolence. It was probably nonsense. Probably he had his servants chopped in two for missing a spot. But it was difficult to feel that looking at him.

"I'd have to think about it," Cohen said.

SLIPPING BEAUTY

The avenues of the Emirate were wide and bright, and the construction never stopped. Workers swarmed and pecked and hammered. At night, lanterns hung from the rails and made the scaffolding wink. Cohen stood at his window in a cashmere bathrobe. His calls home had gone unanswered. It was Saturday night, Sunday morning. He wished he'd packed Chantal's sleeping pills.

He lay on the bed and considered calling his mother. She would think it was about Ruby. He would have to explain. *I'm in an Arab kingdom. No, Ma. It's for work. Yes, I'm eating.* He would tell her he was—what? Frightened? Lonely? The TV channels showed sports clips, models in bikinis, men burning things and laughing.

Cohen didn't want to be any of them. But he didn't want to be himself, either. It was how TV got you.

In the middle of the night, he awoke to find a young woman sitting on the edge of his bed.

"Slipping beauty is awake," she said. Her accent was eastern European, comically so. The girl stood up and lifted her lingerie over her head. Her body, backlit by the TV, was a brutal sculpture. Her scapulae curved like dark wings. "Who do you want to be?" she declared. "We are outside of time."

Cohen's body understood the situation, but his mind was still foggy. The girl leaned toward the bed and made a purring noise. Her breasts shivered. The perfume hit hard. His fingers tensed, then a memory seized him, somewhat cruelly: his neighbor's eldest daughter, Julie Jewett, bending down to pull weeds. She was a plump, lascivious girl, snaggletoothed. A few years ago his mother had called with an urgent piece of gossip: Julie Jewett had become (as she put it) a "streetwalker."

Cohen rubbed his eyes and the girl, the whore, was still there. "I appreciate the offer," he said. "I do. But I should sleep."

The girl began to touch herself. Her fingers made a wet click.

"Please. I have a wife and child."

"Lucky girls," she said.

Cohen gazed at the girl for another moment. Her face was immaculate, as if degradation were merely an inconvenient form of ambition. But she was too thin and too far from home. Her story wouldn't end well.

"Do you need help?" Cohen said.

The girl's neck stiffened. She looked as if she was going to spit at him.

"Please," he said again. "I'm just here for business."

DATA

He left a rather confused message for Mr. Vanderweghe and then inquired of the concierge as to the location of the American embassy. There wasn't a full embassy yet, just a few consular officers. He took a quick shower. When he emerged, the nephew was sitting on his couch, sucking on a fig.

"You got lunch plans?"

Cohen said, "I don't think that's a good idea."

"You're pissed about the girl, huh?"

Cohen shook his head, like it was all a misunderstanding. "I'm not the guy you want."

The nephew withdrew a PalmPilot from his robe and tapped a few buttons. "Daniel Evan Cohen. Born June 6, 1974. New Haven, Connecticut. Social security 421-90-5272."

Cohen's chest fluttered.

"Don't freak out," the sheik's nephew said. "The sheik just wants your advice."

"I don't really have a choice here, do I?"

The nephew looked offended. "You always have a choice," he said.

THE SHEIK (REDUX)

"I offer a second apology. It pains me to imagine a guest unhappy." The sheik plucked an olive from the colossal pile between them and began a dainty inspection. They were in a smaller courtyard. The frescoes along the walls shone violently.

"I appreciate that," Cohen said. "I really do. But I'm not sure—" He paused. "I feel like I might be being held against my will."

The sheik frowned. He tapped his heart with two fingers. "Nothing bad is going to happen to you, Daniel."

"But I could leave if I wanted? Right?"

"Of course." The sheik smoothed the robe over his belly. "Is this what you would like?"

Cohen filled his eyes with the utmost regret, and nodded.

"That is a disappointment to me," the sheik said. "I hoped we might become better acquainted. But I see I have given offense."

"It's only that I don't think I'm the best qualified to advise you."

"Yes," the sheik said. "You have told me there are others whose expertise exceeds yours. I understand. But you are the one who sits before me now." The sheik popped the olive into his mouth and licked his thumb. "Why do you think that is, Daniel?"

Cohen shook his head.

"Because I have chosen you."

"But you don't know me, really."

"I am coming to know you. I know, for one example, that you are worried about corruption. You regard it as an unnatural condition. It offends your morality. But what has been accomplished by our species that didn't involve foresight? Jacob and his birthright. David. Saul. We make the arrangements necessary to honor our covenants."

"I'm really only half-Jewish," Cohen said.

The sheik cast his eyes toward the blue square of sky above them and shrugged gently. "You may leave now, my friend. Of course. It was only a wish that you would serve as my adviser, not a command."

The sheik stood. Cohen was beset by a sudden confusion. He tried to gather himself, but could think only of his father returning home, dampened by rain, and the mood that seemed to blaze around him each night, which Cohen had always taken to be rage but which he now saw was something closer to panic. Once, when he was about ten, Cohen had found his father slumped in his recliner, staring out the window. "Do you want something, Dad?" Cohen said.

"A cold beer and a better life," his father said.

The sheik sank slowly back into his seat. He was still smiling, though his eyes were glum. "I am offering you an opportunity, Daniel. God bestowed certain talents upon you. I recognize them, even if you do not."

The question seemed to be: what sort of life did he feel himself entitled to? Wasn't that what the sheik was asking? Had his father ever been asked such a thing? Cohen's cheeks tingled. He felt a disorienting surge of relief.

"If I knew something were going to happen," he said softly, "a particular event, to a particular country. I'm speaking generally. You'd expect the currency to weaken, obviously. Certain industries would slump. Others would benefit over the longterm—defense for sure, private security—and you'd want to buy call options. You know what a call option is? You'd want to buy a whole bunch at a strike price that seemed insane. That'd be the way to do it, derivatives. Buy in volume through a series of offshores and sell off as you approach the strike. You load up on the stocks themselves, it's too fishy." Cohen paused. "What I'm telling you is what anyone could tell you."

"But you are not anyone," the sheik said. "You are Daniel Cohen."

FLIGHT

He was getting on a plane, escaping. He'd been chased through a series of atria by giant grouse, into a brightly lit tunnel that required him to hunch over. The tunnel turned into an airport terminal, a tarmac, and now this plane where he sat with something bundled in his arms that he wasn't allowed to look at. The engines coughed to life and he closed his eyes. The pilot's voice came over the intercom and it was Mr. Santello, his father's boss. "We've got a problem up here," he said.

Cohen opened his eyes. The dawn was a red blade over the Gulf.

THE SHEIK (A FINAL TIME)

His office was in a small, anonymous building several miles from the city center. It was humbler than Cohen expected. On one wall were photos of the sheik: flanked by two senators, shaking hands with a vice president, gazing shyly at a young pop star as she sipped from a straw. The singer's mysterious death had been ruled a suicide.

Cohen didn't hear the sheik come in.

"Sit sit sit," he said. "You look tired, Daniel. Did you sleep?"

"Some," Cohen said.

"Strange dreams? It happens when I travel. But Daniel is the one who understands dreams, is he not?"

"I'd like to leave," Cohen said. "You said yesterday I could leave if I wanted to."

The sheik looked pleased. "He comes to the court of the Babylonians to advise the king. I don't suppose Daniel was any happier among the Chaldeans. Then the den of lions. Terrifying! Even for a man of great faith."

Cohen had a wild notion: the sheik was himself a dream. The towers and minarets—none of it was real. Soon Ruby, summoned from a fitful sleep, would cry out. He would find her curled against the rail of her crib, rubbing her eyes in the dim.

The sheik said, "Let me tell you what will happen next. The nominal sum that resides with your current firm will remain there. A larger sum will be transferred to a fund and placed under your sole control." The sheik mentioned a sum.

Cohen went white.

"There will be no records, paper or otherwise," the sheik said. "Your namesake, in addition to his talent with dreams, was an exceptional administrator. This is why the sultans employed Jews for financial matters. Jews feel an ethical compulsion. They are, you might say, honest despite themselves."

"I've been with the company less than six months," Cohen said.

The sheik tossed his hands in sympathy.

"What about Mr. Vanderweghe?"

"You musn't worry about him."

"My wife. She told me this might happen."

"Yes, Chantal is it? Shall we call her?"

The sheik took the phone and murmured a few words in Arabic, then jabbed a button and Chantal's quavery voice rang out.

"Allo? Allo?"

"*Honey*?" Cohen said.

The sheik excused himself from the room with a small bow.

"How did you get on this phone line?" Cohen said.

"You called me," Chantal said. "Why do you yell?"

"I want to know what the fuck is going on."

But Cohen could see the situation. The sheik had hired Chantal to seduce him. How hard would that have been? Cohen with his bulging eyes and his nose. She had worn a white sarong the first time he saw her. And now she had a child, his child, his Ruby, and he was bound to do right by both of them.

"How much did they pay you?" he said.

"Dan'el—"

"Don't lie to me," Cohen said.

Chantal began weeping, not the loud sobs of an actress, but soft squealing hiccups, like a dolphin. She sounded like Ruby, that pure in her misery. She had been this way the night she confessed her pregnancy—a former exchange student of dubious means adrift in

America, standing in the middle of Cohen's living room, shivering, her teeth stained by the wine she had drunk to muster her nerve.

"I'm sorry," Cohen said.

"I don't unnerstand."

"Don't listen to me," Cohen said. "I'm just tired."

"What do you mean who pays me?"

Cohen closed his eyes. "I made a mistake. The hours have been very long here and I haven't been sleeping well. I got confused."

Chantal blew her nose. "When are you coming home?"

"Soon. Tomorrow probably."

"We miss you," Chantal said. Her voice was so soft.

"I miss you, too. I miss you both." He would grow old with this woman, her needy aggravations, the way she clung to Ruby as the child fed from her breast.

"Dan'el? Are you okay?"

"Yeah. Don't worry. I'll be home soon." Cohen paused. "Listen, I may get a promotion."

EXIT STRATEGY

Cohen was in a limo. His bags were in the back. Someone else had packed them.

"You deal with me now," the nephew said. He sipped from a snifter of fresh orange juice and something else. "Look: There's nothing you can do about any of this shit. It's happening way above your head. It's happening in some cave you've never even thought about."

Cohen shook his head. "It doesn't make sense. You don't need me."

"Probably not," the nephew said. "But you're a loyal guy. Not everyone is like that anymore. You take care of your family and you do good work at your job, which happens to be making money on investments. It doesn't sound like a bad life, man. Anyway, it wasn't my call."

They drove on in silence. Cohen watched the desert flick past.

"You think we control shit, but we don't," the nephew said. "We didn't put the plankton under the earth. We didn't invent the car or the highway or the dollar." He was a drunk, sociably so. "That kind of luck can't last forever, right? So you diversify. No one's going to plant drugs in your bag or mess with your kid or listen in on your phone calls. Stop worrying. It's just business."

MANKIND

Cohen stared out his window. The plane banked sharply and the latest of the Sura Islands came into view. Workers swarmed over the sand like dark insects.

The sheik had made a gift to him of a bilingual Koran, and Cohen spent a few minutes flipping around in the book, trying to identify the islands before they slid from view.

One of his servers, the loveliest, knelt beside him. "Al-Nas," she whispered.

"I'm sorry?" Cohen said.

She blushed. "The final sura."

"What's it mean?"

"Look it up," she said playfully.

Cohen struggled to look away from her, from the idea—painfully clear to him—that he could have her if he so desired. He glanced at the Koran.

"Mankind," she said. "We ask Allah for protection from Satan." She held out her hand and Cohen handed her the book and she turned to the right page and handed it back, so Cohen could see it in English.

The girl closed her eyes and began singing in Arabic.

In the name of Allah, the Beneficent, the Merciful.
Say: I seek refuge in the Lord of Mankind.
The King of Mankind.
The God of Mankind.
From the evil of the sneaking whisperer.
Who whispereth in the hearts of mankind.
Of the jinn and of mankind.

The girl finished singing and opened her eyes. The plane banked again and she set her hand on Cohen's shoulder and squeezed lightly.

"Who is the jinn?" Cohen said.

"You would say, maybe, 'genie.' A powerful ghost. Something you cannot see that holds you."

The girl asked if he wanted anything else.

Cohen shook his head slowly. He looked down at the page again and read the words and tried to imagine a God equal to the trouble of His creation. The plane hit a patch of bad air and for a moment Cohen was plummeting toward the earth, a small creature, smaller than Ruby, whistling with dumb velocity. When he awoke, the jeweled lights of his city were beneath him. *So this is who I am*, he thought.

Cohen had asked his father once whether God existed. He wanted to know if it was God who lifted your body into heaven when you died. "What you see is what you get," his father said. It was true, like most things his father said, which made it no less cruel.

THE RANGER QUEEN OF SULPHUR

from **vol. 6, no. 2**

Stephanie Soileau

IT WAS NEARLY DAWN. Deana had been up all night disbanding a cult of hooded dwarves who were sacrificing children to a giant eyeball. Her mouth was dry, her eyeballs were fuzzy. There was a tinny hum in her head. But she decided that as long as she was awake anyway, she might as well do as she'd promised and go with her brother to his eight o'clock appointment at the obesity specialist. With at least an hour before she had to leave the house, she packed another bowl into her pipe. She opened her bedroom window, perched the box fan facing outward on the sill, and lit another stick of sandalwood incense, which she sank into the barren dirt of the flowerpot on her cluttered desk. She hit the bowl. She clicked the mouse.

There was plenty of time yet to seek out a curative potion for her druid, who had been struck by a poisoned arrow and was hemorrhaging massive hit points each turn. Whenever the poison took its toll, the little druid avatar, a long-haired, leather-clad figure with a wooden staff, would shudder and go "Hunh!" In five turns, he would be dead. Azama (née Deana), exiled ranger queen, halted her party in a circle of stone ruins and cast a healing spell on her afflicted companion. It was only a palliative, but it would buy them some time. "Hunh!" said the druid, and shuddered.

From the dark beyond the ruins emerged a specter in a purple shroud, its hand held up as if in blessing. There was a bright flash. The trees, the stream, the adventurers—all went eerily still. The specter, moving fast, came to the frozen figures each in turn and touched them with its thin fingers. One after another they silently died, last of all the ranger queen. Now on the screen a human hand floated in a starry cosmos. It turned and stretched its fingers as though its owner were regarding it in wonder. With a spasm, the hand exploded into dust. The game blinked off and Deana found herself looking instead at the keyboarding tutorial she had left open the previous night.

"The fuck?" she said. The timer on the ten-key numeric test was still running, nine hours and thirty-seven minutes later.

Granted, she was stoned and therefore apt to overlook or misinterpret vital details, but a lengthy search through her hard drive revealed no evidence of the game file that represented more than four hundred hours of her life for the last four months—about twice what she'd spent at work, and fifteen times what she'd spent on her classes at the vocational college.

It took another long while (just under nine minutes, according to the typing timer) of watching a red ember burn the incense stick to ash before she began to understand the magnificence of this loss. All of it, she thought, just gone.

MORE TIME GONE GETTING DRESSED, changing clothes again and again, trying to like this body she had inherited from her father and shared with her brother, this imposing colossus that stood five feet eleven with shoulders like a linebacker's, this mighty frame that—despite breasts for which she had to special-order brassieres—looked ridiculous, she thought, in dresses and in most women's clothes. Fine, so clothe it in jeans, a crew neck T. Why fuss over what cannot be helped? Although she was large, yes, dense and big of bone, unlike her brother she was not obese; her body, she thought in her best moments, was the body of a warrior. Her best moments, unfortunately, were few.

She had written the information about Jonathan's appointment around the edges of a pay stub and stashed it somewhere not obvious, not on her desk, not in her wallet. Finally she found it on her dresser, under bras and Coke cans. When she pulled it from the mess, she started an avalanche. She kicked aside the towel that was blocking the crack under her door and gave her shoes a twice-over on the way out, once to see if they were tied (they were) and once more because by the time she looked up, she'd already forgotten whether they were or not.

And she was almost on her way.

Her mother was in the kitchen stirring a pot of roux on the stove, easing the bubbling flour-and-oil brew from pasty beige to nearly black. It filled the house with a charred, ashy tang that smelled both catastrophic and delicious. "I've got the ladies for lunch," she said. The ladies being a set of poof-haired old dames from the local KC hall who invaded each other's homes once a week to confer over crime maps and recipes, to worry each other into a state of panic over cholesterol, and to ask humbling questions of whatever adult children still occupied rooms that should by now have been converted into arts-and-crafts or computer retreats for their retired parents. Deana's mother waved a dishtowel like a fan to drive off a hot flash. Her eyes, behind the fogged-up lenses of her glasses, were distressed. "What do you smell like?"

"I don't know. A billy goat? A puppy dog?"

"I really wish you wouldn't burn incense. It's hard on your daddy's lungs. Are you going to the doctor with Jonathan?"

"Well, I told him I would."

"Don't let him agree to anything expensive, he still doesn't have insurance. Here, I want you to bring him some of this." Into a plastic pitcher Deana's mother poured a murky, brown liquid from the jar that had been sitting atop the fridge for weeks with a gray fungus thick as a pancake floating on its surface. She had doted on this concoction, guarded it nervously, so difficult had it been to get her hands on the mushroom—the "mother fungus," she called it—originally obtained from who-knows-what-witch-doctor and reputed to work as, among other things, a decongestant, antibiotic, digestive aid, energy booster, stress buster, weight-loss supplement, hair thickener, rust remover, and foot soak.

"I'm telling you," Deana said, "he's not going to drink that."

"You tell him I said he better. He needs to do something or he's going to end up like Paw-Paw Curtis." She covered the mouth of the pitcher with a layer of plastic wrap. Then she poured more tea into a mug and said, "Go give that to your father."

Deana's father, a six-foot-five Goliath tethered to his recliner by oxygen tubes that snaked from his nose to a humming generator on the floor, sat watching television in the living room. Above his chair a trio of trophies—deer heads with nappy fur and ponderous antlers—hung alongside the bow that had killed them, back in the days when he could breathe. Since then he had fallen under evil enchantment: toxic rags, brought home in the pockets of toxic work clothes, invisibly powdered with dust from the Plant, which Deana, as a little girl, had thought was an actual plant, leafy and noxious, that her father spent his days pruning and watering. "Those work rags," her mother would say, telling the story for the five hundredth time. "I shook them out in the yard where the kids were playing. Nobody told us not to. I threw them in the wash with everything else."

"Mom wants you to drink this."

Her father reached up through the network of tubes and took the mug. He rasped between short, sudden breaths: "Is this that foul potion she's been. Brewing in the jar? That woman is trying. To poison me." He sniffed it, took a sip, and made a little noise of surprise and delight.

"Is it good?" she said.

"Not bad!"

As Deana turned to leave, he grabbed her forearm and looked at her with pleading eyes, his mouth a pucker beneath the cannula mustache. "Boo, catch me that. Remote control. If I have to watch. Another. *Andy Griffith*. I'm gonna shut this machine off. And die."

*

ON HER WAY TO THE HOSPITAL, still high, Deana imagined liposuction too vividly and knew she was going to have to ditch her brother's appointment. Just last week she'd seen the procedure documented on TV in troubling detail: the tube laced through a hole in the flesh, the slurping, slapping, wet sound as it jabbed and sucked at the curdy fat and siphoned it, yellow and blood-marbled, into a jar. She could not possibly sit next to Jonathan while a doctor described such things. And besides, she was nearly late.

She stopped at a green light. The car behind her honked. She took a left and drove east on the long stretch of road that was Sulphur's main drag. She passed car dealerships, trailer dealerships, dollar stores, and the cross street that led to the hospital. She passed the Payday Loan where she spent most afternoons. After two miles through tank farms and a sloppy complex of hotels and floating casinos, she crossed the bridge to Lake Charles and pulled off, finally, at the beach.

She backed her truck across the sand, lowered the tailgate, and stretched belly-down on the rusted bed. Greenish foam washed up at the shoreline and congealed. On the opposite shore: a petrochemical metropolis, the likely source of this muck. Vista, Olin, City Services. A long white burn-off cloud trailed from a smokestack to join a low blanket of actual clouds, which made it seem the plants and refineries might be the source of all weather and gloom. If Deana had some magic thing of power, a ring of PVC pipe, forged in the fires of Vista Chemical, say, she might breach that dark city, sneak past the guards and alarms, and chuck the ring into a vat of boiling liquid plastic. The whole place would be consumed in its own evil flames. All would bow to the heroine who had broken the poisonous magic: Deana LaFleur, Ranger Queen of Sulphur.

But she was only who she was: A girl who had twice been held back in middle school, having sopped up the bleak conviction that all roads lead to Kmart or the Plant, so why bother. A girl upon whom, at twenty-five, it was only now starting to dawn that certain basic occupational skills might at least rescue her from the lowest forms of drudgery, but who, true to her nature, skipped three in every four classes. In fact, she had a typing class later that morning.

Beyond the tailgate the foul-breathed water kissed the shore. Down the beach, a pair of young men had turned up with a four-wheeler and were skidding out across the sand, shouting. A rebel flag streamed behind them.

"Assholes," Deana said. Then she stood up in the bed of her truck and yelled it: "Assholes! Assholes!" But clearly they couldn't hear her.

JONATHAN LIVED IN A RENTAL HOUSE on Eighteenth Street, in a neighborhood of lonely old ladies and young black families, and thus of cheaper rents and greater freedom to, say, rescue as many greyhounds as he cared to from the track at Delta Downs. So far he had cared to rescue three. The dogs, in varying stages of obesity themselves, ran barking to Deana when she opened the gate, the oldest a stout barrel on spindly legs, the youngest still slim and spry but for arthritic ankles wrapped tightly in gauze. The middle dog leaped up and pushed at her chest with its front paws. She raised the pitcher of tea above her head. "Call off your hounds," she said.

Jonathan sulked in the open doorway. He had to turn himself at an angle to get through. "Why should I?"

"Sorry I missed your appointment," she said, and didn't feel sorry at all, only angry that she should put up with so much and get no sympathy for her own failings.

"Whatever," said Jonathan. He pointed at the jumping dog. "Just knee her in the chest when she does that. Ruthie, down!"

Deana held out the pitcher. "Mother sent you mushroom tea."

"Ew."

"She said if you don't drink it, you'll turn into Paw-Paw Curtis."

"I liked Paw-Paw Curtis."

"I just remember he had no feet."

Jonathan took the pitcher and waddled toward the kitchen. A Big Gulp cup was sweating by the sink, and he popped the lid off and dumped out its watered-down contents. He filled it nearly to the top with the tea, poked the straw in, and snapped down the lid. The youngest dog raised itself, slowly and gracefully, onto hind legs and rested its front paws on the counter. It laid back its ears and twitched its nose.

"Get down," Jonathan said, with no conviction. He swung his hip and bumped the dog to the floor.

"It smells weird in here," Deana said. She shivered, rubbed at the goose bumps on her arms. "And it's freezing."

"So?" Even in the dreadful heat of Louisiana summers, Jonathan wore full-length pants that covered, but did not hide, the grotesqueries that were his legs. His stomach, a thick, drooping apron that hung down to his thighs, was bunched in the voluminous crotch of his pants and swayed when he walked, the great shuffling mass of him bumping walls and rattling the house as he went. He had never, ever been thin, but there had been a time, in his teens and early twenties, when he might have passed as "a big guy" like Deana was "a big girl," with the kind of bulky physique that straddled the line between might and fat. Even then, he had been sensitive about it. Once, when he was twenty-four, still living at home and soon to abandon pursuit of the world-religions degree he had been slowly creeping up on at the local college for seven years, Deana, only thirteen, told him giddily that he looked—with his Coke-bottle glasses and greasy black hair—exactly like her then hero Stephen King. She'd thought this was a compliment, but he slapped shut the textbook he was reading and threw it so hard across the room it left a dent in the wall. "And what do you think you look like, you mean little bitch?"

Now, Deana sat astride the arm of the sofa, wanting to make clear that she had no intention to stay and get high. For one thing, she couldn't bear the smell of these dogs. The newest one leaped onto the sofa and curled up, pressed against her leg. It sighed. Jonathan sat down next to it—the cushions under the dog rising up in a little hill, displaced by Jonathan's great weight—and patted its rump. He took a few tiny, quick sips from his giant cup of tea.

"What did the doctor tell you?" Deana said.

"He said lap-band surgery would be a good option." He set the cup on the floor and started loading the bowl of a pretty little glass pipe.

"Lap band? What is that?"

"They put, like, a rubber donut around your stomach to make you feel full."

"Fuck."

"And if you eat too much, you have 'productive burping.'"

"You mean you throw up?"

"It's 'productive burping.'"

"Gross."

Jonathan took a long draw off the pipe and held his breath. Through the exhale he said, "I guess it works really well. He's known people who lost, like, over two hundred pounds. But the surgery's too expensive."

"How expensive?"

"Twenty-five thousand dollars. So, you know, fuck it. I'll just be fat."

"Um," said Deana. "Why don't you not eat?"

"I wish you would stop asking me that."

"Go back to OA, then."

"Those bitches are assholes."

He passed Deana the pipe and a lighter, and in spite of her best intentions, she took it. She poked the dog until it moved from the couch, and then she settled into the cushions next to her brother. Before she took a hit, she let herself relish just the slightest hint of clear-minded outrage at this brother who would do nothing for himself, who could just relax into his misery, accept his imprisonment. At least, Deana thought, *she* was learning to type.

"Well, it's not like you're a shut-in yet, I guess." She set fire to the bowl.

Jonathan rocked himself out of his seat and went to the cassette tapes stacked two rows deep in towers on the bookshelf, their cases cracked and yellowed. He grabbed too many at a time and held them to his chest, picked through them one by one, examining the labels, many of them home-recorded, inscribed in the handwriting of high school and college friends who had, as far as Deana knew, long ago fled Sulphur. At last he found the one he wanted and shoved the rest back onto the shelf. "I'm digging the Bad Brains lately again," he said.

While the first song rushed from the speakers, beat its chest, bared its fangs, Jonathan shuffled to the kitchen and returned with a container of vanilla icing, a spoon, and a bowl of broccoli florets drizzled with white dressing. He took his place on the couch and balanced these things on his lap and knees, alternating crunchy florets with heaping white spoonfuls of frosting.

"Oh my God, Jonathan," Deana yelled over the pounding bass. "What are you eating?"

"Fuck off."

For the length of the cassette, they sat together on the couch in silence. The dogs, hypnotized by the prospect of food, stood frozen before Jonathan, noses to the carpet, ears alert, waiting for something to drop. When Deana was roused from her stupor by a shaking—rhythmic, constant—of the couch, she turned to her brother and saw him jerking his shoulders, wagging his head, twitching his feet. Somehow he danced under the weight of his weight like he could shake this body off, wriggle out as the thin punk-rock Jonathan who'd been sheltered there all this time.

He bumped the bowl of broccoli to the floor and the dogs lunged. They licked the splattered dressing from each other's paws, from the carpet, from the couch. They bumped each other's thick bodies out of the way and, in their clumsy chaos, toppled the Big Gulp cup. A puddle of mushroom tea spread across the rug. Jonathan gazed calmly upon the mess at his feet, sighed, and scooped up another helping of icing.

Deana stretched out her hand. "Give me some of that."

"Watch out, Dee," he said. "The dread serpent will come for you too."

AT THE PAYDAY LOAN, Deana sat at a desk behind bulletproof glass. Almost always—for the first few hours anyway, before the five o'clock rush—she was unsupervised and alone. She was equipped at her station with a creaky oscillating chair, the cash drawer, a telephone, and, most important, a computer with an online connection for recording transactions, looking up payment history, and, when no one was watching, searching whatever idle phrases came into her head, like *get me out of here* (about 1,340,000 hits) and *I hate Sulphur* (ten hits; eight relevant: "I hate Sulphur, LA, it's a flipping black hole" et al. Two more, not relevant: one by a blogger with a special loathing for sulphur-crested cockatoos and the other by a frustrated chemistry student). Today, Deana positioned her fingers on the keys as the typing teacher had shown her. Sighting and jabbing at letters, she gradually entered into the search engine the phrase *lap band surgery*.

If the first several links gave the same information, albeit in far more sophisticated and detailed terms, that Jonathan had already given her, the last link on the page was something like a revelation. Apparently this surgery, so expensive in America, could be performed for a fraction of the cost—only about forty-five hundred dollars in fact, a hefty but not unreasonable sum—in Mexico. There was a form on the Web site for scheduling consultations. Profound changes were as simple as clicking SUBMIT.

Moreover, when Deana opened another search screen and, surrendering the unattainable ideal of ten-finger typing, picked out with one finger the phrase *border crossing Mexico*, she found that it was no big trick to just *go* there. Mexico had always seemed as impossibly distant to her as New York or China, the only realistic destinations from the departure point of Sulphur being New Orleans, Houston, possibly Memphis, these three the most distant outposts on the rim of her map. But with no passport, almost no money, only minimal plans, a person could simply *go*. Remarkable. Even she could maybe manage this.

Someone tapped at the glass of her cashier's window. It was a plump woman with a lopsided hairdo and a right arm that ended at the elbow. She had first come in five months ago for an advance on her Walmart check and then again two weeks after that, and again two weeks later, and on and on, paying the growing fees and interest but always extending the loan at what was effectively an annual rate of over 3,000 percent. Deana had cashed her checks, minus the fees, and shoved back through the slot in the window an ever-diminishing pittance of bills and change, less than fifty dollars last time, with which this woman must somehow feed, clothe, and house herself for the next two weeks. Then the woman had stopped coming in. The catastrophe that began this miserable cycle—what could it have been? a busted refrigerator, a loss on the dogs, bail for an over-loved son?—now months distant. One crisis exchanged for another.

Sad. Well, what could Deana do? She probably got disability, at least.

"Somebody's been calling my workplace threatening to have me arrested."

"I'm not the one calling, ma'am."

"Well, who is?"

"My manager. But he isn't here." Deana asked for the woman's name and pulled up her file on the computer, making a show of doing something when she already knew there was nothing to be done. She said blandly, "It says you owe $620.75 and you haven't made a payment since February. That's why you're getting calls."

"Six hundred twenty dollars? For a two-hundred-dollar loan?" Her voice was tearful, plaintive, infuriating. "How am I supposed to pay that back?"

"I'm sorry but," Deana recited, as she had been trained to do, "you were given the terms of the loan and you signed a contract. If you fail to pay, we can report you to a collection agency. We can file charges of bank fraud, and"—she always fumbled over this blatant untruth—"we can have you arrested." Like most of the sad sacks who came in, this woman didn't know any better, and setting her straight was not Deana's job. She'd nearly been fired for that before.

The woman slid her purse from her shoulder and pinned it against her chest with the nubby right arm. The purse's strap was wrapped completely in duct tape and it flopped over the half arm while she rooted around. Finally she produced a wadded-up bill. "I can give you twenty right now, and when I get my next check, I'll give you another fifty."

This too was a dead end. "We can't take partial payments unless you give us your checking account number."

"I don't have a checking account."

"So you have to pay in full."

The woman tried to push the crumpled twenty through the slot, but Deana blocked the opening with her hand.

"You're telling me you won't take my money?" The woman turned to a young black man who had come in after her. A very small girl was pressed against his leg and held on to his fingers with both hands. "I don't understand why nobody will help me," the woman shrilled. "I can barely even buy my groceries. Young lady, why won't you help me?" Trembling with rage, the woman delivered to the young man and the little girl and the echoing walls of the otherwise empty storefront a disjointed tirade about Christian charity and a dying cat and a leaking roof and her own missing arm.

"They're thieves," the man said, and looked squarely at Deana. "They don't care about nothing or nobody." Then he picked up his little girl, propped her on his hip, and went on his own tirade. Electric bill. Surgery. Denied unemployment benefits. On and on. "Usury is a sin," he said. "It's a sin!"

Deana rose from her chair and pretended to search for something in a filing cabinet, her back to the window. After all, he was right. She didn't care. Let these people learn to read a contract. Let this woman not have lost an arm. Let them have been born somewhere else, as someone else, or not at all.

"You should be ashamed," the woman said to Deana's back, and left the store.

When Deana had processed the man's transaction and was once again alone, she came from behind the wall of her station and stood at the storefront door, gazing out. It was midafternoon. There was a heavy quiet on the main drag. Now and then a car crept by, fairly tiptoed. Deana locked the door, turned off the lights, and lay on her back right there in the entryway, the widest, emptiest stretch of linoleum in the store. She stretched out her arms and legs. The fluorescent light above her was the saddest thing she'd ever seen.

LATER THAT NIGHT, in the customer-service booth of the Kroger, Deana squatted on a footstool that Jonathan had been using to elevate his ashy gray feet, freed of their shoes but concealed from customers by a wall that enclosed the office from which Jonathan, once ensconced for his evening shift, was rarely called upon to descend. Split open in his hands was a raggedy novel with a snarling, bloodied pair of Dobermans on the cover. He put it aside reluctantly.

Deana shuffled through papers she'd printed from the Internet and explained about the doctor in Reynosa, just across the Rio Grande from McAllen, Texas, practically still the United States, really, and only eight hours away. "Americans go there all the time for prescriptions. It's so freaking cheap," she said. "You could just put it on your credit card."

Jonathan said, "Why is it so cheap?"

"I don't know. It's Mexico. You have a consultation next week." She showed him reviews, testimonials, before-and-after photos, the doctor's credentials, which were, granted, Mexican, their credibility impossible to assess. But there was a photo of this doctor, smiling, mustachioed, trim and clean in a white coat, posing with a smiling patient. She said, "We've got to do something."

A pair of eyes peeked over the tall counter of the booth. "Excuse me?" said a woman, jumping to see over. "Excuse me?"

Jonathan swiveled his chair to face her.

"Do y'all—," she said, sticking a little on the *y'all*, "do *y'all* have wonton wrappers?"

"Wonton wrappers?" said Jonathan.

"You use them to make egg rolls," the woman said. She looked from Jonathan to Deana. "It's the wrapper." She swirled a finger. "Around the egg roll."

"I know what they are," Jonathan said. He picked up the intercom mic but put it back down when he saw the long, curling lines at the registers, only two open—the late-night closing shift. "Just a minute," he said, and leaned sideways to retrieve his shoes from where they were tucked under the desk with his socks stuffed inside them. He took a sock in hand, scrunched it down to the toe, and rocked forward, wheezing, until sock met foot. He sat up again, panted for a while, then went for the other one. He did not bother to tie the shoes. "Let's look," he said. He descended the three steps from the service booth, still out of breath and, waving the woman to follow, shuffled off toward the back of the store. The woman went after him in half steps and pauses, trying not to dart rudely ahead of the slow-plodding fat man.

The woman was actually a girl, or not a girl, really, but young, Deana's age or a little younger, and, judging from the accent, not from around here, or from around here, but more like one of those kids Deana remembered from high school who talked about college as though it was something they'd actually do, and then, lo and behold, did, who would come back from summers chatting blithely about the house at Holly Beach, fishing the Gulf, or, a few of them, about weed in Amsterdam, punk clubs in Prague, who ran for student government or hung out in the art room making beaded necklaces and marionettes out of papier-mâché, who wrote columns, plays, poems, songs, learned guitar, like they thought anyone actually gave a fuck, like they thought they could actually do something. Like they could march into any damn place and ask for any damn thing they pleased.

"Wonton wrappers," Deana clucked when Jonathan was back in the booth. "Jesus! Where does she think she is?"

His feet came out of the shoes again and he stripped off the socks, which required much the same effort as before. "We usually have them. They're just out of stock." He was gasping for air, sweating through his shirt.

"Jonathan," Deana said. "How can you deal with that every day and not shoot yourself? We can go. Did you know that? We aren't trapped. We can just go."

"So you go, then. Bring me back a sombrero and some Chiclets." He picked up the novel again and held it in front of his face. She kept at him for another hour, but he wouldn't budge.

THEY RARELY CAME TOGETHER as a family and almost never as a family with other families. She had overheard her mother's excuses on the phone often enough. Jonathan was said to be shy, Deana busy with school. Of course it was always too hard on her father. Saturday was her father's birthday, however, and thus one of those extraordinary occasions that found them all in one place. Deana had not been warned (or had she?) about the gathering that was to take place in their kitchen and so stumbled into it, having just woken up at the indecent hour of noon, still wearing boxers, an oversize T-shirt, and no bra, reeking of weed.

Her father sat at the kitchen table with a store-bought cake in front of him. He was telling a story—one of his great pleasures, though the going was slow—to the husbands of the KC hall ladies. One of the men leaned against the refrigerator and kept checking his feet to see that he was clear of the oxygen tubes. Two more men were cocked back in chairs at the table, while her mother and three other ladies admired the mushroom tea. They passed it among themselves, mirthful with revulsion, and held it up to the light to examine the pale, webby scum that hung in amber liquid at the bottom of the jar. Jonathan teetered on a little stool in a corner far from the others. He was reading, or pretending to read, the local paper. It fell to Deana, as always, to be the presentable child.

Feeling like a lumbering giantess next to these women, nasty in mood and body, she crossed her arms over her bra-less breasts and said, "It's magic. Did Mother tell you? It cures cancer. It relieves debt. I'm pretty sure it summons demons."

Jonathan snorted in the corner, the only sign that he had been listening at all. The women looked at her like she'd spoken in tongues.

Her mother laughed weakly. "You don't have to make fun."

"Does it really do all that?" one of the women said. They speculated in earnest until an explosion of deep-bellied laughter from the men interrupted them. Her father had finished his story. There was an amiable pause during which they all—men and women—looked from one to the other. Jonathan rattled the newspaper and adjusted his fanny creakily on the stool. The jar of tea had made its way back to Deana's mother. She cradled it in the crook of one arm and said, philosophically and to no one in particular, oblivious to the lull in the room, "I just thought it might be good for Jonathan."

The guests turned their gaze casually to Jonathan, as though genuinely to assess in what sense the tea might be good for him. When he felt them all watching him, he peered over the top of the newspaper, then deliberately folded it and set it aside. If his weight had not pinned him so stubbornly in place, he might have risen and, with dignity, left the room. But then, if such an exit had been possible, he would not have been the subject of this unwelcome attention in the first place. Instead he sat there resting his hands on either side of his enormous belly, face stoic, like a greasy-haired, bespectacled Buddha.

"Well, we're all carrying a little extra around these days," said one of the men.

"You've got to love the body you got, hon," said one of the women.

Her father slapped a thigh with exaggerated enthusiasm and said something about the great-looking cake.

But their mother would not drop it. Flustered by her own faux pas, she grew shrill and angry. "It's a matter of health. His grandfather suffered so bad with diabetes. Do you think I want to see my child go through that? Lose his eyesight? Lose his feet? Jonathan, do you want to lose your feet?"

Jonathan was rocking himself back and forth for momentum. At first it looked like he might topple to the floor, but with one hand gripping the countertop and another braced against his thigh he managed to hoist himself off the low stool. Still wearing an impassive expression but sweating now, either from effort or shame, he said, "Don't be ridiculous. The asbestos poisoning will get us first."

Had Jonathan and Deana been alone together, warding off with jokes the dull terror that, in lighter moments, they had come to call, almost affectionately, the Big Suck, Deana would have laughed. But the acerbic, angry fatalism that registered in her mind and her brother's, paradoxically, as a weird kind of optimism did not sound so much like optimism when others were listening too. Her father's oxygen hiss-clicked. The men looked at the table or their shoes. The women looked at her mother, who squirmed as though she had been accused and then removed herself from the room.

And her father—whose good cheer relied not at all on mean tactics and was uncannily, even supernaturally, inexhaustible—he too seemed stricken and suddenly pale. "I don't appreciate that at all," he said.

Jonathan gave a nervous laugh and looked helplessly at Deana. She offered nothing, and finally, without another word, he squeezed past the men and left the room.

The gathering recovered. Soon her mother returned, red-eyed but wearing again the calculatedly pleasant face she wore for company. She served the cake. Deana's father embarked upon another story in which he was a reluctant and humble hero.

When Deana had sat long enough for propriety, she flopped a big slab of cake onto a plate and went after her brother. He was at her computer, playing the game she thought had disappeared from her hard drive. She felt a pang of joy and nostalgia, a dizzy longing for the familial little band of warriors, alive and battling orcs. She set the cake on the desk and watched over her brother's shoulder while he routed the enemy. When the gasps and groans and clanking armor had finally ceased, Jonathan paused the game. "Okay," he said but didn't turn around.

"Okay?"

"Okay." He wobbled his head, a little no, a little yes. "Okay, fine. We'll go to Mexico."

HE HAD CONDITIONS, THOUGH. They would not tell their parents, or anyone else, about the appointment. If asked, they were driving to Memphis for barbecue. All the way there for barbecue? Yep, all the way there. A weekend of messy, mustardy sauce, and they would come back fatter than ever before. He wanted snacks for the road—Doritos, beef jerky, sacks of bite-size chocolate candies—and a two-day orgy of illicit tasties, truck-stop hot dogs and taquitos, fast food for breakfast, lunch, and dinner. All to celebrate his imminent transformation. They spent almost a hundred dollars at Kroger.

The night before they were to leave, after packing her bag, smoking the last of her weed, and answering a call from a woman speaking first Spanish, then English, to confirm the appointment for Jonathan at the clinic in two days, Deana left a message for her brother to be ready at six the next morning. She was eyeing her computer and, having resisted the urge until now, was considering a celebratory binge of her own when her father, detached from his oxygen machine, tapped on her door frame. He said, "Your mother's at keno. And weather channel says. It's a nice night. How about taking a little ride. Baby doll?"

"Where?"

"I don't know. Anywhere. I ain't been out of this house. In a lifetime."

At night, from the top of the Lake Charles Bridge, the Plants dazzled, a spectacle: merry twinkling lights, fires atop chimneys white and slim and tall as dinner candles. The casino boats floated at their feet, yoked to the town like a couple of water buffalo to drag it out of the sludge pit of the eighties. They rolled down the windows, drove slow over the bridge, turned around and drove back over. She took him to the little beach, parked the truck facing the lake and the lights, and they sat for a while and looked.

"Peanut," he said, "I've been meaning to say. Your mother and me."

She felt a sudden terror that this would be the moment when he would tell her, finally—and it was about time, really—to leave his house and get out on her own, to quit getting high and messing around and squandering the life that he had wasted himself to give her. The oxygen canister, which leaned between them on the seat, released its gas in abrupt, quiet gasps whenever her father took a breath.

"We've been meaning to say," he said at last. "We're proud of you. For going back to school. And for being a good sister. To your brother."

She said nothing and did not look at him.

He reached over and patted her hand, let his fingers rest on hers. "I still know people over there," he said, and she knew he meant that twisted thicket of pipes and tank farms across the lake. "When you get your certificate. I can get you in."

"Okay, Daddy," she said.

"It's fine work, baby doll."

"Okay," she said. Deana withdrew her hand from his.

"Not like it was." The wide lake was spattered with moonlight, casinolight, Plantlight. One of the chimneys at Vista, dormant until now, threw up a hot yellow tongue of flame that sputtered and steadied. Her father took as deep a breath as he could and sighed. "Sometimes it's almost. Pretty."

WHEN DEANA PULLED into her brother's driveway at six o'clock sharp, his house was dark, the door shut and locked. She knocked for a long time. The dogs barked in a frenzy inside, until finally a light blinked on, they settled down, and her brother, hushing them, squinting, wild-haired, opened the door.

"Why aren't you up?" she said.

He yawned without covering his mouth. His pajamas were sweatpants and the biggest T-shirt she had ever seen. She followed him inside and closed the door, kneed the dogs away from her. She looked at her watch, showed it to him, tapped it. "I told you six. Hurry up!"

"I'm not going," he said. Like *I'm not hungry*. Or *Pass the salt*.

"You're going."

"I can't. There's nobody to watch the dogs." He sat on the couch and lolled his head to one side and the dogs piled on. The whole pack of them, her brother and his greyhounds, were still in their morning moods, just this side of drowse. "God, I'm sleepy," he said. "How are you so perky?"

"You said that guy Wyatt could take them."

"He said no."

"You said he said yes."

"He did. And then he said no."

"Then why don't you leave them at the vet, like everyone else?"

"I can't leave them in those little cages." He rested an arm along the spine of a curled-up dog.

"With Mom and Dad, then."

"Are you joking?"

"Then we'll take them with us. Jonathan, get up!" She grabbed his damp, mushy arm and pulled, but he did not budge. He shook Deana off and tried to cross his legs at the ankles, gave up and spread them wide, sunk low in the cushions and smacked his lips. Again the slow yawn, the squinting eyes. "I'm out of weed," he sighed. "Let's drive to Orange and stock up."

Deana glared at him, astonished. "We bought all that food." It was in her truck right now, in the middle of the bench seat, a fiesta in a cardboard box.

One of the dogs sat up on the sofa to scratch its side, and Jonathan slung an arm around it and pulled it close. "Do you need a bath, Ruthie-Ruthie?" He buried his face in the dog's neck and stayed that way for so long Deana thought he must have fallen asleep.

"You're going to get all that shit out of my truck. Right now. Get up."

He did not move.

"Jonathan!"

"Okay, okay."

She held the door open impatiently while he crammed his feet into flip-flops, and when he was finally coming out, she let it slam shut in his face. At the truck she waited again by the open passenger's door. It took him forever to cross the lawn.

"So, Orange later?" he said.

"I have a class."

"What class?"

"A typing class."

"That sucks. Maybe tomorrow, then." Clutching the box of snacks against his belly, he turned away, as though this delivery had been the sole purpose of her visit all along. The dogs wrestled clumsily under the trees. Jonathan gave a quick whistle. All three bounded into the house and he followed them and shut the door without even a good-bye.

SHE THOUGHT BY NOW she might have been dropped from the roster. She expected a scolding at least, but the instructor nodded when she walked in, and gestured for her to take a seat at one of the open typewriters. He scanned the list of names on his roll, finally asked her to remind him of hers, and then got immediately on with it. They were learning on typewriters rather than computers, he had explained long ago on the first day of class, because it would make their fingers stronger, the typewriter keys being stickier, more stubborn. But really, most probably, Deana knew, this crappy vocational school could not afford a whole classroom of computers. Typewriters they had, so typewriters it would be.

The other students were a motley range of ages and colors. Her nearest neighbor was a middle-aged black woman in neat, secretarial attire, and on the other side sat a big white kid who could be only just out of high school, if at all, with thick, immobile hands that had probably suffered in their attempts at fine motor activities since the early days of Legos and shoelacing. The students rolled paper into their machines and waited. Deana did the same. The teacher began to chant:

A space J space semicolon space
R space U space 7 space 5
cat hat rat bat pat goat moat

Pre-words, nonsense, became one syllable, then two, the words became phrases, the phrases proverbs.

Practice makes perfect.
An ant may well destroy a whole dam.
Better to light a candle than to curse the darkness.

And many of the others clickety-clicked right along, had indeed become nimble, or nearly so, even the kid with the impractical hands. Their progress weeks ago had seemed so impossibly, so glacially slow. It felt then, as it felt now, like Deana was accomplishing exactly nothing, going exactly nowhere; that she would never type or drive or toke her way out of this place that pinned her like a boulder on her toe, that could only be named after the stink it produced. It was the plants and the heat and the ruthless mosquitoes, the price of gas, the addictive games, the crappy jobs, the hostile rednecks, hopeless brothers, delinquent cousins, complacent mothers, jobless fathers, spiteful uncles, polluted waters, the stifling reek of sulfur and fast food and tanker-truck exhaust. It was the vague, embedded memory of those desolate eighties, the oil-bust years, the slim Christmases and government-issued "cheese food." The bumper stickers everywhere that read LAST ONE OUT, SHUT OFF THE LIGHTS! It was all of this and it was none of this. And if it wasn't this, what was it? It was her. It was in her. It was something awful in her. What candle could light such a darkness?

All around, the slow, tapping drone rose to a crescendo, an orchestra of swiftly clacking keys. And now, still, she could not hit a letter without looking for it first, and when she found it, she jabbed it with the same rage and hate that she might the eyes of a foe.

THE YEAR OF SILENCE

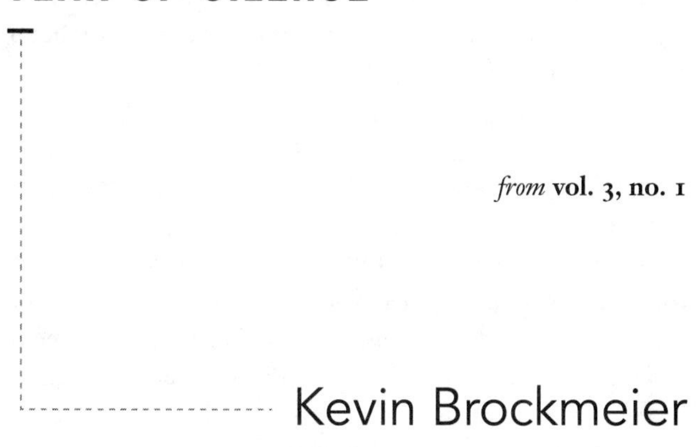

from **vol. 3, no. 1**

Kevin Brockmeier

1.

SHORTLY AFTER TWO IN THE AFTERNOON, on Monday, the sixth of April, a few seconds of silence overtook the city. The rattle of the jackhammers, the boom of the transformers, and the whir of the ventilation fans all came to a halt. Suddenly there were no car alarms cutting through the air, no trains scraping over their rails, no steam pipes exhaling their fumes, no peddlers shouting into the streets. Even the wind seemed to hesitate.

We waited for the incident to pass, and when it did, we went about our business. None of us foresaw the repercussions.

2.

THAT THE CITY'S WHOLE IMMENSE CAROUSEL of sound should stop at one and the same moment was unusual, of course, but not exactly inexplicable. We had witnessed the same phenomenon on a lesser scale at various cocktail parties and interoffice minglers over the years, when the pauses in the conversations overlapped to produce an air pocket of total silence, making us all feel as if we'd been caught eavesdropping on one another. True, no one could remember such a thing happening to the entire city before. But it was not so hard to believe that it would.

3.

A HANDFUL OF PEOPLE were changed by the episode, their lives redirected in large ways or small ones. The editor of a gossip magazine, for instance, came out of the silence determined to substitute the next issue's lead article about a movie star for one about a fashion model, while her assistant realized that the time had come for her to resign her job and apply for her teaching license. A lifelong vegetarian who was dining in the restaurant outside the art museum decided to order a porterhouse steak, cooked medium rare. A would-be suicide had just finished filling his water glass from the faucet in his bathroom when everything around him seemed to stop moving and the silence passed through him like a wave, bringing with it a sense of peace and clarity he had forgotten he was capable of feeling. He put the pill bottle back in his medicine cabinet.

Such people were the exceptions, though. Most of us went on with our lives as though nothing of any importance had happened until the next incident occurred, some four days later.

4.

THIS TIME THE SILENCE LASTED nearly six seconds. Ten million sounds broke off and recommenced like an old engine marking out a pause and catching spark again. Those of us who had forgotten the first episode now remembered it. Were the two occasions connected? we wondered. And if so, how? What was it, this force that could quell all the tumult and noise of the city—and not just the clicking of the subway turnstiles and the snap of the grocery-store awnings, but even the sound of the street traffic, that oceanic rumble that for more than a century had seemed as interminable to us as the motion of the sun across the sky? Where had it come from? And why didn't it feel more unnatural?

These questions nettled at us. We could see them shining out of one another's eyes. But a few days passed before we began to give voice to them. The silence was unusual, and we were not entirely sure how to talk about it—not because it was too grave and not because it was too trivial, but because it seemed grave one moment and trivial the next, and so no one was quite able to decide whether it mattered enormously or not at all.

5.

A STAND-UP COMEDIAN PERFORMING on one of the late-night talk shows was the first of us to broach the subject, albeit indirectly. He waited for a moment in his act when the audience had fallen completely still and then halted in midsentence, raising one of his index fingers in a listening gesture. A smile edged its way onto his lips. He gave the pause perhaps one second too long, just enough time for a trace of self-amusement to show on his face, then continued with the joke he had been telling.

He could not have anticipated the size of the laugh he would receive.

6.

THE NEXT MORNING'S NEWSPAPERS had already been put to bed by the time the comedian's routine was broadcast. The morning after that, though, the first few editorials about the silence appeared. Then the radio hosts and TV commentators began to talk about it, and soon enough it was the city's chief topic of conversation. Every family dinner bent around to it sooner or later, every business lunch, every pillow talk. The bars and health clubs all circulated with bets about the phenomenon: *ten dollars says the government had something to do with it, twenty says it will never happen again.*

When two full weeks went by without another incident, our interest in the matter threatened to shrivel away, and might actually have done so had the next episode not occurred the following Sunday, surprising us all in the middle of our church services.

There was another silence, more than ten seconds long, just a couple of days later, and a much shorter silence, like a hiccup, the day after that.

Every time one of the silences came to an end we felt as though we had passed through a long transparent passageway, a tunnel of sorts, one that made the world into which we had emerged appear brighter and cleaner than it had before, less troubled, more humane. The silence siphoned out of the city and into our ears, spilling from there into our dreams and beliefs, our memories and expectations. In the wake of each fresh episode a new feeling flowed through us, full of warmth and a lazy equanimity. It took us a while to recognize the feeling for what it was: contentment.

7.

THE TRUTH WAS THAT we enjoyed the silence, and more than that, we hungered for it. Sometimes we found ourselves poised in the doorways of our homes in the morning, or on the edges of our car seats as we drove to work, trying to hear something very faint beneath the clatter of sirens and engines. Slowly we realized that we were waiting for another incident to take place.

There were weeks when we experienced an episode of silence almost every day. One particular Wednesday saw three of them in the span of a single hour. But there were others when what the papers took to calling a "silence drought" descended upon the city, and all our hopes for a cessation went in vain. If more than a few days passed without some minor lull to interrupt the cacophony, we would become irritable and overtender, quick to gnash at one another and then to rebuke ourselves for our failures of sympathy. On the other hand, a single interlude of silence might generate an aura of fellow feeling that could last for the better part of a day.

The police blotters were nearly empty in the hours following a silence. The drunks in the bars turned amiable and mild. The jails were unusually tranquil. The men who ran the cockfights in the warehouses down by the docks said that their birds lost much of their viciousness after the great roar of the city had stopped, becoming as useless as pigeons, virtually impossible to provoke to violence.

And there was another effect that was just as impressive: the doctors at several hospitals reported that their mortality rates showed a pronounced decline after each incident, and their recovery rates a marked increase. No, the lame did not walk, and the blind did not see, but patients who were on the verge of recuperating from an injury often seemed to turn the corner during an episode, as if the soundlessness had triggered a decision somewhere deep in the cells of their bodies.

Surely the most dramatic example was the woman at Mercy General who came out of a prolonged coma in the space of a five-second silence. First her hand moved, then her face opened up behind her eyes, and soon after the noise of the hospital re-emerged, she moistened her lips and said that everything sounded exactly the same to her.

The doctors had a hard time convincing her that she was, in fact, awake.

8.

THE SILENCE PROVED SO BENEFICIAL to us that we began to wish it would last forever. We envisioned a city where everyone was healthy and thoughtful, radiant with satisfaction, and the sound of so much as a leaf lighting down on the sidewalk was as rare and as startling as a gunshot.

9.

WHO WAS THE FIRST PERSON to suggest that we try generating such a silence ourselves, one that would endure until we chose to end it? No one could remember. But the idea took hold with an astonishing tenacity.

Local magazines published laudatory cover stories on the Silence Movement. Leaflets with headings like PROMOTE SILENCE and SILENCE = LIFE appeared in our mailboxes. The politicians of both major parties began to champion the cause, and it wasn't long before a measure was passed decreeing that the city would make every possible effort "to muffle all sources of noise within its borders, so as to ensure a continuing silence for its citizens and their families."

The first step, and the most difficult, was the dampening of the street traffic. We were encouraged first of all to ride the subway trains, which were appointed with all the latest noise-alleviation devices, including soft-fiber pressure pads and magnetic levitation rails. Most of the cars that were left on the road were equipped with silently running electric engines, while the others had their motors fitted with mineral-wool shells that allowed them to operate below the threshold of hearing. The roads themselves were surfaced with a reinforced open-cell foam that absorbed all but the lowest frequency sounds, a material that we also adapted for use on our sidewalks and in our parking garages.

Once the street traffic was taken care of, we turned our attention to the city's other sources of noise. We sealed the electrical generators behind thick layers of concrete. We placed the air-conditioning equipment in nonresonant chambers. We redesigned the elevators and cargo lifts, replacing their metal components with a clear, durable plastic originally developed by zoos as a display barrier to prevent the roars of the lions from reaching the exhibits of the prey animals. Certain noises that weren't essential to either the basic operations or the general aesthetic texture of the city were simply banned outright: canned music, church bells, fireworks, ringtones.

10.

WE WERE EXULTANT when the roads fell silent and pleased when the elevators stopped crying out on their cables, but by the time the cell phones ceased to chirp, we were faced with a problem of diminishing returns. The greater the number of sounds we extinguished, the more we noticed the ones that remained, until even the slightest tap or ripple began to seem like an assault against the silence.

A clock ticking inside a plastic casing.

Water replenishing itself in a toilet tank.

A rope slapping languidly against a flagpole.

A garbage disposal chopping at a stream of running water.

The flat buzzing of a fluorescent light.

A fan belt squealing its broken tune.

A deodorizer releasing its vapor into the air.

An ice maker's slow cascade of thumps.

One by one, perhaps, these sounds were of little account, but added together they grew into a single vast sonority, and no matter how many of them we were able to root out, we kept discovering others. Now and then, while we were working to eliminate the noise of a match taking light or a soda can popping open, another episode of true silence would occur, a bubble of total peace and calm enwrapping the city in its invisible walls, and we would be reminded of the magnitude of what we were striving for.

How inexcusably flimsy, we realized, was the quiet we had managed to create.

We redoubled our efforts.

11.

WE WERE MORE RESOURCEFUL than we had imagined. It seemed that for every noise that cropped up, there was at least one person in the city who was prepared to counteract it. An engineer bothered by the medical helicopter that beat by his office a dozen times a day drew up plans for a special kind of rotor blade, one that would slice through the air as smoothly as a pin sliding into a pincushion. He handed the plans over to the hospital, and within a few weeks the helicopter drifted so quietly past his window that he was surprised each time he saw it there.

A single mother raising an autistic son who was provoked to fits of punching by the tone of her doorbell devised an instrument that replaced the sound with a pulsing light. She said that her son liked to sit on the floor watching now as she pressed the button again and again, a wobbly grin spreading over his face like a pool of molasses.

A carpenter designed a nail gun that would soak up the noise of its own thud. A schoolteacher created a frictionless pencil sharpener. An antiques dealer who liked to dabble in acoustic engineering invented a sonic filter that could comb the air of all its sounds before releasing it into a room.

Eventually every noise but the muffled sigh of our breathing and the ticking of our teeth in our mouths had been removed from inside our buildings. The wind continued to blow, and the rain continued to fall, and no one had yet proposed a method to keep the birds from singing, but as long as we did not venture outside, we remained sealed in a cocoon of silence.

*

12.

THERE WERE TIMES when the silence was close to perfect. Whole minutes went by after the early morning light breached the sky when the surging, twisting world of sound left us completely alone and we could lie there in our beds simply following our ruminations. We came to know ourselves better than we had before—or, if not better, then at least in greater stillness. It was easier for us to see the shapes we wished our lives to take. People changed their jobs, took up chess or poker, began new courses of exercise. A great many couples made their marriage vows, and not a few others filed for divorce.

One boy, an eight-year-old who attended the Holy Souls Parochial Academy, left school as the rest of his class was walking to the lunchroom, rode the subway to the natural history museum, and found his way to the dinosaur exhibit. He waited until the room had emptied out and then stole beneath the tyrannosaurus, using the giant ribs of the skeleton to climb up to the skull. He was found there late that evening by a security guard, sitting hungry but uninjured on the smoothly curving floor of the jaw. The boy had left a note in his teacher's paper tray explaining himself. He had dreamed that the dinosaur was still roaring, the note said, but so weakly that the sound could be heard only from directly inside its head. He wanted to find out if it was true.

13.

THE BOY WHO CLIMBED the tyrannosaurus was not the first of us to feel that his dreams were blending together with his reality. There was something about the luxuriousness of our situation that made it tempting to imagine that the space outside our heads was conforming to the space inside. Yet we did not really believe that this was so. It was just that we were seeing everything with a greater clarity now, both our minds and our surroundings, and the clarity had become more important to us than the division.

14.

THE SILENCE WAS PLAIN and rich and deep. It seemed infinitely delicate, yet strangely irresistible, as though any one of us could have broken it with a single word if we had not been so enraptured.

Every so often another natural episode would take place, and for a few seconds the character of the silence would change slightly, the way the brightness of a room might alter as some distant roller in the current surged through a lightbulb. But the quiet we had generated was so encompassing by now that only the most sensitive among us could be sure that something had truly happened.

15.

IN THE ABUNDANT SILENCE we proceeded into ourselves. We fell asleep each night, woke each morning, and went about our routines each day, doing the shopping and preparing our tax returns, making love and cooking dinner, filing papers and cupping our palms to our mouths to check the smell of our breaths, all in the beautiful hush of the city. Everywhere we could see the signs of lives in fluctuation.

A librarian who had worked in the periodicals room for almost three decades began displaying her oil paintings at an art gallery—hundreds of them, all on lending slips she had scavenged from the library's in/out tray, each tiny piece of paper flexed with the weight of the paint that had hardened onto it. The flyers at the gallery door proclaimed that the woman had never had the nerve to show her work before the silence was established.

The bursar at the university was caught skimming money from the school's pension fund. In her letter of resignation, she said she was ashamed only that she had been found out. If there was one thing the silence had taught her, she wrote, it was that any grief that befell a professor emeritus could never be more than a fraction of what he deserved.

A visiting gymnast giving an exhibition on the pommel horse at the midtown sports club fractured his wrist while he was doing a routine scissor movement. But up until the moment of the accident, he reported, the audience in the city was the most respectful he had ever seen, barely a cough or a rustle among them.

16.

GRADUALLY, AS WE GREW USED to the stillness, the episodes of spontaneous and absolute silence came less frequently. There might be a three-second burst one week, followed by a one-second flicker a few weeks later, and then, if the episodes were running exceptionally heavy, another one-second echo a week or two after that.

One of the physicists at the city's Lakes and Streams Commission came up with what he called a "skipping-rock model" to describe the pattern. The distribution of the silences, he suggested, was like that of a rock skipping over the water and then, if one could imagine such a thing, doubling back and returning to shore. At first such a rock would land only rarely, but as it continued along its path, it would strike down more and more rapidly, until eventually the water would seize it and it would sink. But then, according to the paradigm, the rock would be ejected spontaneously through the surface to repeat its journey in reverse, hitting the water with increasing rarity until it landed back in the hand of the man who had thrown it.

The physicist could not explain why the silence had adopted this behavior, he said—or who, if anyone, had thrown it—he could only observe that it had.

17.

A TIME CAME SOME EIGHT MONTHS after the first incident took place when it had been so long since anyone had noticed one of the episodes that it seemed safe to presume they were finished.

The city was facing an early winter. Every afternoon a snow of soft fat flakes would drift gently down from the sky, covering the trees and the pavilions, the mailboxes and the parking meters. Recalling the way the snow used to soften the noise of the traffic made us experience a flutter of helpless nostalgia. Everything was different now. The sound of our footsteps creaking over the fresh accumulation was like a horde of crickets scraping their wings together in an empty room.

Not until we walked through the snow did we really discover how accustomed we had grown to the silence.

18.

WE MIGHT HAVE BEEN CONTENT to go on as we were forever, whole generations of us being born into the noiseless world, learning to crawl and stand and tie our shoes, growing up and then apart, setting our pasts aside, and then our futures, and finally dying and becoming as quiet in our minds as we had been in our bodies, had it not been for another event that came to pass.

It was shortly after nine a.m., on Tuesday, January the twenty-sixth, when a few seconds of sound overtook the city. There was a short circuit in the system of sonic filters we had installed in the buildings, and for a moment the walls were transparent to every noise. The engine of a garbage truck suddenly backfired. A cat began to yowl. A rotten limb dropped from a tree and shattered the veneer of ice that lay over a pond. Ten thousand people struck their knees on the corner of a desk or remembered a loss they had forgotten or slid into an orgasm beneath the bodies of their lovers and cried out in pain or grief or sexual ecstasy.

The period of noise was abrupt and explosive, cleanly defined at both its borders. Instinctively we found ourselves twisting around to look for its source. Then the situation corrected itself, and just like that we were reabsorbed in the silence.

It seemed that the city had been opened like a tin can. So much time had gone by since we had heard our lives in their full commotion that we barely recognized the sound for what it was. The ground might have fallen in. The world might have ended.

19.

FOUR DAYS LATER another such incident occurred, this one almost eight seconds long. It was followed the next week by a considerably shorter episode, as brief as a coal popping in a fire, which was itself followed a few days later by a fourth episode, and immediately after by a fifth and a sixth, and early the next afternoon by a seventh.

We were at a loss to account for the phenomenon.

A cryptographer employed by the police force announced his belief that both the episodes of silence and the episodes of clamor resembled communications taking the form of Morse code, though from whom or what he could not say. A higher intelligence? The city itself? Any answer he might give would be no more than speculation. His hunch was that the sender, whoever it was, had resorted to using noise because we had ceased to take note of the silence. He said that he was keeping a record of the dots and dashes and hoped to be able to decipher the message very soon.

20.

THE CRYPTOGRAPHER'S THEORY bore all the earmarks of lunacy, and few of us pretended to accept it, but it was, at least, a theory. Every so often another event would transpire, interrupting the stillness with a burst of shouts and rumbles, and we would stop whatever we were doing, our arms and shoulders braced as if against some invisible blow, and wonder what was going on. Many of us began to look forward to these eruptions of sound. We dreamed about them at night, awaiting them with a feeling of great thirst. The head of the city's Notary Public Department, for instance, missed the noise of the Newton's Cradle he kept in his office, the hanging metal balls clicking *tac-tac-tac* against one another as they swayed back and forth. The cabdriver who began his circuit outside the central subway terminal every morning wished that he was still able to punch his horn at the couriers who skimmed so close to his bumper on their bicycles. The woman who ran the Christian gift store in the shopping mall designed a greeting card with an illustration of a trio of kittens playing cymbals, bagpipes, and a tuba on the front. The interior caption read MAKE A JOYFUL NOISE UNTO THE LORD. She printed out a hundred copies to stock by the cash register, along with twenty-three more to mail to the members of her Sunday school class.

21.

IT TURNED OUT that in spite of everything the silence had brought us, there was a hidden longing for sound in the city. So many of us shared in this desire that a noise club began operating, tucked away in the depths of an abandoned recording studio. The people who went to the club did so for the pure excitement of it, for the way the din set their hearts to beating. Who needed serenity? they wanted to know. Who had ever asked for it? They stood in groups listening to the club's switchboard operator laying sound upon sound in the small enclosed space of the room. The slanting note of a violin. The pulse of an ambulance siren. A few thousand football fans cheering at a stadium. Gallons of water geysering from an open hydrant.

Afterward, when the club's patrons arrived home, they lay on their pillows unable to fall asleep, their minds spinning with joy and exhilaration.

22.

THE EPISODES CONTINUED into the spring, falling over the city at intervals none of us could predict. Whenever we became most used to the silence, it seemed, the fundamental turmoil of the world would break through the tranquility and present itself to us again. More and more people began to prefer these times of disruption. They made us feel like athletes facing a game, like soldiers who had finished their training, capable of accomplishing great things in battle. A consensus slowly gathered among us. We had given up something important, we believed: the fire, the vigor, that came with a lack of ease. We had lost some of the difficulty of our lives, and we wanted it back.

23.

THE CITY COUNCIL DRAFTED a measure to abolish the silence initiative. After a preliminary period of debate and consideration, it was adopted by common consent. The work of breaking the city's silence was not nearly as painstaking as the work of establishing it had been. With the flip of a few switches and the snip of a few wires, the sonic filters that had sheltered our buildings were disabled, opening our walls up to every birdcall and thunderclap. Scrapers and bulldozers tore up the roads, and spreading machines laid down fresh black asphalt. The cloth was unwound from the clappers of the church bells. The old city buses were rolled out of the warehouses. A fireworks stand was erected by the docks, and a gun club opened behind the outlet mall. A man in a black suit carried an orange crate into the park one evening to preach about the dangers of premarital sex. A man with a tattoo of a teardrop on his cheek set three crisply folded playing cards on a table and began shuffling them in intersecting circles, calling out to the people who walked by that he would offer two dollars, two clean new, green new George Washington dollar bills, to anyone who could find that lovely lady, that lady in red, the beautiful queen of hearts.

24.

IN A MATTER OF WEEKS, we could hear cell phones ringing in restaurants again, basketballs slapping the pavement, car stereos pouring their music into the air. Everywhere we went we felt a pleasurable sense of agitation. And if our interactions with one another no longer seemed like the still depths of secluded pools, where enormous fish stared up at the light sifting down through the water—well, the noise offered other compensations.

We became more headstrong, more passionate. Our sentiments were closer to the surface. Our lives seemed no less purposeful than they had during the silence, but it was as if that purpose were waiting several corners away from us now, rather than hovering in front of our eyes.

For a while the outbreaks of sound continued to make themselves heard over the noise of the city, just as the outbreaks of silence had, but soon it became hard to distinguish them from the ongoing rumble of the traffic. There were a few quick flashes of noise during the last week of May, but if they carried on into the summer, we failed to notice them. In their place were dogs tipping over garbage cans, flatbed trucks beeping as they backed out of alleys, and fountains spilling into themselves again and again.

The quiet that sometimes fell over us in movie theaters began to seem as deep as any we had ever known. We had a vague inkling that we had once experienced our minds with a greater intimacy, but we could not quite recover the way it had felt.

25.

EVERY DAY THE SILENCE that had engulfed the city receded further into the past. It was plain that in time we would forget it had ever happened. The year that had gone by would leave only a few scattered signs behind, like the imprints of vanished shells in the crust of a dried lake bed: the exemplary hush of our elevators, the tangles of useless wire in our walls, and the advanced design of our subway lines, fading slowly into antiquation. That and a short item published in the Thursday, July the eighth, edition of the morning newspaper, a letter detailing the results of the log the police department's cryptographer had been keeping, a repeating series of dots and dashes whose meaning was explicit, he said, but whose import he could not fathom. Dot, dot. Dot, dot, dot. Dash. Dot. Dash, dot. Dot, dash, dash. Dot. Dot, dash, dot, dot. Dot, dash, dot, dot. Dot, dash, dot, dot.

THE WAY YOU HOLD YOUR KNIFE

from **vol. 6, no. 2**

Rebecca Makkai

ANN RESENTED HOW BEETHOVEN'S NINTH thumped from the speakers in the bog museum, making it impossible to feel anything but triumphant, uplifted, Germanic. And Harry had preferred jazz, to begin with. Two little boys ran across the floor, and the red lights in the heels of their sneakers flashed in time to the music.

On the wall it stated in Danish, then English, then German, then French, that clumps of sphagnum moss from the bogs had been used as bandages during World War I. She stared out the bay of east-facing windows at what looked from up here like an Iowa prairie, solid enough to walk on, the brown of dried blood.

Ulf, the museum director, whose hand she'd shaken on the way in, who had offered her a sympathetic and conspiratorial nod, announced loudly from the information desk in Danish, then English, that the museum would close in ten minutes. A few people began to leave—the boys with the sneakers followed their parents toward the exit—but there were still twenty people now, maybe thirty, clustering together near the windows, feigning interest in the wall plaques and photos of carnivorous plants.

"I'm certain this is completely illegal." A man with a British accent and a thick white beard had leaned in over Ann's shoulder.

"Of course it is," she said, and continued staring at a chart that placed bog water's acidity between the juice of an orange and the juice of a lemon.

"Do you believe Harry would appreciate spending eternity in a pool of fruit juice?" the man asked.

"I assume he knew what he was getting into."

Ann moved on to another panel, one about Celtic sacrifices. She squinted at the photos of the tar-black mummies, their deflated bodies, their faces preserved down to the wrinkles in the lips. The girl in the glass case in the corner—Stora Girl, she was called—Ann had avoided since she'd come in, but her slow circuits of the room had several times brought her close enough to see the shape of the girl's head, the arm, flat and leathery and bent at the elbow, the rough cloth of her dress. She'd tried hard, in her early field work, to get over her squeamishness about bones and even hair, but she knew herself well enough to realize that if she saw the dead girl's hardened face, she'd be up with nightmares. Although she didn't read Stora Girl's plaques as she skirted the exhibit, she had read the pamphlet Ulf had handed her at the door, about the two-thousand-year-old teenage girl's discovery by Danish farmers, in 1952, the leather strap that circled her throat, the barley and other seeds found in her intestines. She must have seen pictures of the girl many times back in Harry's office, although the intervening fifteen years made it all so hazy now. And this was apparently a second-rate bog mummy, incomplete and damaged and poorly preserved.

Ann was sure Harry's favorite had been Tollund Man, the eerily perfect sacrifice victim whom some of these mourners had traveled to the larger Silkeborg Museum to see yesterday. (They had chartered a van. Ann, still on California time, had stayed in the hotel, looking at the pictures in a Danish tabloid—someone else's celebrities, someone else's scandals and sagas and public tragedies—and trying to sleep.) It was Tollund Man's picture on the cover of Harry's most important book, which was a merciful choice, really—he looked quite peaceful for a mummy.

She remembered a day quite early on, maybe sophomore year, when Harry had beckoned her into his office to show her an article about the "bog brains" down in Florida, where for some reason the skeletons had disintegrated, leaving only what used to be the mind. It wasn't quite in his wheelhouse—his foci after all were theory and northwest Europe, not bog juice—but he obsessed about those brains all semester. "That's *something*," he'd said, and hit the xeroxed article with the back of his massive hand, as if willing her to see what he could. She stood behind his desk chair, loving how he smelled like book glue. "That's *something*." She'd always felt as if he were waiting for her to guess what, exactly, it was. Surely he already knew.

Harry was one of those professors who simultaneously exuded youth (though he wasn't that young, just younger than most) and classic scholarliness, the kind they'd all seen in the movies. He was the subject of a million rumors: he had trained to be a priest, he dealt drugs, he had a twin, he was independently wealthy. Students would lurk at his office door, hoping for small talk. Then they would see, with evident chagrin, that Ann was already there. The boys might make their awkward way in to ask about grades or sports or the Ireland trip—but the girls could see it was pointless. The territory was marked. There was Ann sprawled on the couch. There was Professor Browner laughing and leaning and wiping his eyes. The girls would hesitate or smirk or glare, depending on how many times they'd seen this same tableau, but they all slunk off down the hall, and Ann loved what they assumed.

She had made the mistake once of asking under what circumstances Harry believed Tollund Man had died. He sighed and looked at the ceiling. "Asking *why* is very dangerous, Ann. It's voodoo. The only question allowed us as archaeologists is *what*. What are his clothes made of? In what country were the fibers grown? But we can't just make up some story. We'll leave that to the *historians*, yes?"

"That's not what I meant," she said.

THE BEETHOVEN SHUT OFF NOW, abruptly, before the chorus had a chance to finish, and the group gathered in the middle of the room. In the hotel bar the night before, Ann had visited stiffly and briefly with the few mourners she knew, the professors and grad students from Indiana back in the late eighties, and Harry's wife, Ellen. The rest were strangers, tweedy men around Harry's age and curly-haired women with chunky necklaces made from rhinoceros horn or kente cloth beads.

Ulf returned to the room carrying a white bedsheet, which he spread over the glass case that contained an ornately carved knife and sheath—this museum's only other treasures. "How civilized," someone whispered near her. "Like a picnic." A woman at the edge of the cluster began to cry loudly.

"We considered to use a metal case," Ulf announced, "which frankly would not rust, due to the absence of oxygen. But Dr. Browner wished the scenario to be as nature." Ulf was about thirty, pale and thin-nosed, with both his sleeves and his brown pant legs an inch too short. Whatever money Harry had willed to the struggling museum or to Ulf personally must have more than made up for the legal and ecological objections. Ulf might even have hoped that whenever Harry was excavated, it would give his little three-room pit stop a chance to outshine the Silkeborg: Come, witness the mystery of Modern Bog Man! Was he murdered? Did he fall? Behold his perfectly preserved shoes!

Ulf placed on the cloth a beat-up, brown leather briefcase that until then Ann had assumed was his own. When she'd gotten the phone call last week, she'd thought they would be putting together something between a memorial and a time capsule—what Harry's colleague had asked for were "small modern artifacts"—but she knew Harry well enough to realize now that they were assembling what he must have considered his last and greatest joke. In fifty or a hundred or a thousand years, these objects would be displayed beside his blackened body in a case. Associate professors of the future would write articles for small peer-reviewed journals on the contents of Modern Bog Man's briefcase. They would try to piece it all together with some story—and maybe this was Harry's point, that it couldn't be done.

Harry had said to her early in her junior year, as he lay back on the couch in his office, Indonesian pillow over his eyes, that he'd told Ellen never to bury him in a graveyard. "They get plowed under," he said. "Twenty, a hundred years. I'd rather give someone the pleasure of *discovering* me." He lifted the pillow when he heard her laughing. His face was young and tan, but covered at the time by a brown beard with soft curls that she wanted to wrap around her fingers. She was in his rolling chair, her feet on his desk, shoes off ("Put your feet up!" he'd told her, so she had), half listening to the Art Tatum record he'd put on. "If your heart is really in this, you'll end up wanting the same." She was never sure what he meant by "this": archaeology, or their hypothetical affair. But she was twenty-one years old and in love and unable to sleep at night. She decided to take it as a challenge on both fronts.

She remembered leaving his office that day, finding a red-faced boy in a parka staring at the framed map of South America in the hallway. "Brownnosing?" he said, and slung his backpack onto his shoulder. She must have glared at him. "Get it? Dr. *Brown*er?" He advanced into the office, already starting to whine his way into a paper extension, sounding like someone Ann was supposed to babysit.

She had continued visiting Harry past the end of the semester, and she began, tentatively, calling him by his first name. They wrote twice over the summer, and the next fall, he phoned her at home over Thanksgiving break, introducing himself to her skeptical father as "Ann's friend Harry." He took her to dinner at Affamato early that December and told her how the diet of the !Kung women was making them infertile, and how, counterintuitively, the soil was less rich in rain forests than savannas. She ate salad and polenta because he was a vegetarian, and it was the first time she had ever left a lipstick stain on a wine glass.

That same weekend, he asked her to watch a Japanese movie with him in his office. He showed her the VHS box, which stated on the back that the film was "taut and intense, a sensual thriller and a masterpiece of Asian cinema." There was still no affair, but she nonetheless lied to her roommates that she was studying with a girl from her Sociology and Gender seminar and might stay the night at her apartment. Harry left his office door open half an inch, and they sat side by side on his couch in the dark. At first, the movie seemed to be about a war. Then there was a romance. Ann paid minimal attention to the subtitles, focusing instead on Harry's running, whispered commentary. "Watch what they'll do: they can show everything but body hair. *Anything* else goes, but the hair is taboo. Sometimes the porn actors shave themselves completely." Ann watched Harry lean closer to the movie, concentrating, while a man took off a woman's raincoat and blouse. The dark office made her brave, and generous enough to risk the first move. It was something she knew Harry couldn't do, and so she'd do it for him. She felt almost like the more adult party, like the one who could show him the way. She made herself stare at the screen while she reached over and rested two fingers on his knee.

But rather than melt under the light pressure, he coughed and tightened and moved away. He watched the small remainder of the movie from the far corner of the couch, his legs crossed widely, foot twitching. His foot was all she could see, and the blurring TV screen became more a strobe light than a picture, just a random blue illumination of the infinite time and silence and humiliation contained in that little office between the present moment and the end of the videotape.

When it was over, Ann got up and grabbed her backpack—such a childish thing, a backpack, she suddenly saw—and got to the door before he could turn on the lights and see her face. "Well, now I've seen a Japanese movie!" she said, and stumbled out into the glaring fluorescent buzz of the hall. He was behind her in the door, and she could see from his cringing eyes, his fingers pulling his beard, that he was going to feel the urge to explain it all to her, to break the news that had already been broken. So she blathered on as she backed down the hall, asking if he thought she should sign up for 322 or 343.

"I won't be teaching either one," he said, as if she'd asked, and his voice was deep and professorial and horrifyingly patient. As if she were a little girl who'd proposed to her uncle and had to be told that wasn't how the world worked. "I look forward to hearing your decision, though. Certainly."

She walked back to her dorm and sat outside in the snow for half an hour, crying onto the knees of her jeans.

For the last two weeks of the term she avoided his office, practically running past it on the way to turn in her final sociology paper. After break she began halfheartedly dating the first senior boy she could find. But then that spring Harry recommended her for the departmental scholarship, introduced her at the awards ceremony, wrote her an old-fashioned letter of introduction to the woman who would become her thesis advisor at Yale. Whether he felt bad for her, or guilty for his near indiscretions, or simply admired her work, she decided she'd take the help. It occurred to her only at the end of grad school why he'd done it. How many other girls in her position, humiliated, might have run out of that office screaming rape? Or at least that was the mythology among male professors: reject a student and she won't rest till she's taken your child's college fund. Harry had only helped her because he was scared of her.

In any case, in the many hotel lobbies of university towns in which they ran into each other over the next fifteen years, on their ways to the same lectures on what Ann's current boyfriend called "Skulls and Bowls," Harry Browner was affectionate, introducing Ann to passing colleagues as "the most promising young woman I ever had the pleasure of educating." Past a certain point in her career, she didn't appreciate "promising" and "young," but then at each meeting she was so surprised by some new sign of age in Harry—a forward tilt to the shoulders, a wilting of the eyes—that she *did* feel young, or at least desperately wanted to.

And what had been eating at her ever since she heard the news, the whole sleepless flight across the Atlantic, was that her primary reaction to Harry's death had been relief. An incident that had for fifteen years been kept alive in someone else's memory, out of her control, was now utterly erased. It belonged to Ann alone—and if it existed only in one person's mind, it was no more real than one person's dream. It felt like a washing away.

"Each guest is now stepping forward, please," Ulf was saying, "and is proclaiming several words of memory, and then is giving to the case."

The sobbing woman stepped forward first and took a few false starts before she launched into a story of Harry helping her through "a very dark time." The woman clutched a small, unlit candle in her hand, which she kissed before placing in the briefcase. Did this woman get the joke? How many of them did?

Ann watched Ellen Browner, small and white-haired, smiling grimly at the edge of the little crowd. Ann had first met her when Harry invited his junior seminar to his house for lasagna at the end of the term, and there had been Ellen, in an actual apron. Ann was offended at how she cleared plates while Harry poured the drinks and held court from the couch and got up only to change the records—Hawkins to Parker to Monk. Somehow, in her undergraduate mind, she had concluded that Harry, too, must have been dissatisfied with Ellen's regressive housewife mind-set, must have craved someone more modern who shared his politics. She'd assumed this was why she'd never seen Ellen before, on campus; he must have kept her hidden out of embarrassment. It was humiliating to remember that she'd ever thought this way, that she'd had the world so thoroughly, and so wrongly, cataloged. Ann had wondered in the hotel bar last night whether Ellen truly remembered her, remembered that she was the one Harry had called at home, the one Harry had watched movies with in his dark office, the one who used to call the Browner house and hang up the phone when Ellen answered, after a pause deliberately long enough to arouse suspicion.

She had seen Ellen several times after that first night, but she couldn't remember exactly when or where. Even her memories of Harry had slipped alarmingly away. It hit Ann that from this distance of fifteen years, if she actually added up all her specific recollections of her time with Harry and played them back-to-back, it wouldn't add up to more than ten minutes. Surely she had spent hundreds of hours with the man: maybe an hour a day, four days a week, for a school year. Plus years of dinners at conferences, brief phone calls of congratulations whenever one of them published a book. What was left of those now but fragments of fragments?

Harry saying he enjoyed her article on California mission gardens, some unkind joke about Richard Leakey, his ordering a Scotch. If she could watch that dinner in that Italian restaurant her senior year of college, watch it like a movie, would every word wrench back a memory? Or would they land echoless, the dull thuds of ideas and questions and jokes her brain had not just buried but eradicated?

One at a time, the mourners brought their artifacts forward—an ornate magnifying glass, an ancient floppy disk, a beer bottle, a carved jade monkey. Many had brought notes, which Ann guessed would soon be rendered illegible by the bog juice. Ellen herself silently contributed the white knight from a chess set—a reference, Ann guessed, to Harry being her knight in shining armor. She couldn't believe, though, what she'd learned last night in the hotel bar, about what he'd put Ellen through at the end: insisting they move to Denmark as soon as he learned of the cancer, making her deal with his doctors in Danish and broken English. They lived for two years in Copenhagen, where Harry worked on his last book until he couldn't write anymore, and where Ellen had no friend but, eventually, the hospice nurse. And all the while Ellen hadn't known why they were really in Denmark, hadn't heard a word about the funeral arrangements, until he was dead and she opened the envelope he'd given her months before. Then the poor woman had to phone everyone in Harry's address book and try to convince them to fly overseas on the whim of a dead man. Not even a destination wedding, the kind Ann had deftly avoided several times, but a destination funeral. She was amazed anyone had come at all. She was amazed she'd come herself.

The briefcase was almost full. Any future archaeologist would have to assume, upon excavating Harry, that he had robbed a curio shop, then drowned as he tried to evade the police. Ann was stalling, but she was one of the last few left and would very soon have to decide not just what to say, but which artifact to put in. She had in her purse an academic journal from ten years back, in which Harry had published a landmark article on the child bog mummies of Ireland. She had rolled it up in a rubber band and sealed it in a Ziploc, unsure whether this would protect against the bog, but unable to think of anything better. She had considered bringing an LP, in memory of the turntable on its huge wooden stand that lived in the corner of Harry's office. Every time she visited, he'd clear the clutter off the plastic lid—coffee cups, ungraded papers, pens—and put on some singer from before her time, then ask if she knew who it was. After a while, she learned them all. Vaughan singing Gershwin, Kitt singing Porter, Holiday asking how she knew her true love was true. But the only ones Ann had been able to find, hunting through the used bookstore's one little cart of records, were classical or Motown or horrible late-eighties pop. She'd chosen a Bach recording, one with the composer scowling out from under a tightly curled wig. At the last minute she left it on her bedroom floor, when it wouldn't fit in her carry-on. And the journal, she decided, was far better anyway.

But this was all back when she had pictured some kind of time capsule, something more legitimate. She had even imagined a sort of marker near the bog, indicating Harry's final resting place and giving a date on which his memorial could be unearthed. But now that she got the joke she realized that the journal, if it was still legible when they dredged it up, would lead the police of the future straight to the truth. Tracing the author of the only mummy article, they would soon have dental records to compare. They'd rule it a suicide, or they'd find the records of his medical treatment and figure he was placed here after the fact. The police always got first crack at human remains. No one ever thought, on seeing the bones of a human foot jutting from a riverbank, to call an archaeologist. By the time scholars got a look at what might have been the key find of the century, the police had usually torn the thing to shreds. The journal would date him, identify him, and reduce him to a box of evidence in a Danish police vault. She couldn't do that.

She considered what little else she had in her purse, besides her wallet. Lipstick. Five euros. A taxi receipt. A ticket stub for the museum. The taxi receipt should work nicely, especially sealed in the Ziploc. It would be another red herring for the excavators: Modern Bog Man arrived by taxi. Based on the fare, his point of origin must have been around ten miles away.

The man with the British accent who'd spoken to Ann earlier was placing a deck of cards in the briefcase. "I've learnt in the museum today," he said, "that the words *heathen* and *bogeyman* both have their origins here in the bogs. Harry Browner was nothing if not a heathen."

"Hear, hear!" said a man, and several others echoed him, though they had no glasses to raise.

"A bogeyman he was not, though I'd like to imagine Harry haunting my closets in the future." The crowd laughed. "I had the good fortune to be Harry's editor, and I thus look forward to a lifetime of spooking from our dear heathen bogeyman." Applause. There really should have been drinks. The sun had sunk low enough in the sky to reflect off Stora Girl's case, and Ann wished she'd picked the other side of the circle to stand on, so she didn't have to see the halo of light over the girl's small black head. It was a horizontal case, and the girl was recumbent, the pieces of her legs—Ann couldn't help now but notice—laid out like pieces of an incomplete puzzle, awaiting their connectors. She knew from the pamphlet that the leather strap was still around her neck, but she couldn't see it from here. Why they always assumed these people were sacrifices, she couldn't understand. Even Harry, who prided himself on objectivity. What was so far-fetched about a good old-fashioned murder? A girl someone wanted to shut up?

Ellen Browner looked around the group, seeing who remained. Her eyes found Ann. "Allison, dear, would you say a word?"

It knocked the breath from her chest. She searched Ellen's face for signs of malicious triumph and found none. The other mourners, the ones Ann knew, didn't even seem to register the mistake. Ellen looked at her expectantly. *I nearly tore your marriage to shreds*, Ann wanted to say. *I could have tried harder. I could have thrown him down on the couch.* She was a bit shocked to find that wretched college student still inside her, crystallized and vicious. Regardless, she was an adult, and stepped forward like one. She thought of beginning by stating her name, but she might as well remain Allison now. Ann was never here. Ann did not know Harry Browner. Ann's neck did not itch wildly every time she saw his name cited in an article. The phone had not glued itself to her palm every time they spoke.

"Harry Browner was my first mentor," she said. What else could she say? That he had lectured her about Japanese porn? She opted for a story she often shared with students in her intro courses. "On the first day of my first class with Harry, he handed us each a penny, and asked us to imagine it was the only surviving artifact from an otherwise unknown culture. We all concluded that Abraham Lincoln must have been their god. It was a lesson in how signs that seem so clear can mean something entirely different, and it was one that Harry would never tire of teaching us." And perhaps in the end that was all their year-long flirtation had been. Maybe he had recognized a talented student who needed to learn once and for all, the hard way, not to trust the way things seemed. If that, in his twisted mind, had been education, it had worked.

Ann could think of nothing more worth sharing, so she dropped the taxi receipt into the briefcase, not bothering to slip it in the Ziploc. It wouldn't last, but what would it matter? Ann was never even here, anyway. She stepped back, dizzy and dry-mouthed, and when no one else volunteered, Ellen concluded by thanking everyone for coming such a long way and inviting them to spend a few more minutes taking in the museum before the burial. She called it that, "the burial." The mourners started talking and hugging and peering into the briefcase as if it were another museum display.

Ann made her way back to the windows, and was almost there when she felt a hand on her back. "That was so sweet of you," a woman said. It was someone from the hotel bar, a middle-aged white woman in a purple sari. "What a wonderful idea, to put a penny. And it won't even rust!" Ann smiled, horrified, and thanked her, and then thanked her again when she couldn't think what else to do. She wanted to yell at them all, the whole crowd, that they'd gotten it wrong. That it wasn't a penny, and her name wasn't Allison, and the poor girl in the corner wasn't sacrificed but murdered, and her name wasn't Stora Girl but something else entirely, and they hadn't even understood Harry's last request. Instead she embraced the anonymity Ellen had bestowed on her. She slipped away to find the water fountain in the hall. She swallowed a cold mouthful and rested her head on the metal edge. Somewhere a vacuum started up.

If her memories of Harry totaled only ten minutes, what about his of her? It had to be even less—because while he had been a monumental figure in her young life, she was just one of many students to him, an unfortunate incident, a girl who decided not to get him in trouble. Still, he must have remembered the important parts, the hand on the knee. But no, she had to remind herself: he had no memories of her, because his memories were gone. If she could forget, by will, that night in his office, that entire year in his office, in what way would it even have happened?

She sat on the carpet beside the water fountain, head on her knees. It was the way an angry college student should have sat, not a tenured professor. Her mind looped the end of Beethoven's Ninth again and again, as if deeply troubled by its truncation—but of course her memory of the score wasn't sufficient to complete the whole symphony, and she couldn't hold all the layers of harmony in mind at once. She knew it would bother her across the entire Atlantic, until she could get home and listen to the whole thing full blast. Her freshman year, in Archaeology 103, Harry had asked a hapless baseball-hatted boy in the first row to read aloud a xeroxed passage from some dry theorist, and when, embarrassed, the boy stopped mid-sentence, at the bottom of the page where the words ran out, Harry laughed into his beard and said, "A bit of coitus interruptus there, yes?" How had she even known what that was, at eighteen? But she had, and it was Harry's ease in addressing them all as adults, at forgetting they had only just discovered sex within the past three months, that first made her love him, if only as a professor. Had her entire career sprung from that suggestion of unfinished business? Had *that* been the thread that led her to more of Harry's classes, to declaring her major, to graduate school, to her own research and teaching posts and books? For nearly twenty years she had heard those words whenever her phone cut off mid-call, or music was silenced mid-song. "A bit of coitus interruptus there, yes?"

And here was Harry again, from the beyond, refusing them all closure, denying them the end of the sentence. There was to be no gravestone with an end date to his long and perplexing life. There was only the promise of future confusion, future students of archaeology humiliating themselves with their false assumptions.

She unfolded the museum pamphlet and laid it out on the floor beside her. Strangled girl, knife and sheath, please donate today. She imagined a museum in Bloomington filled with choice and

IN THE DAYS AND YEARS THAT FOLLOWED, Ann's memory of the sinking itself would become less distinct than her picture of that overflowing briefcase on the floor of the hall, Ulf's body curved over it, thin and fumbling. She would not remember how they all got to the edge of the bog, only how Harry's body, wrapped in a gray blanket until the last moment, was carried out the back of a large van. There were more words officiously spoken there at the bog edge, but even a few hours later those would be gone entirely. She would remember her shock at Ulf walking directly onto the spongy peat moss that covered the bog, unafraid of sinking, and at the large pair of scissors he used to cut a two-foot-long slit in the brown tangles. He reached in where he'd cut, the scissors vanishing with his hand, to slice through another layer, and another, until he was in to the shoulder. When he stood up, his coat sleeve was soaked through. Ulf and another man carried Harry out onto the bog, unwrapped the blanket, and pushed him through the slit, feetfirst. Harry wore khaki pants and a sports coat, just as he had in life. He went down slowly. His arms stayed stiff at his sides, like those of a reluctant child refusing to be stuffed into his pajamas. At the last moment, Ulf slid the handle of the briefcase over Harry's hand, jamming it firm on his wrist so it would sink with him.

"Look at his face," someone said beside Ann, in the long seconds before Harry's head went under. It was the British editor again. She'd been avoiding that very thing—Harry had been dead five days, and despite the refrigeration he had arranged, she didn't want to see a face that had for that long been absent a soul—but now she couldn't help it. "Look at that coy bastard. Outsmarted us all, hasn't he?" And yes, that was the look, if you could call it a look at all, on Harry's face: smug, content, bemused. "Joke's on us." She could feel the editor's breath on her neck, although it really wasn't his fault. They were all huddled together there, on the bog edge, against the cold and the wind and the strangeness. "Normal funeral, you know the body's eventually going to evaporate into the earth. We don't even have that comfort." She understood. Harry, from the moment he had laid the plans for this horrible party, knew he could trump everyone there: he would outlast them all, suspended below the surface, that half smile frozen on his face to the end of the planet. If the human race wiped itself out before anyone found him down there, he would be one of the last of his species—the Peruvian ice mummies, the men of the Celtic bogs, some scattered bones, and Harry. And even her little rolled-up journal couldn't beat that final ace.

The top of his head finally disappeared below the moss. Ann couldn't help, despite everything, feeling as if he were drowning down there; she couldn't help panicking a little more at each passing second when he didn't resurface, gasping. But no, he was simply sinking—like a rock, a secret, a boat in a storm.

ONCE SHE WAS UP IN THE AIR and over the Atlantic, Ann ordered the drinks she'd wished she had at the funeral, one after the other. She had expected to feel better, in some way, after slipping the journal in, but instead found only guilt and stupidity piled onto the regret and disgust she'd been stewing in all weekend.

She pulled the blanket around her in her seat and leaned her face against the hard plastic of the window cover. There were fifteen channels on the earphones that plugged into the armrest, and although three of them were classical, the guide in the seat-back pocket didn't list Beethoven's Ninth on any of the playlists. It would follow her, then, incomplete, all the way back to Berkeley. She settled instead for "Soothing Sounds of Swing," which would, after all, remind her more of Harry's life than of his burial. *The way you wear your hat!* There was Ella Fitzgerald, and there was Ann's third vodka tonic, delivered by the smiling flight attendant. *The way you sip your tea!*

She recognized a couple from the museum, across the aisle and down a few seats—two of the crunchy field-archaeologist types. The woman was sleeping on the man's shoulder. They looked perfectly blissful, as if they hadn't just attended the world's most horrifying funeral. A moment later a man laughed loudly and said, "No, no, of *course*!" in a loud British accent, and she looked back to see the editor, making his jolly way, for some reason, to New York. She felt as if Harry had somehow followed her back onto the plane, and how dare he? Here were all these beatific mourners, and here was an article in the in-flight magazine about the Silkeborg Museum, and here was this song about the endurance of memory. (*The way you haunt my dreams*, Ella sang.)

Had she really thought her little journal in its flimsy Ziploc would matter? Harry knew what he was doing. For God's sake, he'd *invited* people to identify him, each in their own way, with those stupid objects. And then down he went with their little knickknacks, and they could never have them back. He was the one holding the case.

She willed herself to fall asleep, to hear nothing but the buzz of the plane's engines. She told herself she would not dream about Harry or his acid grave, and she would not open her eyes until it was time to change planes at JFK.

In a thousand years, she imagined, an intrepid young archaeologist much like herself would dredge up Harry Browner from the bottom of the bog, and add him to the small but growing gallery of the murdered and the lost and the tossed-aside. In her less academic moments, perhaps, this archaeologist would wonder not about the manufacture of Harry's briefcase or the wear on his soles but about who had left him there like that to die. She'd wonder if his enemies, his children, his lovers, his friends had known his fate, or if they had spent the rest of their days searching the Danish countryside, calling his name.

The archaeologist would lock Harry in a little glass case and put him on display for the gapers of the world, but what would really intrigue her—more than the mummified chess knight, more than the way the case was crammed onto his wrist, more than the small, soft-covered book so black and solid, even in its bag, that it could not be pried open—would be the question of *why*. She'd settle at the small desk in her book-cluttered office and begin to write her article, but every so often she'd stop and stretch and drag the students in, the promising ones. She'd hit the photos with the back of her hand and ask them what they thought it all meant.

They would try so hard to answer as scholars, but she'd care less about their answers, less about her article, even, than about the irretrievable memory, the one that didn't even exist anymore, because no one was left to remember it: the story of what grotesque chain of events had brought that nameless man to the bog's soft edge—what murder, what betrayal, what strange and unfathomable sacrifice.

THE WRECKERS

from **vol. 5, no. 1**

George Makana Clark

December 17, 1820

Dearest Ezadurah,

With luck, this will reach you before I'm missed. Time comes when a man has to rattle his fortune and see what shakes out, so says my new fast friend, and by God, with my lungs filled with sea air, the salt spray in my face, I reckon he's right.

You're likely still in a temper, but hear me out. When I return, it'll be at the front door, not skulking at your window like a baboon outside a sweetshop. And I'll have money enough to buy your freedom. Here's what's happened since I left your bed. I'll tell it straight, in the plain words of a soldier, without any flash and spangle.

After you and I quarreled, I stomped off to the Prince William Tavern, my blood still in a boil. I meant to drink off the anger before my money ran out, but I threw dice with some jumped-up little macer and got swindled. At the table next, a sea captain noticed I wore the green and black of the Cape Corps and offered to share his brandy. He took keen interest on hearing I command a company of Negroes. "Takes a tough old sweat," says he, "to lead a mob of armed savages into battle."

My new friend's a stout Welshman of easy manners. Before we reached the bottom of his brandy, I was already on about you. He squinted at the bar girl and told me he'd loved a Malay once, a whore at the company lodge in the days of the Dutch East India Company. For a moment he seemed not to know where he was. He put down his glass and asked if I wanted to prosper in life, as he could put me on the short road to riches. He wouldn't state the nature of his expedition, nor did I press him, having learned enough in life to know that honest work never paid well. I had to decide on the spot, for he sailed that very night. A subaltern's pay barely keeps a man in drink and clean linen—if I didn't follow my fortune, you'd forever remain a slave, and so our unborn child.

We spilled into the street, the captain and I, arms round each other's shoulders for camaraderie and balance as we made way to the docks, both of us singing, *I'll go no more a roving*, until we fell into laughter. See, it hadn't set in that I'd really go.

Waiting at the quay was a dreggy mob of sailors the captain had mustered in the taverns, newly released criminals and old men with teeth like broken bottles, the residue of opium etched into their wrinkles. A few shouldered sea bags, but most came with only the contents of their pockets.

The darkened ship appeared lifeless, silhouetted by the stars. She was wide below decks, her hull sheeted with copper. A flat-bottomed yawl hung abaft. Not a word was spoke as we ventured up the dock. One of the deck apes refused to board a ship whose name began and ended with an *a*, and a mate appeared from the shadows to wrestle him up the gangway. When another saw the ship's naked prow, he whispers to me, "A vessel without a figurehead'll certain lose its way." There in the dark, surrounded by those luckless thugs, such superstitions put me in a funk.

I turned back to where two men stood guard at the foot of the quay, pistols drawn. Above the harbormaster's office, I saw the roofline of the Prince William and suddenly wished only to be back in that convivial place, enveloped in the heat of the fireplace, a throat full of brandy, you in your bed waiting for me to crawl back.

The captain turned at the top of the gangway and braced my shoulders. "Go back to your Malay slave girl," says he, not unkindly. If not for this reminder of your servitude, I might've quit the expedition then and there. But the hand of fate had grabbed hold of me, and I was bound to go. The captain sent the ship's boy to fetch my swords and pistols from the unmarried officers' quarters, with a note to the watch sergeant that I'd been lucky at dice and would be taking a room at the Prince William.

A wizened fellow dragged a box up the gangway, a feat complicated by a matted fur coat draped over his arm. The fastener sprang, spilling out tools, but he waved me away when I stooped to help. "A sail-maker's tools are his life," mutters he, raw cabbage on his breath. The coat on his arm shot me a look, and I realized it was an enormous cat.

When the boy returned with my kit, I rummaged it for ink and paper to write this letter and came upon my uniform. It turned my insides just to look at it, pressed and starched so as to seem that it stood at attention without me in it. I knew I'd never wear it again. I might've pitched it over the rail and into the sea but for your seamless mending where the sleeve had come apart, its black facings newly dyed by your hand. No one would guess it was original issue.

Shadowy figures cast off the bowlines and silently hoisted the mainsheets, and in this furtive manner I left Cape Colony, a deserter to king and corps and to you and the child in your belly.

That's the short and the long of it, written down while it's still fresh, nothing held back, save that the captain's asked me not to mention his name in case this letter falls into the wrong hands, nor should I record the name of the ship that's taken me away from you, a prudency, says he, as we'll be sailing in Portuguese seas. God's blood, but all this secrecy's got me strung.

The silhouette of Table Mountain retreats from sight in the

false dawn. The captain's promised to pass this letter to the first ship we meet headed back to Cape Port, that you won't wonder long what's become of me. Forget all that rubbish I said before I left—you know how I get when I'm in a stink. Never mind if the child favors me or your master, I'll love it as my own.

Roland

December 24, 1820

Ezadurah,

Forgive the plain salutation, but I'm no good with flowery language. Did you get my letter? I reckon you didn't have any trouble with it. Remember the hours spent under your blanket in the candlelight while we worked on your reading, our scattered clothes a floor for the makeshift tent, your sister slaves only a few feet away, pretending to sleep?

Last night I camped on the aft deck, my back pressed against the planks, arms restless and empty, eyes fixed on the Southern Cross, the very constellation that shines through the transom over your door. A week at sea, and I've settled into the rhythm of shipboard life, my spirits lifting and falling with each swell that cants the deck, that makes the masts groan against the keelson and dictates the cadence of the sailors' endless chant. The sail-maker's been teaching me the lingo, and already I sound like an old salt. The currents fight against us as if bent on turning back the expedition, the shoreline unbroken, league upon league of desolate coast backed by cliffs. Each moment carries me farther away from you and our child.

When not on watch, the deck hands are ordered to lie below, confined to their bunks. I've no stomach for life deep within a rolling ship, and the captain wants company when he opens a bottle. We sleep where we drink, our coats for pillows, eyes shut to the moon and the sails, stirred only when the sun spills over the railing or we feel the prodding toe of the sail-maker, who on occasion takes it upon himself to assay whether we yet breathe. This arrangement's set the crew to grumbling, as they think it poor luck for a captain to abandon his rightful quarters and upset the order of things. Some throw plugs of tobacco overboard to supplicate the olden gods who still hold sway over the sea.

Through the opaque skylight, I've discerned shapes moving within the captain's cabin. Some of the deck apes speculate that the secret passenger is an assassin engaged by the Spanish viceroy to slit King George's throat. Others claim he's the emperor of the Kongo himself, traveling with enough gold to buy back Loanda—fortress and guns—from the Portuguese. The sail-maker says it's no man at all, but a demon out to collect souls. The captain refuses to speak of it.

The seabirds skrike while the coxswain lends filthy lyrics to an old ballad, his plaintive voice at odds with the words. Waves gather and spend their force against the prow, gently rocking the sturdy vessel, a cradle for me and my dissipate brethren. The laundry's closed tomorrow, and I imagine your mistress'll open her vast wardrobe and present you and your slave sisters each with a cast-off frock to last the year. Then off to church to thank God for your master's blessings. Happy Christmas.

Roland

January 1, 1821

Ezadurah,

I write this beneath the starboard lamp, my back against the taffrail, the world spinning, and not just from the drink. Better if I throw this letter in the sea than upset you with its contents, but I've sworn to hold nothing back. To do otherwise is to put even greater distance between us.

Twice I've seen ships moored offshore, sails furled on the yards. When I asked the sail-maker what they were up to, he looked away. "Same thing as us, I wager," says he. "Take a hard look at this cursed vessel. What cargo requires such a wide hold? She flies the Scandinavian Cross, though I doubt she's showing her true colors. If you rummage the captain's quarters, you'll certain find a double set of ownership papers." Blow me, but didn't I know all along what this expedition was about, only I kept it tucked away in the back of my head.

The captain got in a right stink when I broached the subject, so I ventured below deck for more agreeable company. There I discovered an empty hold filled with shackles and benches, where sailors take their opium. They offered some in exchange for my silence. Lice teemed in the darkness away from the light and salt spray. Lost in the pipe, I watched them hop about in the candlelight. A couple of sailors fell to buggering one another listlessly against the bulkhead, their desire blunted by the opium. Again, pardon the coarse language of a soldier, but I've promised not to braid the truth.

My father once told me that at the time of my conception his seed had been spread so thin among his many sons that nothing good remained. I tried to rise from the long bench where I lay entranced, but the sail-maker's black cat kneaded my chest with its oversize paws, jade eyes staring into mine. From the shadows, I felt the weight of thousands upon thousands of slaves who'd been carried away from kin and village on this unclean vessel, and I imagined your young mother, through some whim of destiny, shackled to the very bench where I lay, and I began blubbering to God and the cat for my salvation from the boundless darkness of that hold.

This business'll go on without me, nor can I sign off the expedition mid-voyage. If any good can come from the slave trade, it'll be your freedom. It's a new year, yet the world seems tired and played out. Forgive me.

R

January 7, 1821

Ezadurah,

The sun's just risen over the sea, the second anniversary of the morning after you first let me into your room. I imagine you outside heaping linen and shirts into the steaming cauldron, me still on the edge of your bed, watching you through the window as I tug on my boots, knowing I've stayed too long.

Yesterday we met a ship bound for Cape Colony, and the captain told me he passed over the letters. The currents are speeding them to you.

I spent this morning at the rail, spewing into the ocean. Without your tempering influence, I drink more than I ought. There I tumbled over that black cat the sail-maker keeps for omens and luck, a hulking, tailless creature with extra toes on its forepaws. I watched the sail-maker's needle loop through the canvas with the delicacy of a dragonfly, his hands broken from arthritis yet never missing a stitch. The thread drove his pet to frenzy.

"Playful cat," says the sail-maker. "Fierce seas ahead."

We've crossed the Tropic of Capricorn. The air grows oppressive, and the naked sun so heats my tin cup that I wrap a kerchief around its handle, the rum within hot as tea. Dark clouds form ranks and march across the sky, and the ship falls dead silent but for the rats that scurry inside the bulkheads in a hopeless attempt to escape the coming blow. The sail-maker touches his ear to make certain of the gold hoop, a burial payment to any stranger who finds his drowned body washed ashore.

The helmsman has turned the ship's bow into the gale and set the sails to flapping. It puts me in mind of the day I first clapped eyes on you gathering linen from the lines, your thin worn Christmas dress erased by the lowering sun, silhouetted body appearing and disappearing between the sheets. God strike me, but I never realized how strong a memory that made.

R

January 9, 1821

Ezadurah,

There's a sail on the northern horizon. It's the forenoon watch, and I picture you and your slave sisters working at the mangle box, squeezing out rinse water, flattening uniforms so they can be pressed dry, the corded muscles of your forearms bulging against the narrow sleeves of your dress. I'd trade the salvation of mankind to feel our child stir within your belly.

All's calm now, a miracle we're still afloat after the storm. Nothing like a good blow to show you your place in the universe. Just before the squall, the captain entered his cabin for the first time during the voyage and returned with a bottle of good Scotch, as he didn't want to see it go to the bottom without tasting it first.

Cliffs of waves crashed over the deck, and the rain seemed to stop midair with each flash of lightning. I remained topside for fear the ship might sink, and me trapped below with no chance of making my way back to you. A bolt knocked down the mizzenmast, and a wailing chorus rose from the crew: "She sinks!" Some of those sorry hands recruited from the taverns of Cape Colony lowered a longboat and pushed off into the heaving sea, the captain hollering after them that they'd die without a grave. No sooner had the storm swallowed these words than a funnel was conjured, and I plugged my ears to the screaming wind as it moved over the boat, spraying kindling and broken sailors.

We wound ratlines round our waists, and the captain corked the bottle with his thumb while we counted the seconds between the waves that broke over the pitching deck. At the height of the storm the tally reached twenty—twenty seconds to fill and drain our cups, six more to hold our breath as the sea buried the deck and plunged us into a dark, prolonged silence, until God saw fit to restore us to the world of the breathing. I became beastly drunk and lost count, and the waves took me unawares, carrying away the whisky before it reached my mouth. Before long I was unable to distinguish air from seawater, my lungs awash. Sailors'll claim drowning is a pleasant way to go, and perhaps it's so, providing there's nothing to hold you to this world.

Incited by thunder, drink, and the fear of drowning, the captain delivered a confession into the face of the storm—he'd killed his Malay whore out of jealousy. "I tried to ignore the rumpled bedclothes," screams he into the wind, tears and rain streaming, "the damp sex rags on the floor." I ought to strike this bit out, but you and I are beyond pretending that slaves are the masters of their own bodies.

When the ship's naked bow ploughed under the sea, I thought certain we'd sail straight to the ocean floor. At such a time, if a man bawls out to the sea and sky for mercy, snotters hanging from his nose, who can judge him? The captain threw the dregs of the bottle overboard, an offering of peace to the sea, and the ship found her feet and rose again, her bowsprit and forestays covered in weeds. Dawn found us afloat on a calmed ocean, still tangled in the ratlines.

The ship's come alongside, a Portuguese frigate. The sail-maker's fashioned a rope sling suspended from the mast, by which a half dozen strong backs will hoist the plump Welshman to the other vessel. I'll sign off now, that he'll have this letter in his hand when he goes over.

R

January 14, 1821

Ezadurah,

The sky's starless, the ocean without horizon. A sailor plays the smallpipes during the dog watch while the sail-maker keeps time with his limberjack. The wooden doll's limbs flail as it dances its clackety jig.

The cat's grown stout and nests in scraps of canvas at the sail-maker's feet. I ask what sort of luck a pregnant cat brings on board. The sail-maker answers that it's bad luck for her pups, as a ship can house one cat only, else it invites infestation.

I game with the crew below deck, throwing dice into a serving tray illuminated by four lanterns to ensure there's no cheating. As we toss, our hands cast shadows in all directions. Once, through some trick of light or drink, I saw mine in four places at once: there, gathering the dice from the tray; at a child's writing desk in Cornwall, knuckles swollen by sharp raps from my father's cane; in garrison in Cape Town, disassembling and cleaning my pistols; and stroking your hair in some faraway land where you and I lived freely together.

We continue up the coast, me on the foredeck, cheeks flushed by the sun, rum, and a growing hope that all this might yet come out well. The captain and I hold buckets over our cheroots to keep them lighted against the wind. Either he's too embarrassed to speak of his confession, or the Scotch has wiped the memory clean. He fills my cup with rum and asks me to describe you, and here on deck I conjure your presence behind a curtain of steam, your iron snaking through rows of pewter buttons, tracing the black facings, the captain charging my cup with each new detail.

Are you yet slogging through Wordsworth's ballads? That sort of writing hardly seems like poetry at all. If I want plain verse, I'll turn my own hand to it, as it can't be much harder than soldiering. Wait for me.

Roland

January 17, 1821

Ezadurah,

It's mid-watch—I remember rapping lightly on your window at this hour, heart thumping.

Last week I discovered the identity of our mysterious passenger, the personage so important as to dislodge a captain from his own quarters. My curiosity got the better of me one night, and I stole below deck to fiddle the cabin lock.

At the open threshold, my eyes adjusting to the darkness within, I heard whispers in some foreign tongue. A lantern lit, and an outlandish creature bounded toward me, unsheathed cutlass in hand. He was a mulatto, wide across the shoulders, his brow heavy with scar tissue, face covered with white powder that stank of sulfur. Enormous teeth forced his lips into a bizarre smile. I fell arse over tit against the boards as he pressed forward, his cutlass a downward blur, the outsize chompers flashing, and me suspended between the deck and eternity.

"Parada!" comes a voice from the interior of the captain's cabin, and I thought it was Jehovah commanding me to let go of this world and follow him into the next. My eyes crossed as they focused on the cutlass frozen an inch above my nose.

"Forgive my man," says the voice. "His Negro blood gets the better of him." The mulatto went stony at the mention of his African heritage, but he sheathed his blade. I regarded this second stranger, who'd stayed my execution. He was aristocratical, beard trimmed in the manner of the Iberian, though he squirmed a bit in his flash clothes, and scurf lightly dusted his shoulders.

He poured two whiskies and handed me a tumbler. "I apologize," says he with odd, tight-mouthed diction. "In British seas, I travel in secrecy to protect our trade interests." He introduced himself as a Portuguese resident, the governor's trade representative in Mozambique. Books in all languages were strewn across the captain's table, their margins notated with foreign words and ciphers. There was a physician's bag made from black horsehair, but the clasp was shut and I couldn't see its contents.

I took a swallow from the tumbler. "Your man comes at me again," says I, courage on the rise, "I'll slice him from throat to crotch."

"I shouldn't provoke him," says the resident. "As a child, he boxed in the harbor streets up and down the eastern coast of Africa. His father knocked out his first teeth, that he wouldn't choke on them in the ring—touted him as the 'Wild Boy of Sofala.'" The resident pushed his thumbs into the mulatto's mouth, exposing the grotesque smile. "These teeth belonged to the father—he wears them in remembrance of the day he beat the old man unconscious."

The resident reached into his tunic and caught a louse between his fingers. I realized the dandruff on his shoulders was alive. "Such adaptable little beasts," says he. "They've been found inside the tombs of Egyptian mummies, their mandibles locked onto the desiccated flesh." He pinched the insect until it popped.

I drained my glass, but the resident made no offer to refill it. "You're a bit old for a lieutenant," says he. "Conduct yourself well, and you'll advance in rank beyond imagination. My man will escort you to the top deck." I handed the mulatto the empty tumbler on my way out.

When I told the Welshman about my encounter with the resident and his mulatto, he became distant, like a guard who'd grown friendly with a condemned prisoner but could no longer stomach the sight of him on gallows day.

Today we sailed by the fortress São Miguel, grey and bristling with guns on a hill overlooking the town of São Paul de Loanda, my field glass filled with the power of the Portuguese in Africa. So ends my first month away from you.

R

*

January 20, 1821

Ezadurah,

Damn me, but hasn't fortune finally gotten round to smiling on the luckless? I've been promoted. In a natural harbor some leagues north of the fortress, we took on one hundred and eighty African soldiers. The resident ordered them to crowd before me on the deck, their arms and faces scarified. Still they stood straight as the king's own Life Guards, their muskets cleaned and oiled. The resident reached into his horsehair bag and produced a brass star, which he pinned on my collar as a badge of authority. "These Negroes," says he, "will follow your every order, brigadier." Me, the fifth son of a drunken schoolmaster, a brigadier at twenty-nine!

My spirits were dampened when the resident told me my soldiers would be housed in the slave hold. The men turned to me in hopes I might intercede, were that I could. I commanded them to surrender their arms, and they obeyed from habit, sullenly queuing up to descend the ladder into the hold. All their military training had led them to this. A pitiful wirra rose from the planks when the hold was sealed, and the sun glinted on the sea like a million angry eyes.

"Don't be soft-headed," says the resident, noting my distress. "The Negro doesn't suffer like you or I. He lacks the alchemical, complexifying force to have developed a soul." I once smashed a bottle into a man's teeth for saying as much regarding the souls of Malaysians, and under different circumstances, I'd've paid the resident the same.

I wish I could study your face as you read these letters. Would I see understanding there, or revulsion?

We're anchored near a rocky headland overlooking a shallow bay, waiting for the sea to flood its shoals so we can lower the yawl. The captain's promised to deliver this letter to the next ship that appears on the horizon. "Look to your own soul," says he, looking out at the deserted coast, "as it can be snatched away without your knowing."

The resident paces the deck, spouting scripture for what he calls his "Modern Testament," while the mulatto scribbles it all down.

He drifts from one language to the next, as if his ideas are too big to be expressed in a single tongue.

We make landing this morning. This will be the last time you hear from me for some time, as my letters from the interior won't be sent until I return to the ship. There's a faint starboard breeze, and it suits me to pretend it's your breath on my neck.

Brigadier Roland Turnbull

January 21, 1821

Ezadurah,

I'm off the lush! No more will I leave your bed to carouse at the Prince William, God strike me.

We rose at the crack of a sparrow's fart, when the dew still clung to the rigging like crystals on a chandelier. While the sailors readied the yawl, the mulatto lugged a stone cross onto the deck and balanced it in the center of the yawl. He's uncommon strong, I'll grant him that. The deck apes lowered the yawl, and the waves pushed the laden craft against the ship's hull, threatening to swamp it. I clambered down the rope, and we set off, the sail-maker calling cadence to the oarsmen, the black cat beside him, her litter writhing within. The resident sat next to the cross, clutching his black horsehair bag. I looked over the gunwale into the ship's oily waste, my wavering image staring back at me as if from the ocean's bottom.

We beached at the river's mouth, the mangroves thick with mosquitoes. Damn me if land, be it mud, doesn't feel good beneath a soldier's boots. The mulatto smiled at me with those awful teeth, gums dry and bone-white, and whispers that Angola's a dangerous place and I should look out for myself. His sulfur face powder stinks like the floor of hell.

As we unloaded, the cat leapt from the yawl and disappeared into the mangroves. "There goes our luck," says the sail-maker, glum.

The resident strode onto the beach, his face flushed with fever and excitement. "Keep sharp, young brigadier," says he. "The shore's inhabited by a bold race of wreckers."

The yawl ferried muskets and powder ashore while I drilled my troops on the beach, teaching them commands in English. They looked right smart on that narrow strip of sand, ready to march into the sea had I not called halt. Yet their eyes flash resentment when they think I'm not looking. I ought to have insisted they sleep on deck.

On the resident's orders, the mulatto carried the stone cross up the bluff. I strolled beside him to enjoy his misery, but blow me if he didn't somehow manage it. We erected the cross at the bluff's edge, upon a flattened, ash-covered rock, where the wreckers light bonfires to lure ships unto the shoals. "This cross," says the resident, "is a replica of the one that marks my grandfather's grave in the Cemetery of Pleasures, in Lisbon. May it serve as a navigation point, that in death he continues to point the way for the living."

Then he says to me, "A commander needs personal discipline," and he ordered me to kneel before the cross of his ancestor, a knight of the Order of Christ, and take an oath of temperance. I never cared a fadge for God, yet I swore the oath in fear I'd never see you again, but that I reform. The dying sun carved shadows into the bluff, delineating the world, light to light, darkness to darkness, as I knelt in the ash, the cross blood red in the sunset, surf pounding against the beach below.

We strike out for the interior tomorrow. The sail-maker refuses to return with the yawl and will accompany us on our expedition. "I can't abide life aboard a ship at anchor," says he, "sails furled, floating on our own waste."

Through my field glass, I watch the captain pace the empty quarterdeck with only rum and the ghost of his murdered Malay whore to keep him company until we return.

Above camp, the wreckers gather on the bluff to build a bonfire. The flames backlight the cross of the Order of Christ, throwing its elongated shadow over us. A day without drink, and I'm in the sweats. There's something that sings in a man when he's on the piss. Already I miss it.

R

February 2, 1821

Ezadurah,

It's been a while since I last took up pen and paper. I've been saving ink, as I have only what was in my kit, and I'll be damned if I ask the mulatto for any.

When you stop drinking, it's like waking from a dream. The bed sweats have ended and I sleep now like a bishop.

Our first night ashore, the sentries captured one of the wreckers as he crept into the camp with intent to fire our powder. The saboteur wore, entwined in his beard, a baptismal medal stamped with the image of Saint Bento d'Avis.

"The scoundrel likely took it from a murdered castaway," says the resident. He produced a protractor from his horsehair bag and measured the slope of the wrecker's head. "Through cranioscopy we've learned that, in most cases, the frontal lobe of a Negro is not sufficiently developed to house a soul. They can be taught to pray and observe the sacraments, but there's no spirit behind it." It got my back up, imagining those foul instruments touching your face. I asked if he'd ever measured the mulatto's skull, and he seemed taken aback, as if it'd never occurred to him to do such a thing.

We impressed the captured wrecker to serve as our guide inland. He seemed glad enough to be alive, and he sang a bit of nonsense as we set out, the notes falling in time with his bare feet. We push through dim, terraced forest, the river always in sight, hands held before us, else we run full face into spiderwebs or risk stepping on mambas, which nest in the deadfall. The resident counts each pace, compass in his open palm, its needle wavering east by north.

The captured wrecker speaks a guttural language understood by my soldiers. They've made a fool of the man, dressing him in scraps of uniforms, a cocked hat with no brim, a faded coat flapping over his naked buttocks. A soldier taught him to sing a fado, and they roar as he struggles with the strange words.

The forest abounds in game, and we roast steaks of giant sable and ostrich. The resident, served by his mulatto, dines on a camp table with china, stemware, and candles. After dinner, the mulatto plucks nits from his master's hair and bedroll. My men are also plagued with lice, but because I slept on deck in the sun and salt air, I'm clean. I continue to sleep apart from the expedition, and each night I scrub my hair and skin with sand. The mulatto's also spared infestation, though he seems to take no precautions. Each night he lies at the foot of his master's teeming bedroll, fully clothed, naked sword in hand, face still powdered. The only concession he makes for his own comfort is to remove his oversize teeth.

This next bit is hard for me, as I imagine it is for you. But when you begged me to teach you to write, it was so that your life as a slave would not go unrecorded. Likeways, I commit the captured wrecker to paper, that he won't disappear from the world.

When our prisoner could lead us no farther, the resident ordered him hanged as a robber. The wrecker sang his nonsensical song as he followed the sail-maker up into an iron tree. The latter tied a rope around a branch and loosened the noose to facilitate a hangman's fracture, a kindness of sorts. But the rope was short, and when the wrecker got the push his arms and legs flew in all directions, putting me in mind of the sail-maker's limberjack and its juddering, mindless dance. As custom dictates, we let the man hang an hour while we stared at the horizon.

When we cut him down, the resident knelt beside the corpse and removed from his horsehair bag a small arced saw that conformed to the curve of a human skull. He drew it in long sweeps across the wrecker's brow, its tiny teeth quick in the flesh, slow with the bone. Again he dug through the bag until he found a scalpel, which he used to scrape the brain from the bowl of the skull. Finally the resident produced a tiny druggist's scale on which he weighed the organ, its grey folds overfilling the metal dish. "God, in His wisdom, determined that the races should have different origins," says he in that queer, clench-lipped way of his. "Through the modern sciences, we can trace the development, limited though it may be, of the African peoples over time and geological distance." He recorded the weight in his medical journal, seemingly satisfied with the results. That night, staring into the fire, I nearly lost my resolve to give up drink.

Next we captured a Negress who wore around her neck a wooden idol. "Once our God was only a shabby doll like this, bound by the narrow limits of our savage imaginations," says the resident as he examined the trinket. When, late in the second day of her employment, the Negress found herself lost, the resident measured the angle of her brow, gave her a carved ivory comb from his black bag, and set her free.

"Why do we need guides?" asks I. "Don't you know where we're going?"

The resident consulted his compass. After a time he says to me, "My earliest memories are of Angola, journeying into the interior with my grandfather. When he sent me away to Lisbon, I near died of suffocation in that dust-filled sewer of mobs and narrow streets and hot schoolrooms. I looked on my residency in Mozambique as a way back to this place, never imagining my grandfather might die before I could rejoin him." He wiped at his sweaty brow, the fever which I had noticed earlier on the beach upon him again. "Here I am at last," says he, "walking in his steps." It was the most the resident had ever said to me, and he seemed to regret it. He strode ahead, his neck red with embarrassment.

I've used too much ink. The false dawn spreads across the horizon, and I picture you rising to fetch water and stoke the fire beneath the cauldron. Do you wait for me still?

R

February 14, 1821

Ezadurah,

Happy Saint Valentine's Day. Where are you now? What are you doing? I've ink enough left for two, maybe three letters.

Nearly two weeks since we've left the coast, marching up an ever-rising series of hills, mountains, cliffs, and waterfalls, league on league under the hard sun, calves knotted, the river little more than a series of converging streams broken by falls. There is, in the thin highland air, a sense of watchful expectancy.

The men struggle to keep some semblance of formation as they hump our provisions up the escarpments. Soldiers travel by company, not by individual, and I'll be damned if I'll let them straggle. A rope burned a soldier's hands, and he dropped a chest down a rock face where it burst open in a jumble of shackles and chain.

When I saw those emblems of my new trade strewn below I near threw myself after the chest but for you and our child.

The sail-maker mends our boots and britches by firelight. "I'd never've come," says he, "had I known it'd be such hard going. Still, if I'm to be damned to hell, I ought to be there for the offense." Even the mulatto's showing fatigue. He's ditched the table, cutlery, stemware, candlesticks, and china, and the resident now dines on a tin plate.

We've left the shade of the forest canopy. Sunlight's an ancient, deistic force—like gravity, magnetics, wind, or desire—capable of suspending flies, dust, the glum notes of the soldier who sings fados. Beads of sweat stripe the sulfur powder that lightens the mulatto's complexion, and his skin grows swart under the sun, indistinguishable from the Negroes he so hates.

"Careful," says I one day, "or the resident'll order you hung by mistake."

Well blow me if the mulatto doesn't give me a slap—more of a tap really, looking back on it. But my nerves were worn down from this ugly business and all the sleepless nights filled with loneliness and worry for you. I set at him with bare knuckles, using my elbows and forehead when he tried to come inside, peppering his face with long jabs when he kept his distance, turning my fists so I wouldn't break them on his face. I let fly a mighty right as he ducked, taking my punch on his crown, and I felt the crush of nerves against bone. Suddenly the bruiser was pounding my belly like a butcher with a slab of coarse meat. He huffed with each blow he landed, his breath whistling through those ghastly teeth. It was sunrise before I came to, face down, nose plugged with a paste of dirt, snot, and blood.

The mulatto was gone, retired into the bush to defecate, as he did every morning—never have I met a man so regular in his habits. The resident looked up from his compass to inspect my swollen puss, and for the first time I saw him grin. "I see you've had a set-to with my man," says he. I noticed something odd in the smile—his teeth weren't rooted to the gums, but, rather, joined together with silver wire. They were the first teeth of a child. "Nothing like a good fistfight to promote mutual respect," says he. The mulatto emerged from the bush, and as he helped the resident to his feet, it dawned on me that I was looking at son and father, each wearing the other's teeth.

Yesterday we met an old Negro goatherd. My troops slaughtered and salted his livestock to sustain us on our march. After he had led us through a pass hidden in the folds of the escarpments, saving us much time and effort, and after the resident had measured the slope of the old man's forehead, the goatherd, like the wrecker before him, was hung.

Thus the expedition proceeds into the interior, always keeping to the easternmost tributaries, the resident staring at the compass as if it points to his very destiny. As each guide reaches an unfamiliar horizon, he's either hung or he receives some bauble and is turned loose, depending on the results of the resident's measurements. I ask by what rationale our guides are condemned or rewarded, and the resident replies that he employs the very same criterion as God, who judges each of us before we're born into the world, our souls stamped upon our skulls.

Today we came upon a mission station which, according to the resident, houses a priest of the order of Saint Bento d'Avis. In addition to a thatch-roofed chapel and rectory, there's a kitchen pavilion that emanates the smell of fresh bread and roasted pork. I had hoped to dine on Christian food and sleep in a proper bed, but the resident ordered us to bivouac on the blind side of the mountain. He stowed his compass and stared down on the mission station as if looking back to his childhood.

Late at night, the mulatto came to me with an open bottle. "No harm," says he, nodding toward the resident, who lay in a blind fever. I'm a devil for brandy, but I stuck to my oath. The mulatto drank himself batchy, and I marveled that only a few months earlier I'd've behaved likeways. How the sober look down upon the drunk, the drunk upon the sober. Each knows truths shielded from the other. We listened to the somber voice of the fado singer, and I joined my voice to his, the words no longer strange in my mouth, and the mulatto wept without shame as the sentries came in from their posts, each with his own heartache, the firelight throwing our features into bas-relief.

I'm put off sleep tonight, unable to shut my eyes without seeing your master creep into your room. I swear on my beard, I'll strangle him with his own entrails if he hurts our child. I'm near out of ink, and I won't trouble you further with these thoughts.

R

February 15, 1821

Ezadurah,

I've been right pleased with myself since swearing off the piss, but damnation, my sobriety seems nothing when set against the wickedness committed this day.

I woke to a distant hymn and joined the resident on the crest overlooking the mission station. Through my field glass, I counted more than six hundred Negroes—men, women, and children—queued up on the banks to be baptized. There was something familiar in their hymn, and I recognized it as the very tune the captured wrecker had sung in ill-remembered Latin as he went up the hanging tree. The priest draped medals around the converts' necks as they emerged from the water by ones and twos.

"After the christening," says the resident, "the priest will command each of them to make a pilgrimage up this mountain, that they might be closer to God."

The converts stared up at the clouded sky, their baptismal gowns grey in the overcast, as they marched the path up the mountain to where my soldiers were lying in ambush. The early sun glared through a break in the cloud cover, and the river shimmered as if being brought to a boil.

The first new Christian to crest the mountain was still caught up in the rapture when my soldiers sprang from the rocks, beat him, and forced his wrists into manacles. The face of Saint Bento d'Avis had been stamped on his baptismal medal, a twin to the one entwined in the wrecker's beard. "There's no good face to put on it," the sail-maker said, and he turned back to his mending, I to my shave. Maybe it was the angle of my mirror, but my forehead appeared receded, lacking behind it space enough to house a soul.

All day, the converts made their ascent, only to be clubbed, chained in pairs, and bound together into the coffle, baptized into slavery.

Last up the hill came the priest, who strode past the resident's empty embrace. The resident stared at the old man's back, then produced from his horsehair bag a small box of white sand, which he took as a purgative, the grit audible between his teeth.

We've secured the coffle and now wait until dawn to begin our long march back to the coast. I see the slaves in silhouette, the setting sun halved on the horizon. It's easier to look upon them in shadow than to meet those blunt stares. Their voices swarm in the growing dusk. "They pray for salvation," says the priest. If I had any Latin, I'd join them.

R

February 22, 1821

Ezadurah,

The captain's made a monkey of me with his shite promises. When we return to the ship I'll settle that bloated Welshman, I swear it, I'll cut out his fat guts and feed them to the sharks.

This morning, while the resident tossed in fever and his mulatto relieved himself in the bush, I rummaged the horsehair bag for ink and paper, as they seem to have an endless supply. I found all the letters I'd written to you aboard the ship, their seals broken. The captain must've turned them over rather than risk sending them.

I'll take a breath, steady my pen. God's blood, but this gets under my tits. You must think I've died or abandoned you. The resident's kept the letters, I suppose, for his own amusement, a laugh at the expense of his gulpy brigadier, his faithful little lap bitch! I thought to confront him, but to what end? I'm too ramped up to sleep. There's no trusting the resident now. He might just as easily order his mulatto to slit my throat while I sleep as pay me off, once this is all over.

I've pocketed the opened letters. God willing, I'll deliver them to you myself when all this is over.

R

*

February 25, 1821

Ezadurah,

We march on a dead bearing to the coast, you and the child weighing heavily on me. If the resident noticed that the unsent letters went missing from his bag, he hasn't said anything. Have I lost you? The thought of it stops my heart.

The coffle winds back to the eastern horizon. If I fired a musket, the ball would fall to the dirt before it could pass the last slave. They no longer look up at the sky but stare instead at the shackles wrapped round their ankles. Some tear strips from the hems of their baptismal robes to bandage their blistered feet. Our captives grow more fearful with each league we put between them and their homes. A rumor's spread among them that we're a cannibal race.

We no longer stop to enlist and hang native guides, a relief. Often I follow the priest as he strides the length of the coffle, reading aloud from a silver Bible that must weigh as much as a cannonball. I catch him staring at the resident, who's become so feeble that the mulatto is obliged to carry him pick-a-back.

"He's the dead spit of his grandfather," says the priest of the resident, "a burden on all mankind. Would that I'd been strong enough to stand up to the elder."

The priest dresses with all the care of a camp whore, his cassock wrapped round his waist like a sarong. I've knocked glasses with enough tavern clergy to guess at his story: a second son thrown into the church against his will, the inevitable disgrace and exile to the colonies, and so on.

As we re-traverse the mountains, I sense that the ground on which we tread bears witness against us. Disease has passed over the expedition like the sun and stars, leaving my soldiers burning and shivering in turns. They crush lice between their thumbnails and forefingers, only to scratch days later at the next generation. We dispose of the dead where they fall. The resident believes that to arrive at a cure, one must first find a substance that produces the same symptoms in a healthy body. He experiments on the mulatto, feeding him concoctions of foxglove and rue, but after a violent purge, the boxer's sturdy constitution defeats every substance.

I'll continue to write these letters with stolen ink and paper, not knowing if you'll ever see them. They're a testament that I still exist, and that I'll somehow find my way back to you.

R

April 1, 1821

Ezadurah,

I'll keep this to a page, as I'm down to my last few sheets of the resident's paper.

Today the sail-maker sniffed at the air and said we're nearing the sea. It might yet all come out well. When our cargo's delivered in the Americas, I'll return to Cape Colony to purchase your freedom, and we'll sail away to Brazil, where they say the races mix freely.

We broke our march with the gloaming, and the priest built a fire over which he turned a spit of burnt meat. He refuses to eat the fresh game my soldiers provide unless he's twice cooked it. "When the world's set on fire," says he, "I'll already have the taste for char."

He's cracked from living so long in the interior, but I've learned more from madmen than ever I did from the sane. I sat down beside him, posing the question that troubles me so. "How do you make peace with your part in this expedition?"

The priest stared at the meat in the fire. "The resident will take his slaves, with or without me," says he at last. "At least I provide them some small comfort." He rose from his acrid dinner to walk among the slaves, reciting scripture from his open Bible. I suspect he invents most of what he reads to his chained congregation, as there's little in the existing testaments to help reconcile them to their new lives.

The distant sea breeze fails to lift my spirits. The sail-maker reckons the slaves will be sold secretly in Louisiana, as foreign slave trade's now illegal in America, and the value's driven up. I could spend the rest of my life in atonement, and my scale would still tip toward damnation. Yet, if you'll have me, some good can come of this still.

R

*

April 3, 1821

Ezadurah,

I've made a mess of this already, but my supply of paper's run too low to begin again. The blood's from my hand, a lost finger, the stain black in the firelight. All's quiet in the camp, but for the moans of the wounded or the blind salvos fired into the darkness by our twitchy sentries.

Everything's gone down the bog. Last night there was a rain of arrows, followed by the pounding of bare feet. The wreckers were upon us. I managed to bully my troops into a square, where they loosed volleys in all directions. Our attackers ran forth from the darkness as if animated by some bellicose god. Several tried to murder the resident in his bedroll, but the priest stepped up to save him, his blade and halo of white hair bathed in moonlight, looking like an angel of God come to set fire to the world. The mulatto and I fought back to back, each braced against the other. There's a strength imparted to a man of low character when there's no way out but full forward, cutlass flashing, and for a moment he rises above himself. If only I'd fought like this for you.

Our attackers have withdrawn for now. The fires are stoked, their towering flames illuminating our perimeter. The sentries shake off exhaustion and boredom to watch over the coffle, slaves guarding slaves. The resident dictates new scripture to the mulatto in a host of tongues. "If man evolves," says he, falling into English, "then so must God, as we are made in one another's image, each pushing the other in an upward spiral!"

I can't look on this letter anymore. My eyes are drawn instead to the reflected image of our modern God, His cheeks and sockets sunken in shadow, His rat-like teeth crimson in the firelight, a universe of lice contained within His pointy beard. He stretches a hand toward the sky, traces a lazy spiral against the galaxy of stars.

R

April 6, 1821

Ezadurah,

I'll write while the fire lasts. The sentries peer into the pitch, straining their eyes, heads cocked as they listen for the hiss of arrows, their palms flat on the earth to detect the pounding of the countless bare feet that signals the next attack. The expedition is decimated.

My missing finger won't let me sleep. I think back on what I've done in life, corpses of bushmen stacked chest-high, bonfires built at the mouths of caves where escaped slaves hid out, all the money wasted on drink and dice that might've bought your freedom three times over, and now this filthy business. If I'm improved over my ancestors, it's only in my capacity to do wrong.

The resident squirms in his sodden bedroll, clutching his medical bag, its glossy horsehair alive with lice.

The mulatto sleeps sound, his powdered face shining in the moonlight. Perhaps it's the sulfur that keeps him free of lice. The old priest sits at the fire and blackens a spit of game. A rustle of chains moves down the coffle like a sour breeze.

We spent the past three days in full retreat, the wreckers harrying our flanks in a running battle back to the coast. When I call formation, I discover another soldier has gone missing; whether from desertion or a cut throat is beyond my ken. Each night the wreckers charge at us until their progress is arrested by a storm of musket balls. During one of these assaults, the sail-maker took an arrow through his neck. He pulled me near enough to feel his rattle breath, unfastened the gold hoop from his ear, and placed it in my palm, payment for a burial I had no time to provide.

The wreckers seem insensate to their casualties, their bodies stacked on the perimeter like books spilled from a shelf, their faces unreadable in death. In the pre-dawn, I recognize some as former soldiers in the expedition. Others wear the medal of Saint Bento, baptized by the priest between slaving expeditions, I reckon. It's clear to me now that they aren't robbers, but, rather, the broken clans of the stolen. Unable to free their own kin, they fight to save others.

Each morning the resident walks unsteady among the piled corpses, stooping to measure the skulls of deserters with various apparatuses from his horsehair bag, gauging the distance from nostril to ear, jawbone to brow, the depth of the sockets, the length of the crown, drawing a cranial map of each soldier's betrayal.

It's nearly dawn and the wreckers have failed to launch their nightly attack. The resident's fallen into delirium. "God," murmurs he, petitioning a deity descended from Babylonian idols, "may King Miguel the Absolute beknight me into the Order of Christ, that my grandfather and I might abide as equals in heaven!"

Earlier, the mulatto crept over to the priest. "Please, Father," says he, gesturing toward the silver Bible, "might I borrow this?"

"Take the blasted thing," answers he. "May it serve you better than ever it did me." I looked over the mulatto's shoulder as he opened the book, eight generations of slavers scrawled in its facing, all sharing the same surname, the resident's name beneath that of the priest.

The coffle's chained to an ancient iron tree—the very one from which we hanged the captured wrecker at the start of the expedition. They strain against its trunk in silence, save for the stirring of chains and baptismal medals. The tree groans, its massive roots half wrenched from the ground. I'd convinced myself I could do this thing for you, that it wouldn't touch me.

R

April 7, 1821

Ezadurah,

I stare now at the cross of Santa Maria whereupon I'd forsworn drink. If there's some spiritual residue imparted to this object, it no longer resonates for me. I hear a wawling from the bush, and I reckon the ship's cat has begun a new feline race on the coast of Portuguese Angola. The priest, the resident, and the mulatto sleep nearby, shoulder to shoulder, three generations of slavers, and in repose I recognize the features of the sons in the fathers.

When we crested the final hill and I saw the coast, I thought myself free and home. But now, as I look out from beneath the shelter of a rock shelf, I see row on row of coffled slaves, a half thousand souls huddled in the mud, adults standing over children to shield them against the pounding rain.

The ink bleeds on this sodden paper, no use writing any more. A better person might think of the woman he loves and their unborn child, but I see only the misery of strangers. Blast and damn me for what I'm about to do. I never deserved you.

R

My Ezadurah,

The drowning tide's coming. Its currents eddy at the river's mouth. The mulatto's buried me to my ears in a sandspit in full sight of the ship, a warning to the captain that the resident yet has some bite. I can't see much along the darkening coast. Better to shut my eyes, imagine you asleep on your straw bed, as you were the night I quit Cape Town.

I'm interred standing at attention in full battle kit: pistols, cutlass, the green coat and black facings of the Cape Corps. The collar still smells of the lavender you put special in the wash. The mulatto's offered to write down this last testament and send all my letters to you on his arrival to the Americas. He says there's little harm can come of it then. Don't read them to our child. Say instead that I was lost at sea.

Last night I cut the watch sergeant's throat and allowed the other sentries to run off. I worked the tip of my saber into the chains, finding weak links. Those I freed vanished into the bush, new wreckers to stand against future expeditions. I'm no slaver. Tell our child that.

When the mulatto rose for his morning defecation, there were hundreds yet to be saved, and me still trying to force the broken tip of my blade into those stubborn chains.

The yawl approaches for the mulatto. Soon the ship will make passage to the Americas, and I am proud the slave hold is half empty. The prow at last supports a figurehead, freshly carved from the hardwood of the mangroves, each detail purchased with the captain's rum and rendered exactly as I described. The face is a perfect likeness of your own.

The beach glows red in the gloaming. The wreckers have set a bonfire of kelp and driftwood on the bluff where they now conduct rites for their dead. Its flames cast a shadow of the stone cross over me, marking my grave. Of all my sins, the words I last spoke to you weigh the heaviest. I never meant them.

The sea will soon haul me before God. I've asked the mulatto to fill my mouth with sand to save me from gibbering for mercy. I'll hold my breath as long as I can, God give me strength, in order to remain here under the same sky as you and the child I'll never meet.

I can feel the salt spray on my cheeks. Oh God, look at the golden moon. The red sand. The black advancing sea. The light's finished and these are my final words, written in the hand of my murderer on this day, April 8, 1821.

FALLING

from **vol. 8, no. 1**

Andrew Tonkovich

THE SIR JAMES TEMPLEMAN I KNOW liked nothing better than to instruct the groundskeepers to dig another foxhole and install into it another atheist. We had at the plantation at the time of the "accident" 145 full-time nonbelievers enrolled in the campus's subterranean residency program: skeptics, freethinkers, atheists, agnostics, some of them scientists and some academics, and some just sad, angry, bitter individuals who took Sir James up on his offer of free room and board, as it were, and a generous stipend upon completion of the program, one of many grants, fellowships, and endowed chair positions sponsored by the International Templeman Prize for Faith in Science.

There had been only five vacancies that summer, though we at TempleLand held every confidence that they'd soon be filled too.

The holes had since the program's inception become quite elaborate, cozy even, each with carpeting and satellite, Wi-Fi, and hot meals delivered by our on-site service staff, island locals who live in the small fishing village at the far end of the bay. Among the professional and academic anti-God crowd the place had become, I was told, something of an easy prize, low-hanging fruit on the foundation and conference and grants circuit. Most of them didn't take the challenge at all seriously, and TempleLand's complex of palm-circled foxholes was considered by them, cynically if you ask me, a de facto artist's colony or even a kind of writer's retreat. It was a free tropical vacation away from the lab, classroom, or lecture hall, a respite from what must be for these cynics the exhausting if otherwise unrewarding work of setting good people against the divine, the miraculous, the unknowable. And, after all, as Sir James liked to point out privately, nobody listened to or compensated them adequately for their atheism, humanism, or rationalism, not the secular foundations or the government—not at the rates he did anyway—nobody except a sincere old man who loved and feared his Jesus.

Still, considering we had graduated only three scholars in five years of the program, it must be conceded that this was never what you'd call a particularly successful experiment. Lacking what they called a control model, the secular critics asked, how would results be measured? Faith, answered Sir James, is not of the quotidian or the calculable.

This was a problem, of course, or would have been except that the problem of calculating the unknowable, the unseeable, had as far as I could tell most always worked *for* us, not against us, had worked to our advantage as believers and to the disadvantage, it seemed, of the nonbelievers, who demanded more.

Sir James liked to speculate further that, although the results of the program would be, like the divine itself, indeed difficult to quantify on the skeptics' terms, these results would nonetheless exist, publicly documented or not. There would be, he was confident, deathbed conversions and secret confessions, children of our alumni baptized in private. There would be doubt and prayer, and submission and redemption, that no one would ever, ever know about except, yes, our Lord and Savior. Hard hearts would be softened. For that possibility Sir James Templeman, philanthropist, was willing to spend a few million dollars of a fortune one hundred times that size, built on faith, and yes, on prudent investing in commercial real estate and mutual funds.

We were located on a private island in the West Indies, with guest houses, a dining room, library, landing field, swimming pool, golf course and lawn bowling, a small chapel and on-site medical support, in addition to the magnificently restored colonial mansion in which Sir James, a widower, resided. I had my own comfortable apartment in the carriage house, with a view of the sea on one side and the hills from the other. Sir James took his tea each morning in the solarium of the main residence, among his beloved prizewinning orchids, often with a personal guest who was staying with us just then, a congressman, member of Parliament, college dean or chancellor, writer, minister, rabbi, lama, or mullah.

After breakfast they often toured the grounds together, Sir James and the visiting senator or journalist or clergyman, stopping occasionally to chat briefly with a subterranean-dwelling nonbeliever-in-residence working in his or her quarters. Walking with the aid of a cane, Sir James would point out a foxhole, sitting inside it a well-known prizewinner, esteemed scholar, PBS host, investigative journalist, or somebody else unable to resist what must have seemed the jackpot of free time to conduct research, read, collect no-strings-attached fellowship money—round-trip airfare from anywhere in the world included—just to show up the famous philanthropist even while, yes, the scholar humbled himself before God if also perhaps humiliating himself in the eyes of his colleagues back home. So, yes, the conversations were brief, if mostly cordial.

A residency lasted forty days, the same period Christ wrestled Satan in the desert. If the participants left early, they naturally forfeited the money. But if they completed their underground tenure, when they stepped out of their foxholes each received generous compensation and could take the opportunity to elaborate on the mystical or, as more likely occurred, exercise their God-given (as Sir James liked to remind them) right to brag that they still rejected the Spirit, had found no evidence of it, and so had cheated the foundation after enduring five weeks in a luxurious burrow.

We were proud of our successes, however few. The three men who'd indeed come to embrace the divine, to find faith, were a Danish chemist, an American MBA, and an Indian hydrologist. They used their time in the foxhole to study Scripture, search their souls, and write scientific papers that affirmed a spiritual dimension in, respectively, the areas of chemistry, the free market, and the study of water movement, distribution, and quality. The title of the hydrologist's report, "Living Waters," delighted Sir James.

The three scholars had looked for and found scientific proof of the hand of the divine, and were eager to share it. Their subsequent proposals to fund research in this important work were accepted by the Templeman Science Institute in Colorado Springs, Colorado. They eventually left their home institutions and were given permanent positions, fully endowed research chairs at the institute, and they and their work were featured on our website.

You might have heard that Sir James had plans beyond the foxholes and the universities. Yes, there were other big ideas in the works: a privately funded manned space launch, a faith-based interplanetary satellite exploration program, an all-Christian professional baseball league. Mystery may be found and experienced everywhere, Sir James always said, and the Templeman Fund helped to sponsor the search for it. I looked forward to helping him realize this dream as his secretary, his trusted confidante. But this was not to be, not after the disappearance of the atheist Dr. Simon Killacky, aged forty-eight, a part-time geology instructor, speech team faculty advisor, and women's softball coach from a small community college in Orange County, California. He had been at the estate fewer than three days. An unattractive if gentle man, Killacky had been welcomed at the landing field on a Friday, provided a lei and a Bible, been driven in a golf cart to his assigned hole, and clocked in by noon, thus beginning his first day. I myself did not speak to him beyond reviewing the rules. I observed him sign our standard legal agreements, answered a few routine questions, and had no interactions with him on Saturday at all. He seemed tired, perhaps anxious, when I met him, which is what I later told the investigating authorities, who reconstructed events based on evidence found in his foxhole, which is to say very little evidence at all.

It seems Dr. Killacky ate his early evening dinner on both Friday and Saturday nights, read portions of Scripture and sections from textbooks and scientific journals (passages still marked with Post-its), made some notes, sent a handful of e-mails, called his lawyer on his cell phone, used the small bathroom facility, and then pulled the fiberglass roof over his hole and, it seems, went to sleep. Thus he passed his first two days, giving no indication of any behavior other than we anticipated.

Indeed, on the second night, the authorities concluded, he retired at about the same time, though, of course, there were no witnesses. Individual foxholes are purposely distant from one another, perhaps fifty meters apart, and neither of the two nearest residents, a black lady Marxist historian from Oakland or a botanist from Winnipeg, noticed or heard anything. In retrospect, we might have installed sensors or even surveillance cameras, but, even now, these seem an intrusion and a violation of the spirit of the wager, the contract, the premise of what was, to Sir James's mind, both a scientific laboratory and hallowed ground.

On Sunday morning at eight, the staff delivered Dr. Killacky's breakfast tray at the edge of his as-yet unopened residence. An hour later, observing the breakfast untouched, and concerned that he had not yet awakened, the server summoned the security chief, who pulled back the opaque roof to discover Dr. Killacky missing, and in his place a new hole, situated in the center of the foxhole, about a meter wide. This second hole, clearly much deeper, was very dark. The radius of this perfect circle—there is no other way to say this—was of a human torso.

All items in Killacky's accommodations remained, untouched, the laptop and Bible and his personal notebooks, the scene suggesting that the atheist had dug down a few feet for some reason and was perhaps trapped down there, or even hiding.

Alas, investigation of the hole quickly established that this was not at all the situation. Security summoned me almost immediately and, skeptical, I soon had to concede what was obvious if unbelievable: that this was a very, very deep hole, perhaps indeed bottomless, as our security chief, a local man, would insist over and over. And which would later seem to be proven.

And, yes, certain facts could not be denied even early on: absent footprints or other evidence, it seemed Killacky had to still be down there, deep down inside of the hole, however shallow or deep. Feeling foolish, if desperate, I directed the staff to secure first one ladder, then a longer ladder, then a length of stout rope. Then they tied that rope to a longer rope, weighted with a hammer of all things, the handiest object available, lowering and lowering the whole contraption until we soon ran out of line, forty, fifty, one hundred meters, neither locating Killacky nor reaching bottom, and hearing and seeing not a thing.

News of Killacky's disappearance leaked before I could notify his wife or the embassy, and soon the media arrived, the print reporters and TV people with cameras. I apologized to Sir James, who personally supervised the rescue attempt from his wheelchair, parked at the edge of the site, but he understood and agreed that we should cooperate and provide the press complete access. "We have nothing to hide," he said.

The scene soon became a familiar one, day and night, quickly developing into the "Atheist Lost in a Hole" story and the "Earth Swallows up Nonbeliever," with the twenty-four-hour cable stations sending their celebrity anchors and investigative reporters, these familiar on-camera personalities standing on the lawn wearing khakis and guayaberas, attempting to answer for their viewers the question of how this was possible and who Killacky was and, of course, where we were and what the Institute's work was. They reminded viewers and listeners and readers of Sir James's remarkable biography, the life story of a southern-born gentleman, Rhodes scholar, lifetime Presbyterian knighted by the Queen of England, who had renounced his U.S. citizenship and moved to the island for tax reasons and to promote the investigation of the universal and divine, to advance the consideration of the holy as part of a new model of scientific inquiry.

Soon we at the compound were working with the national police and the Red Cross, and had contracted an outfit to assemble heavy equipment toward facilitating Killacky's rescue: a crane—an industrial block and tackle pulley, really—generator, lights, and seismic listening devices. Ten hours went by, then nightfall. Soon it had been twenty-four hours, when arrived the second tragedy.

An overeager rescue dog put to work sniffing for Killacky's scent jumped into the hole, or fell, and soon Jo-Jo, a German shepherd from Wyoming, became the second subject of the search-and-rescue operation, her photograph appearing below Killacky's on the television screen and in the newspapers.

This continued for some days, all of it of course profoundly disrupting life and study in TempleLand, not to mention the nearby village, so that we were soon forced to send the other resident scholars home. I chartered a small jet and handed them envelopes as they departed, a check for each, thanking them for their good-faith effort and inviting them to visit again. Yes, I assured them, they would receive credit for days in their hole so far and could pick up at a time convenient to them. Each expressed their various concerns for Killacky, some angrily, insisting that he had been kidnapped, even murdered, most likely by us, by me or by Sir John, speculating, as these scientists will, that what now appeared to be a seemingly perfect, symmetrically-bored vertical chasm, a tunnel really, must certainly have been there before Killacky had been installed in foxhole number 139.

As for Killacky, facts soon emerged painting an alternately gratifying and unflattering portrait, and pointing to motives that led to jokes about his handiness with a shovel or his need to disappear, and fast. Yet the notes and diagrams, scribblings and mathematical equations left in his hole suggested that his reason for being at TempleLand went well beyond the grant. There were calculations and a timeline, and rough sketches, all of which seemed to point to serious scholarship regarding the actual age of the planet and examining the record of a prescientific history which likely corresponded to that story outlined in, yes, holy texts.

But, disappointingly, it also emerged that Dr. Killacky had needed cash to pay off a student blackmailing him after he had done things to her in his office, nasty and wrong things that she'd memorialized on her cell phone's camera feature, and that she'd threatened to share with his wife and then with the world, to spin on her website, like straw into gold. In my immediate postdisappearance discussions with Sir James, we agreed that Dr. Killacky perhaps had not been the very best choice among applicants, and that the staff and I might have vetted him more thoroughly. Sir James was, naturally, disappointed, but he was never angry, and

I value even now that moment when he took me aside one afternoon and explained that God worked in mysterious ways and that we might be witnesses to a phenomenon right here on the grounds that was well beyond the reckoning of mere man, and that Killacky himself was perhaps playing a role important to the moment, which might be a kind of revelation—about what he could only speculate, but would not—a revelation that would no doubt point further to the connectedness of spirit and science.

"And so," he promised, "ultimately contribute to the success of our endeavors here."

Killacky's wife, Mrs. Judith Killacky of Rancho Santa Margarita in Orange County, felt otherwise. She arrived on a special flight we chartered. Mrs. Killacky resembled a well-known blond movie actress who'd once been young and sexy but who now, middle-aged and fat, appeared on late-night television commercials pleading on behalf of starving and dying African children.

She'd recently filed for divorce and had not even known her missing soon-to-be ex-husband was staying with us at TempleLand. Mrs. Killacky—"Jude" she called herself—was of little use to the authorities, had long suspected her husband's infidelity, and so was the subject of plenty of media attention. There were the couple's small children at home, four of them, and a suspiciously large life insurance policy, all of these reliably tawdry details assembled to provoke curiosity and inspire contempt. Even more attention was paid, most of it speculation, to those available details of Dr. Killacky's work in the area of the geological record of the earth and, surprisingly, the New Testament stories of the birth of Jesus of Nazareth. This was an unexpected development, at least to me, but Sir James seemed unsurprised, and was encouraged. "The direction of Dr. Killacky's scientific work," he said, "will redeem him, and will vindicate our own."

Meanwhile, after just two weeks, the young woman student in possession of the sex video shared it with a British tabloid, which printed stills, for which she was compensated, it was widely believed, quite generously. Then she herself disappeared, on the same day the whole thing appeared on a porn site online.

After four full weeks of searching and waiting, after using sonar and radar, after taking X rays and employing a psychic and bringing in medical forensics experts from around the world, after lowering a camera and losing not one but two mini-robotic units, we still had not found the actual bottom of the hole, or established the existence of a bottom, or located either Killacky or the dog. Neither had any evidence at all been discovered of either, not in the hole or on the steep walls of the chasm or anywhere else. There was no shovel, no disturbed earth. There were no footprints.

Bit by bit the press corps abandoned the story and left the island. Embarrassed, frustrated, the authorities seemed to give up too, the local police and military, Interpol, the FBI, the army of private investigators we'd hired, all of them packing up, defeated, and likely convinced that, in the absence of evidence to the contrary, TempleLand, Sir James and I, somebody on the plantation, Killacky himself, had somehow contrived to make him disappear, perhaps for the insurance money, or arranged a hoax.

With the departure of the media and the police, the area around the hole was cordoned off, a round-the-clock pair of guards posted, and a single klieg light left to illuminate the site at night.

We at TempleLand held a small commemorative service in the chapel, where Sir James himself paid tribute to the lost man, offering generously that he believed in his own true heart that Dr. Simon Killacky might indeed have become number four on our roster of scholar converts, and might yet. Our Lazarus, Sir James called Killacky, someday to be revived, resurrected, and reborn.

He further lamented the cruel attacks on poor Dr. Killacky, who had been revealed not only, it seemed, as a philanderer and sexual predator, but as a poor scholar too, having done little research or writing, it turned out, in his field prior to his brief stay with us. The newspapers reported that he'd actually published only one paper, not in a juried scientific journal, and had in fact never completed his doctoral work, so that he was not a PhD after all. None of this mattered to us, said Sir James, or to an island, a nation, a world that cared so deeply for his journey, ongoing, or to those who loved him, and certainly not to the Creator who directed the lives of us all.

The miraculous had occurred, Sir James insisted, although we had at first not seen it, not recognized it, this marvel, not at all an "accident," he assured us, no, not in the mechanistic way of our secular world. The mystery would still teach the world somehow. God had chosen His servant Simon, as he'd chosen Saul and Simon Peter, on whose name and shoulders He had once built His own church, the rock on whom was anchored the faith of millions. That Killacky was, he pointed out, a teacher whose subject was the history of rocks, was further promise and assurance of His plan.

Geologists and seismologists, geophysicists and earth scientists of all stripes responded predictably to Sir James's remarks and to his interview on *60 Minutes* with anger, skepticism, speculation, with theories and more questions, suggesting the unlikelihood of an anomalous fissure. They pointed to what they called the "obviously sculpted" shape of the hole, its perfect, precise route straight down, the centerline of a cylindrical crevasse, the smoothness of the walls. They mocked us, and others, suggesting that maybe, yes, something or someone had reached up from the earth's center, maybe a giant or demon with a machine or device as yet unbuilt had drilled up to the surface. This image appeared in an editorial cartoon, as did many others, ridiculous and yet tapping into something exciting and appealing, which Sir James chose to celebrate.

Indeed, there was always an artist's rendering, a sketch or a digitally assembled cutaway of the earth, on television or printed alongside the newspaper articles. There was an illustration of the shaft with Killacky and Jo-Jo falling, and mathematical equations of velocity, speculating how long it would have taken them to fall, minutes or hours or days. There was the color-coded journey, always with a tiny cartoon dog and cartoon man, through the crust to the upper mantle, then the outer core, and finally to the inner core where the man and the dog would reach the impossible heat and be melted, as if to engage the problem and the premise, and at the same time the impossibility of each.

There were interviews and commentaries by oil-drilling experts and spelunkers, hydrologists—including our own born-again prizewinner—survivors of underground and underwater falls and cave-ins. The constant printing and airing of that image, of the tiny man in free fall and the faithful dog above him, must have caused many, as it did me, to see them as eternally falling, and to understand falling as a journey and not an end, and to begin to appreciate that journey as somehow infinite despite, of course, being reminded, over and over, that science was working hard to find an ending—in their deaths.

But not Sir James, who insisted on the infinite. He offered that this was all God's plan, for He has a plan for us all. For He is not done with us here, and neither is His work complete. He is in control, He has used His servant Dr. Killacky, and He will reveal in His time the meaning and purpose of this phenomenon, this miraculous moment, this scientific experiment, this bringing together of the nations, of his disciples, to witness the power, glory, love, and caring of a Creator who can do whatever pleases Him. Remember, said Sir James, that He has counted the sparrows and numbered the hairs on our heads and created this very world, seen and unseen, so that our job, our duty, is to marvel and to wait for Him to further make real a revelation.

"Dr. Killacky is with God, and with us, somewhere," offered Sir James. "As is Jo-Jo. Because God is everywhere, on the earth and inside it as well." And that place, he insisted, is forever, is infinite.

Yet soon Sir James was forced to direct me to terminate the foxhole program altogether, in part on orders from the authorities, and to have the remaining holes filled in. I sent letters to those scholars whose research we'd been forced to interrupt, apologizing again and including a second check and the requisite legal paperwork removing from TempleLand any further liability or responsibility.

The two security guards remained, even as the holes were filled in, every landscaped berm razed and squares of new grass laid in. Life as we'd known it resumed, if tentatively, with Sir James steadfast and confident, even happy. This is the Sir James I knew, who again greeted with smiles and a wave those remaining on the grounds. The disciples, we called them, those faithful hundreds who'd arrived at the site almost immediately and who still camped on the perimeter. They cooked meals on small camp stoves and built jolly fires at night, sang and prayed and held vigil. Most seemed to have chosen to wear white, often with a skein of gauze wrapped around their heads. They decorated the great lawn with crosses, candles, cans of dog food.

The earth had swallowed up a sinner, some said. God was testing a man, and mankind. Like Jonah in the belly of the whale, or

Daniel in the lion's den. Some argued that a prophet, heretofore unknown, unrecognized, had been taken from us. Either way, it was a test. God had expressed His will and would not be mocked or questioned, would only be worshipped. The disciples were there to witness the awesome power when Dr. Killacky, God's servant, reappeared or that great if immeasurable authority, revealed.

It was a surprise then even to me, a challenge to my own understanding of His power and requirement of faith, when the first disciple leapt into the hole and the others quickly followed her. Apparently nobody else had expected this either, stupid in retrospect, a failing, a misunderstanding for which I blame myself.

The woman who jumped did not even bother to distract the two guards, who sat eating their suppers at sunset just a few meters from the edge of the short wall around the hole and the yellow warning tape. Eating plates of red beans and white rice, yams, roast pork, and plantains, they observed her approach from the darkness, walking into the splay of the artificial white light, thinking perhaps that she might be heading to the portable facilities we'd organized or adding another candle to the hundreds of votive lights that flickered and waned, the smell of their wax and the heat of their flames suggesting an outdoor cathedral under the palms.

They continued eating as she approached and, as they later reported, heard only the gentlest ruffle of air in between forkfuls of dinner. They looked up, surprised to see the tape broken. A note lay on the ground, its message written in bold, elegant, and clearly feminine handwriting on a sheet of blue-lined notebook paper: FOLLOW ME. And the small space that had briefly been occupied—by a young woman, was all they could say, veiled, slight—was left a vacuum now somehow larger than anything that surrounded it, the lawn, the palms, and the night itself.

These were local men, island men, untrained, unarmed. They called out for help, then screamed into their walkie-talkies. One ran to the main house to summon Sir James and me, leaving the other guard alone at the hole. The man could offer little resistance when the rest of them, the dozen other devotees who'd hid at the perimeter of the light until they'd seen Sister Alpha, as she'd called herself, leap into the hole, then rushed forward themselves, running together past the lone guard and disappearing one after the other, one onto another, down the redemptive oblivion of faith and mystery, a narrow, deep hole in the ground wherein, it was assumed, they meant to find not only evidence of their faith but perhaps, in their action, faith itself.

And so the police and the news crews returned. A handwriting expert quickly confirmed the woman's identity not as an island local but as Sarah Melissa Jean Hoolihan, aged twenty, Killacky's former community college student who'd gone missing after selling the dirty photographs and the video taken on her cell phone.

Her parents were flown to the island and spent some days with us, living in a guest cottage adjacent to the house in which Mrs. Killacky stayed. They were longtime practitioners of Transcendental Meditation and each morning and evening sat cross-legged near the hole for fifteen minutes, humming and being still. They otherwise cooperated with the authorities, showed little anger toward us or toward Killacky, and were concerned that their daughter, a "good girl," a "shy girl," had somehow inspired or convinced others to jump.

The Hoolihans were still there a week later when the authorities, confounded again after renewing and then abandoning the exploration of the hole, accepted Sir James's proposal to construct a viewing platform and a small amphitheater, with a thick Plexiglas barrier around the hole. Men in hard hats poured cement pilings and trimmed lumber, built steps and a turnstile.

It was important, Sir James insisted, that the hole itself be left open. "They might be anywhere. They might be here, with us even now."

We sat together in the rose garden, he in his wheelchair. I had been taking Paxil for a week, prescribed by Sir James's own personal physician, and yet I was still not sleeping well. I was not myself. My own faith, in the divine, in the unknowable, in Sir James, had been shaken, I don't mind telling you, and there was also the matter of a civil suit filed against us by Judith Killacky and her four orphaned children, who appeared every morning at breakfast but otherwise stayed in their quarters.

Sir James tried to comfort, to reassure me. "These children of God," he reminded me, "they also are scientists in their way. They are astronauts, explorers. Of another realm perhaps, but on an adventure we can only dream of, and envy." Sir James, aged eighty, did not hesitate. His hands did not tremble. He spoke softly but firmly: "I only wish that I could join them."

"Do you really, sir?" I asked. "Do you?"

He looked at me, this man of faith, his pale blue eyes searching my face. And where I had always imagined he'd found something deep, had encouraged and affirmed it in me, his mouthpiece, his servant, his friend and fellow worshipper, I saw that now he looked quickly away. I was, I felt, no longer the receptive pool, the reflection, the loving gaze. And, not finding in me the reciprocity of understanding and faith and wisdom, the pool into which this great man-prophet might drop a pebble of his knowledge, I saw that he glanced away, out the window, and I knew then that I risked losing him.

And so I got up from the roses and left him there in the garden and walked slowly but deliberately in the direction of whatever he might have been seeing, summoning, that element no one had proven, the dimension unseen, the realm into which I had invited myself to dwell, had been invited by Sir James, a place that for me had been as real as the plantation, the sea, the orchids in the solarium, the roses in the garden, the palms, the very stars above. Needing to know myself whether I might be reclaimed, whether I could live there again and always, I walked across the lawn, greeted the two guards and a dozen workers in boots and hard hats, passed under the frame of the platform under construction, considered not one moment further that I would do this, removed the plastic tarpaulin that covered the hole, and leapt.

I fell and fell and fell, and must also, in my falling, have fallen asleep. I had no sense of time, which was to me a relief, and I found it easy enough to hold my arms tightly at my sides so as not to limit my progress or hurt myself. I had time to think, to remember. As a child I was taken to Disneyland, not far from Professor Killacky's former home, and to a ride sponsored by the Monsanto Corporation in which visitors to the Magic Kingdom entered what appeared to be a giant microscope, ostensibly to be shrunken to microscopic size in order to visit the internal workings of the human body, the molecules and cells, or to explore the atom, the universe, I could not recall exactly now. Such, however, was my vision of myself descending, as of a grown man reduced to the size of a small one or a child, even as it seemed to me the diameter of the hole itself also narrowed, gradually.

This could have taken days, this journey, yet my vision, in direct opposite proportion to my shrinking size, only broadened as I shrank and the tunnel shrank. And so I saw all around me a giant tableau of history, time, faith, layers and layers of geological strata corresponding, yes, directly and precisely to the story of our Creator's handiwork, the destruction, the birth, just as the missing scientist had explained in his paper and no doubt further detailed in his notes for those who knew how to read them.

I was Jonah, and then Daniel. I was Jacob, climbing down a ladder. As I fell I knew I was also on top of, above, and behind Dr. Killacky and the dog Jo-Jo, that I was borne on the tailwind of Sister Alpha and the twelve other disciples, even, lo, on the bodies and spirits of multitudes. I seemed not to be falling faster. My body would, I knew, reach free fall, a point where I would not drop any faster, but I was not sure if this was true for falling down holes, or of how gravity worked miles and miles under TempleLand and the island. I had entered the portal to another world, if not yet entered that world itself, by looking into Sir James's wise, ancient eyes and finding nothing of myself left. I needed to be here, for him as much as for myself.

I woke after some time to darkness and coolness, reached out gingerly to touch the slick, wet walls of the tunnel, brushing them barely with my fingertips, at a speed of what felt sometimes fast, but sometimes so slow I might not be falling at all. Proximity to what must have been the earth's core began to warm the tunnel. It was dark there, but not as dark as you might imagine.

And who, I wondered as I fell, is anyone to judge me, or science, or Sir James? I heard his voice as I fell, and felt relief, peace. I wondered now what everyone, except Sir James, had been so scared of. I felt more alive than I had ever been, or felt, in my life up above. Still, I expected only more, and I looked forward to reaching the end.

I heard my own voice. There was no echo here. There was no beginning after a while, not that I could recall, not to me and not to my journey. There was no end, not to believing, not to faith, not yet anyway, and I fell, fell, fell confidently, which is a feeling unwelcome to those on the surface, frightening, but which I assure you was the anticipation and excitement of arrival. "Remember this always," was all I thought, spoke, heard, all three of them the same expression.

And when I woke, here I was in, yes, this small chamber in the very center of the planet. I had indeed become smaller, and so fit perfectly with the others, and I took my place standing in the crèche. The scene was arranged as it should have been, with Dr. Simon Killacky standing on one side, wearing a beard and robe and carrying a staff, Sister Alpha sitting in her blue gown, and Jo-Jo guarding the manger.

She smiled at me, this young and beautiful Sarah Hoolihan, and then beckoned, and the humiliating scenes of her on the video and in the photographs were no more. I approached, welcoming her invitation, and peered inside the humble cradle to adore the infant and to feel, at last, the complete joy and assurance of the sight of him, here, in the world at last, that world rediscovered by a man of science and a man of faith and, lo, there he was, Sir James, a tiny baby at rest in swaddling clothes, laid in the warm, dry straw. Around us knelt and prayed the rest of the disciples wearing their purest white, with candles burning eternally around us, the grotto illuminated by the tiny flames as well as by the bright blue eyes of the child.

And after I had adored him, and been found again in those strong and gentle eyes, I returned to my own station, where I am now, kneeling forever and eternally, together with the others here in the enduring and real world where science and hydrology will never, ever find us and cannot deny us, no, not hidden deep in the earth's core.

THE TREE

from vol. 5, no. 1

Benjamin Percy

THE STORY BEGINS when a pinecone raises its knuckles and abandons its nuts, losing them to the birds and the chipmunks and the wind, only one of them taking hold in the earth. This is in spring, after the powdery snow has turned to a hard rain that makes the rabbitbrush go yellow and the cheatgrass green and sends floods of brackish water surging through canyons.

This particular nut, buried and dampened by the rain, opens softly and releases a green-tipped stem that, like a finger pointing the way, uncurls and stiffens and presses its way upward until it breaks the soil and takes in the warm air and the warm sun, so thrilled by them both that it grows three inches that day and three more the next. Its roots mine the soil, burrowing downward, extending like capillaries, drinking up precious moisture and gobbling up nitrogen, phosphorus, potassium, knocking aside worms and grubs, feeding, feeding, feeding off everything, so that several other nuts can find no sustenance and wither and eventually break down into particles the tree consumes as well.

It is so hungry.

The tree grows, and growth remains its principal concern. It is a ponderosa, thick-waisted, towering already, with three-needled fingers and scab-colored scales of bark, black lining the crevices between them. For so many years its branches stretch skyward and its roots grope downward and it drinks with great thirst, allowing no neighbors except sagebrush and cheatgrass, knowing no company except for the turkey vultures that roost in its branches, and the ants and the beetles that scuttle in and out of its bark, and the occasional cow that takes rest in its shade.

The cows—and the tree, for that matter—belong to the Mosses, a family that for several generations has ranched this acreage. When the old man doesn't wake up one morning—a bloody starburst filling one of his open eyes—his family begins to parcel the land to developers who build, on two-acre lots, homes of a similar neocolonial design, with rustic touches such as river-rock facades and wide-board hardwood flooring. Big bay windows look out over the patchwork of sage flats and alfalfa fields that stretch to the upthrust of the mountains.

Though the tree at first views the front-end loader and the concrete truck and the flatbed carrying lumber and the big-bellied men wearing tool belts as invasive, as if they form a strange garden that might steal nutrients from its soil, and though it at first spits sap and drops pinecones like bombs and makes of its interior a groaning complaint when anyone comes too close, really the tree is cautiously interested after so many years of nothing but the birds and the bugs for company. It has not realized up to this point its hunger as a kind of loneliness.

Its hunger—once consigned to sunlight and rain and subterranean nutrients—suddenly transforms when one day a moving truck followed by a bullet-shaped car crawls up the driveway. The car door kicks open to reveal a little girl with hair the color and curl of wood shavings. There are a mother and father, of course, but the tree sees only the girl, who immediately runs to it and balances on a snakelike root and places a warm little hand on its trunk and asks her father if he might hang a swing from one of the branches. Aside from a construction worker who crushed out a cigarette against its bark, this is the tree's first human contact, as welcome as a warm rain.

"It's talking to me," the little girl says.

Soon a swing with yellow ropes dangles from one of the lower-reaching branches and nearly every day the girl pumps her legs and bends her body to reach higher and higher, as if she hopes to toe the clouds from the sky. She reads books in the tree's shade. She plays with her dolls and stuffed animals in the tangle of its roots.

Nights, it scratches at her window, delighting in the way she startles, her eyes wide, her arms out before her and then falling to her side in relief when she realizes it was only a branch, only the tree.

In the winter, her father pulls from the garage a box full of blinking colored lights and wraps them around the tree's trunk and along its branches. The tree doesn't mind, not when it sees her mouth open in wonder, her eyes a glimmering reflection of the lights, the tree as though it is a part of her.

When the wind blows, the tree dances—its branches bending—and sings—its needles hissing, its trunk moaning, *crick-crack*—for her. As a child the girl claps and giggles. And then as a teenager she gives a half smile and maybe hums something back at the tree before turning to a magazine, her phone. She still swings, but lazily, her bare feet and painted toenails gently scuffing the ground, its roots, an almost-caress.

After so many years she knows the tree and the tree knows her.

And then one day she shoves the car full of suitcases and duffel bags and hastily taped cardboard boxes and rolled-up, rubber-banded posters. A window fan. A computer with cords dangling from it like roots. When she slams shut the trunk, she stands looking for a long time at the house and the tree, and then she and her parents vanish into the car and the engine roars to life. They hurry down the cinder driveway and the tires kick up a reddish cloud that rises again a day later when the parents return without the girl.

She has left before—usually for a weekend, sometimes for a week, even two—vacationing somewhere exotic, returning to the tree with her skin smelling of salt and coconut oil and glowing from too much sun—but never for this long and never at this time of year, when the alfalfa is being reaped, when the aspen's leaves go golden. Without the girl, the mother and the father continue to watch television in the living room, to heft groceries from the trunk of their car, as if nothing has changed. The air grows cooler and when the wind rises the tree sheds many of its needles and empty cones like tears.

In a hollow where a woodpecker once burrowed for grubs there is now a wasp's nest, and the tree threatens to crush the larvae into a yellow paste if the wasps do not do its bidding and find the girl, *find her*. In a buzzing rush they rise from the hollow and wander many roads and wind currents to peer into cars and houses and caves alike, hunting for her. A week later one of them returns to the tree—its wings tattered, its stinger limp from a run-in with a robin—sputtering out the girl's location, far away from here, over the mountains, in a dormitory on a college campus.

Of course the tree does not understand why she has left, only that she has left, has begun another life far away. The tree wishes that its roots could uncoil, that it could slither like a wooden octopus across the many miles that separate it from the girl and deposit itself outside her window and tap at the glass and earn once more the warmth of her smile.

Since it cannot, it schemes other ways to earn her attention, hurrying the sap through its system and opening its buds a season early to send spores on the wind. The spores follow a maze of updrafts and downdrafts to finally find her. They arrange themselves on her window in a constellation of pollen, a foreign alphabet whose letters she does not understand. She wipes them away with a damp paper towel and when they reappear the next day wipes them away again.

The tree seizes a crow and whispers splintery threats into its ear, and sends it off with a nut tucked under its black feathers like a jewel to carry over the forested foothills, the snowcapped mountains, the green expanse of farmland interrupted by clusters of alders and oaks, until the crow finally swoops down onto the campus. Outside a brick dormitory, on a lawn shaped like a half moon, the crow pecks a hole and deposits the nut and then flutters past the girl's window, a black cackling shadow. The soil here is rich and dark, and almost immediately the nut cracks open and begins its probing ascent, like a periscope, to spy the girl, to seek her out. But on the third day a shirtless man in jean cutoffs sits on the seedling and strums his guitar, singing off-key songs for a good two hours. And on the fifth day a lawn mower snarls across the lawn and lops off the green shoot at its head.

Back at the girl's home, the tree's bark begins to darken and grow knotty. Its branches twist. Its roots curl. Spiders and beetles creep out of its hollows. A vulture roosts in its crown and screeches all night its rusty music.

Winter comes. The sky goes gray. Ice clots the ditches. Frost steals across the windows of the house and the figures inside become blurred shadows. The sagebrush and rabbitbrush wither into dry wigs. The ants and wasps die with their eggs and become the food of next season. Geese fly south in flocks the shape of a spearhead.

When the first snow falls, the tree knows the father will soon drag from the garage the box full of colored lights to weave around its branches. And he does. And the tree is ready. A ragged *crack* is the only warning before a branch the size of a missile falls from above and crushes the father's skull, a red smear on white snow. His legs twitch. The colored lights blink. The tree pleasures in the taste of blood warming its roots.

And the girl comes home, as the tree knew she would. She looks different somehow. Her face squarer. Her body longer. Her hair a different color, the yellow of the mullein flower. Her black clothes match the black bags beneath her eyes. She stands for a long time looking at the tree. A wind rises and the tree dances for her, waving its empty branches, moaning out a song. She does not clap or smile. Her face grows more pinched and severe. She goes into the garage and emerges a moment later, not with a fistful of lights, but with a chain saw. She yanks the cord, and the chain saw coughs a cloud of black smoke before settling into a full-throated growl.

The tree does not fight the blur of the machine's toothy blade, even as sawdust covers the ground like newly fallen snow, even as it bleeds and weeps trails of sap, so hungry for her final touch, its loneliness repaired.

ALAMO PLAZA

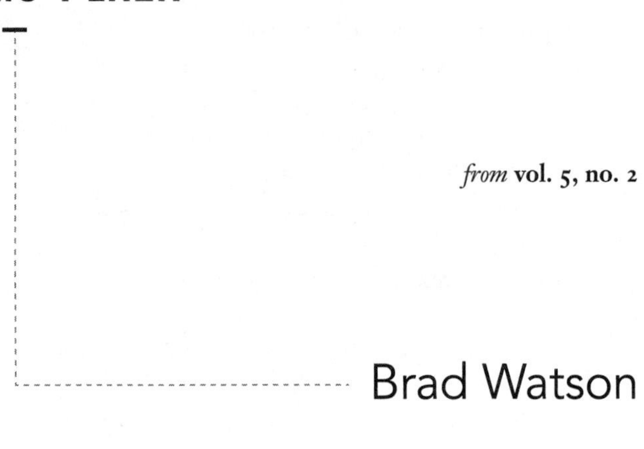

from **vol. 5, no. 2**

Brad Watson

THE ROAD TO THE COAST was a long, steamy corridor of leaves. Narrow bridges over brush-choked creeks. Our father drove, the windows down, wind whipping his thick black hair. Our mother's hair, abundant and auburn and long and wavy, she'd tried to tame beneath a pretty blue scarf. He wore a pair of black Ray-Bans. She wore prescription shades with the swept and pointed ends of the day. He whistled crooner songs and smoked Winstons, and early as it was, no one really talked.

This was before things changed, before Hurricane Camille, the casinos.

My older brother, Hal, slept sitting up, his mouth open as if he were singing silently in a dream. My younger brother, Ray, had been left with our grandmother, too young for this trip, too much trouble most of the time. He was just two, and the youngest of three, and his sharp, hawkish eyes constantly sought their prey, which was inattention, which he would rip to shreds with tantrums, devour in small bloody satisfying chunks of punishment or mollification. I was so very glad that he was not along.

By noon we smelled the brine-and-fish stink of the bays. The land flattened into hazy vista, so flat you could see the curve of the earth. Downtown Gulfport steamed an old Floridian vapor from cracked sidewalks. Filigreed railings, shaded storefronts, not a soul out, everyone and everything stalled in the heat, distilling. The beach highway stretched out to the east, white and hot in the sun. Our tires made slapping sounds on the melting tar dividers and the wind in the car windows was warm and salty. We passed old beach mansions with green shutters, hundred-year-old oaks in the yards. A scattering of cheap redbrick motels, slatboard restaurants, bait shops. The beach, to our right, was flat and white and the lank brown surf lapped at the sand.

The Alamo Plaza Motel Court's white stucco fort facade stood flanked by low regular motel rooms around a concrete courtyard. The swimming pool lay oddly naked and exposed in the middle of the motel's broad front lawn, one low diving board jutting over the deep end like a pirates' plank.

We stopped in the breezeway beside the office and went inside where the floor was cool Mexican tile, lush green plants in large clay pots in the corners, and a color television on which we could watch, late afternoons and evenings after supper before bedtime, programs unavailable back home. I have a vivid memory of watching a Tarzan movie there in which Tarzan, standing in the crook of a large tree, is shot right between the eyes by a safari hunter's rifle, and he doesn't even flinch. Is it possible this is a true memory, not invented or stretched? Would even Hollywood in the thirties—for this was an old movie even then—have Tarzan being shot directly in the forehead with a high-power rifle, the bloody spot at the point of entry jumping out on his skin, and him not even blinking his eyes? I was, I am, as incredulous as the safari men on the jungle trail below, holding their high-power rifles and gaping at this jungle god, who just stared coolly back at them with the bullet hole in the center of his forehead.

WE RENTED A BUNGALOW in the rear of the Plaza. In the mornings we went to the beach, joining hands to cross the white concrete path of US 98, the beach highway, to the concrete steps that led down to the beach on the Sound. It was not an exhilarating beach, as Gulf beaches go, its white sand dredged from beyond the barrier islands twenty miles out to cover the naturally muddy shore, where the natural flora included exposed roots of cypress and mangrove. Huge tarpon, an almost prehistoric-looking fish, cruised here between the river and the sea.

Our father, my brother, and I waded far out into the Sound, where the water was still just knee-deep to a six-year-old. We turned and waved to our mother, who sat on the white sand on a beach towel, the pale blue scarf on her head, the cat-eyed sunglasses perched on her nose. She did not swim, and though one reason we came to Biloxi instead of the more beautiful beaches in Gulf Shores or Pensacola was the cheaper prices at motels, the other reason was her fear of the water. She felt safer sitting on the edge of the Sound, which was more like a lake, than she did near the crashing waves of the Gulf. The year before, standing near her beach towel in the sand at Gulf Shores, Alabama, as if it were her sole tentative anchor to the dry world, she had seen a young man drown trying to save his little boy from a rip current. She'd watched as the rescue squad dragged the man's body onto the beach. A year later, and for many years after that, the terror she felt still welled up in her with a regularity as steady as the ticking minute hand on the clock, and with that same regularity she forced it back down, into her gut, where it fought with her frequent doses of Paragoric.

I can still remember her in the swimming pool, at the country club they'd struggled to join, before the hard times forced us to drop out. She would step into the shallow water with a look on her face that now I understand as terror but which then I took for simple cautiousness and uncertainty. A slim hand out as if to steady herself from some unknown that could unsteady the whole deal. A cream-colored bathing cap covered her dark curls, as if she were going to plunge in with the boldness of an Olympic diver, though her pointed, blue-framed sunglasses still rested on her slim nose. And before the water reached above her waistline she would bend her knees and, holding her head up on her neck as far as she could stretch it, push herself gently forward and dog-paddle around the shallow end, her toes bumping the bottom and pushing her forward every few little strokes. Knowing her now, I'm astonished she had the courage to get into the pool, with others there who might see her and laugh at the fact that she couldn't really swim. All those club people, who might laugh and think what a country girl she was—Did you *see* that? Can't even swim! And my admiration for her swells in some proportion to my sense of her loss in the intervening years.

BUT THERE WE STOOD, far out in the tepid brown Mississippi Sound, waving to her. She was not actually distinguishable to us as herself, that far out. She was a figure who occupied the spot where we'd last seen our mother, apparently wearing the same pale blue scarf on a head of short dark hair, with the same pale skin, and waving back for a moment, then falling still. A figure in the light of the moment just a millisecond away, her image reaching us far out into the Sound, yet gone as if she'd been gone for a dozen years.

IN THE EVENINGS, we went out to eat oysters on the half shell, platters of fried shrimp, fish, french fries, and hush puppies, and returned to sleep in the luxurious window-unit air-conditioning of our room. Our mother would almost never let us use the a/c at home, as it cost too much on the power bill.

Mornings and late afternoons, we went over to the beach and frolicked. I so love that word. Sand castles, not such artful ones, of mounds, moats, and tunnels. A tall woman with big blond hair and breasts like pale luminescent water balloons walked by in a green two-piece bathing suit, walking so carefully she seemed to be treading along the shore through a very narrow passage only she could see. We glanced at our father, and he bobbed his eyebrows. We fell over into the sand, yipping like hyenas.

I once told my mother of being propositioned by a lascivious young country girl at a filling station in Buckatunna, Mississippi, on my way home for a visit. I'd been filling up my little Honda coupe and this woman kind of ambled over and stood there leering at me. You sure are good-lookin, she said. I'm having a party at my house, you want to come on over?

Did you go with her? my mother asked me when I told her the story. Of course not, I said. I didn't know her from Medusa. Well, that's the difference between you and your father, she said.

At this time they had been divorced for about seven years.

MY BROTHER AND I DANCED BAREFOOT across the white-hot parking lot to the center of the Alamo Plaza's interior court—its *plaza*, I suppose. There beneath a small shed roof sat a humming, sweating ice-making machine. We would tip open the canted lid to the bin and scoop out handfuls of ice crushed so fine it seemed shaved. We packed it into snowballs and threw them at one another, tossed them into the crackling hot air and watched them begin to shed water even as they rose and then fell to the sizzling concrete, melting instantly into a wet penumbra that shrank and evaporated into smoky wisps. We opened the bin again and wedged our heads and shoulders in there for the exquisite shock of freezing cold. For at least a few moments as we reeled in the white-hot courtyard on burning bare feet, our heads felt as dense and cold as ice cubes on top of our icicle necks.

WE DROVE TO A GROUP OF SMALL CABINS on a cove and a grizzled man rented us a skiff. Our father sat at the stern and gunned the motor, buzzing us out into the stinking Sound, bouncing us through the light chop, our mother holding on to her sun hat.

We drifted a half mile or so off the shore, baited hooks, and cast out. For a while there was nothing, just the little boat rocking in the gentle waves of the channel, the hazy sky, gulls creaking by and checking us out with cocked heads, a beady black eye.

My brother pulled up the first fish. He swung it over my head and into the boat. It was a small fish, with an ugly face. As soon as it popped from the water it began to make ugly, froggish little sounds. Croaker, our father said. He unhooked it and tossed it back into the chop. I asked about the strange noise it made and he said it was the sound they made trying to breathe out of water.

The truth is the Atlantic croaker makes its sound by tightening the muscles around its swim bladder, and uses the sound for general communication and to attract a mate. It's said to be a "prodigious spawner."

I reeled one in, the fight leaving it. Up it came, into the boat. *Croak, croak*. A brownish fish with a little piggish snout. A small mark on the back of its eye gave it an angry look, a what-are-you-looking-at? kind of look. These fish looked pissed off to be interrupted in the middle of their prodigious spawning.

Soon we were all pulling in croakers. The boat floor crowded with flapping, croaking fish. A chorus of their dry frog noises rose around us. After a while, my father had had enough and started tossing croakers overboard. Some smacked dead on the surface and floated away. Others knifed the water with a final croak and were gone, back to their spawning and general communication with their kind.

WHEN I WAS TOO YOUNG TO REMEMBER, now, how young I was, I began to have a recurring dream, or nightmare. The air in the dream was electric, very much like the electron-buzzing screen of our television when the station went off the air. Jumping with billions of little black dots. A charged, nervous air, the atmospheric equivalent of the feeling you get when you knock your funny bone. In the dream I felt very weak, and very heavy, as if my mass were compounding, draining my strength. I was aware of a hellish din of angry voices, though there were never any distinct words. I began to see I was in a very small room, the only door a tiny one in the corner, little larger than a mouse hole. Other times, the dreamscape changed to one of dreadful empty vastness, all gray, in which the horizon seemed impossibly distant and I seemed very small, and the pressure of the air was heavy upon me. I suppose it was a simple dream of anxiety, though I have sometimes fancied it a latent, deeply buried, sensorial memory from the womb, and who knows but that this is possible on some level? I was too young, it seems to me, to create such a memory from what little I'd heard about gestation. I probably knew nothing of that when the dream began. I may have been told where I came from. I don't remember. In any case, I have no firm idea where such anxiety in one so young, where *that* could have come from. Except that I'd had, from a very young age, the sense and fear that my parents would divorce and force me to choose between them. Maybe I had picked up on some general unhappiness. I don't know. But I spent much of my alone time worrying that something terrible and heartbreaking would happen.

AT THE POOL there were a couple of ladies laughing and sipping drinks at the little round table beneath the green-striped umbrella, and a very big fat man, not overly fat but very big, was taking huge vaults off the diving board, leaving it bouncing on its fulcrum like a flimsy plank of pine siding as he hit the water in a cannonball, showering the laughing ladies with water, again and again. The ladies cried out, Stop! Oh, stop it! Their laughter rose and drowned in the humid salty darkness and the *clacka-clackity-clacka* sound of cars cruising past on the cooling white-slab highway along the beach. I listened to the cars long into the night, in my bed, along with the faint surf, my father snoring lightly, my mother and Hal lying still as the dead. The Gulf breezes puffed against the windows, slipped through seams, and drifted through the chilled air of the room like coastal ghosts released from their tight invisibility, sustained for a while by the softly exhaled breath of the living.

MY BROTHER MET ANOTHER BOY and began going off with him, around the Alamo's grounds or at the pool or, when I'd followed them there, across to the beach, where I couldn't follow without an adult. He became more of an absence, and so I drifted into the same safe quietude where I spent most of my time, anyway, where most middle children spend their time.

At some point in my childhood I wanted out of my family, although I loved my mother and father and tolerated my brothers as well as anyone else. I didn't want never to see them again, but it would have been nice to live with some other family, possibly across or down the street, instead of my own. An imaginary one, maybe. When you are quiet, you are different, which makes everyone a little nervous and suspicious, if you are the only one that way. I was at ease if left alone in my room to read comics, or alone in the large tract of woods bordering our cul-de-sac street. I loved spying on others walking in the woods when I was hidden and could see them without their seeing me. Sometimes I looked into windows at night, but only at ordinary things. People eating supper, or watching television. No undressing or showers or such. I only wanted to experience the mystery of seeing things as they really were, when you yourself did not enter in. It seemed frank and honest in an exciting way. There was nothing to fear in terms of yourself in such moments. If you were quiet and still, it was almost as if you weren't there. It was like being a ghost, curious about the visible world and the creatures in it. As if you were dreaming it, and not a part of the dream but there somehow, unquestioned.

ONE DAY HAL ASKED PERMISSION to go out with his new friend's family on a charter fishing boat. They would have to leave very early, before dawn. I determined to rise then, too, and see him off. But I wasn't able to, and no one woke me, so I didn't get up until light was seeping into the sky over the Sound. I rushed outside onto the motel lawn, stood there barefoot in the dew and cool heavy breeze, and looked out across the water. On the horizon I could see the gray silhouette of a ship, a big ship, which in my memory's surviving image appears to be a tanker of some kind, an oceangoing vessel. But at that moment, on the lawn, I thought it must be the boat Hal had gone on with his new friend and family—these people I'd never spoken to, whom I'd only watched from across the lawn, complete strangers to me and already fast friends with Hal. Watching the ghostly ship far out in the Sound, I had the strongest feeling that he'd gone away and would never return. It was something I couldn't quite grasp, just yet, someone going so far out in the water on a boat that you can't see them anymore, and then coming back in. I was very sad, I remember, thinking that he was gone forever. And I have lost the memory of his returning from the fishing trip to the motel. I've wondered why I felt so much sadder then than I did when he died. Anticipation is expansive in the imagination. Memory is reductive, selective. And any great moment must be too much to absorb in that moment, without the ameliorative power of genius or mental illness. When

Hal died, years later, it seemed like the completion of something I'd been watching and waiting for all that time.

His last words, I was told, were a blurted, Look out!

My father's last words, I was told, were, Something's wrong.

If my mother had any last words, they are a secret, as she was old and alone. And if any words were formed in her mind as she lay unconscious and slowly dying on her bedroom floor, no one will ever know what they were.

IT'S HARD TO REMEMBER HAL in very specific ways. He was a small boy, and then a small man. I did not remember him that way, since he was nearly four years older and so until I was into my later teens he was larger than me. I remember how shocking it was when, a couple of years after his death, I went into his room and tried on one of his shirts. It was tight across the shoulders, too short in the sleeves. This was shocking because I had thought he was at least as tall as I was and stockier, but he was not. He had always carried himself like a larger boy and man.

A second child will always feel displaced by the first. People say it's the other way around but it's not. Later in life there are the photographs you discover of your older sibling, before you were born, with one or both of your parents. It's then, after you've had children yourself and know the experience in your own life, that you understand the bond between the new, young parents and their first child. You understand how miraculous and illuminating it is. You know how the experience has remade the whole world for the parents, and how the only child's world, entirely new in the magnificent, solipsistic way only an only child's world can be, eclipses all else, and when the second child comes along it is only as if the eclipsing body has moved aside, moved along in its path. The wonder has passed, leaving the washed and dazed sense of deep and cathartic change, an experience that will never be repeated for anyone in that little world. And, in truth, it leaves everyone feeling a little bit diminished. You realize this, when you are older and you have memories and these memories are informed, in a slow infusion of understanding, by the old photographs taken before you were even conceived.

Hal was a prodigy, in many ways a typical first child in that he was precocious, gregarious, fearless, bestowed at birth with the grandest, most natural sense of entitlement. Every first child is a king or queen. A prince or princess, an *enfant terrible* of privilege and favor. And Hal was talented. When he was three, he learned the words to the popular song "Davy Crockett, King of the Wild Frontier" and sang it so adorably that our parents secured a recording session for him down at a local radio station.

He was introduced by George Shannon, a local radio and television personality. I imagine Hal wearing his cowboy outfit, a black hat and black, sequined shirt, black pants, black, filigreed cowboy boots, a toy six-shooter in a toy holster on his belt. He probably wasn't wearing this outfit, since it had nothing to do with Davy Crockett, but there's a framed photo of Hal at about that age, wearing that outfit, that hung for decades on our mother's living room wall, and so that's how I see him, then. A musical cousin, Doc Taylor, strummed the song's tune on a guitar, and Hal sang the song in his piping voice.

Born on a mountaintop in Tennessee,
Greenest state in the land of the free.
Raised in the woods so's he knowed every tree.
Kil't him a b'ar when he was only three.
Davy, *Daavy Crock*ett.
King of the *weeld* frontier.

I write "wild" that way because that was how he pronounced it, like some kind of flamboyant elf.

In the background on the recording, toward the end of the song, you can hear a baby crying a little fitfully, fussing. That was me, only a few weeks old, trying as would become usual to assert myself, to little avail.

This recording was of course a precious possession, always, but it became all the more so after Hal's early death, when he was a young man only recently married. It disappeared after the accident, and my mother bitterly accused Hal's widow of having taken it for herself. I took this for the truth. And then, many years later, after my mother's death, I found it beneath a stack of papers and documents in a dresser drawer in her bedroom.

Well, no, said one of my cousins. It was never lost, not that I know of.

She never told you that Sophie had taken it?

No, my cousin said. She never said that to me.

I could have sworn she'd told me the recording was missing, stolen, possibly destroyed out of spite. But even the memory of her telling me that comes from so long ago, now, that I can no longer be sure.

OUT AT THE ALAMO PLAZA'S POOL the next day there were a few people, a woman with two toddlers down in the shallow end, a few grown-ups in loungers along the apron. The big fat man who'd been jumping and doing cannonballs the night before was again on the diving board, leisurely bouncing and looking around, as if this were simply his place. He bounced easily, the board bending beneath his great weight and riding him slow as an elevator back up again. His toes hung over the end, his arms hung at his sides, and he nodded to us as we walked up.

Across the highway the beach was empty. The Sound lay flat and brown in the sun's glare.

Morning, he called out to our mother. She smiled and nodded back. Morning, sir, our father said in his clear baritone sales voice. From my spot at the three-foot mark, I called good morning to the man, too, and he called back with a little salute and a wave, Morning, young man.

Standing there bouncing.

A long, big-boned woman lying flat out on a lounger with a big broad hat over her face called to him. The voice came from her, but you couldn't see her face. The hat didn't move. Harry, she said to the man. Don't go splashing all over creation.

The man looked at her, still bouncing, then looked at me and smiled and winked. He walked back to the base end of the board and turned around.

Harry, the woman said.

The big man rose on his toes. It looked comical, the action of a much lighter, fitter man. He spread his arms like a ballerina, ran tiptoeing down to the end of the board, came down heavily, and the board slowly flung him up. He came down in a cannonball, leaning in the woman's direction, and sent up a high sheet of water that drenched her pretty good. She sat up and adjusted the wet floppy hat on her head. Harry swam to the pool's edge and grinned at Hal and me. I turned around and looked at our mother. She stared at the man and woman, her mouth cocked into a curious smile. She saw me looking and picked up a magazine and started reading it. Our father sat in a deck chair in his swim trunks, his elbows on his knees like a man watching a baseball game. A can of Jax beer rested on the concrete apron between his white feet.

I heard a loud *thawongabumpbump* and a broad shapeless shadow darted onto the dimpled surface of the pool. There again was Harry suspended in all his bulk high in the air, a diving mule pushed off the circus platform. At the last second he tucked his head and rolled over onto his shoulders, sending an arc of water toward the mother with her two toddlers in the shallow end. They screwed up their faces and recoiled. When the water settled they all three turned, dripping, to stare at Harry, the mother annoyed, the children bewildered.

That's enough, Harry, the woman said. She'd snatched her hat off and I saw she was wearing a man's heavy black sunglasses, like our father's, and her wide mouth was painted bright red. Her hair was frizzled and graying.

All right, sorry, Harry said.

But as soon as the woman had pulled the hat brim back down over her eyes, Harry was up and tiptoeing back to the diving board. He made shushing gestures to all of us, a finger to his lips. At the shallow end, the mother hustled her toddlers from the pool, grabbed up their things, and headed for their room.

Harry was poised at the base of the board. He spread his arms, rose on his toes, and pranced down its length. He swung his arms above his head, scrunched his big body down like a compressed spring. The board bent almost to the surface of the water, seemed to hesitate there, then cracked and split down its length and tossed Harry awkwardly into the air.

He hit the water with a loud, flat smack. The split board bounced a couple of times and lay still. Harry floated motionless as the rocking water lapped the edges of the pool. A little scarlet cloud bloomed around him. Then he jerked into a flurry of motion. His head rose up and he bellowed, then sank down again.

The big woman shouted and stood up from her chair, her hat tumbling into the grass. The two men standing poolside leapt into the water. They managed to subdue Harry and pull him to the pool's edge. The woman stood rigid, watching them, her mouth hanging open. Then she closed it with a clap and her face took on what looked like a long-practiced expression of disgust. Other people came and helped drag Harry out onto the concrete apron. He made a groaning, desperate sound. Blood leaked from a wound on his foot. One of the men who'd helped rescue Harry from the pool pulled a car around, and he and the other man helped Harry into it. The woman got into the back seat beside Harry and they drove away, to the hospital I suppose.

I walked over to the diving board, leaned down low, and looked at the split board, its two pieces splayed, blond splinters sticking out like bleached porcupine quills. Hanging there jammed tight in the split, a small blunt wedge drained of color, was what appeared to be Harry's little toe.

It was fantastic. It made the whole trip.

OUR MOTHER WAS HORRIFIED, of course. One year, a drowning. The next, a dismembered toe. Not so disturbing as a death, but awful in its own way. I think it settled deeply into her subconscious, an augury somehow of vague misfortune looming.

For our father, who was her opposite in terms of being able to live in the moment instead of living each present moment with a terrible awareness of the past and a foreboding sense of the future, the accident had a different effect. He would remember it with a kind of morbid humor, closing his eyes and pursing his lips and shaking with silent, wincing laughter. Ooo, shit, that had to hurt, he'd say. I still remember the time, riding with him in the car when I was a boy, and I had my arm out the passenger-side window. He glanced over and told me to take my arm into the car, that he'd heard about a man riding along with his arm out the window who was sideswiped by another car that took his arm right off at the shoulder. Ever since, I've never been able to leave my arm out a car window if there are other cars present within anything close to striking distance. I live with a combination of my mother's constant fear of danger, and my father's irreverent appreciation of it.

ANYWAY, YEARS LATER, I wasn't even sure if the incident with the poor man's toe had really happened. It had been so long ago, and I had been so young, and I hadn't thought about it in some time. But I had been remembering it and trying to recall the details when I had the disturbing thought that I may have invented it all. I asked my mother if she remembered it. She was eating a piece of toast at the breakfast table, so I suppose my timing wasn't good. She stopped chewing, as if stomach acid had suddenly boiled into her esophagus, and her eyes took on that vaguely alarmed and unfocused look she got when she was presented with something horrible. But then it passed, and she swallowed.

It was his big toe, she said.

I found that hard to believe and said so. I asked was she certain.

I'm certain, she said. That's what made it so horrible.

I saw my father a couple of weeks later, though, and put the question to him. I told him what my mother had said. He scoffed.

It wasn't his big toe, he said, that would've been impossible. It was his little toe.

I didn't say anything.

It's just like your mother to make it into something worse than it actually was, he said.

SO, WE WENT BACK HOME that very afternoon of the accident, and a storm had passed through. A tornado had hopped right over our neighborhood, which was in a low area between two modest ridges, and had snapped off the tops of several tall pines. One of the pine tops lay in our backyard, another in the street in front of our house. The air was gray and you could smell the spent, burned residue of destructive energy in the air, feel it prickling the skin, as if we were inside a big discharged gun barrel. Green leaves and small limbs were strewn across yards and in the street and on rooftops. A telephone pole leaned toward the ground, the wires on one side taut, those on the other side loose and hanging low toward the damp grass. Everything was wet and smoking.

Some incredible violence had occurred, and yet almost everything remained intact. There sat our little brick ranch-style house. There, the pair of mimosas in the yard where I crouched concealed in the fernlike leaves, dreaming of Tarzan. There, the azaleas beneath mine and Ray's bedroom window where every year our mother took an Easter photo of her boys, our bow ties and vests and hair flipped up in front. There, the picture window of the living room we used only at Christmas or when she and our father hosted their supper club. There, the inexplicable everyday, the oddness of being, the senseless belonging to this and not that. I was barely able to contain myself. Something in me wished it had all been blown to smithereens.

OUR POINTY BOOTS

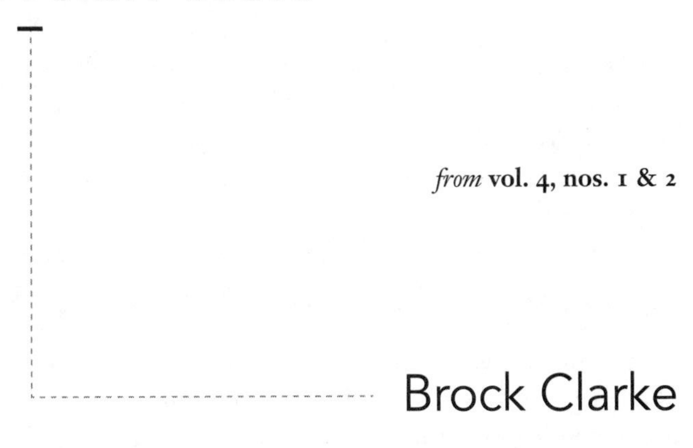

from vol. 4, nos. 1 & 2

Brock Clarke

THE REPORTERS STAND BETWEEN all fourteen of us and our transport; they put their microphones and cameras in our faces and say, "You're going home for Christmas. What's the first thing you're going to do when you get home?"

We ask, "What are our choices?"

"The usual two," the reporters say. "Are you going to hold your babies and sweet babies real tight? Or, are you going to lay your fallen comrade to rest while the chaplain conveys the gratitude of the president and the entire nation and then prays to God for the state of your comrade's immortal soul?" Then they consult their notes and ask, "You do have a fallen comrade, don't you?"

"Yes," we say. "Saunders."

"Well," they say. "What's the first thing you're going to do when you get home? Are you going to bury him? Or, are your going to hold your babies and sweet babies real tight?"

"Neither," we tell them. "The first thing we're going to do when we get home is put on our pointy boots and parade around the Public Square."

BEFORE WE GRADUATED FROM HIGH SCHOOL, before we met and married our sweet babies, before we had babies with our sweet babies, before we got the jobs that we didn't want to work at for the rest of our lives, before we realized that we probably *would* work at them for the rest of our lives if we didn't do something about it, before we did something about it and joined up, before we went to Iraq, before what happened to Saunders, before any of this happened, we were sitting around on a Friday just before graduation, skipping school, which, as graduating seniors, we were of course expected to do, feeling bored, feeling like we were missing something in our lives. And so we decided to go to the Public Square, to the Bon Ton, which had a little of everything, to see if they had what we were missing.

They were terrified of us at the Bon Ton because we were young and noisy, and we seemed even noisier than we were because we were the only customers in the store, because the store was the only store left on the Public Square that hadn't pulled out and moved to the mall, and they were terrified of us because we couldn't, at first, find what we were missing, and this disappointed us and so we let them know about it. They tried to sell us fedoras in the Men's department, and we put our fists through their tops and then wore them around our wrists like bracelets. They tried to sell us stirrup pants in the Ladies' department and those of us who are Ladies said stirrup pants were an abomination and so we all liberated the stirrups with our hands and feet and teeth and then reshelved what remained with the other, normal pants, thus diminishing their retail value. We wondered what the people at the Bon Ton had to say about *that*. The people at the Bon Ton didn't have anything to say; they scattered, hiding in dressing rooms and locking the slatted doors behind them, or crouching behind checkout counters, armed only with their bar code guns. And so there was no one to help us when we entered Footwear and saw the rows and rows of boots, their pointy toes pointing at us, as if to say they wanted us as much as we, we realized, wanted them.

ONCE WE'VE FINISHED TALKING to the reporters, we get on the transport that takes us to Germany and then another one that takes us home. We get off the transport and there, standing on the base's tarmac, are our sweet babies, waving at us. We can see that our sweet babies don't have our babies with them, for which we are grateful. Because that means there's one less person between us and our pointy boots. The tarmac has been cleared, but the snowbanks surrounding it are ten, fifteen feet high, high enough that you can't see the electric fences somewhere on the other side of them. It's sunny out, the sky is crystal blue, but it's so, so cold that our eyes start to water, immediately, the way they did when we first got to the desert and sand got into our eyes and they started to water, immediately. This is one of the things we've learned: not that people are the same wherever you go, but that we don't change, no matter where we are. We shoulder our duffel bags and walk toward our sweet babies. As we get closer, our sweet babies stop waving, run toward us, arms out in front of them, preparing to hold us. Their faces look hopeful, but nervous. Because they know that Saunders is dead, and they also know about the usual choices, know that we could choose him instead of them. When they get close enough, they put their arms around us and hold us real tight. But we don't hold them back. We keep one arm to our sides; the other keeps shouldering our duffels. When our sweet babies realize this they push themselves away, like they're the ships and we're the shore.

"You bastard," our sweet babies say to those of us who are men. "You bitch," our sweet babies say to those of us who are women. "You chose Saunders, didn't you? You chose burying Saunders over holding us real tight."

"We didn't choose Saunders," we say.

"Well, you obviously didn't choose us," they say.

"That's true," we say.

They look at us, confusion displacing anger on their faces for a second, before they figure out what's going on, before they figure out what we've chosen. "Oh no," they say.

"Oh yes," we say. And then we ask them to please take us home, where our pointy boots are in our closets, waiting for us to put them on and parade around the Public Square.

WE HAVE SEEN AND DONE SOME THINGS: When we first killed an enemy, we were glad, because for the first time ever we found that we could actually do what we were trained to do; when we first killed someone we weren't sure was an enemy, we were happy that the word *enemy* existed so that we could call him one anyway; when we first saw one of our own comrades killed, we were ecstatic that it wasn't us; and when we were done being ecstatic, then we were so, so ashamed. We've seen and done all of that. Plus, there's Saunders. But we're truly ashamed of only one thing: that once we first saw the pointy boots in the Bon Ton, we had a fight over what kind we should get.

Those of us who grew up on a farm refused to buy Lucccheses for fear of being mistaken for wops. Those of us who were Italians refused to buy Fryes for fear of being mistaken for rednecks. Some of us didn't want to get Acmes because they sounded like joke boots. Some of us didn't want to get Bearpaws because the name was too close to the name of the pastry. Some of us had no trouble getting Durangos except for those of us who had trucks that went by the same name. We all, finally, agreed on Saunders, except for Saunders, who said it was a stupid name for a boot. It was like giving a dog a human name, he said. "I would never name *my* dog Saunders," one of us said, and then Saunders wanted to know what the hell *that* was supposed to mean. And how does life turn out this way? How does the thing that promises to be different, the thing that promises to make you feel good, end up making you feel as bad as everything else? And when that happens, do you take it out on the thing that has promised so much, or do you take it out on yourself for believing the promise?

We did both: We took it out on ourselves and on the boots. We hurled them at each other, at close range; we gouged each other's eyes with the pointy toes; we clubbed each other with the hard heels; we put the boots over our hands, like gloves, and then boxed each other with them; we fell on the floor and wept at how pathetic and ridiculous we had become, how pathetic and ridiculous we always had been and always would be. And then, after we had wept but before we could figure out what else to do that we might later weep over, we were quiet, just for a moment, just long enough to hear one of the salesladies say meekly from behind her locked, slatted dressing room door: "What I'm hearing is that it doesn't really matter what *kind* of boots you're wearing, just as long as they're pointy."

It was like hearing the voice of God: not a vengeful God, but a practical, reasonable God, a God who didn't keep tabs on all the bad things you did, but who listened, really listened to you while you did those bad things, so as to help you get what you wanted so you'd stop doing them. When you hear that voice, you don't stop and ask how it got so wise, or question its wisdom. You just do what it tells you to do. We did what the saleslady told us to do. We gathered up the boots, found their partners. We located our size and our preferred brand and put them on, no matter how damaged they were, how damaged we had made them. Then we lined up and proceeded past the locked dressing room door; as we went past the door, we put our mouths to the slats and thanked the saleslady for her help. "I guess you're welcome," was her blessing. And then we left the Bon Ton and went out onto the Public Square.

ONCE OUR SWEET BABIES figure out what we've chosen, they say, to themselves, "Poor Saunders. Poor us." And then, to us: "You fuckers can just go ahead and walk home," and then they run to their cars and lay rubber out of the parking lot. So, we reshoulder our duffels and start walking.

Just outside the base, on the other side of the street from the entrance gate, are two protestors, both dressed head to toe in insulated camo, layers and layers of it, with only their faces uncovered. One, a woman, her cheeks round and fiery red, her gray hair peeking out from under a camo ski hat, is holding a cardboard sign with the words NO MORE WAR written on it in red marker, with a green peace symbol drawn underneath. The other protestor is a man. Ice hangs from his gray beard, and snot from his red nose, like Christmas tree ornaments. He chants "NO MORE WAR" into a bullhorn, drowning out whatever it is the woman is chanting, which is also probably "NO MORE WAR." They are exactly like us: there should be more of them, and they should have better ideas, and they should have better ways to tell people about their ideas. When they see us walk out of the gate, they stop chanting and come over to talk with us.

"Welcome home," the guy with the bullhorn says, although not through the bullhorn, which he holsters in what looks like an enormous, weird-looking widemouthed wine sack.

"We're proud of you," says the woman, who is probably his wife. "We feel it's important you know that."

"Okay," we say.

"This"—and here she taps her sign with the hand that's not holding it—"this doesn't mean we're not proud of you."

"Thank you," we say.

"We know you don't want to be there any more than we do," she says.

"But we volunteered," we say.

"You didn't think you were volunteering for this," she says. She looks at her sign and points to the word WAR, so we know exactly what's she's talking about.

"What *did* we think we were volunteering for, then?" we ask. We know the answer, and she doesn't, but even if she did, she'd look at us the way she looks at us now—in huge disappointment, as though we're not the people she thought we were, not the people she needs us to be. Still, she's not quite ready to give up on us. We know this, because we know her. She really is the kind of person who wants to give peace a chance, and since she's giving peace a chance, she figures she might as well give us one, too. "*We*," she says. "You keep talking about yourselves as 'We,' and not 'I.' You poor people. I bet the army taught you to talk like that, to think like that."

"Actually," we tell her, "we've talked and thought this way ever since the day we first put on our pointy boots and paraded around the Public Square."

"What?" she says, but she doesn't wait for any answer. She slowly backs away from us, and across the street, where she stands holding her sign over her chest with both hands, as though out of modesty. "Are you coming, Harold?" she shouts. But Harold is not coming, not quite yet.

"Tell us something about what it's like over there," he says, eagerly. We know him, too. He's the kind of guy—with his camo, his questions, his bullhorn, his homemade holsters, his gear—who spends every minute he's not protesting the war fantasizing about what it's like to be in one. "Tell us something we might not have heard from someone else."

"Well," we say, "one of the things you might not have heard is that when we're interrogating someone we say that if they don't tell us what we want to know, we'll cut off their heads and then fuck their skulls."

"Always?" Harold asks.

"Every time," we say.

"You say it in English?"

"No, we don't say it in English," we say, even though we do say it in English. Because we trust that if we say it the right way, whomever we're saying it to will get the point, more or less.

"Has anyone ever told you what you wanted to know?"

"No," we say.

"I wouldn't think so," he says, then glances at those of us who are women, then looks away from them before they see him looking. It's too late; they see.

"What?" those of us who are women say. "You got some kind of problem?"

"No, no problem," the guy says, his hand moving instinctively to the bullhorn in his holster. "I just have a hard time imagining it, that's all. Can, you know, a gal actually do that, physically? I mean, it's not much of a threat, is it?"

"That's *it*," those of us who are women say. They drop their duffel bags and charge Harold. Those of us who are men have to restrain them while he retreats across the street. He stands next to his wife and shouts through his bullhorn, "It's kind of funny, if you think about it," and then his wife snatches the bullhorn out of his hands and tucks it into her parka.

"Saunders wouldn't have thought it was funny," we say.

"Who is Saunders?" Harold's wife wants to know.

"Saunders is dead," we say. "We're going to lay him to rest tomorrow."

"I bet Saunders didn't think he was volunteering for *that*," the woman says.

"No, he didn't," we say as we start walking home. Because we know what Saunders thought he was volunteering for. He thought he was volunteering for the same thing we did: for the chance to feel the way we felt when we first put on our pointy boots and paraded around the Public Square.

IT WAS LUNCHTIME when we got out of the Bon Ton that day and onto the Public Square. It was sunny, hot, almost summer. The county courthouse workers were sitting in the shadow of the statue of our locally significant Revolutionary War general with their bagged lunches, struggling to unwrap their cellophane-wrapped meat and cheese sandwiches. The guys from the halfway house were lying back-down and shirtless on the grass, wolfing their cigarettes, then lighting their new butts with the remainders of the old without once opening their eyes. The bail bondsmen stood near their storefronts, across the square from the courthouse, sipping burnt coffee out of Styrofoam cups, eyeing the cuffed as they were led into the courthouse, making bets on how much their bail would be, on who would end up jumping and who would not.

And then there was us, fifteen teenagers, boys and girls, standing in front of the Bon Ton. For a while, we did nothing but look down and admire our new pointy boots. There is no love so true as one's love for one's new pair of shoes, and we loved our pointy boots even more truly than that. We turned our feet this way and that, watched as the boots glinted in the sun; we squatted down and traced our fingers over the stitched patterns, or if we'd chosen boots with no patterns, we ran our fingers over the smooth, stitchless surfaces; we stuck our toes into the smallest sidewalk cracks and marveled at how pointy the toes really were. We looked around the square, and saw that no one else was wearing anything remotely like them. We pitied these people. Because this is what it means to be in love: You feel sorry for people who aren't. And then you feel happy that no one feels sorry for you. You feel so happy that it's not enough just to sit there and admire the beloved. You have to do something that shows the beloved how much you love it. And if you love your pointy boots the way we loved ours, you show them so by parading in them around the Public Square.

We did that. We proceeded loosely, not in formation, as we later learned to do at the base; not single file, or on our hands and knees, as we learned to do in the desert; but some of us in twos and threes, some of us by ourselves, some of us stopping, momentarily, to admire our boots in the windows of the empty storefronts, or to wipe some dust or dirt off our pointy boots, and then moving on again. Around and around we went. We did it for the joy of the thing, and not necessarily to be noticed by the poor people who were not us. But they noticed us anyway. The county courthouse workers looked up from their sandwiches, the bail bondsmen from those who might soon be bail bonded; the guys from the halfway house actually sat up and opened their eyes and let their butts die out without lighting another. One of the most fully gone of the halfway house guys even got up and started parading with us. He wore sweatpants—with one sweatpant leg down to the ankle, the other pushed up to the knee—and beat-up white leather high-top basketball sneakers with no socks. He brought his knees up high as he marched and waved his unlit cigarette like a baton. He was mocking us, probably, and we let him, rather than kicking his ass, which we could have done, easily. We practiced restraint. We figured ass kicking was unnecessary, figured he'd get tired sooner or later and return to the grass with his halfway house brothers. Which is exactly what happened. After a lap or two around the square, he went back to the grass and sat down and watched us. Everyone did. We knew what they were seeing: They were seeing fifteen teenagers, some boys, some girls, parading together but not together, all wearing pointy boots but not the same pointy boots. Fifteen individuals, but also a group, a group people could identify and admire: those kids who paraded around the Public Square in their pointy boots. They could see what we, and they, and everyone, were told in school was all around us: a nation of individuals, united. They could see the promise of America, in other words, made flesh by us and our pointy boots.

*

IT'S DARK BY THE TIME we get home. We knock on our front doors, and our sweet babies unlock them and let us in. But before we're able to get our boots out of our closets and on our feet and start parading around the Public Square, our sweet babies try to stop us. We keep aiming for the bedroom, for the closet where our pointy boots are waiting for us, and they keep edging in front of us, blocking the room, asking us questions. They ask us if we want something to eat. They ask if we want to take a rest, or watch some TV, or maybe play a board game. They ask us to admire the Christmas tree (there is a Christmas tree, in the corner, next to the TV, a pretty, droopy Scotch pine with colored lights and presents piled underneath it and a wooden nativity scene with baby Jesus and His mom and dad facing outward and the donkeys and wise men facing the presents). They tell us that they were waiting for us to get home to put the star on the top of the tree. They ask us if we'd like to put the star on the top of the tree now or a little bit later. Why don't we do it a little bit later? our sweet babies say. But for right now, would we like some hot chocolate? We know what they're doing. We know they've taken a seminar, at the base, about what to do when your soldier comes home. We know they've been warned to expect us to be a little different. To be a little *off*. We know they've been told to be patient with us, not to force us to talk about things we might not want to talk about. We know this because we were made to take a seminar at the base in Iraq, telling us to expect the same thing about ourselves, to treat ourselves with the same caution, the same care.

When we don't answer any of their questions, our sweet babies put their hands on our shoulders and look into our eyes and say, "We missed you."

"Yes," we say.

"I bet you miss Saunders," they say.

"Yes," we say.

"Poor Saunders," they say.

"Yes," we say. And then: "About those pointy boots..."

"*Fine*," they say. They take their hands off our shoulders, step to the side, and make a sweeping motion with their arms in the direction of the bedroom, the closet, the boots, as if to say, *It's all yours*. We can see the hurt on their faces. We can see what we've done to them, what we've always done to them. We are not heartless, and to show we're not heartless, we say, "Sorry."

"You've always cared more about your pointy boots than you've cared about us, haven't you?" they ask.

"Yes," we say, and run past them, into the bedroom.

AT THE END OF LUNCH HOUR, the county workers finished their sandwiches and went back into the courthouse. The bail bondsmen finished their coffee and went back into their storefronts. The halfway house guys finished their cigarettes and went back into their halfway houses. And we, we finished our parading and sat down at the foot of the statue of our local Revolutionary War general. We'd paraded for almost an hour, but we didn't feel at all tired, not even our feet, which we would have expected to feel tired, considering we'd been parading in brand-new pointy boots. But we didn't have one blister, one strained arch, one bruised heel, one rubbed-raw toe. We felt *good*. And if we felt so good, some of us wondered, if we weren't tired, if we weren't footsore, then what did we think we were doing, sitting down? Let's get up and *parade*, for crying out loud, some of us said. But others of us said no. Because hadn't we felt good before? Hadn't we felt good on the basketball court, or while smoking cigarettes behind the art room, or while sitting on the hoods of our parents' second cars on the dirt roads outside town and drinking beer, or while doing things to each other—in the cornfields next to the dirt roads—that we'd always wanted to do but couldn't get up the nerve to without the help of the beer? And hadn't we then ruined those good things? Hadn't we then taken and missed a terrible shot we had no business taking, at exactly the worst possible moment, and lost the game, or smoked an extra cigarette and got caught doing it by the art teacher, or drunk ten beers too many and then later wrecked our parents' cars, or before we wrecked those cars done things we shouldn't have with each other in the cornfields and then regretted it afterward? Hadn't we ruined good things before? some of us asked. And it should be said that Saunders was one of us who asked it. Looking back, you would think, after everything Saunders had done in Iraq, that he was one of us who wanted to get up and parade and ruin our good feeling, but no: He was one of us who spoke eloquently about not ruining it. He was one of us who said that we should always keep the memory, the vision, of our parading around the square in our pointy boots close by, and we shouldn't ruin it by going out and parading around the Public Square in our pointy boots whenever we felt a little sad, a little lonely, a little useless. He said that we should try to find that feeling somewhere else—through our work, through our marriages, through *whatever*—that we should go looking for that feeling everywhere. And even if we never found it, even if our lives ended up as lousy as they'd been before we put on our pointy boots, then at least we'd have the memory of that time when it wasn't lousy, when we felt *good*; at least we'd have the memory of the one good thing we *didn't* ruin. And no matter what, we should agree to do this together, to do everything together, as one. Then, those of us who hadn't wanted to parade again asked, Agreed? And those of us who had wanted to parade again said, Agreed. Then we went home and took off our pointy boots and put them in our closets. We polished them regularly, religiously, treated them more tenderly, more lovingly than we ever did our sweet babies, which our sweet babies never failed to notice and comment upon. Whenever we moved, we took the boots with us, moved them from bedroom closet to bedroom closet, but we never put them on, not once, until now. Because we promised Saunders we would wear them when we laid him to rest.

WE'RE SITTING ON OUR BEDS, trying to put on our pointy boots, which is difficult, more difficult than we remember, more difficult than it used to be, because our feet have been in round-toed boots for so long they've stopped being the kind of feet that will slip easily into pointy boots. A few seconds later we hear soft, muffled, thumping sounds coming toward us. We look up and see our sweet babies standing in the doorway. They have crazed, I'm-determined-to-try-one-more-time smiles on their faces, and in front of them, in front of us, stand our babies, wearing overlarge T-shirts that read DADDY'S LITTLE GIRL, or MOMMY'S LITTLE BOY, or DADDY'S LITTLE BOY, or MOMMY'S LITTLE GIRL, depending. Our babies are so much bigger than the last time we saw them; they hardly even look like our babies anymore. Our babies turn

babies, wondering if they *really* want to know. Do they really want to know what the two protestors know: that we are the kind of people who, when interrogating someone, shove our rifles in his face and say, "If you don't tell us what we want to know, we are going to chop off your head and fuck your skull"? Do they want to know what the two protestors don't know? Do they want to know that we are also the kind of people who then, when it comes down to it, will not do what we've threatened, except for Saunders, once, kind of? We say "kind of" because the woman was already dead. She was already dead. We had killed her while storming the house, or someone in the house had shot her beforehand, or during, or she had shot herself. In any case, she was dead, slumped against the wall. There was a small hole in her chest and there was a lot of blood still coming out of it and staining her robes. She was wearing so many robes, so many layers of clothing, even though it was so hot; her headscarf had slipped down and was covering her face. We removed it. Her face looked like ash, but we put our hands inches from her mouth to feel if she was breathing; we put our fingers on her neck to see if she had a pulse. She wasn't and didn't; she was dead. Her son (we assumed he was her son; he was the right age, around ten or so) was still alive, face down on the floor, hands behind his head. There was no one else in the house; we'd checked. We assumed we would do what we normally did: We would tell the boy who was still alive that if he didn't tell us what we wanted to know we would cut off his head and fuck his skull. And then, when he didn't tell us, we'd bring him to the people who did the real interrogating, the people we knew nothing about except that they used better threats than we did. Or, they used the same threat, just more effectively. But before we could say what we usually said, Saunders blurted out, "If you don't tell me what I want to know, I'm going to fuck your dead mother's skull." And then, before we could give him hell for deviating from the script, Saunders dropped his pants and tried to do what he'd threatened. Do our sweet babies want to know that? Do they want to know that, when Saunders started to do it, we laughed? That all of us laughed? Maybe because we were so startled that he deviated from the script, or that he tried to do what he'd threatened. Or maybe because he kept saying, "It's not working, it's not working," and we said, "Well, *of course* it's not working, Saunders, she's dead." "That's not what I mean," Saunders said. "I'm talking about *it*. *It* isn't working." "Well, Jesus, Saunders," we said, "of course *it* isn't working." And then we laughed, we couldn't help ourselves. Because it *was* kind of funny, if you thought about it. Do our sweet babies want to know that? Do they want to know that we are the kind of people who laugh at Saunders trying and failing to skull-fuck that dead mother? That we are the kind of people who laugh harder when Saunders, his pants still around his ankles, the *it* that wasn't working hanging out for anyone with eyes to see, waddles over to the son, his rifle in his right hand? The son is lying face-down on the dirt floor of his house—if it is his house, or if you can call it a house, just a stack of cinder blocks with planks of wood resting on top, really. The son is crying, the dirt around his head getting wet from his tears, his hands still clamped behind his head, keeping his head still while the rest of his body shakes and writhes and convulses, like a snake with its head nailed to the ground. "Look at me," Saunders says to the son. The boy turns his head in Saunders's direction. "You're next," he says, cupping his crotch with his left hand, and we laugh harder. *That's* the kind of people we are. Or maybe that's *not* the kind of people we are. But it is the kind of people we've become.

But our sweet babies don't want to know this, any of this. So, instead, we say, "We are the kind of people who, when we get home, before we do anything else, put on our pointy boots and parade around the Public Square." And then, finally, we cram our round-toed boot feet into our pointy boots, and go do that.

IT IS HARD SLEDDING, getting to the Public Square. For one, it's snowing, again, again, and there is nowhere left to put the snow—the snowbanks are too high already—and so the walks are unshoveled, the roads unplowed. For another, our pointy boots have shit for traction and we slip and fall, a lot, as we walk. By the time we all get to the Public Square, we are soaked and sore from all the falling. Cold, too. Because all we have on are our travel camo pants and jackets, our berets, and, of course, our pointy boots—which are at least waterproof, and a good thing, too, because they're completely buried in the snow. It is dark, after six o'clock. The county office building's windows are dark; everyone has gone home. On the corner of State and Lewis, the bail bonds office has an illuminated Western Union sign in the window, but otherwise the place is dark as well. The guys from the halfway house are nowhere to be seen. It's possible that the halfway house has closed. It's possible that they've joined up, too, that the army is where the halfway house guys are sent when the halfway house closes. The Bon Ton is no longer the Bon Ton, is no longer anything, but the city has decorated its front windows with white blinking Christmas lights. The streetlight poles are wrapped with green garland and red bows. The statue of the Revolutionary War general is buried up to the waist in snow, the falling snow piling up on his plumed hat. Other than him, we are the only ones on the square. It is not how we pictured it, not how we remembered it. For that matter, we're not sure how we pictured ourselves, how we remembered ourselves. We do a quick head count and find that we're not all here, not even close.

"Where the hell is everyone?" we ask. But we know. We can see them putting the silver stars on top of their Christmas trees; we can see them holding their sweet babies real tight; we can hear their babies calling them by name, each and every one of them.

"Those bastards," one of us says.

"Those bitches," another one of us says.

"This is ridiculous," the third of us says.

"Maybe we should just go home," the fourth of us says.

"Our poor babies," the fifth of us says.

"Our poor sweet babies," the sixth of us says.

"Poor Saunders," the last of us says, and then we remember why we can't go home. His funeral is at nine in the morning. We can picture it: His sweet baby and baby will be there, trying to be brave, trying not to cry while the chaplain conveys the thanks of the president and prays to God for the state of Saunders's immortal soul. We'll be there, too, wearing our pointy boots. Because we promised Saunders, right before he died. He said, "When you lay me to rest, will you please wear your pointy boots?" We promised we would. But first, we need to do what we've come here to do. We have fifteen hours to parade around the Public Square in our pointy boots, fifteen hours to forget what happened to Saunders, so we can help bury him.

"Are we ready?" we ask each other. And then we start parading around the Public Square. We walk slowly at first, take tiny steps, because of the footing. But then we start going faster. We don't mean to. It's the blinking Christmas lights: They blink too fast and when we look at them, they make us walk too fast, too. Right in front of the Bon Ton, after only one lap around the Public Square, we slip, and fall on our backs, and because it's impossible not to laugh when someone slips and falls in the snow, we laugh. Then we remember laughing at Saunders and we stop laughing. Then we remember when we stopped laughing at Saunders and looked around. There was the mother, lying on the dirt floor faceup, the way Saunders had left her. There was the son, lying there, his face down and to the side, still weeping, still looking at Saunders, who was still grabbing his crotch with one hand and holding his rifle with the other. But Saunders wasn't looking at the son, or at the mother, or at us. His eyes were closed, his face pinched in concentration. We knew what he was doing: He was trying to picture the day we'd paraded around the Public Square in our pointy boots; he was trying to replace the picture of what he'd just done with the picture of us, our boots, the square, us parading around it, people watching us, us feeling so good. We knew that's what he was doing, because we did the same thing: We closed our eyes and tried to picture it, tried to remember it. We tried so hard. But the harder we tried to picture the boots, the Public Square, the office workers and bail bondsmen and halfway house guys, the farther away all of that was. All we could see was the mother, Saunders kneeling over her, us laughing; Saunders getting up and waddling over to the son, us laughing even harder. Go away, we told the memory we didn't want. Please come back, we told the one we did. Please come back, we begged our pointy boots. But they didn't.

We opened our eyes. Saunders was lying on his back next to the son. They were both crying now—the son because he didn't know what was going to happen, Saunders because he did.

"I'm sorry," Saunders said.

"I am, too," each of us said.

"Will you promise me something?" Saunders said. "When you lay me to rest, will you please wear your pointy boots?"

"We will," we said, and then without saying another word, we aimed our guns at him and one by one—Carson, Marocco, Smoot, Mayfair, Penfield, Rovazzo, Zyzk, Palmer, Reese, Appleton, Exley, Scarano, Loomis, Olearzyck—we shot him, and then we shot the son, too. Then we closed our eyes again. But we saw the same thing as before, except that there was another Saunders in it and another son, and they were both dead and we'd killed them.

"Are you still seeing it?" we ask ourselves. But of course we know the answer. We lie there, in the snow, waiting to see whether one of us, any of us, will get up, brush off our pointy boots, and try again.

THAT WINTER

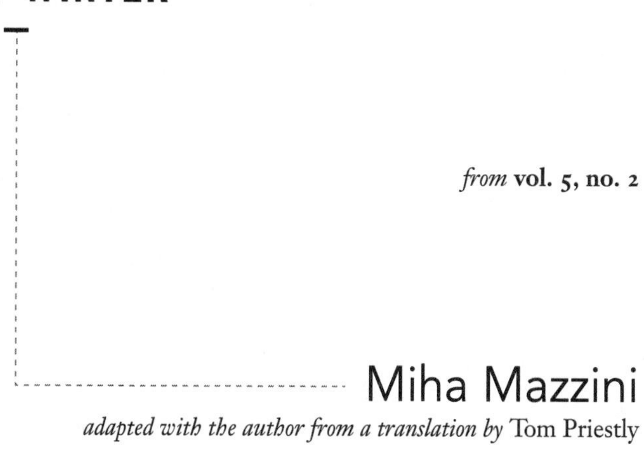

from **vol. 5, no. 2**

Miha Mazzini

adapted with the author from a translation by Tom Priestly

THE PRISONERS RELEASED before me had flown home from The Hague in airplanes sent for them by their states. I was the first one who wasn't a national hero. The guard just handed me a train ticket to Sarajevo and some pocket money for travel expenses. I greeted him with "Tot ziens" and he answered with "Tot nooit, hopelijk!"—an unsubtle indication he didn't want to see me again.

In the train I couldn't take my eyes off the window: moving, everything was moving. Houses, cities, gliding by, going away, a constant flow of change after eleven years of immobility.

Waiting for another train in Düsseldorf, I felt like a ghost returning to the world for the first time. I moved out of the way of a person talking to himself, a sure sign of madness at the time of my imprisonment, whereas now everybody had headphones and their mouths were empty of cigarettes.

After Munich the landscape got more and more orderly. Austrians took symmetry and tidiness for beauty, their windows vomiting carnations from houses built to last forever. The train entered the tunnel and came out in Slovenia. I expected to see the big steel factory, once the pride of Yugoslavia, but only one chimney still stood, covered with ads for supermarkets and foreign brands.

Nobody entered my compartment—Slovenia was now part of the EU and there were no more border policemen or customs officers in Europe. But at the Croatian border I was asked for my papers. A pair of Slovenian officers browsed my documents: "Den Haag—The International War Crimes Tribunal for crimes committed on the territory of the former Yugoslavia." They looked momentarily bewildered, until the policeman, still a kid, sucked air into his spreading chest, soaking his words in venom. I looked into his eyes and the air left him. His partner, the customs officer, elbowed him out the door. The Croat officers didn't know how to react and quickly went away; they had their own war with the Muslims and some of their heroes had been my prison buddies.

When the train stopped in Zagreb, I bought myself some newspapers. The Croats had buried one of their fascist commandants from the Second World War. In his camp they had killed at least seventy thousand people. Though he fled to Argentina after the war, escaping hanging, he had been in prison, unrepentant, for the past decade, after having finally been extradited. At the funeral the priest said the prisoner had slept peacefully throughout his life, since he knew that God had forgiven him everything.

The train entered Bosnia on the Serbian side of the country and when I offered my papers to the officers, they stood at attention, saluting me like windup toys, while they retreated backward. The staff of the small border station started walking up and down the platform, pretending to be running errands, stealing glances through my window.

I dug into the corner and shame covered me like an icy blanket.

The Sarajevo train station looked forlorn, as though no one had used it since the war began, sixteen years ago. Cigarette smoke drifted from the cafés in front of it. I waited on the abandoned platform until my bus arrived and I almost ran for it, my head lowered.

I had not called anybody in my village to let them know I was coming. The last time I had seen my former wife was in court, on the witness stand. She was talking about how she had begged me to dissolve the factory but I had beaten her into silence. I stopped listening to her. The knowledge that this must be the same lie my daughters were hearing from her dripped from my heart through my body like acid, leaving just burnt hollowness inside. For her testimony she got a change of identity and money for them to start over. I received the divorce papers in prison, signed them, and put a letter on top asking her not to ever mention me to my girls. She didn't answer.

IN SOCIALIST YUGOSLAVIA, those in power wanted to change even the hill farmers into workmen, and they built factories everywhere. Every politician who had grown up in some dirt shack wanted to give his native village a factory and the people expected it; the size of the new industrial building was the measurement of the politician's status in the party. Our benefactor was a lower official in Sarajevo, so the factory was small. Like every other one, it produced something simple, so the former farmers could adapt quickly. Then capitalism discovered a work force in China adapting even faster and cheaper and the political factories fell into ruins.

I was the only person who got off the bus at the stop in my village. The walls of the factory were caved in, the barbed wire rusty and sagging. I didn't want to look at it, but I couldn't stop. I expected memories to attack my eyes and ears, but only the wind was whispering, exhausted. A summer storm had just passed by, the wet hair of clouds still hung over a neighboring hill. Veins of tiny streams furrowed the sand on the road, and I had not yet gotten my feet wet when I was surrounded by the men who came running from the village.

I recognized them at once and at the same time was amazed

that they, like me, had gotten old. Larger bellies, sagging belts, grayer hair on heads and bodies, more marks on their skin. Only the slightly soiled sleeveless T-shirts and the stubble on their faces were still the same (shaving occurred only before Sunday mass). We had received Bosnian papers in prison and the other prisoners had used their mobile phones as well, telling me the news that wasn't printed, so I had heard that Jovo had hanged himself and Milojko had died. The remaining seven stood in front of me now, only Nikola was not there.

They looked at me. Behind their backs, from the village, I could feel the looks from their wives and children, and also from those who had not been a part of our group.

I realized that my next movement would decide the kind of reception I would have.

I smiled. It felt false, mechanical, just the lengthening of the corners of my lips, but they did not notice.

There was shouting, more like roaring, slaps on my shoulders and back. The smell of unwashed bodies, of farm animals, machine oil and gasoline. Somebody took my bag for me, we walked, I was hemmed in among them. They were offering me cigarettes, I kept on refusing, and they were shouting "Europe! Europe!" in wonder. We entered Cane's Inn and the tall owner didn't hit his forehead on the doorpost like he used to do; the years had curved his spine from a bow to a question mark. The interior hadn't changed: the bar was in the corner, small and insignificant, tables occupying most of the room, for people to sit and talk. I don't know why, but in prison I had loved to browse the glossy magazines about interior decoration and I noticed that bars outside the Balkans are different, big central monsters in the middle of the room, for lonely people to hang around them, looking at themselves in the mirror behind the bottles.

Cane brought brandy, fiery-strong, and we started drinking toasts. We were just lifting glasses in the air above us, nobody turned to the picture on the wall. It used to be Tito for decades, Milošević afterward for a few years, and now Saint Sava, his expiry date much more lasting.

They brought a serving of lamb, the meat cold and slimy. The noise and the pouring of drinks went on and on. I did not wish to get drunk, I just sipped the surface of what was in the glass. They must have noticed, but they did not want to stop making a ruckus. If they did there would be silence and they would have to talk.

I asked them how they were, what they did, and I had to repeat myself several times before they began to talk—about being farmers again, or Pavle being a mechanic. He rubbed his dark and oily hands at the sides of his paunch, leaving only the middle of his T-shirt white, like the center of the target. They talked about the way they smuggled Chinese goods and sold them again in the three-boundary region, between Croatia, Bosnia, and Serbia, and how in this way they were getting by, slowly, getting by. They told me and then they told me again, and then once over. They kept shifting as if on the edge of a precipice. They were in danger and did not want to take the next step: asking me how I was, how it had been. And the crucial question: why had I turned myself in? They did not dare. Branimir, with his foxy face and sagging cheeks, was in a hurry to speak each time it appeared they would run out of breath. I could not recall him ever speaking so eagerly.

When there was really nothing left to say and when they had described every method of smuggling, when I had learned the contents of every market stall, they got up and accompanied me to my home. They told me they had kept watch to ensure that none of *them* had come even close. They handed me the key, I let myself in, and they did not follow me inside.

You go away for a couple of weeks and when you get back the apartment is dusty. After many years the dust has become fixed, it has stopped accumulating and just sits there, the years fly past, the particles hold their peace, only the smell which floats above them counts the days and knits them into a special stuffiness.

My wife had taken everything that could be driven away, including the washing machine where she had put my bloody clothes every morning that winter without saying anything. She did not even leave the objects that had belonged to *them*, the ones I had stolen. For a long time she made me seethe in prison, but some nights I understood that maybe she had made a good deal for my daughters, who were growing up somewhere out of these countries where history is a tool for revenge, not for learning. I felt happy for them but at the same time this was part of my punishment:

what I had done I had done for them. How old had they been that winter? I thought back—three and four years old. Now they probably don't even dream in my language anymore. I try not to think of them but they're always there when my mind goes floating, in waking, before sleeping, looking out a window.

I carried everything left into a single room: an old couch, a squeaky chair, the table from the cellar that had before been good only as a workbench. I turned on the water at the mains and let it run for a long time before it was free of rust.

What now?

I went for a walk. The clouds were dragging their very last tails across the mountains. The sun that had been hot in the valley was no more than a caress up here. Behind me I heard a stifled cry of fear and when I turned I clearly saw a woman's back and the movement of her elbow as she hurried behind a corner.

Had she crossed herself, seeing a ghost?

We had burned all of the Muslim houses—every single one—and I expected to see the same blackened stumps, decaying teeth biting at the sky, as when they had taken me away, but very few ruins were left. They had begun to rebuild most of them. Concrete supporting slabs stood among the debris, with a wall or two. As if somebody was indicating that he had not given up, he was still here.

Where?

I walked past our houses and people from my group loudly and hollowly greeted me. The rest retreated. In front of me doors closed and drapes fell, and as I walked on they opened up again and I felt the looks. A short way from the village had stood the factory. I could not go that far. I turned back to Nikola's.

Bits of plaster and some tiles had fallen off his house and joined the trash in the yard. I knocked on the open door—no reply—and I stepped into the stench.

He was lying in a corner and snoring. I sat on a bench and placed my foot on one of the empty bottles. His potato-like nose had collected lots of veinlets in the intervening years, and his cheeks shook while his jaws pumped air inside, the lungs answering with a protracted whining, almost like a dying echo of the songs we used to sing at the factory.

Evening was coming on when Nikola awoke. He raised his head, it swung to and fro as though fighting for more space for itself, his eyes narrowed a little and when he recognized me, he cried out.

"No! I'm not going on guard duty! NO!"

"Nikola, it's over, nobody has to do guard duty anymore."

His coughing stretched into puking until finally there was not even mucus left to fall to the floor.

"They let you out?"

"Yes."

We were silent.

He went on all fours into the next room and came back with a full bottle and swallowed almost a third in a single gulp.

"Did you meet them yet?" he asked, and waved toward the village. For the first time he looked me in the eye.

I nodded but my eyes escaped his and slipped toward the entrance.

"Why did you come back?"

I sighed and could not find any simple words.

He answered in my place: "Because you want to see how they are... what about you?"

"I cannot sleep," I said.

"Me too, I am never awake. Will you?" he said, offering me the bottle.

I shook my head. "If I'd had a lot of that in prison, the first year, then I would. Not now, no."

"Did you hear about Jovo? Dead!" His limp and soft body made just one surprisingly quick and savage gesture, slashing his index finger across his neck. "Milojko died, too. He just"—Nikola stabbed the fingers of both hands into his stomach and they sank into a burrow of his gut—"withered," he said, finally finding the right word. "Listen to me, boss, listen. Let me state it clear: the first option is to die. You can choose only the speed: fast or slow. The second option is to forget, like the others from our group did. But, boss, you said you can't sleep, so you're not like Cane and the others." He gestured toward the inn, but in the wrong direction. "Why are you still alive? How will you kill yourself?"

I opened my mouth to speak but he didn't let me.

"Boss, nobody wants you here. Nobody waited for you. You're a ghost, a reminder. Please, do us a favor."

Nikola seemed to want to burst out laughing, but just screeched. He bent over across the bed, I thought he was going to throw up again, but he dipped his head into a pile of trash and rummaged through it for a long while. Twitching, he turned around and flung a coil of rope in my direction, missing by a good yard.

"Did you enjoy posing as a model on your way to becoming an international star? How the fuck didn't you spot that creep photographer and shoot him!" Again he screeched and between the stumps of his teeth gleamed traces of enamel. "Commandant!" he added, as if spitting.

I could feel the hate radiating from him in my belly. I did not react and so he lost interest. He tilted the bottle and allowed it to decant into him. He threw it at the wall then, it shattered and he lay down on the bed, rolled himself into a fetus, and showed me his back.

Silence.

Socialism had wished to fertilize us, and sometimes, even into our hills, some theater troupe or other came on tour, usually an amateur one from a nearby town. Their exaggerated movements and gestures always repulsed me. But when you are locked up and cannot hope to sleep, then the day is long enough for you to remember everything, including theater performances. Do the men in our nation get drunk so often in order to show what they're feeling? They behave in the overwrought fashion of bad actors. I remembered my own drinking sessions, friendships until death after the first round that change into angry hatreds after the second one and into miraculous reconciliations after the third, then the same cycle all over. And once you are no longer someone who drinks but a drunkard, true feelings have fled and what is left is just grotesque sentimentality and, finally, bathos.

I got up and the bench sighed below me.

The house stank. Twilight was slowly eating away Nikola's body part by part, only his legs and one hand still visible. Like those bodies the earth had begun to return after that winter. Cane had mentioned them first. He said it was the same as when his Deepfreeze broke down. Except for the crows. I went to the field between the factory and the forest and *We did this?* crossed my mind for the first time. Because the ground was frozen throughout the cold months, each time we dug we hadn't been able to bury the bodies deep enough, and with the thaw, foxes and other animals had started excavating them. Remains protruded from the soil, a hand here, a leg there, a torso, a head, gnawed bones marking the way toward the trees. Crows jumped around, picking the meat off the bones, too full to fly, arrogantly moving just out of reach of my steps. I have always felt there was something aching in the vapors of plowed earth but this smell nauseated me. I closed my eyes and fought with my stomach.

I never saw the American photographer hidden in the forest. We later learned he'd been crossing the hills, trying to get to Sarajevo, bribing each border guard he came across and sharing a drink. When his stomach couldn't stand it anymore he asked his guide to stop the Jeep and went behind the trees, noticing the crows and following them.

The first picture he took was of me in my moment of nausea. I remember feeling disgust and horror, but in the photo, which appeared the following week in foreign newspapers, something about my face makes it look as if I'm enjoying myself.

I returned to the factory that night and told the others we must dig again and rebury. We couldn't prepare ourselves to do it until the following week, the same time the photos began to be published. Then how we dug! And we burned the bodies, taking the remains down to the valley and throwing them in the river. It wasn't that we feared foreigners. The West was impotent and weak—they did not intervene even at Srebrenica, years later. But among the bodies of Muslims, there were some of our weekend warriors as well. People who left their jobs in Serbia on Friday afternoon, took guns and drove across the border to Bosnia, robbed a house or two, killed some Muslims, and returned to work on Monday morning. Occasionally these armed men came to our village and we told them that here were just our Muslims, that they and their stuff belonged to us. Most of the intruders went away, but some had been too drunk and too courageous, and we did not want their bodies to be discovered.

The darkness took Nikola's body completely now.

I bent down to pick up the rope as I went.

*

THE NEXT DAY I went for another walk around the village as soon as I was awoken by hunger. I caught sight of Branimir bringing a heavy cardboard box around the corner of his house. When he saw me he backed away immediately, as though on a rewind button. I waited by the open trunk of his car, but he did not appear again.

In Pavle's mechanic shop—not registered, unofficial—I met only his legs. He peeked from under a vehicle, apologized that he had essential work to do, whatever I might say he would listen. I walked on.

I was the only customer at Cane's Inn. He brought me some uncut bread and put a piece of roast meat in the microwave. My glance fled to the big roasting spit which used never to stop turning. Cane flourished his dishrag as if to say: once a week or once every two weeks is nowadays quite enough. Since the war the families don't come to his inn on Sundays anymore, he said, and his eyes got big, like a hurt child's. I remembered coming here with my ex-wife and daughters and I wondered again: three and four years old that winter, do they remember anything? Do they remember me just as a presence in their childhoods, have they forgotten my face? Do they fall for a boyfriend who reminds them of me without knowing the reason? They would still be sleeping in the morning when I returned from the factory and handed stolen stuff to my wife. Sometimes somebody helped me bring in a TV or a fridge or something big from one of the Muslim houses, some days I just went to the bathroom and threw my bloody clothing on the tiles. I slept most of the day and ate supper with my family, read the girls an evening story and went back to the factory. To work, as I told them. Usually I drank a coffee with my wife in the kitchen, and I remembered now with sudden and bitter anger how she would sometimes carefully mention that we needed a new car or a video player or hi-fi, something nice she had just seen at some Muslim family's, her finger caressing the rim of the coffee cup, sending the smell into my nostrils.

I looked at the shelf in the corner. Five vases full of plastic flowers were still standing there, though dust had taken the bright colors away. During the week this had been a place for men only, but on Sundays, Cane put a vase on each table, providing a nice family setting, as he explained it. He used to sit down with every customer and drink or snack on something, in this way obeying the law of the correct innkeeper. Now he stayed behind the bar and wiped glasses. When he brought me my warmed-up food he was on the point of sitting down. A reflex of his body swung his ass toward a chair, but he caught himself, moaned a little about work, and went back behind the bar.

"Do you ever remember that winter?" I asked him.

"What?" He looked wide-eyed. "Winter?"

I pointed my finger toward the factory, just a corner of its wall was visible through the window.

"Oh...oh..."—he flapped his hand—"that's water under the bridge...sorry...you suffered...you are a hero...but for us ordinary people..." Droplets appeared on his forehead. He mumbled a bit more.

"Don't you have dreams?" I asked.

"No." Droplets also on his upper lip.

"No nightmares?"

"No. Please, Commandant, please! It's gone, they were different times, strange times...something was in the air, this won't happen again. It's like when you get a flu or something. You're not yourself...but then, a week, or...winter passes and you're your old self, healthy. Commandant, you'll destroy yourself if you won't let it go."

"Cane, don't call me 'Commandant.' You know I was just your foreman. When we...started this, at the factory, we started it together."

I didn't need to tell him the rest: the generals had wanted somebody to be responsible for our small unit, and it was me who became commandant.

Cane got his hurt-child eyes back: "But...you were the boss. I was so unimportant!" He searched for another word, then stopped abruptly. "You see! Don't mention it anymore!"

I started eating. For a while he was so tense that I expected to hear a glass crack under his hands, but he slowly calmed down and the dishrag again slid over the glasses, which he was cleaning for the second time. I finished eating and wiped my mouth and fingers with a napkin. From time to time Cane stole a nervous glance in my direction, appearing afraid of further questions.

"And what about those new houses, the renovated ones?"

He burst out in relief: "Did you see them? It's unbelievable! They could have stayed in our village, that's how it was written down in the peace agreement, but they just went and now... Commandant, you won't believe it. Those Muslims are like gypsies, they have settled in large numbers all over the world, but the men come here in the summers. They are here a week or two and they build walls. They sleep in the car, they bring materials from the valley up in the trunk and they build walls. That's how they spend their vacations! Their food they buy in the valley, too. They do not come to me! We get nothing from them. You will see for yourself, the first of them will arrive any day now."

He wanted to say something else, but his open mouth could not find the words.

"How much do I owe you?"

"Commandant, that's okay! Actually, we talked yesterday, if you wish we'll set up a collection campaign and help you start over. In the three-boundary district the work is great! We'll arrange a market stall for you. Just let us know: are you most interested in technical things, music, clothing? Maybe helping to traffic Chinese or Africans into Europe?"

ON MY WAY HOME I STOPPED in front of the bare concrete pad where once Sead's house had stood. I placed my palms on the dusty surface and through the warm epidermis felt the interior cold of the building. Only a few of the Muslim inhabitants of our village had left immediately after the siege of Sarajevo started. Most of them believed, as I did, that our village would be something special, an exception, that our bonds would hold. I had gone to school with Sead, his father had taught me a trick with a coin and a dog, brotherhood and unity was the slogan of Tito's Yugoslavia. But in the summer of '92 we were at Cane's, watching the news. The Russian writer Limonov had come to visit our troops on the hills above Sarajevo and he started firing a machine gun on the city. Mother Russia was with us, the announcer said.

Cane's palm slapped the table. "Right," he said, "it's for the mushrooms."

Everybody turned toward him, our heads traveling slowly through the alcohol.

"Do they come in the fall? Do they?" Cane lifted his finger almost to the ceiling. "Do they come to our village and park on your field?" he said, pointing at Branimir, who nodded. "Do they crumple your grass? Go into our forests and pick our mushrooms? Do they sometimes even have picnics here, on that grass, and bring everything with them? Leave us nothing but damage and expenses! City people! People of Sarajevo!"

"You're right, you're right," we said, nodding.

He continued: "These city people... they look down on us! They think they're something more. For them we're all backwards idiots! They're like Turkish invaders. For centuries they've robbed our lands, conquered us, taken our money, bled us with taxes—those Muslims! Now revenge is ours. Cities must burn!"

I can't remember much more from that night, but soon, one by one, we became weekend warriors, occasionally for a few days on the hills above Sarajevo, until that winter when we brought the war home.

By then, half of the Muslim villagers had fled on bus convoys, begging their Serbian friends to watch over the possessions they left behind. Some of us really did look out for them. Others started slowly taking their things or even moving into their houses. By that winter, the Muslims left in the village were stuck between the front lines. Some tried to go away: during the night, over the hills. We never heard from them.

Sead's father had stayed out of stubbornness. He said he had to guard the compressor in his garage. In December the compressor at Pavle's mechanic shop broke down and we came for Sead's father's. We took him to the factory. He was our first prisoner. Others followed—in The Hague, after I turned myself in, they proved five killings and seven imprisonments had happened under my command during that winter, until in the spring a humanitarian convoy evacuated the village of all remaining Muslims. I think we could have gone on beating and torturing them, because we really believed they were spies for the Muslim army, and therefore traitors. But our belief was like a balloon, we had to pump it up all the time with shouts, with frenzy, with constant movement, never stopping, never thinking. Some of our neighbors confessed. Sead's father didn't. He died after three nights of interrogations.

I walked to my house now and made a noose. One's hands never forget. The rope slid smoothly.

How many times had I pondered how the others could bear what we had done? I came to see it all from close-up; Cane had been the innkeeper, Pavle the mechanic, Branimir a farmer, and so on, then along came the idea of our great country and we did what we did. Now Cane is again the innkeeper, Pavle the mechanic, and Branimir is a salesman of Chinese goods, since it does not pay any longer to live off the land. And here I am. And was that all? Like a flu, as Cane had said, something came and infected us.

There was something escaping me that I wanted to find out before I went. Nikola's second option: to forget. Was it possible?

I HAD LET CANE KNOW that I would take him up on the offer of a market stall, and that we should meet that evening, all together, have something to drink and a snack, and talk about the jobs.

When I went in the inn and cheerfully said "Good evening," they raised their arms and the air expanded with relief. "Boss! Boss!" they shouted, and Cane ran up with glasses in his arms like a row of newborns.

We embraced and someone shouted loudly for music.

Cane put on a CD and for a while we just drank. Branimir began to sing quietly along with the female vocalist, sometimes too early or too late. Tears spurted from his eyes and with the palm of his hand he splashed them onto his forehead.

We embraced.

They told me about some gimmicks for selling the Chinese goods more effectively, just to Europeans, as we called those belonging to the parts of the former East that had joined the Union. You had to keep T-shirts and the inscriptions separate, and imprint them according to demand. Pavle added that you had to do the same thing with auto parts. Some clients were so unpleasant that they wanted only original ones for their money.

Even more embraces, again a song, tears, fresh glasses.

"And what about those Muslim house builders?" I asked. "What do they buy?"

Grumbles, curses, they don't do any buying, no sir!

Forgetting that he had complained to me already, Cane told me everything over, twice. There was nothing to be gotten from them.

"And is that right?" I shouted.

No, there is no justice, not anywhere on this earth!

"And is that what we fought for?"

Howls. Denials. A fresh round, down in one.

"And are we pussies to put up with the injustice they're causing us?"

We are not, no!

"And will we suffer the way we've been suffering for so long?"

We shall not, no way! What they're doing to us! Shame on us!

"Will we let them trample on our heroic thousand-year-old history?"

We shall not! Lead the way! Let's go!

I walked to the door and opened it wide. The men were breathing behind my back, sweaty, heated, shaking with excitement. With my arms I jammed myself against the doorposts, imprisoning them behind my back. They were stuck in that narrow room.

"What's up? What's up?" someone yelled behind me.

I turned and looked them in the eyes.

Cane was the first whose arms gave way, he began to scratch his waist. They quickly followed his example, scattering around the room, moving the tables about, straightening the tablecloths, picking their caps up off the floor—waiting for me to move away from the door.

I SAT ON THE COUCH and rocked the noose between thumb and forefinger as if I was fishing. How many times before had I thought about what had happened to us, not to everybody but to enough of us in this village, in other villages, in towns? It looked like madness now and whenever I recalled the slogans that we used to shout I was always ashamed. But didn't they once, in Spain, fight war shouting "Long live death!"?

How can grown people change so that they become animals

for vain, empty words? We live alongside one another until words connect our feelings and turn us into a crowd, an organism with its own needs and greed. And when the spell is broken, some people can step out of the organism with a clear conscience: It wasn't me, I'm not guilty. Nikola was wrong: there is no forgetting. People who claim they've forgotten are always reusable for another crowd.

I tossed the rope over a roof beam. I was totally at peace. I got up onto a chair and put the noose around my neck. With my left hand I checked to see whether the noose was sliding smoothly, and I was about to kick the chair.

Then a car coughed and through the window I caught sight of an old Vauxhall with British plates stopping at Sead's house. The engine died, I thought the driver's seat was empty, but the door on the right side opened and Sead emerged. He started inspecting the wall he had built the previous year. I couldn't tear my eyes away from him. From the trunk he fetched a brick, took some mortar from a small red container, spread it on, and gently put the brick in place. Over and over. He did not look around. Almost completely bald, stooping slightly, he carried brick after brick. He fixed them, overlapping, in a corner, a first row, a second, a third…

He was going to build a house in which nobody would ever live. A husk, a ghost reminding the torturers that even if they forgot everything, somebody else would not. What did his family think about these vacations of his, about the long journey? Did they consider him an eccentric, did they understand him?

I forgot the noose, moving my head forward to see better, and the rope tightened.

I was merely a dead cell, a flake of dandruff that had fallen off and from which there would never come any benefit. I was insignificant, I could kill myself now or later, with a rope or with alcohol. However, something else…something else…There had to be something other than Nikola's two options.

I took the noose off and jumped to the floor. I walked to the door.

I cannot, I cannot, how can I manage it?

I began to tremble and sweat, to glance toward the noose. Was it really easier to kill again than to ask forgiveness?

As I walked toward Sead I wondered what I might say to him,

how I could tell him that no hour passes without my remembering that winter, that I cannot sleep, that my memories are devouring me…

When I reached him I could not speak.

He did not turn around. He carried on rebuilding his wall.

I fell to my knees and burst out sobbing. I wept and knelt in front of him, but Sead carried on setting bricks on his wall until he had emptied his trunk, and then he collected his tools and drove away without looking at me.

ONLY CONNECT

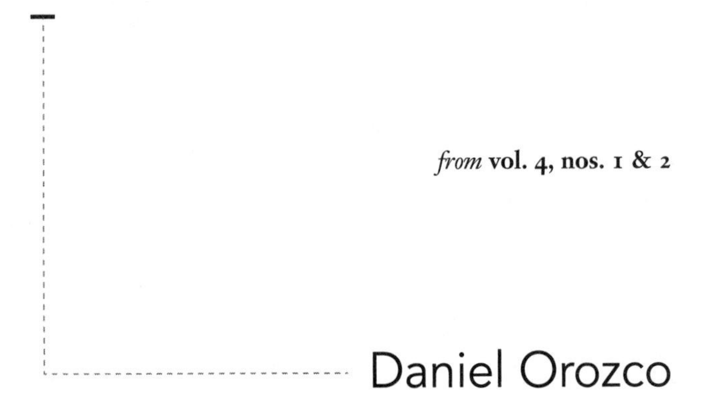

from **vol. 4, nos. 1 & 2**

Daniel Orozco

TWO MEN FOLLOWED A THIRD MAN up the street one night. His name was Bennett, and he had just left a party where the woman who'd invited him used him to flirt with somebody else. She worked with Bennett in the labs at the medical center. They were both researchers on the same projects, doing cutting-edge work in psychopharmacology, where the big bucks were. They made very good money, but her apartment was much nicer than his, and he wondered if she made more than he did. She lived on the northwest slope of Capitol Hill, in a secure building that was a hundred years old and meticulously restored. It had a lobby with thick, bloodred carpet and stamped copper panels on the ceiling, and a cage elevator that rattled and clanked pleasingly as it took you up. Her apartment had many windows, and they all looked out over Lake Union and the boats huddled in their slips, and at the Olympic range beyond. As the party progressed, dusk settled and you could watch the snow-drape on the mountains sparkle in the last light before sinking into shadows. You could watch the Space Needle brighten, shimmering and upright in the clear night. It was his first time in her apartment, and he liked it, the spectacular view and the tasteful and elegant minimalism of the decor, uncluttered and clean. He had hoped something would come of this invitation, that being invited by her might mean something. But she had a lot of friends, and the place was teeming with strangers. Bennett was born here, and although she had been hired less than a year ago, she knew more people than he ever did.

He had somehow ended up with her in a corner of her crowded kitchen. They were seated across from each other at a tiny breakfast table, and she was telling him about a trip she was planning over Christmas, a trek along the Inca Trail in Peru. He was asking her questions to keep the talk going, and she was answering them, when a man detached himself from a nearby clique, smiled briskly at Bennett, and leaned against the wall behind her, holding a beer bottle in his hands. Bennett recognized him. He was a popular barista at an espresso bar at the medical center. He was young, narrow and pale, with lank black hair that flopped into his eyes. He wore one of those expensive secondhand bowling shirts that you find in expensive secondhand clothing shops.

"I heard it's not so dangerous down there anymore," Bennett was saying to her. "Not like it used to be, I mean."

She shrugged. "It's dangerous everywhere."

"I suppose."

"It could be dangerous right here." She leaned forward, toward Bennett. "You never know where danger lurks."

He looked at her and smiled. When Bennett was confused, he smiled. Her eyes glimmered. She smiled back. She was playing with him.

"I could be in danger right now," she said. The barista behind her was grinning, picking at the label on his beer bottle, and Bennett realized that he was the one she was playing with. Two women appeared and tugged her out of her chair and swept her away. The barista looked at Bennett, toasted him, and tipped his beer back. Bennett watched the cartilage in the barista's neck bob up and down. Then he got up and left.

He slammed the cage door shut and stabbed at the buttons. He would not be her go-between. He was no flirting conduit. "Fuck her," he said. He liked hearing the words. "Fuck that shit," he said, alone in the elevator that ticked like an old clock as it carried him down. He stepped outside into a cold autumn night. He couldn't quite remember where his car was. He had drunk several beers really fast, and he was still buzzed. He guessed uphill, so up he went, chanting "Fuck her" in cadence to his steps. He could see his breath in the air before him. Maybe it was the brisk night air, the bracing uphill trudge. Maybe it was the cathartic power of the F-word, spoken aloud, over and over. But soon he wasn't angry anymore, only embarrassed. He'd probably had six conversations with her in the past year, mostly work-related, and from them he had constructed the framework of a relationship and conjured the hope of something more. But between his conversations with her she had a life all her own and, before them, an entire history he was not a part of. You can't know anybody, not really, not in the brief overlaps of flimsy acquaintance, nor in any of the tenuous and fleeting opportunities for connection that we are afforded. It was a bleak little moment of clarity, but it was for Bennett a certainty he could find comfort in. He felt better, tramping the streets of the city he was born in, pondering opportunity and connection, gauging his prospects—the next disappointment, perhaps. But maybe not. And suddenly he remembered where his car was parked—clarity begets clarity!—when a voice very close behind him asked: "Fuck who?"

Bennett turned around, and two men were on him, shoving him swiftly backward and crowding him into a gap of hedge and against the wall of a brick building.

"Wallet. Money. Now."

He looked at the one who spoke, a tall young man in a dark hooded sweatshirt, holding tight fistfuls of Bennett's jacket and pushing hard against Bennett's chest. He looked at the other man, who was shorter, and older. He wore a sport coat and slacks, and he was pressing a pistol into Bennett's belly. Bennett had never had a gun pointed at him before. He thought it would be bigger.

"So are you deaf or what?"

He looked back up at the man who'd said this, the younger one, the one without the gun. Shouldn't the one with the gun do the talking? Bennett was not deaf, but he wasn't sure which one to tell this to. He looked from one man to the other and back. The face of the younger one was an inch away from his. His breath was sweet, cloying and thick, like rotted candy. Bennett felt sick. He couldn't breathe.

"What are you going to do?" he gasped. "Shoot me?"

It was his most immediate concern, and a legitimate question, although maybe not one you ask out loud. It was the wrong thing to say. Bennett was a little drunk, and suddenly very afraid, but also confused. So he smiled.

It was the wrong thing to do. The younger man loosened his grip. "Shoot him," he said.

SO COSTAS SHOT HIM.

They were driving to Astoria, Costas and the kid, to get ahold of some methamphetamine. They had dipped into their buy money, splurging on rib eyes and dirty martinis at a Black Angus in Bellingham, and they needed to make that up. They pulled off the I-5 in Seattle, parked the car, and walked up this hill until a man came out of a building, and they followed him.

Every four weeks or so they made a run to Pasco or Yakima, or as far south as Ashland if they had to. But Astoria was their favorite. Yakima was touch and go these days. The town had gone all fancy and upscale with the winery boom. There were too many strangers, and the supply was not always steady. And Pasco was just a fucking chore. The Mexicans they dealt with were quarrelsome and ill-tempered. They enjoyed needling the kid—*maricón* this, *maricón* that—and got a kick out of it when he invariably flared up and Costas had to settle him down. But Astoria was steady and mellow. The connection in Astoria was *tranquilo*. They always looked forward to that run. Costas drove, and the kid would stuff the CD changer with Led Zeppelin, slapping John Bonham's drum work on the dashboard and screaming the lyrics out the open window into the rushing night. They pulled into rest stops, where they would do more lines, and the kid would go down on Costas, who hung on, knuckling handfuls of hair, bucking and groaning, and astonished still at the good fortune of this boy in his life.

They had met six months earlier when Costas went down to the carport one night and climbed into his car and started it up. He turned to back out and looked into the rear seat and saw this boy sleeping hard, dead to the world. It was a cold, damp spring, the usual in Bellingham, and Costas brought him inside and made him pancakes, and one thing led to another, and the boy stayed. Would it last another six months? Would it last through Christmas? What lasts, anyway? But it would do for now because that's what matters, after all—the Right Now. Money in your pocket, and cocaine's rush and buzz, and this beautiful boy's head in your lap.

Astoria was their hideaway, their love nest, whatever you want to call it. They would stay an extra night or two at a Red Lion down along the river, where every room had a balcony with a view of the marina and the Astoria Bridge, a very narrow two-lane steel structure that shot high over the Columbia to the Washington side. In the evenings, when mist whirled and settled onto the water in the distance, the bridge seemed in its trajectory to fall short of the opposite bank and plunge into the river, a bridge to nowhere.

Some nights they drove across into Washington, to a seafood restaurant in Chinook. It had once been an Episcopal church, and the nave was now the dining room, overlooked at one end by a stained-glass window of wooden ships on a storm-tossed sea. They ordered cioppino, and it came in a huge bowl with clams and mussels and crab parts sticking out. They put on bibs and used tiny tools to get at the meat and sopped up the broth with crusty bread. They lit up cigars and took a late-night stroll to walk off their meal. It was a small, narrow town, maybe five blocks wide, and made up mostly of vacation homes strung along a riverfront highway. Costas was a dog lover, and he kept kibble in his coat pockets to toss to the pooches that ran along the fences they walked by. Sometimes they set their lit cigars on the curb and stepped between the darkened houses, moving through open garages, peeking into the glove boxes of unlocked cars. Back doors were invariably unlocked, and they went inside just to see how easy it would be here, listening to the folks asleep in their rooms somewhere, and pocketing an insignificant trinket or two—a magnet off the refrigerator or a TV remote control—with only the dog of the house sniffing solemnly at Costas's pockets for more treats.

But usually they stayed in Astoria. They got a bottle of Hennessy and a bucket of fried chicken and lay in bed watching cable TV late into the morning. They smoked cigarettes on the balcony and flicked the butts into the water and watched the gulls fight over them. They went to a bar on the main drag that was underneath the bridge. The boy marveled, running back and forth, gawking overhead like a rube in the big city. A massive three-storied slab of concrete anchored the trussed roadway above, and he pressed himself against it and peered along its vertical surface up into the crossbeams and struts as if drawing a bead on the secret of bridges. Then he ran into the bar to report to Costas, who was playing liar's dice with the barkeep. Outside, then in again, tugging on Costas's sleeve like a child, nattering about smallness and bigness, and vastness and scale. "Bolts the size of your fist!" And then mile-by-mile replays of bridges he'd crossed—Pontchartrain in Louisiana, the Seven Mile Bridge in the Florida Keys, and one in the Chesapeake Bay that he swore to God dipped underwater and became a tunnel, then rose out to become a bridge again. And then in movies—the rope bridge quivering over a sheer ravine with a warlord hacking at one end of it, a bridge in Europe strapped with dynamite as Nazis swarmed across it, bridges that rattled apart in awesome earthquakes or got bent and twisted under the magnetic power of alien forces. He was jacked on coke and speed, wound tight and motormouthing, and so in and out, in and out, until the barkeep begged Costas—whom he knew from prison in Vacaville many years before—to please shut the boy up. "Put a leash on your pup, Costas!" And it was a good laugh for everybody, even the boy joining in with gulping, ratcheting hiccups of laughter. But back at the motel he wanted the gun so he could go shoot that fat fuck bartender in the mouth. Costas was rolling around in a tight ball on the carpet with his gun pocket underneath him, the boy kicking at his head and ribs. Then he tried for the car keys, but Costas got to them first, and the boy jumped up and down on Costas's fisted hand until the bones broke. Costas was tenacious. There was nothing you could do to him that had not been done to him before. And even as cranked as the boy was, he relented, heaving and exhausted, and settled for the wallet on the nightstand. He took all the cash and left. He turned up in Bellingham two weeks later, grimy and red-eyed. "Happy to see me?" the boy said, pushing past Costas into the apartment, glancing at the cast on his hand. He pulled off his clothes and headed for the bathroom, reeking of the street and of whatever he'd gotten into. "What, you gonna cry?" he said, watching Costas watch him, standing naked in the steam and letting the hot water run, then stepping into the shower stall.

Inconstant moon. Costas didn't remember where he'd heard that, but that's what the boy was. One day, he would not come back. So the boy showers, and grateful for his return, Costas cries. He is enthralled, and he knows it. Would he do anything for this boy? Well, no. Not anything. But, okay, he might. All right. Yes. He would.

Shoot him.

So Costas shot him. The gun was small and didn't make much noise, two benign pops, like the rap of a knuckle on window glass or the click-crack of a walnut being opened. Costas hated the gangbangers with their huge pieces and all their stopping-power bullshit. Up close, a .22 stopped you just fine. He shot him twice in the belly and put the gun away, and they both eased him onto the ground. The man was watching them go through his pockets, then he said a woman's name and closed his eyes. They got around sixty dollars, plus ATM and credit cards. The cash would cover them tonight, and they knew somebody who'd pay a hundred dollars for each card.

They took two steps out of the hedge and another step over a grassy strip and stood on the sidewalk nose to nose with a woman staring at them. She was a chubby, moonfaced girl, all big-eyed and O-mouthed. She dropped a small paper bag that hit the pavement with a tiny thud, then rolled in a half circle and began to wigwag down the hill. The kid retrieved it before it got away. He opened the bag and peered inside. He pulled off his hoodie and looked into the woman's face and smiled. "Chunky Monkey!"

"C'mon," Costas said. "Shake a leg."

The kid rewrapped the bag carefully and held it out to her. She took it. "Thank you," she whispered. He flipped his hoodie back up, and they walked past her and loped down the hill.

"What's the matter with you?" Costas said, and the kid only grinned. She had gotten a good look at his face and he didn't even care. Costas thought a moment: if, when he turned around, she was still standing up there goggling at them, then he would trot back and pop her. But when he looked, she was gone. All the better. They needed to get to Astoria. Their buy was going down and they could not dillydally.

WHEN SHE GOT HOME, she dumped the ice cream down the sink and crawled into bed in the clothes she was wearing. She lay there listening to sirens in the night, to jets passing over on approach to the airport, to the drunks stumbling home from the bars on Capitol Hill. She heard the birds at sunrise and the garbage trucks wheezing up the streets. When it was light, she got up and used the phone. She left a message at work, then changed her clothes and went outside. It was a clear and cold fall morning, and she had her down jacket on. She could see her breath in the air. She walked three blocks and spotted a patrol car parked across an intersection just ahead. The street behind it was cluttered with more cars—blue-and-whites and unmarked sedans and a gray windowless van up on the sidewalk. She asked the policeman sitting on his car what happened. He said nothing happened and told her to go on to work. "I called in sick," she said. "I'm not going to work today." The cop stared at her until she walked away. She tended to be overly thorough in conversation in a way that made her seem insolent or flip. She tried too hard, believing that being as precise as possible about what you thought and felt was how you connected with people.

That afternoon she read in the paper that somebody had been shot and killed. She sat at a small dining table in the kitchenette, drinking a medicinal tea. Because she had called in sick, she now felt sick. She lived in a basement apartment, and feet went by in the slot window above her dining nook—people coming home from work, footsteps and voices approaching and receding, approaching and receding. The man had let her get a good look at him. He had pulled back his hood and smiled into her face. He held her ice cream out to her. She took it. She thanked him. *I should be dead.* This is what she was thinking when she ran home last night and as she lay in her bed until the sun came up. This is what she was thinking now, running her hand across the newspaper spread on the table, smoothing it out. She believed she would never forget his face. She believed it would be sliced into her memory forever.

I should be dead. But I'm not.

She called in sick the next day, and the day after that. Maybe he was out there, looking for her. She stayed home and indulged in fearful fantasy. She peeked out her window at the steps that led down to her door. She jumped when the mail dropped through her mail slot. She gazed anxiously at the phone, which did not ring. She drank tea and dozed fitfully through the day, awaking at dusk to her darkened apartment. She kept the radio turned off. She did not need to hear about what had happened. A man was dead, and his killer was out there. She imagined staying in her apartment forever—the Woman Downstairs. But the romance of her fear soon dissipated, and she grew restless and bored, and ran out of tea, and after three days she went back to work.

Her name was Hailey, and she was a paralegal assistant at a successful real estate practice. Long ago, in her first months out of paralegal school, they'd had a Christmas party where one of the lawyers she worked for had taken her into an empty office and kissed her for ten full minutes. He was twice her age and married, with three children in college. After the holidays he'd taken her to lunch and apologized, all stammering and shy. She hoped he would call this week, ask after her, wonder where she'd been for three days. But he didn't. She was twenty-nine years old, on the brink of her next decade, and in love with a man who did not call her after she saw somebody die.

She never told anyone. She moved gingerly through the weeks and months that followed, as if stepping from foothold to foothold to balance the secret she carried inside, the thing that no one could know. She was different now. Words no longer came tumbling out of her mouth, rushing to fill a silence she had once dreaded. She was contained, withheld. At first she had felt guilty, had been laden and bleary with it, and people at work had asked if she was all right—even her lawyer. But the guilt lifted quickly, and then she felt guilty about that, until that went too, and soon she felt only clean and new and grateful, as if, climbing out of bed from a long and frightening illness, she now stood blinking in bright, clean light. She felt lucky. She was alive.

Years passed. Hailey waited for her lawyer. She watched him grow old, divorce, marry again. Then he died, and she was alone once more. His son stepped into his father's shoes at the firm and treated Hailey with kindness and respect. She was an esteemed figure in paralegal. "My father always liked you," he told her. And she thought: *so he did remember.*

She moved north, across the canal to Green Lake, and every evening, rain or shine, she walked the path around the lake in the park. She had seen other old women walk the lake, striding briskly past, all vital and vibrant, nodding and saluting at everybody. Who were these fast walkers, these show-offs? Where were they going so fast? Hailey was in no hurry. She kicked through swaths of fallen leaves. She sloshed into deep puddles in her waterproof boots. She stood in downpours to watch red-winged blackbirds flit crazily through the reeds along the bank, or to follow the progress of an intrepid swimmer cutting the rain-pocked surface of the water. She stopped for shaved ice at the snack shack, gave her change to the regular panhandlers, sat in evening's last light watching the kids on the monkey bars. Mothers smiled solicitously at her and she smiled back. Near the small boat launch she peered at a map of the park and eavesdropped on boys and girls on first dates teasing and cajoling each other into rowboats. She spotted a walking stick once, a slash of green against a brown thicket, and she stopped for an hour, drawing a small crowd that joined her to observe the insect step gravely along a narrow twig. Hailey was alone, still. She had never even gotten a pet, neither dog nor cat nor bird. Pets were substitute companions, and she would have a real one or none at all. She had read somewhere, long ago, that solitude was not a sad thing, but a vital and transformative phase, in preparation for love. She didn't believe it anymore. But she still remembered it.

One day at work, Hailey was going over preliminaries with a client entering into a commercial leasing arrangement with her son-in-law. She was a silver-haired woman who sat regal and straight-backed in a chair across from Hailey, who was taking notes. She was saying that she loved her daughter, but did not like or trust the man she had married. She called him a heel, and an ass. She was from the South, and when she spoke, she elongated these words into two syllables: *hee-uhl*, *aa-uhs*. She was saying that she wanted the legal arrangement to be rock solid and unimpeachable, to protect herself and her daughter from certain ruin. She stopped talking midsentence. Hailey looked up from her notes. The woman was crying.

Hailey capped her pen and took off her reading glasses. She looked from the woman's face to the window behind her, and the woman turned in her chair to look as well. They sat in a conference room on the nineteenth floor of a building downtown, and through the plate-glass windows they had a spectacular view of the Sound. It was late afternoon, the end of a hectic week, and the office was still. Outside, gray clouds hung in panels across the sky, and the light moved behind them. The water changed color from blue to green to silver. Shafts of light tilted down from nowhere and tracked the surface and disappeared. Tiny ferries docked and departed. Finger-sized cargo ships slipped seaward. The conference room grew bright and dim, bright and dim—the vast and languid heartbeat of sunlight itself. The woman reached a hand out behind her, and Hailey looked at it for only a moment and reached across the table and took it, and she did not let go.

SHE DID FORGET HIS FACE. Everything fades. Everything goes. Long after the woman she loved had died—after brief, good years that Hailey had thought she'd never have with anyone—there were moments when he would come back to her. A cold fall night, the sweet rot of dead leaves, the thrum of far traffic in a city's teeming silence—these would bring him back, not like a photograph but, rather, the memory of one, as if someone were describing his photograph to you, and you listen and think: *oh yes*. His smile was sweet and taunting. He held the bag out to her, daring her. And Hailey—long ago, on a Saturday night ice-cream run—reached out and took it from him and thanked him, and meant it. She was alive.

CANDIDATE

from vol. 2, no. 2

Karen E. Bender

IT WAS FOUR THIRTY IN THE AFTERNOON, and Diane Bernstein knew that the phone was about to ring. She had just paid the babysitter, the third one to quit this month, extremely polite when she quit, blaming it on other issues—sorority functions, heavy schoolwork—as though the boy had not unnerved her at all. When Diane had walked through the door, Liza, the baby girl, had fallen into her mother's arms, weeping so hard she began to choke. The boy, Johnny, was curled up in his bed, rocking himself, for he had scratched the babysitter in a fury ("I wanted to play the radio," she said, "and he just went insane") and the young woman had shut him in his room. Why hadn't Diane found a better babysitter? It was not a question she allowed herself anymore. She had long stopped worrying about forgiveness, of herself or others. When the therapist had told her, again, that it was not her fault, she laughed; everything was her fault; everything was everyone's fault. "Even if it was his fault," she said, meaning her husband, to the therapist, "what would it matter? He's gone."

Diane had to figure out who to comfort first: the two-year-old, Liza, who clung to her, frantic with love, unwilling to peel herself from her mother after their long day apart, or Johnny, curled up in his bed, a knot of frustration. "They're cute kids," the babysitter called back, apologetically, pulling her long sleeves over the scratches the boy had given her; clutching her fifty dollars, she got into her Jeep and drove off.

Diane had spent the day working in the remedial writing lab of a private university in the Southeast. She hunched in a dimly lit cubicle with the undergraduates, glossy, overfed children who drove SUVs that were gifts from their parents and who could not correctly use a comma. Their essays, which were supposed to address the presidential election, involved passionate, ungrammatical declarations stating why the Republicans should win. *Lazy people should not get my tax mony*, they wrote, or *I dont want any gay agenda on my family. Marriage is between a man and a woman.* That day, Diane sat with a young woman dressed like a prostitute, with shiny gold shorts, her pink Spandex halter top stretched across her breasts. Her hair was styled in two pigtail braids. The girl smelled of the beach, of coconut and salt. She had written a diatribe about how the United States should take over not only Iraq but Saudi Arabia, Egypt, Russia, and Japan, as revenge for Pearl Harbor. It was an extremely long and angry run-on sentence.

"Do you worry about how other countries might respond to this?" asked Diane.

The girl glared at her. "The terrorists want to kill me," she said.

The girl's previous paper had recorded her frustrations about her parents' divorce, the insensitivities of her superiors at Walmart, the cheap gifts her boyfriend had given her. It had been a more interesting paper, though it too lacked consistent punctuation.

"The terrorists would come to Briar Wood College?" Diane asked, before she could stop herself.

The girl's eyes narrowed. Then, as though suddenly aware of her grade, she smiled and said sweetly, "You're just from the North," which was true, though "the North" seemed to imply anywhere slanting north or west; Diane had moved here from Seattle.

Diane closed her eyes; the school where she worked had raised tuition too many times, and faculty had been cautioned not to discuss politics with the conservative students. They lurched about campus, students and teachers, ignoring each other's pins and T-shirts. She had done what she could: covered her car in bumper stickers and stuck yard signs in her lawn that were later torn down.

Now, at home, Diane thought it was best to unplug the phone: then she would not have to decide whether to answer it. The father, who was now residing in Florida, was not supposed to call at this hour; he was supposed to speak to the children only in the morning, for his voice upset them when it was time for dinner and bed. She carried the girl up to the boy's room and sat on his bed. The children both fell upon her. Liza put her head on Diane's leg and closed her eyes, quiet; her breathing became calm. The boy did not like to be touched, but was generally soothed by coloring in squares in black and yellow. She gave him crayons and paper and he sat up, filling each box in with a startling measure of love.

Diane listened to the silence and envied the girl's belief that she had been rescued. It was an acute misunderstanding between parents and children, one that sometimes comforted her, but also felt like a joke. She sat in her son's bedroom and was overcome by loneliness so crushing she could hardly breathe. Liza's tiny hands fumbled to grab her mother's waistband, and Diane was still as the girl gripped her, as though Diane was waiting to be pulled to a safe place.

SOMEONE WAS KNOCKING at the door. Diane jumped up, holding Liza, and she and Johnny ran to the door. She opened it and found a man in a crisp white shirt and navy pants standing on the other side. He held out his hand as though slicing the air in two.

"Hi there," he said. "Woody Wilson here. Running for state legislature. I want to represent you."

Before he said his name, he was just an ordinary stranger, slim, brown-haired—a salesman of encyclopedias or cleaning equipment—standing there with the belligerent, trudging optimism of someone who went door to door. After he declared his name, she hated him. This shift in feeling was so abrupt that her heart felt like an emptied balloon. His face seemed to glow the way a famous person's would, as though it was an accident that he was walking around on Earth. He lived most fully in the newspaper ads and on billboards all over town. WOODY WILSON, REPUBLICAN FOR NORTH CAROLINA STATE SENATE.

"And what's your name?"

"Diane," said the boy.

"Man," the girl said, looking up at Woody Wilson.

It was late afternoon. The house smelled like a rotten melon. The afternoon was weighted toward night. The autumn light already held an undertone of darkness. Diane had read what he stood for and she hated all of it. It would be so simple, so luxurious to slam the door on him! But she did not. His eyes were clear and blue as a baby's. Her heart began to march as though she had been waiting for him.

"Diane, can I have just a moment of your time?" he asked. He kept smiling, but his face was red from the heat. "I can see you're a family person." He stepped back and began to arrange the plastic vehicles scattered across her front porch. He put Big Wheel behind sedan. "I have a family too. How old are your kids? I have two, eight years old and five." He laughed, brokenly; it almost sounded as though he was weeping. "I've come to ask for your vote, Diane," he said. "I am for family. We are what makes America great." He swept his arm toward her in a grand, appropriating gesture; she stepped back from him. "What does your family need? If you want more money in your wallet, I have the answers. If you want better schools, I can answer that, too."

She tightened her arm around Liza's waist. She knew that her ideas were opposite to his in all political realms. "And how are you going to make the schools better?" she asked.

He heard the blade in her voice; his eyes narrowed. The pale clapboard houses behind him seemed to be melting in the heat. "Good question, Diane," he said, speaking quickly. "We want to bring faith back to our schools. Every child should be allowed to pray. No cost to the taxpayer." His words sounded a little breathless.

"Pray to what?" she asked.

He blinked. "I'd say Jesus," he said. She was silent. "But it's a free country," he said. He sounded hesitant on that one, she thought. He tapped a rolled-up leaflet against his hand.

"I believe in separation of church and state," she said, crisply.

He nodded vigorously, as though by making this movement he could ensure their agreement. The optimism in the gesture was ridiculous, almost moving. But then he handed her the leaflet. "Some folks may say it's hard to know whether to choose me or my opponent, Judy Hollis. So I wanted you to see this."

DID YOU KNOW THAT JUDY HOLLIS IS A LESBIAN?
THAT SHE IS BRINGING HER GAY AGENDA TO RALEIGH?
VOTE FOR WOODY. FAMILY VALUES.

She looked at the ad and her heart began to pound faster. She had seen it earlier that day, in the local newspaper. She set the baby down; she'd heard enough of the hate masquerading as congenial agendas.

"Diane, our campaign is getting the word out," he said. "Judy is bad news for our state."

"Because she's gay?" she asked.

"Yes," he said. "We don't want them coming here. I stand for values, Diane, family values. You know what I mean—"

"No, I don't," she said. "I don't want to hear this bullshit. Just stop."

Woody blinked but did not move. The boy glared at Woody Wilson as though he were an animal the boy wanted to eat. Johnny regarded most men who were tall with brown hair this way—it was the simplest way he could describe his father. The boy lay on the floor and rolled from side to side. Why did they work, the ways he tried to comfort himself? He rolled and screeched and turned; they were strategies that adults had found somewhat tolerable at age two but that now made them turn away. Liza gazed at him. The girl's love for the boy poured out of her; she could not help herself. She stretched herself on top of him. She screeched and tried to lick his lips. "Stop!" the boy roared, trying to push her off. She clutched his foot as he tried to crawl away from her. Diane plucked the girl off the boy and set her on the couch, where the girl began to scream.

"Please," Woody Wilson said, "Let me say—" His face went white. Then he toppled forward onto her living room floor.

THE GIRL LET OUT A PIERCING SHRIEK of delight, as though the man was entertaining them. The boy jumped back, his hands pressing his ears. "Stop!" he bellowed. He rolled into a ball on the floor.

Woody was lying face-down across Diane's hardwood floor. He seemed as incongruous as a whale washed up on a beach; she looked down at him, afraid. Diane lightly tapped his shoulder, then she rolled him over. His shoulder was soft as an avocado. He had recently had a mint and his breath was medicinal.

"What'd he do?" yelled the boy.

She jumped up and grabbed the phone off a side table. Woody's eyes opened, and he was staring at them.

"I'm calling a doctor," she said.

"Don't call anyone. I don't want them to know." His presence on billboards made the mundane facts of his humanity strange and troubling. His forehead was pink, with creases in it like clay. There was golden hair on the backs of his hands. He touched his eyebrow; a dark bruise was forming. She was afraid of him, which translated into a great and useless pity. She rarely pitied anyone but herself now, so that superiority was somewhat enjoyable.

She left the front door open. Moths flew in. Woody Wilson put a hand on his forehead. "Ow," he said. He took a deep breath. "Exhaustion. That's what the doctor said. Nothing wrong at all. He said if it happens, sit down for a few minutes, take some breaths, and keep going. I have to keep going."

"Okay," she said, reluctantly. She felt vaguely afraid of being blamed.

"I don't know what happened," he said. "But when I feel strongly about something, sometimes I see black. I feel my heart churning. Perhaps the Lord is telling me something. Ow," he said, softly.

What did he mean, the Lord was telling him something? She sat in her cubicle every day, convincing her students: Evidence. A clear and organized argument. Sometimes she heard herself ranting about evidence, concrete examples, and she felt herself sweating, pathetically, with her own zealotry. He rubbed the bruise on his forehead. She went to the kitchen and brought him an ice pack. He sat up and pressed it to his face.

"Why are you running for office?" she asked.

"He told me to do this. Woody Wilson. I will stand for values. Speak out. The town needs to know your name."

THROUGH THE OPEN FRONT DOOR the clouds were knitting together in a searing, bright sky. She could see the houses on their lawns, each life parceled out into its plot of land, the determined, clipped order of flowers and shrubbery. There were two registered Democrats on her street that she knew of, and four Republicans. They went in and out of their houses, shaving their lawns, picking up their newspapers, remarking on the weather. They would all walk into the voting booths, educated and uneducated, intelligent and dumb, and their votes would be worth the same. They sat, diligently filling in bubbles on paper, and, she thought, because of the voters' impulsive, careless yearnings, wars started, debts soared, the land grew barren, and their great-grandchildren would starve.

The bump on Woody's head was growing larger and darker. It made Diane ashamed, as though it somehow implied something sinister about her. The phone began to ring. Her husband felt most lonely around dinnertime. He did not love them, but did not know who else to call.

"I'm sorry," said Woody Wilson. His right foot tapped on the floor like a rabbit's. "A minute. I'll be on my way." He paused. "Does it look very bad?" he asked.

"I don't know," she said. "Maybe you should keep the ice on it."

The phone rang ten times and then stopped.

"Thank you very much, Diane," he said. He tapped his fingers on the floor rapidly. "I'll just be here a second. I'm a person who does best when he's busy. No one can say I don't have plans."

"All right," she said. "While you're here, I just have one question," she said, suddenly breathless. "Why do you hate so many people? Why so intolerant? I just want to know."

"I do not hate them," he said. "Listen. I am trying to help them from leading lives of so much pain—"

"Why do you assume that people who are not like you are in pain?" she asked.

"I know a lot about pain. My momma died when I was eight," he said, briskly. "My father had to work three jobs. He was always tired. He was so tired he fell asleep on elevators, between floors. I had to get a job working a paper route when I was a small boy. I worked hard. I worked my way up, the good days and the bad. Hard work and faith, that's what got me to college, law school, where I am today."

He recited his litany solemnly, as though it were a prayer. Everyone was competitive in terms of their pain. Whose pain was the worst? Did it matter more that Woody's mother had died when he was young or that Diane's husband had left the family? Was a troubled, problematic child a worse pain than infertility? What about the fact that Diane's hours working as a composition instructor had been cut in half, the sudden eczema that spread across her skin, how did that weigh in compared to being diagnosed with cancer, losing your family in a war, fearing that you might not make love to another person again?

"You were lucky you succeeded," she said. "Some people don't."

"It was not luck," he said sternly. "It was faith. Let me tell you something. A few months ago, before I decided to run for office, I was waking up one morning and I swore I saw a pit bull rush toward the bed. It wanted to eat me. It had a huge, pink mouth. It had been waiting for years for me. It was probably a dream, but it looked real. I said 'Jesus' and it disappeared."

The boy noticed Woody's bag of buttons and stickers. He began, methodically, to take them out and count them. The phone rang again.

"Don't you need to answer that?" Woody asked.

HOW DID ANYONE KNOW the right way to live a life? Diane's husband, at forty-five, had begun to feel pains in his chest. The pains were nothing, the doctor said, but anxiety, but her husband felt, abruptly, the slow, inevitable closing of his own life. He had awakened one night, damp and trembling, after dreaming that Johnny was strangling him. In the dream he had peeled his son's hands off his throat and risen up, free, into the sky. She had these feelings too, for she had had her own disappointments—it had not been her dream to berate undergraduates about commas, for one thing—but she was going along with what was given them, and when she tucked the children in she had not thought there was anything else to do. But suddenly her husband believed that their family was killing him. He was almost gleeful in this—a solution. He was a large, healthy man, but after the dream, he began visiting doctors, checking not only his heart but his lungs, his kidneys, his skin. He said that something was dirty in his blood. No doctors found anything. He searched the Internet for remote adventures; he logged on to sites that described trips into mountains, forests, deserts barely developed by human hands. He said he wanted to go somewhere clean. His home office—he was a freelance reporter for a variety of computer magazines—was papered with posters of Tibet, mountains white, iridescent with snow.

This business had intensified shortly after the doctor had explained to Diane and her husband that testing had placed their son on the autism spectrum. The boy, he said, loved rules so intensely it could be difficult for him to get married or live with someone. He might be tormented in public school, so make sure to explain his issues to the teachers. He could receive therapy to help him understand when another person was happy or sad. On the bright side, the boy would be proficient at math.

After they had heard this, her husband asked her to drive home. She stared at the shiny, broad backs of the cars in front of them. His silence made her aggressively talkative.

"I don't know if he was the best guy," she said. "We could see someone else."

He sat, hunched, arms wrapped around himself as though he were freezing.

"Don't you have anything to say?" she asked sharply, in the tone she sometimes used, despite herself, with the children.

He glanced at the dashboard. "We're low on gas," he said.

THE PHONE STOPPED RINGING. She counted; this time it took twenty rings. Woody lowered the ice pack. "Someone wants to talk to you," he said.

"No," she said. "Actually, he doesn't."

The boy looked up. "There are fifty-eight Woody Wilson buttons in your bag," he said.

"Really?" said Woody. "There are, I think, 108 signs all over town. Yard signs, billboards. I drive around counting them. My wife, Tracy, helped me put up the signs. She did a good job. It was a good day for her." He pressed the ice pack to his head and closed his eyes. "I am her rock," he said. "I am her anchor in troubled water."

The hope in his face, his desire to be seen in this role, made her look away.

"You are your husband's rock," he said eagerly. "I can see it." He picked up the ice pack again. "My wife used to work in real estate," he said. "Did I tell you? She sold a house three blocks away." He paused. "She was very happy," he said. "We had wine and steaks at the Port House." He was staring at his shoe with the frozen gaze of someone banishing other thoughts from his head. Then he quickly looked at her. "And what kind of work does your husband do?"

"I don't really know anymore," she said.

She did not yet know how to answer this. Should she say he was dead? "He left six months ago," she said. Telling Woody was practice, she told herself. She hated other people's pity; their sympathy, she felt, was a way of flattering themselves. She tried to laugh, a hollow, cheerless sound—why? She did not want him to be afraid of her. She was certainly afraid of herself. "That was him on the phone."

"I'm sorry," he said.

A MONTH BEFORE her husband had left, she had told him that she was picking up some milk at the supermarket and checked into a motel instead. It was a one-story chain motel with a small aqua pool, one she had often passed, wondering who frolicked inside there, and this time she put her own key in the door. She had no idea what she would do in the room, as she was not meeting anyone there, but she bought a bag of chips from the snack machine, walked into room twenty-seven, and sat on the bed. She ate each chip slowly, trying to make the bag last. The room whitened with light every few seconds from the passing cars. She undressed and looked at her naked body in the mirror over the dresser. She did not look much different than she had ten years ago; that was before she had met her husband. The fact that she did not look different seemed absurd. She lay on the bed. She tried to imagine an alternative life that she could have, but her fantasies were surprisingly clichéd: tipping champagne glasses in a fancy restaurant in a hotel, floating on a gondola on golden water. Why did she think these things would give her the feelings she wanted? She lay in the dim room and understood that her longing would never end. She lay in the darkness for half an hour. Then she got dressed and went home.

"When I'm feeling troubled," said Woody, "I let Him in my heart. I put myself in the hands of the Lord."

"What does that even mean?" she said. "What hands? What are you talking about?"

"I call his name when I cannot take another step." He looked at her as though she would understand this. "Do you ever feel that, Diane? Who do you call when you cannot take another step?"

She called Dr. Dawson, a woman in her sixties, who had a doctorate in clinical psychology. They sat in a drab, spare room in a mirrored office building, and Diane talked for fifty minutes to this woman who had red hair that was stiff like a meringue. The woman laughed at her jokes, listened when she cried, was quiet when Diane yelled at her. Occasionally Dr. Dawson would tell Diane facts about herself, such as the fact that she had enjoyed math as a child, or her own desire to write erotic poetry; somehow, these facts were always disturbing. But Diane never wanted to leave that room when the hour was up—not even for what relief she had gained during that hour, but the mere hope of it.

"I call Dr. Dawson," she said.

He blinked. "What does Dr. Dawson say?"

"She tells me that I am not my parents," she said.

"Who else would you be?"

"I don't know," she said.

He laughed carefully. "Have you thought why you have not given God a chance to mend your heart—"

"I'm my own responsibility," she said. "Now I don't have to act out the failings of my own parents. I am responsible for my own future. I know I can rely on myself." What did all of this mean? Did it mean simply getting up in the morning, driving the boy to school, handing the girl to the babysitter, making sure they all had enough to eat, sitting in her cubicle for the appointed number of hours, driving home? What was that? Did it mean she could make herself happy? "So your wife sells real estate," she said lightly.

"She did until a year ago," said Woody.

He put down the ice pack and stared at it. When he looked up, he stared through her, as though another person was simply a clear window to some better view. "She won't get out of bed. She stays there with the curtains shut. She says the light hurts her hair," he said.

She looked at Woody Wilson, the blazing whiteness of his shirt, the way his hair was parted very neatly in the middle. She imagined him standing in front of the mirror that morning while his wife lay silent in the dim bedroom, drawing his comb tenderly through his hair. "I'm sorry," she said. "It sounds hard."

"Hard," he said, and laughed, a sad laugh. "Life is hard. But you know, marriage is a sacred union."

"Fine," she said, thinking that this was what she resented most of all, the lack of specifics, the cheerful vagueness, "but, you know, I think that each person has to give something."

"I give her my devotion," he said, sitting up, excited, ready for a debate. "She does the best she can. I wake up in the morning and sometimes I look at her face, and I just want to know what she is thinking. I tell her she needs to go to church. God will help her." His face was naked, a boy's face, the pale, terrible lids of a child. "I want people to see that I'm trying. I want people to say that Woody Wilson was a good man."

A FEW WEEKS BEFORE her husband had left, Diane had heard him crying at odd moments: when he was in the bathroom shaving, when he was in the garage taking in the trash cans. His crying was soft, private, not meant for her or the children, and each time she came upon it she felt both wounded and enraged. He never wept with her, and she knew that this meant she was not supposed to comfort him. One night during this time, she had woken up and made his lunch for him. In the dark kitchen, she put a peanut butter sandwich, an apple, a stick of string cheese, and a cookie in a brown bag and left it on the counter. The next day, he took the bag to work and when he came back, he said, "I took your lunch today. Sorry."

She was suddenly ashamed of her gesture. "I know you did," she said, and they were both more familiar in this, the feeling of deprivation, their quiet, growing anger toward each other. The next morning, when she woke up, that same lunch was on the counter; he had made it for her. She had wept, and had begun to eat it slowly; after a few bites, she stopped. He would be leaving soon; they both knew this. She sat in the empty kitchen and wondered at the point of these gestures, their ultimate selfishness.

The phone was ringing again. Woody clapped his hands over his ears. The boy suddenly stood up and went into the kitchen. The girl wandered off to join him. There was the scream, "Stop!" by the girl, followed by the boy yelling, "Give it!" and then the sound of a body falling in the kitchen. "Oh, no," Diane said. She ran into the kitchen. She heard the candidate stepping behind her.

The boy had the girl pressed to the floor with his body. She was coughing. He was trying to unpeel her tiny closed fist. "Give it!" he growled.

"I want it!" screamed the girl.

"Get off her!" Diane yelled at the boy. She grabbed his thin shoulders and tried to shake him off, but the boy would not move. "Now!"

Diane imagined how Woody Wilson saw them, the disheveled middle-aged woman in the putrid kitchen, wrestling with the enraged son who was stronger than she was. Legislate against this, she thought. The girl opened her mouth to bite the boy's hand.

Woody grasped the boy's hands. "Let go of your sister," said Woody quietly.

"She stole it!" screamed the boy.

Woody held a hand out, as though to calm the air. "Now wait, everybody," he said. "Wait." He reached into his pocket to pull out a Woody Wilson sticker. "I'll trade you." He handed the girl his sticker. "Vote for me." The girl grabbed it. She was already possessed of a startling rage, as though she foresaw the difficulties her own beauty, her brother's rantings, and her father's fumblings would bring her. When the girl stared at someone, as she did at her brother, Diane saw how she would someday regard a lover, the assumption that the other would feed some endless hunger inside of her. She gazed at Diane with the same expression, and Diane whispered to her, ashamed before its vastness.

The boy broke away from the girl. Woody pressed the boy's sticker back into his outstretched hand. The boy turned from him and hunched over his sticker. It had the green, smiling face of Shrek on it.

"Where'd you get this?" Woody asked the boy.

"At school. They called my name in the cafeteria," the boy said. "I heard my name. They said it like this: John. Nee. Bern. Steen. They chose me. They said I could go home. The lady gave me this when I walked out. She said hold this and go right to the car. I held it the whole way."

Diane remembered this from the day before, the first time she had picked up her son by car at school. The car riders waited for their mothers in the cafeteria, while their parents, in cars at the traffic circle, told their names to the pickup coordinators, who called their names on the walkie-talkie. "Johnny Bernstein," Diane had said to the coordinator. She imagined her son's name floating over the loudspeaker in the cafeteria, where the children were sitting on long steel benches. She pictured all the children, Johnny and Keesha and Juan and Christopher and Sandra and the others, hunched over the tables, waiting to be summoned back to their lives. How many times would they sit like this, waiting to be called—for work, for love, for good fortune or bad, for luck or despair? What joys or sorrows would each of them be chosen for? She wished she could see how her son hurried down the dingy, dim brown public-school corridor, how he walked to the doors that burst open to the afternoon light.

She was relieved when she saw him coming to her car; it was as though he had just been born. "What happened?" she asked. He had told her the same thing: "They said my name like this." Her son cupped his hands together and spoke into them: "John. Nee. Bern. Steen." He said these words with awe, as though they had been spoken by the voice of God. She watched his young face in the rearview mirror, blank but suffused with a new brightness, and she wanted to touch his face and feel what hope was in it, but she simply drove on.

Now Woody leaned toward the boy. "John. Nee. Bern. Steen. You did a good job," Woody said.

The boy nodded at Woody's correct pronunciation. "Yes," he said.

"Your parents will be proud," Woody continued.

"My father calls in the morning," Johnny said. "I hear him, but I don't see his face."

"He must miss you," said Woody. Stop, she thought. Don't pity him. Woody rolled up his shirt sleeves. He bent so he was looking into the boy's face. "Johnny," said Woody, "I know how you feel. When I was a boy, I woke up and the house was quiet. No one called me. Johnny, I didn't have a mother. My father was at work long before I got up." He ran his hand through his hair. "I dressed and got myself to the bus stop. I rode the school bus. I waited for it to pick me up. Some days it took a long time. Sometimes I said my name, too. *Woody Wilson*. I said it over and over. *WoodyWilson. WoodyWilson. WoodyWilson*. There was a bar beside the bus stop. Sometimes a couple men would be sleeping in the doorway. They looked dead. They smelled terrible. Johnny, I said my name so many times it was like a prayer. *Woody Wilson*, I said, *you are not those men. You are yourself.*"

HIS VOICE HAD BECOME QUIETER as he spoke to Johnny. The boy gazed at him, strangely lulled. She felt the little girl grab her leg and Diane touched her hair. How many more moments would Woody speak to her son? And how had her life come to this, hoarding minutes of kindness doled out to them by strangers who knocked on her door? She wondered if this would be the future texture of their lives, this hoarding, and she wished Woody Wilson would leave, but also appreciated the fact that someone else was in the room. She looked away from his pale, thin hair, his shirt rolled halfway up his pinkish arms. She was suddenly afraid that her son would ask him to stay.

But the boy suddenly turned his back to Woody, squatting over his stickers with a fierce expression. "Johnny?" Woody asked. "Are you all right?"

"I don't care," said the boy sharply. "Guess what? I don't care."

She did not know what would comfort him; she barely knew what would comfort herself.

"Well," said Woody. "Hey." His voice broke a little, and he laughed, a hearty, rehearsed laugh. "Well, you never know what will work with kids, what will help them. Never hurts to try, right, Diane? Got to keep trying?"

He touched his hair as though to check that it still existed, that he was all here. He wanted to be reassured, and so did she, and for what? They were soft, graying, halfway to their deaths. They both knew that no one could understand another person's love, parent or child's; they both knew that everyone would die alone.

"Okay," she said carefully, and shrugged.

"Thank you," he said.

The tinny sound of "The Star-Spangled Banner" burst into the room. It was Woody Wilson's cell phone. Woody's face assumed a stern expression as he held it to his ear. "Yes. Still on Greenfield. Yep." He turned it off. "Well," he said. "Time to go."

He picked up his briefcase. "Thank you for your hospitality, Diane," he said brightly. The politician's voice burst out of him as though he were on the radio; he seemed almost surprised to hear it. He smiled as he had in the billboard, holding out his hand. "Good-bye," he said.

"Good-bye," she said, shaking his hand, the firm, remote grip of a stranger. She felt his pulse jump and it startled her; she let go and stepped away.

Standing on Diane's front porch, Woody Wilson slipped his briefcase under his arm. The bump on his head was dark and monstrous. "What should I tell people?" he asked. "How did this happen?"

"I don't know," she said. "Tell them you tripped."

"Yes," he said, brightening, as though delighted by the simplicity of this idea. "I just tripped."

Silence bore down on them; there was nothing more to say. Woody Wilson hurried up the sidewalk to the next house, lifting a hand to knock on the door. Outside, the sunlight was dying. His lips were moving; she believed that he was murmuring his name.

She heard the phone begin to ring again. Quickly, she stepped out the door into the cooling, pink air. She looked at the signs for all the candidates stuck into the green lawns. They sat, arranged in rows under the sky, fluttering in the low wind. She stood for a moment, reading the names displayed there; then she turned and went back into the house.

NEW ANIMAL

from **vol. 8, no. 1**

Douglas Watson

ONE DAY IN HOLLAND a new animal was invented. It was a miniature racehorse with a jet-black coat and, supposedly, a docile nature—the perfect horse for children to ride. Watching it gambol about the laboratory for the first time, Van Roost, the junior of the two scientists who had produced the creature, felt his face relax into a grin. The horse was his first breakthrough as a professional scientist. Soon the Dutch premier was on the phone, offering congratulations, and in bed that night Van Roost's girlfriend, a public-interest lawyer from Luxembourg, acted five or ten percent fonder of Van Roost than she ever had before. Van Roost hoped that she might now leave her other boyfriend and devote herself exclusively to him.

It was a good time to be alive, Van Roost thought.

Which, if true, did not apply for long to the miniature horse's very first rider, a seven-year-old named Greta who, when the horse threw her, sailed twisting through the air and landed in the worst way and broke her neck.

All of Holland went into an uproar. Protesters encircled the laboratory and demanded that the horse be euthanized. This demand was soon met—by a sobbing Van Roost—but the horse's demise sparked the ire of a different brand of protester. By day three of the turmoil, the premier had tightened child-safety regulations, the Dutch legislature had proclaimed that humans ought not to play god with animals, and the European Parliament had reprimanded Holland, saying its legislature lacked the authority to weigh in on so lofty a matter. Then came the girl's memorial service, attended by neither Van Roost nor the senior scientist. Both men ought to have been there—public-opinion polls were clear on that point—but the opinion of the police had been that their safety could not be guaranteed. Van Roost stayed at home the day of the service with the blinds drawn and a recording of tropical surf playing on an endless loop.

Just when it seemed as though the furor over the girl's death would never die down, it did. A few days after the memorial service, some new scandal, something to do with finance or a crashed plane, diverted the public, leaving Van Roost to confront, for starters, the unprecedented difficulty he was having making love to his girlfriend. They tried all kinds of positions, some from Luxembourg, some from Holland, some from other EU countries. Nothing worked, not even the position his girlfriend called the raptor. Finally one day she told him that she had decided to devote herself completely to her other boyfriend.

"What about me?" Van Roost said, and then he thought how pretty she was when she smiled sadly and apologetically and a little bit impatiently.

The next day, an EU regulatory commission scolded Van Roost and the senior scientist for their "negligence if not outright recklessness" and suspended for one year their scientific licenses. Muttering that the girl's death hadn't been their fault, the senior scientist packed his bags and emigrated to America to work for a pharmaceutical company. But it was our fault, Van Roost said to himself. The bureaucrats indicated that he could spend his year away from science either doing community service or studying philosophy at the university in the town where he lived. Van Roost, who didn't know any better, chose the latter course.

The first philosopher he was asked to read was a Scot named David Hume. Hume was, or had been, at pains to prove that it couldn't be proved that the sun, on any given day, was a whit more likely to rise than not to rise. What nonsense! Van Roost thought as he slammed the book closed.

Many nights, instead of doing the required reading, Van Roost would open a bottle of red wine and sit in his kitchen rereading the newspaper stories he'd clipped about the girl who'd died. Greta. Though just seven, she had already begun a serious study of the flute, the papers said. They had all put the same photo on the front page, a photo of this grim-faced child holding a flute to her mouth, her wispy blond hair sticking out in all directions as though it were trying to get away from her. She was playing, according to the papers, one of Mozart's melodies for young people. Van Roost went out and bought a CD of these melodies. He listened to it only once, and that just halfway through. He had never liked classical music, and even these simple melodies struck him as still being classical music. It actually helped him, for a brief moment, feel a little less bad about what had happened, thinking that however many times these melodies had been played in the world and would be played until the end of time, that number would be the tiniest bit lower now, thanks to the miniature horse he had helped invent. Of course, this thought was insane, and Van Roost felt bad about having come up with it.

Another thing he felt bad about was that he couldn't help noticing, from the newspaper photos, that Greta's mother was very attractive. Her thin, pretty, intelligent face was beset by a tangle of blond hair. In the photo Van Roost liked best, she clung to her broad-shouldered husband, whose face was cut in half by the edge of the photo, and looked directly at the camera. Van Roost felt that she was not looking at just anyone: she was looking at him. Had it really been necessary, her eyes were saying, to invent a miniature racehorse? Yet there was also a trace of humor in her face, he thought, humor or resignation—perhaps around the mouth, Van

Roost wasn't sure. Maybe he was reading too much into the photo. At any rate, she was pretty.

He wanted to tell her how sorry he was about what had happened. He even pictured himself knocking on her door, telling her in person. But it wasn't *her* door, it was *their* door, and anyway, he thought as he looked up the address in the phone book and scribbled it on a scrap of paper that he tucked into his jacket pocket, it was unlikely that these people had any desire to hear from him. Surely they just wanted to move on.

Van Roost tried to move on too. He'd been a philosopher-in-training for a month now, and his first examination was nearly upon him. Did death, his professors wanted to know, give meaning to life, or did it strip life of meaning, or did it have some other, totally surprising effect, something no one but Kierkegaard could have anticipated? Van Roost had no idea. He hadn't even realized the class had moved on to Kierkegaard. He went in search of the work in question, a collection of the Dane's essays the editors had titled *Kierkegaard: Necessary*, but the library's copies were all checked out, and the three bookstores in town were also out of stock.

With the illicit glee of a sentry abandoning his post, Van Roost absconded from university life and tried, for a week, to become a drunk and an idler. For seven days and nights, he idled along the edge of a dock by the canal that cleaved the town's heart in two. He drank gin, because why not? When he finished a bottle, he tossed it in the canal, an extremely un-Dutch thing to do. No one seemed to care. Hour after hour Van Roost lay curled upon the dock next to the languid waters of the canal, in whose surface the unthreatening clouds overhead were reflected. It was crushingly boring, he decided, being a drunk and an idler. Still, he finished out his seven days in good faith.

When the week was over, he went home, washed himself, ate a tremendous breakfast of eggs with chives and thick white toast, drank three mugs of strong black coffee, and then set out on foot to see if he could reacquaint himself with the world outside his skull. This would take a bit of time, he soon realized. Day after day he walked through town, never toward the university, never toward his old laboratory, never, indeed, anywhere in particular, or so he thought. It was spring. Everywhere he walked, Van Roost saw children running, biking, shouting, crying, throwing dirt at one another—all the things children did in the spring. This was on nice days. On rainy days, he was one of a legion of adults walking through the town under umbrellas of various hues. His was black. Greta, the girl Van Roost's horse had killed, would never join this adult legion. She would never get to choose an umbrella color. Not that being an adult was so great, Van Roost thought, but at least he, and these other adults walking around with their umbrellas, had had a chance to discover that. Greta was not even able to discover what her fellow children were talking about this spring. Walking past the playground in her neighborhood—for his steps took him more and more often down streets near the one on which her parents presumably still lived—Van Roost would wonder whether any of the children he saw had known Greta. Did they see guilt written in his gait as he walked by? Did they, or might their parents, recognize him from the newspaper stories at the time of the accident?

It made Van Roost sad to watch the children playing. He had once been as happy and carefree as they seemed to be, or at least that was how he remembered his childhood. Don't grow up, he wanted to say to them—then flinched, thinking just how tainted a piece of advice that would have been, coming from the inventor of a child-killing horse.

So. One Thursday, after a lunch of cream cheese and cucumbers on pumpernickel, Van Roost set out on not just any walk but, he knew, the walk that would lead him to the front door of Greta's parents' house. It was a brilliant day, one of those blue-sky wonders when, after a night of rain, the world seemed freshly scrubbed and brighter and lovelier than one remembered was possible. But so many things were possible, Van Roost said to himself as he walked along a sidewalk strewn with damp cherry blossoms knocked down overnight by the rain. Looking at the cherry petals, he recalled a scene from an art film a young woman whose attentions he had once craved had made. In the scene, a man gets on a subway car, the floor of which is strewn with flower petals. Someone has dropped a bouquet of flowers and simply left it there. The man takes a seat, and as he rides, listening to the clatter of the train wheels along the tracks, he thinks, in voice-over and without knowing why, that the flower petals are a sign that someone somewhere has died.

Van Roost couldn't remember how the film had ended or even whether the young woman had finished the project. It didn't matter now, he thought as he turned into the narrow side street on which he hoped, or feared, Greta's parents still lived. It hadn't really ever mattered, he thought. The street was lined with two-story brick row homes with tile roofs. Van Roost's steps slowed as he neared number sixty-four, Greta's parents' house. It was a house just like the others. Pansies—not Van Roost's favorite flower—grew in wooden boxes below the windows to either side of the black front door. Didn't pansies have something to do with death in some cultures? Hadn't he read that somewhere? Or was it love they symbolized?

Van Roost stood on the sidewalk, thinking he should really be somewhere else—at home, for instance, getting his life up and running again.

But, no, this was his life. He had come here to apologize, and he was going to go through with it.

He took a deep breath and went up to the black door and knocked.

After a moment the door swung inward, and there she was, Greta's mother. She was shorter than Van Roost had imagined her, which meant that her husband, who'd stood beside her in that newspaper photo, was also shorter than he'd supposed. She wore a red cardigan over a flower-print blouse over smallish breasts, and her jeans revealed a trim figure. Her thick blond hair was perhaps a half-measure beyond stylish disarray. The shadows under her eyes must have been attributable, Van Roost thought, to the grief he'd caused her.

"Yes?" she said, looking at him far more guardedly than she had in the newspaper photo.

"Mrs.—" Van Roost said, and with a kind of horror he discovered that he'd forgotten the family's name. So he said, "You're Greta's mother."

The woman recoiled, raised a hand along the door's edge. But she didn't close the door. Her eyes (gray-green, as Van Roost had been unable to tell from the newspaper) held his, and her mouth curled slightly, though she was not smiling.

"You're one of those scientists," she said.

Not this year, I'm not, Van Roost wanted to say. He wanted to say, I'm sorry, I'm sorry. He glanced away up the street and thought, My god, this is real, isn't it? A breeze moved through the cherry trees, and the dappled light danced on the sidewalk.

Greta's mother's hand brushed his forearm. He turned toward her, and she smiled politely and said, "Come in."

"I hope it's no trouble," he managed to say.

She held the door for him, and he followed her into a small sitting room whose walls were lined with books. He accepted an offer of coffee, and she disappeared through a doorway to the kitchen. There was no sign of the husband. Van Roost sat down in a leather-upholstered chair in the corner of the room. He could still feel where she'd touched his arm. He scanned the room for photographs of the dead child but didn't see any. There was nothing on the walls but bookshelves and nothing on the shelves but books—serious books. Plato, Heidegger, Proust. A whole shelf of Sontag. Oh, and there it was, *Kierkegaard: Necessary*, the book Van Roost had needed for his philosophy exam.

Greta's mother came into the room holding two mugs. She asked him how he took his coffee. Black, he said. She handed him one of the mugs and then sat down in a chair opposite his, on the other side of a coffee table cluttered with books and papers. A slender volume called *Grief, Sex, and You* caught Van Roost's eye. Greta's mother crossed her legs, sipped her coffee, and looked at Van Roost—again, guardedly, he thought—then looked away, possibly at a clock he couldn't see in the next room.

He blew on his coffee. Surely there was a right way to begin this conversation. He took a sip of the coffee. It was a dark roast, bitter and strongly brewed, just the way he liked it.

"Good coffee," he said, raising the mug as though he'd said, To your health.

Greta's mother nodded, frowning slightly, or perhaps Van Roost imagined the frown because of his anxiety. He crossed one leg over the other, then noticed that his foot was jiggling. He uncrossed his legs and was on the point of telling Greta's mother that he'd been looking for the very Kierkegaard volume she had on her shelf when he heard himself say, instead, "Your husband is not in?"

"No."

Will he be away long? Van Roost wanted to say, and: Is he gone for good? Heat washed over him; he was blushing. He thought about telling Greta's mother that his girlfriend, a public-interest lawyer from Luxembourg, had left him for another man and that he imagined she regretted it. He didn't really imagine any such thing, but he thought it would sound good.

Greta's mother began smoothing her right hand along the top of her right thigh, down toward the knee and then back up again, down, then up.

Van Roost sat up straighter and said, "I came to say how sorry I am for what happened."

Her eyes met his. Her mouth, when it smiled, surprised Van Roost. If I were in her shoes, he thought, I certainly wouldn't be smiling. A little pocket of gladness opened up in his chest, a little bubble of expectation.

"I'm Emma," she said, extending a hand.

That was all. Not thank you, not it wasn't your fault, not get out of here this instant.

"Van Roost," Van Roost said.

Her grip was firm and her hand warm.

Van Roost sipped his coffee, which was cooling. Emma. What a pretty name.

"I want you to know," he said, leaning forward a little, "that it was considered highly unlikely that the horse would exhibit such severe skittishness."

Greta's mother—Emma—looked darkly away and ran a hand through her hair, which really was quite a tangle. "Please," she said in a thick voice. "Talk about something else."

Shame lanced through Van Roost. He blew on his coffee forcefully enough that a drop splashed over the rim and onto his hand. It wasn't hot enough to burn. The husband could come through the front door at any moment, Van Roost thought. What would he think to find the two of them sitting together in awkward silence? Once more Van Roost's eyes settled on *Kierkegaard: Necessary*. He wondered if Emma were familiar with Kierkegaard's position on death. He wasn't about to ask, though, and anyway she had drained the last of her coffee and now leaned forward to place the empty mug on the coffee table between them. Her bra was turquoise, Van Roost saw as she bent toward him, or at least the edge of it was.

"May I show you Greta's room?" Emma said, rising.

Okay, but—why? Van Roost thought as he followed her down a carpeted hallway. He liked the way she held her shoulders when she walked: she thrust them back in a way that seemed to him very proper.

She stopped in the doorway to a small bedroom. Van Roost came up beside her. Sunlight slanted through a window at the far end of the room and glinted off—Christ, Van Roost thought, it's the girl's flute. It lay across a desk in the farthest corner of the room, the sun upon it like a spotlight, but of course one didn't want to think of a spotlight, there being no Greta to pick up the flute and perform. Nearer at hand was a twin bed, and Van Roost registered a second shock when his eyes took in the collection of stuffed horses arrayed on the white bedspread. Beside the bed stood an antique dresser, on top of which sat, there was no way not to notice, an urn—presumably (Van Roost couldn't block the thought) no more than half full.

"She loved horses," Emma said, and then, smiling sadly up at Van Roost, she took his right hand and placed it squarely upon her left breast.

The air caught in Van Roost's throat. Emma's eyes shone darkly, and she leaned into his body, which offered its own response even as his mind jumped away. Look at her eyes, he thought. And he had a point, they were quite extraordinary, they were eyes you could study for a long time without understanding what was going on behind them. The eyes were what Van Roost would remember later, their luminous opacity, and not, say, the breast in his hand, whose feel he was, in any case, too agitated to pay much attention to.

What did command his attention was his rising panic as this woman with married hand began fumbling with his belt buckle. She's crazy, he told himself as she undid the buckle and the top button of his jeans and tugged at the zipper—which caught—and in the next moment he fled down the hallway, zipping and buckling as he went, and on out into the sitting room, where, scarcely slowing his stride, he grabbed, for reasons that were unknown to him, the Kierkegaard volume, and then he clambered out the door and, running, looked back at the pansies under the windows (danger was what they symbolized, he decided) and then ran up the street to the end of the block and rounded the corner and slowed to a walk, his ragged breathing splitting the tranquil air of the quiet street, the sort of street on which nothing was supposed to happen.

Walking home, he crushed underfoot the cherry petals strewn wantonly everywhere.

That night, safely housed behind double-locked door and with a bottle of red wine open on the table before him, Van Roost considered what he had to fear from Emma or her husband. It seemed to him there were three possibilities. One of them was that he had nothing to fear. The second was that the husband might try to hurt him, and the third was that Greta's mother might tell the newspapers that one of the scientists who'd killed her daughter had showed up unannounced at her home and made a pass at her.

All of Holland will believe her, he thought.

He got up from the table and crossed the room to the stereo. He put on his tropical surf recording, and then he sat down and refilled his wine glass. *Kierkegaard: Necessary* glared up at him from the table where he'd laid it. He'd stolen it, he realized with a start. Why had he done a thing like that? He had never stolen anything before. Was he really that curious to know what Kierkegaard thought about death?

Van Roost opened the book at random and read: "Is despair an excellence or a defect?"

Strange question. Van Roost listened some more to the ocean waves breaking. It occurred to him that the sound had no meaning—it was just the sound energy made when, having moved through water, it continued moving through earth and air. Despair was a kind of energy, Van Roost decided. It spread outward from its source in waves. It was probably a defect, but it was hard to avoid. He read on:

> Purely dialectically, it is both. If only the abstract idea of despair is considered, without any thought of someone in despair,

> it must be regarded as a surpassing excellence. The possibility of this sickness is man's superiority over the animal, and this superiority distinguishes him in quite another way than does his erect walk, for it indicates infinite erectness or sublimity, that he is spirit. The possibility of this sickness is man's superiority over the animal; to be aware of this sickness is the Christian's superiority over the natural man; to be cured of this sickness is the Christian's blessedness.

Van Roost closed the book. He got up and went out into the living room and over to the window. Outside, the evening light—energy filtered through dust and water vapor—slanted across the neatly swept sidewalks and against the modest brick homes of the street. Van Roost hadn't known that Kierkegaard was so determined a Christian. He hadn't known anything else about the man either, except that he was Danish and dead, but this new knowledge filled Van Roost with despair. No doubt he was being unfair to Kierkegaard (just as, he'd read somewhere, Kierkegaard had been unfair to Schlegel)—after all, you couldn't judge a writer by a single paragraph—but to watch a great thinker retreat into the waiting arms of dogma was depressing.

Emma's pass at him that afternoon was depressing too, Van Roost thought as he turned away from the window. He thought: No one knows what to do about death. Emma lost her daughter and doesn't know what to do; Kierkegaard peered into the void and didn't know what to say; and I?

I don't know what to do about life, he thought.

He went over to the table and corked the wine. He felt he'd been right to flee Emma's touch and her house, but he wondered, a bit, whether he mightn't have run away at least in part because his most recent attempts at lovemaking, with the public-interest lawyer from Luxembourg, had gone so poorly.

"Fuck it," he said out loud for some reason. He walked over to the stereo and replaced the tropical surf recording with an album by a Belgian rock band he liked. Guitar chords jolted into the room, and Van Roost began jumping around like a teenager. "Give me some money or I'll give you my soul!" the band members shouted in unison. Van Roost shouted along with them. For the first three songs he was a madman, grinning, shouting, jumping around. Then he got tired and, no longer smiling, sat on the couch as the drums and guitars punched and stabbed the air.

When the album ended, Van Roost didn't get up to put another one on. He didn't get up for hours. Deep into the night he sat listening to the faint buzzing in his ears. He felt he was waiting for something.

SOMETHING LIKE THE RESURRECTION

from vol. 7, no. 2

Maggie Shipstead

THE DAY WAS TOO HOT; the muffins that Jeffrey's Chinese wife had taken so long to bring back were stale; a dead spider dangled from a scrap of web in the corner of the ceiling; one of Denny's boys had spilled grape juice on the white carpet; Cynthia kept talking on and on about the latest man who did not love her; Father Patrick, who usually said Mass on TV, had been mysteriously absent, replaced by the nasal Father Roland, and she, Agnes, was dying. Clumps of proteins had infiltrated her heart, replacing the muscle, and now the whole thing was enlarged, lopsided, struggling. The diagnosis was cardiac amyloidosis, or "stiff heart syndrome," a name that had made Cynthia snort with amusement through her tears when Agnes broke the news. The doctors told Agnes the proteins were the reason she was up and down to pee a thousand times a night and why her ankles had gotten so fat. She was short of breath too, and always tired, but she had thought that was just because she was old.

Her children had more or less rushed to her side, except Jeffrey had tried to delay because of a business meeting. After all, he said, the doctors gave her a year. She wasn't going to die tomorrow. "They said *up to* a year," she told him. "I could very well die tomorrow, but then at least you won't miss your meeting, which is the important thing."

"Fine," he said. "I'll see if they'll do a conference call instead. Even though the reception up there is crap."

So her three children—Jeffrey, Denny, and Cynthia—packed up her eight grandchildren and flew from New York and Colorado and Florida, working their way up to the north woods, to the house on Lake Michigan where Agnes spent her days reclining on her blue davenport, watching the water out the window and listening to the television. Carlotta came in the mornings to help around the house and remind her to take her pills. "Your ankles will only get fatter if you don't take them," Carlotta said when Agnes pretended not to see the tablets, sized for horses, on the edge of her breakfast tray. In a few months she would need a full-time nurse but not yet. Having Carlotta do the dishes and cook and clean—why had Carlotta missed the dead spider? it was hanging there plain as day—was enough for now. Perhaps, too, in a few months she would not be able to go into town on Sundays for Mass, and one of the deacons would have to bring Communion out to her, a consecrated Meal on Wheels. But for now she could still go, chauffeured by her friends the O'Conners, and on the other days she watched Mass on TV with the volume up loud enough for Carlotta to hear wherever she was in the house. Denny had watched with her this morning and endured Father Roland, but now he was out by the lake with the rest of them.

When, also in the morning, Jeffrey's wife had offered the wrinkled white bag of muffins, Agnes had peered through the opening and said, "Well, what are they?"

"All different kinds," said Mildred. *Mildred.* One of those names immigrants gave their children.

"Any zucchini?"

Mildred hesitated, looking at the bag. "I don't think they had zucchini."

"This will have to do, then," Agnes said, choosing a blueberry muffin. "Whatever it is."

Hours later the muffin still sat on a plate on the coffee table, untouched except for the small chunk she had sampled from its dome. Her bathrobe, the white one that zipped up the front, was hot and itchy, but she could not bear the trouble of changing. The grandchildren were down on the beach, digging in the sand and sorting through the rocks while their parents lounged on the sunny dock: Jeffrey and Mildred, Denny and Pam, and Cynthia in a too-skimpy bikini. Brandon, Cynthia's son fathered by God-only-knew-who, was lashing the cedars with a jump rope. Cynthia maintained that the conception had been an accident, but Agnes didn't believe a word. The year before she got pregnant, all Cynthia could talk about was her impending infertility.

"I'm mossing over," she had declared. "My tubes are as tight with an egg as my mother is with a buck." She thought she was being funny. She said these things anywhere she pleased: in front of Carlotta or in the ladies' room after Easter services or at dinner with the O'Conners and their successful, divorced son. "What is a woman," Cynthia asked Mrs. O'Conner, "who doesn't have a child? I don't even know if I can produce milk. It's something you always assume you can do, but what if I can't? What then?"

Agnes liked a fruitful womb, but she had groomed her daughter to be a wife first, thinking there would be a little time before Cynthia needed to be made into a mother, a little warning. Agnes had sent her to cotillion, bought her nice clothes, steered her away from that horrible hippie college, gotten her a secretarial job in an office full of bachelors. Cynthia *could* have married, Agnes had seen to that, but instead she'd spent decades throwing herself at men who barely noticed her. Then had come the silent smugness, the sudden contentment, the Christmastime announcement. Agnes had lost her temper, and Cynthia had screamed that Agnes never let her do anything she wanted, not ever, that Agnes always wanted her to be miserable. *All I wanted was for you to have a good life*, Agnes had bellowed back. Phillip had still been alive, and he told Agnes to knock it off, there was no need to yell, Cynthia could have a baby if she wanted one, husband or no husband. But Phillip had always spoiled Cynthia.

Agnes's pregnancies had been so much more matter-of-fact than those of the next generation: no circus of gifts, no soul-searching and second-guessing, no planning the birth to the smallest, most gruesome detail. And yet she had been so young, only twenty when Jeffrey was born and twenty-six for Cynthia, with Denny in between. None of her children had managed to reproduce before the age of forty. Jeffrey and Denny were late bloomers who married younger women (and, in Jeffrey's case, remarried an even younger woman). Cynthia had conceived Brandon as an act of foolish defiance. In the shade of the cedar trees, Brandon's puny arm cocked back and jerked forward. He didn't move his feet or change his balance, poor boy, just flailed his bird arm back and forth. The trees probably hadn't lost even one flake of bark.

Agnes's children were already starting to grow old, separated from their own children by a wide gulf of years. Four kids for Jeffrey, three for Denny, one for Cynthia. Jeffrey's eldest was twelve: Katie, the only girl. First Katie and then the long, victorious streak of boys, seven of them, ending with Jeffrey and Mildred's toddler, the almond-eyed half-sibling digging in the sand with a red shovel. Katie was a drab girl who wore the clothes of a younger child and had an aversion to hairbrushes, lipstick, and brassieres. She didn't seem to understand that womanhood must be wrangled, contained, buttressed, painted, curled, and sopped up. Girls needed hairbrushes and brassieres the way lion tamers needed whips. No one was helping Katie, no one was arming her. When would she consent to wear a bra? When would she take an interest in grooming? Would she find a husband? Might she be a lesbian? Agnes would have to die without knowing. *Hail Mary*, she thought, distracted, as happened so many times a day, by the specter of her demise. As a younger woman, she had thought God would loom larger and larger as she approached death. And yet her faith had become an old marriage, a threadbare passion practiced by rote. Her prayers escaped by their own accord: abbreviated, habitual emissions that stirred no emotion. She gestured at the Hail Mary with two words and thought *Our Father* and then nothing else. No art in heaven, no hallowed name. She daydreamed through the televised Mass, watching swans float down the lakeshore.

A cloud of laughter rose from the adults down on her dock. Lucky for them her bad news had coincided with a streak of perfect summer days. Come outside, Mother, they said. Sit on the dock. Enjoy the sun. Enjoy your grandchildren. But she was past enjoying the sun, and the grandchildren might spray her with sand or catch her with a wayward rock. Phillip had swum in the frigid lake every day between June and October. A small island, prickly with pine trees, floated in the middle of the bay, and he would swim halfway to it, so far out she lost sight of him. She asked him to wear a reflective cap, but he laughed at her. His college ring, a fat gold and onyx memento of Vanderbilt engraved with his initials, had been lost on one of his swims. The cold shrank his fingers, and it slipped off. He thought it was somewhere near the dock, but a dozen expeditions with a metal detector yielded only a door hinge, some rusty fishhooks, a fifty-cent piece covered in green slime, and a garden trowel. For Christmas one year the children had gone in together on a replacement ring, but he lost that too. Something in the lake had an appetite for Phillip's rings. Agnes had thought he might drown eventually, pulled under by whatever kept clutching at his fingers, but he died on an airplane. The woman sitting beside him thought he was asleep, as indeed he had been until an unnoticed moment somewhere over the Great Plains. He was already partway to heaven: all that was needed was a simple upward wafting through the aluminum ceiling.

She watched Katie fold down the corner of her book, rise from her towel on the beach, and walk toward the dock. The skirt of the girl's purple swimsuit did little to conceal the thickness of her thighs. On the day everyone arrived, Agnes had suggested to Jeffrey that they talk to Katie about her diet, but he said he didn't want to give her a complex.

"Don't give her a complex, but don't give her so many cookies, either," Agnes said. "No girl wants to be fat."

Jeffrey had sighed in a show of patience. In his office on Park Avenue, his diplomas (he had four) hung in an authoritative row across one wall. Sometimes when he spoke to her, Agnes could tell he wished he could simply point to the four embossed pieces of paper and end the conversation right there. Like Cynthia, he had preferred his father and resented Agnes for outliving him. Only Denny loved Agnes best. "She's fine," Jeffrey said about Katie. "I don't want her to turn out like Cynthia."

"Cynthia's in terrific shape for a woman her age."

"We want Katie to worry about more important things than how she looks."

"Then I hope you're happy when she's a fat, braless spinster."

"I'll be delighted," Jeffrey said. "I'll be over the flipping moon."

Mildred still braided Katie's hair in the mornings, twining the clumps into one long rope while the girl ate sugary cereal. Agnes had been able to French braid her own hair by the time she was seven, and before she turned ten, she could cook breakfast for her younger siblings and iron clothes and haggle with the grocer. But Katie was as much a child as her little brothers, and Jeffrey and Mildred saw nothing wrong with that.

Agnes hated the sight of the pointed, sore-looking protrusions under the unicorns and princesses on Katie's T-shirts, and, last year, back when she was still driving, she had gone to Penney's and bought the girl a training bra—pink with a blue rosette between the cups. When Katie came in from the lake that day with a pack of her cousins, the bunch of them trailing sand all over the white carpet (what a mistake that carpet was), Agnes had presented her with the paper bag. Katie had looked inside and then up at Agnes, her eyes full of tears. Shame how that boy of Denny's had torn the bag from Katie and waved the bra, which cost fifteen dollars, in the air before wrapping it around his own naked little torso. Still, why hadn't Mildred convinced Katie to wear the damn thing? You could see her nipples plain as day.

"She'll wear one in her own time," Mildred always said.

Agnes had tried to phone Katie's real mother, Jeffrey's ex, but her number had changed and Jeffrey would not give her the new one.

Katie stepped out onto the dock and proceeded carefully down the planks, maneuvering first around Jeffrey and her stepmother—Jeffrey had one hand on Mildred's bare stomach—and then around Denny and Pam and then Cynthia, who was talking,

talking, talking to Pam, heedless of Brandon, who had left the cedars and taken up pitching rocks into the lake with the same broken overhand. Katie walked with her arms held out at her sides in a way that would have been like a ballerina's if she weren't so stout. Phillip had always run headlong down the dock and leapt off in a shallow dive angled to keep him clear of the big rocks on the bottom, ratcheting his arms forward into a long blade and bending at the waist just so before cutting into the water. At her snail's pace, Katie was finally nearing the end when one of Denny's boys raced out after her. He hurdled the adults in four quick leaps, running full-tilt down the boards like Phillip. "Don't," Agnes cried, smacking the window with her palm. "Don't do that!"

But the boy had already darted around Katie and was down in the green water with a mighty splash. The lake was shallower than in Phillip's day. The big snows had stopped coming. Ugly weeds and skinny saplings grew up through the rocks where before they would have drowned. Twenty years ago, the first section of the dock could be on pure sand and the far end would reach water deep enough to swim. Now there were ten yards of rocks to be traversed between the beach and the dock, as though the lake were pulling away, forsaking the house. Jeffrey and Denny had made a kind of gangway there, slimy boards flat on the rocks. More boys, inspired by the splash, abandoned their rock castles and holes to China and went whooping and running after the first one. Katie lowered herself over the dock's edge and stood waist-deep in the water as they thundered past. The boys were jumping too soon, too quickly. The water wasn't deep enough for so many lemmings, that was obvious, but Jeffrey and Denny and their wives did not stir. Cynthia shaded her eyes and watched the children vanish off the end. Brandon was still on the beach, throwing rocks.

"Carlotta!" Agnes called over the television. "Carlotta, I need you! Carlotta!"

Carlotta appeared at the crook of the stairs in yellow cleaning gloves.

Agnes deplored her finger for trembling as she pointed out the window. "Tell them they can't do that. It isn't safe. They'll break their necks. Go out and tell them."

Tugging off her gloves, Carlotta came down the stairs and went out the sliding door onto the narrow balcony. "Hey! Hey! Hey, listen!" Carlotta's accent was stronger when she was shouting. "Grandma wants you to be careful!"

Denny called something up that Agnes could not quite hear. "What did he say?" she demanded when Carlotta slid the door closed again.

"He said thanks. He said they told the kids to be careful already."

"No." Agnes was shaking her head. "No, they didn't tell the kids anything, and I didn't tell you to tell them to be careful. I told you to make them stop. Would you go back out there, please, and tell them to stop."

Carlotta looked unhappily out the window. Agnes knew she was being crotchety and ungenerous, an old lady, but she didn't know what else to be. Most of the time, she did not notice her own ill temper, or at least she didn't have to feel bad about it, because only Carlotta was around. The boys had swum out into deep water and were splashing and dunking each other. Brandon, who could not or would not swim, had given up throwing rocks and returned to whipping the trees. Mildred's toddler was being dangled by Jeffrey over the edge of the dock so his toes plunged in and out of the water, and Katie was wading through the shallows, bending now and then to retrieve an interesting pebble. Carlotta went outside, this time pulling the door shut behind her. She spoke over the railing again, and Jeffrey pushed himself up on one elbow to listen. Agnes tapped on the window, then again, harder. Jeffrey heaved himself up and came walking up the beach.

"What did you tell him?" she said when Carlotta came back in.

"I said you wanted them to stop. Now I'm going to make your lunch, and then it's time for me to go home."

Jeffrey's step crunched on the gravel path. Agnes turned up the volume on the television. A news program was on, hosted by a man who felt like Agnes did: that the world was being overrun by the stupid and the immoral.

"You don't have to worry, Mom," Jeffrey said when he came inside. "Why don't you come down? The fresh air will do you good." He had to speak up over the TV. Jeffrey looked at the screen and shook his head in that mournful, superior way he had. "Why do you watch this nonsense?"

"He doesn't suffer fools."

"He gets the fools all riled up."

"So your mother is a fool."

"You and Dad campaigned for Kennedy, for God's sake. For all the Kennedys."

"Not for Teddy," Agnes said. "Not for president, anyway."

"Dad wouldn't have watched this crap."

"Jeffrey, what's the point of talking about what a dead person would watch on TV?"

He didn't bother to hide his exasperation. "I'm just wondering what *happened* to you."

"I grew up," she snapped. "I learned the world is complicated." Idealism irritated her now. The man on the television, his face flushed in anger, offered a kind of companionship. She would not tell Jeffrey that she had simply been in love with JFK. She had campaigned for him so she could spend entire days talking about him. He was the most charismatic man alive and a Catholic to boot. She hadn't known about the womanizing, or how his tan was a symptom of Addison's disease, or that his speechwriter had probably written *Profiles in Courage*. When he was killed, she had transferred her love to Bobby, who had seemed like a consolation from God, something like the Resurrection. And then Bobby was shot, and her faith had wavered—she could not see the plan. And then Teddy was disgraced and now dead, too. Even John-John, that poor little boy saluting his father's casket, was dead. God's plan was full of red herrings, double crosses, blind sacrifices. What if Jack had lived to become frail and liver-spotted with the other ex-presidents? What if Bobby had not been shot? What would have happened to Nixon and his tape recorders? Would Phillip's youngest brother have died in Vietnam? Would her grandchildren live in a world of peace and justice, or, through some incalculable twist, would they all be gone, lost in a nuclear annihilation kept down a silent hallway of unutilized destinies? How benign Vietnam and Cuba seemed as countries now, how insignificant. Perhaps her children's fears about a new set of far-flung places would someday seem quaint. Hope for the future lay in the impotence of the past. She had to believe that God would only *hint* at annihilation.

Jeffrey said, "I guess it doesn't really matter."

Agnes's attention had drifted to the lake, the boys swimming back to shore. "What doesn't matter?" she said.

"You're not an elected official. You're not a policy maker. You can watch what you want."

"You're saying it doesn't matter what I think."

Jeffrey folded his arms. "Not on a practical level."

"I vote," she said.

A wry expression traveled across his face, and, too late, he pursed his lips to hide it. "Go on," she said. "Say it. Say, 'Not for long.'" Carlotta, eyes down, brought a sandwich on a plate and a glass of iced tea and set them on the coffee table beside the muffin.

Jeffrey heaved one of his long-suffering sighs. "Why don't you come down to the beach?"

"They could come inside if they wanted to see me."

"They're little kids," Jeffrey said. "They like the beach. If you were cooped up in here with eight kids, you'd be apoplectic."

A shout from outside. Katie was charging though the water, holding something high above her head.

"What's she have?" Agnes said.

"How should I know?" said Jeffrey.

Katie came tearing up the beach and up the gravel path and burst through the kitchen door. Dripping water onto the white carpet, she said, "It's his ring! I found Papa's Vanderbilt ring."

"No," Agnes said.

"Look!"

The ring, when Katie dropped it into her palm, was still cold from the lake. Agnes's stiff heart struggled in her chest.

"Mom?" said Jeffrey. "Are you all right?"

The ring was an ill omen, a memento coughed up by death.

"Did I do something wrong?" Katie asked, looking to Jeffrey.

Agnes made herself smile. "Oh," she said, breathless, "isn't it wonderful? What a wonderful surprise."

CARLOTTA WAS GONE, and Agnes had forgotten to tell her about the spider. A stray breeze caught the bit of web, up in the corner, and for a second the creature trembled and seemed to be alive. Jeffrey and Denny had taken the children to town in the boat for ice cream even though their dinners would be ruined. They had promised to be careful, to watch all the children at all times, to make everyone wear life vests. Only the women were left: Mildred and Pam down in the basement going through old family photographs of people they would never know, and Cynthia in the kitchen fixing dinner and talking about the new man who did not love her. "It's good I'm away for this week," she said, shouting over the evening news and the sound of her own knife on the chopping board. "Let him see how he likes it when I'm gone."

Phillip's ring was on the windowsill. The onyx was scratched and the lake had buffed away the engraving. Only the V, DER, and IL were legible; Phillip's initials had been entirely effaced. The gold, though, once Carlotta had rubbed it with some jewelry cleaner, was still lustrous. Everyone thought Katie's find was a miracle, but Agnes could not shake the feeling that the ring was the short straw, the stopped clock, the black butterfly. Upstairs in her jewelry box she still had the fifty-cent piece Phillip had found near the dock with his metal detector, and although she had scraped the algae from Kennedy's profile, a dark, oxidized rime had appeared in its place and refused to budge. Poor Phillip, buried without his ring. She was tempted to throw it back into the lake, but that would only disappoint Katie. She would have to remember to request that the ring be buried with her, next to Phillip, and that would have to be close enough. When she had first been diagnosed, friends said she could *beat this thing*, even though the doctors had made it clear that there would be no beating of the thing, that the thing could only be mollified, distracted, bribed. Bit-by-counterfeit-bit the walls of her heart were being bricked up with alien proteins. What did people think, that even if by magic her heart did not harden into an immobile knot she would sail on forever? The inevitable was the inevitable. She had never been a procrastinator. *Hail Mary*, she thought, turning the ring over in her hand.

When Agnes had called Cynthia to tell her about the diagnosis, Cynthia had wept bitterly. "How can this be?" she had warbled. "I never imagined it this way."

Agnes had been confused. "What way?"

"I always thought I would die first. Since I was a little kid I've had a gut feeling that you would outlive me."

"Cynthia, that's ridiculous."

"No, it's true. Whenever I thought about death, I saw you at my funeral, and then I thought that I would be there to welcome everyone to heaven."

Leave it to Cynthia to want to be the tragic flower mown down too soon, to imagine the afterlife as a cocktail party with herself as gracious hostess, offering around pigs in blankets. "You'd better get busy, then," Agnes had said.

When Agnes told Jeffrey what Cynthia had said, he said, "I'm sure she didn't mean anything by it. Death is pastel fantasia for most people. No one ever quite believes they won't find a way out of it. But it's the simplest fact that there aren't different degrees of mortality. Everyone is equally doomed from the second they're conceived."

"Don't you think I know that?" Agnes replied, irritated.

How had she raised children who were so afraid to grieve? They were strangers on the other end of the phone, banging around the iron tunnels of grief for an escape hatch. Cynthia would prefer to be mourned than to mourn. Jeffrey styled himself as an unimpressed Hercules or Odysseus or Dante returned from the underworld, all-knowing and blasé. Only Denny, gentle Denny, the lone believer among her children, had said the right thing. God was waiting for her, Denny said. God would take care of her. Agnes had been driven almost to distraction by the moans and whimpers of her own dying mother. She had wanted to tell her to bear up, to quiet down. Mothers, whose bodies are tunnels from the first underworld, are expected by their children to lead them into the grave with stoic acceptance. Parents are supposed to face their deaths with good humor so their children might be reassured. If the mother, crying and clutching, clings to ebbing life, then what of the terrified, bereft child when she is finally swept away? What child could stay close to God after such a trauma? Agnes wanted to die bravely, to show her children how she trusted in God so that they might also trust in God, but they were making it difficult. She feared they would make a mess of everything once she was gone. Phillip had not needed to be brave. Phillip had snored his way into heaven.

"We talked about it once," Cynthia said, crossing to the liquor cabinet with a tumbler of ice and wiping her eyes with the back of her wrist. "He said—God, onions absolutely kill me—he said he wasn't sure he believed in love. And I said, 'What is there to believe? Look around you—love is a fact. Love is everywhere.' But how do you convince someone of that, you know? My theory is that he expects love to feel different than it does, like those women you read about who think they have indigestion but are actually pregnant. He thinks what he's feeling is nothing, but really he's feeling everything. It's just his expectations are too high."

THE BOAT RETURNED when the afternoon had gone slanted and yellow. Something was wrong. The children, who would ordinarily be pouring like rats onto the dock while Jeffrey was still maneuvering the boat onto its lift, sat motionless, crowded together in their too-big orange life vests like survivors of a disaster at sea. One of them must be dead, drowned to punish Agnes for her self-pity, her false forbearance, her secret conviction—despite all her protests—that her death was something special. Her heart contorted itself in time to a limping beat. She pressed a hand to her sternum. Then Denny, dripping wet, stepped onto the dock with Brandon in his arms, wrapped in something blue. Cynthia was standing at the sink, ambushed into stillness by the sight of the boat. Then she was out the door, down the path.

Brandon was not dead. Denny set him down on the rocks, where he stood chewing the edge of his blue wrapper. Cynthia billowed up with flailing arms. Denny spoke to her, explaining. Cynthia dropped to her knees, took Brandon by the shoulders, and shook him twice, hard, before clutching him to her.

In 1963, Agnes, tight as a drum with Cynthia, had become convinced that the baby would be stillborn. She had taken Jeffrey's toy stethoscope and pressed it to her belly, straining for a heartbeat but only hearing the whooshing currents of her internal sea. All day she lay in bed on her back, letting Jeffrey and Denny run wild. Phillip had come home without calling out his usual hello. He seemed to take a long time to hang up his hat and coat, and when he came into the bedroom with the boys in a rowdy, hungry procession behind him, he had lain down beside her, smelling of booze, and put a hand on her belly. He didn't want her to get excited, he said, but something had happened. Could she promise to stay calm? Yes, she said. Kennedy was dead, he told her, shot, and she was flooded with relief that the baby would not be stillborn. She had misinterpreted the sadness radiating from God. Phillip had not understood why she smiled.

Cynthia had been born two days later, on the day Jack Ruby killed Lee Harvey Oswald, almost at the same moment. While Cynthia was being pulled into the world with forceps and the assassin sent to his reckoning, Agnes had been under anesthetic, drifting through a purple nothing. Afterward, returning to consciousness, she had become aware of someone crying. A nurse was sitting in a chair not far from her bed, a white shape with a bowed, white-crowned head, like a swan, one arm crossed over her waist and the other folded against her chest, her knuckles against her eyes.

"It's dead?" Agnes had whispered, able to think of only one reason anyone would cry.

"Oh!" said the nurse, startled. "You're awake."

Agnes tried again. "The baby is dead?"

The nurse dabbed around her run mascara with a handkerchief. "What?"

"Why are you crying?"

The other woman hesitated. Her lips trembled and stuck out like a bill. "It's too much for me," she warbled. "Someone went and shot Lee Harvey Oswald. It was on TV and everything. Shot with the cops right there and everything, like a dog. He got what he deserved, if you ask me, but it's all just too much."

"But the baby is fine?" Agnes said.

The nurse blew her nose. "Yes, yes, of course. A healthy girl."

Agnes subsided onto her pillows. She saw Lee Harvey Oswald, conceited-faced and with hair like a schoolboy's, looking at Kennedy through the gates of heaven, reaching through the bars like a beggar. Kennedy was smiling and wearing a white suit. He would forgive Oswald, but God would not. The nurse opened the door to leave, and Agnes roused herself.

"Nurse," she said. "You won't let my husband in here until I've had time to put on my face, will you?"

"Of course not," the nurse said.

*

ON THE WAY BACK FROM TOWN, Brandon had wriggled out of his life vest, leaped off the back of the boat into the wake, and sunk beneath the surface.

"He looked right at me before he went under, Ma," Denny said, shivering in his wet clothes. "It was the strangest thing."

Jeffrey put in, "I didn't even know anything had happened. I just heard the kids scream, and by then Denny had already gone in after him."

Brandon was sitting at the end of the davenport, just beyond Agnes's slippered feet. The blue cloth—Jeffrey's windbreaker, stitched with the crest of his golf club—was still over Brandon's shoulders. The other boys, stunned into quiet, sprawled on the floor. Someone had turned off the TV. Katie, in her skirted bathing suit and orange life vest, sat in an armchair, her hands clamped between her plump knees.

"Why did you take off your life vest?" Cynthia demanded of Brandon, bending over him. "You *never* take off your life vest. You could have died. You nearly gave your uncles a heart attack." She glanced at Agnes, sorry to have mentioned heart attacks.

"Why don't you ask him why he jumped?" Agnes said, feeling cruel. "Isn't that the important question?"

"He has these impulses," Cynthia said defiantly. "He walks into the road, he climbs onto the roof, he jumps off boats now. I don't know how to make him understand that he can't *do* these things. He doesn't understand that the real world is different from his imagination. He's a time bomb. What can I do? What can I do? Brandon, what can I do? I would be so lonely without you. Mommy would die without you, Brandon."

Brandon watched his feet in their Velcroed sandals strain for the edge of the coffee table and then flop back to dangle above the white carpet. He looked up. "Why didn't you eat your muffin?" he asked Agnes.

"Because it was stale."

Mildred picked up the plate and carried it into the kitchen. She dumped the muffin in the trash and the plate in the sink.

"What's 'stale?'"

"You know what 'stale' means," Cynthia said. "Don't pretend you don't."

"All of you go on for a while," Agnes said. "Let him sit here with me."

Recognizing an order, they left. Mildred led a weeping Cynthia down to the basement, and the others drifted back outside to catch the last light, or upstairs for the first shift of baths, except for Katie, who stayed in the armchair.

"What's stale?" Brandon asked again.

"It's when bread gets old and dry and tastes bad," said Agnes.

"I knew he was going to do something on the boat," Katie said abruptly. "It's why I stayed in my bathing suit, so I'd be ready to help. I had a feeling."

"Everyone's safe now," Agnes said. "You can take off your vest."

Katie played with the straps, but left it on. Her face hung in the brilliant orange rectangle as though in the gallows. "Isn't it weird when you have a feeling that turns out to be right? Like today I had a feeling that I would find Papa's ring, and I did. Don't you think there's something weird about that?"

"Just coincidence," Agnes said. "No one can see the future."

Katie looked at her shrewdly, puzzling through something. "I can't see the future, but sometimes I think I can feel it. I like that kind of stuff—stuff that's halfway between real and imaginary."

"Like what?" said Brandon, who was staring out at the lake and had not seemed to be listening.

"Well," said Katie, "like aliens, or shadows, or dreams that come true." She nodded, satisfied with her examples.

"You're not psychic," Agnes told her. "No one is."

"Except God," Katie said.

"God's not psychic, he's omniscient," Agnes said, studying her granddaughter with new interest. "Do you believe in God?"

"Oh, yes," the girl replied with fervor. "I do. I absolutely do, but don't tell Daddy because he doesn't like it. Mildred understands. She promised to keep it a secret. We tell Daddy we're going out to brunch, and then we go to church."

"To a Catholic church?"

Katie's head tilted sideways in the life vest as she thought. "I don't think so. It's a Christian church."

"Catholics are Christians."

"They are?"

"You should know what kind of church you're going to."

"I'll ask Mildred."

"I think," Agnes ventured, "that sometimes when we're especially close to God, He gives us these feelings about the future."

"I thought of that," Katie said, lighting up. "I thought God might be behind it."

"Yes?" In spite of herself, Agnes was eager to know if Katie's feelings were anything like her own. But she was wary of giving the child false hope, convincing her she was a prophet. She looked at Brandon, but he had his cheek down on the davenport's armrest, his hair still damp. "What else?" she asked Katie. "What did you think God was trying to tell you?"

"Just that something bad might happen. I don't know. Like I should be prepared for something bad."

Agnes studied her granddaughter's round, earnest face. Denny was the believer, but Jeffrey had fathered the believer. Agnes's blood was strong. There was hope for this girl, even though her willingness to believe in her own premonitions made Agnes uneasy. Who could tell what was a false alarm of the nerves and what was the voice of God? Who could distinguish destiny from accident? Sometimes she felt exasperated with God for not speaking more plainly.

A whacking noise came from outside. Jeffrey was standing on the end of the dock, hitting golf balls into the lake. Agnes pounded on the window with her fist. Brandon woke with a start and sat up. "Jeffrey! Jeffrey!" she shouted. "Don't do that!" Jeffrey swung again. A tiny splash rose up in the distance.

"Why shouldn't he do that?" Brandon asked.

"He's polluting the lake."

"Polluting?"

"Making dirty. Filling with trash."

The boy nodded, watching her. "Would my mom die without me?" he asked.

"No," said Agnes, "but she would be so sad."

"She always says she would die without me."

"She wants you to be more careful."

"Why did you jump?" Katie asked.

Brandon frowned at his sandals. "I just wanted to," he said.

"Sweetheart," said Agnes, fearful of his answer, "did you think you wanted to drown?"

Brandon looked up and smiled. "No, I thought I could swim."

LATER JEFFREY AND DENNY BUILT A BONFIRE on the beach even though Agnes told them it was too breezy. The sparks could fly into the cedars and start a fire. The house could burn down. Pam had found graham crackers and a package of Hershey bars in the cupboard, and Mildred went out to buy marshmallows. The children ran around the beach in the twilight trying to find the perfect pointed sticks. Agnes turned up the television.

The sky was dark and the fire had burned down to a smoldering heap of orange and black when the first bottle rocket went up, trailing yellow sparks and a high whistle. Then there was another one and another. Jeffrey had promised her no fireworks. The children could lose their fingers. The house could be burned to nothing. Around the fire, the children had sparklers, and beyond the spitting balls of light she caught glimpses of their orange faces, clouded with smoke. She tried to pick out Katie but couldn't. On the dock, Jeffrey lit something that shot up with a boom and released a shower of purple fire. The beach looked like a battlefield. A cheer went up from the children. Agnes rapped on the glass.

Shimmering trails of champagne bubbles fell from the sky. *Boom, boom, boom.* Agnes felt the percussions in her chest. A pinwheel screeched and spun on the dock, its fractured reflection spinning in the water. The sparklers danced around the fire. She pounded on the window with her fist, but the explosions continued. Red, blue, green, white, pink. "Stop it!" she shouted. "It's dangerous!" Her heart lurched, but she gave the window one last thump. Well, to hell with them. They couldn't even tell her the truth about the fireworks. They just did what they wanted, trusting she wouldn't be able to stop them. They didn't care if she was angry.

Another boom, a luminous rain. She couldn't stand it—she would be heard. Trembling with effort, she pushed herself up off the cushions. Her intention was to go out the sliding door and shout down at them until they stopped, but once she was on her feet, a crippled ox started galloping in her chest. The tightness was too much. She wobbled, and then she was falling backwards. In the window was the reflection of the television and beyond it a red firework bloomed and faded. She landed on the coffee table and tumbled over, coming to rest on the white carpet with her legs up in the air, her bathrobe bunched around her thighs. Damn Jeffrey and his fireworks. She tried to cry out but found she could not. A spark ascended and burst into a canopy of light. As her heart hesitated, she tried to remember a prayer.

WINTER ELDERS

from **vol. 8, no. 2**

Shawn Vestal

THEY MATERIALIZED WITH THE FIRST SNOW. That was how Bradshaw would always remember it. He was standing at the living room window, listening to Cheryl shush the baby, when he saw specks fluttering like ash against a smoky sky, and then caught sight of someone on his front step, though he hadn't noticed anyone coming up the walk. He could see about an inch of a man's left side at the window's border—an arm in a dark suit and a boyish hand holding a book bound in black leather. He knew instantly that there was another suit and another leather-bound volume out there, a companion to complete the pair: missionaries.

Bradshaw opened the door and blocked the frame. Body language was everything. Announce it—*you're not coming in.* On the step were two kids in suits, short hair, name tags. One was tall—taller than Bradshaw, maybe six foot four—and the baby fat on his face had begun to jowlify. The shorter one was younger, with avid eyes and scraped cheeks.

"Brother Bradshaw?" the tall one asked as he looked into the house. "Hi, we're here from the Church."

"I can see that."

"We're just wanting to check in, see if there's anything we can do for you."

"You could clean out my gutters," Bradshaw said. "Or rake the yard."

The little one chuckled, but the tall one looked up at the gutters, spilling over with leaves and twigs. The falling snow had thickened.

"Don't think we won't," he said.

His name tag read ELDER POPE. He would not drop his smile or avert his eyes. There was something stubborn in him and, deeper, the sense that he was proud of his stubbornness. Bradshaw was impressed, a little.

"After you're done you could change the oil in my car," Bradshaw said. "So long as you're just wanting to help."

Elder Pope nodded softly, and pointed with his chin toward the inside of the house.

"Maybe we could come in and discuss your list of chores," he said.

"Right," Bradshaw said.

The littler missionary—his name tag read ELDER WARREN—said, "Could we just talk to you for a few minutes about Jesus Christ?"

"You could not just talk to me for a few minutes about Jesus Christ," Bradshaw said, pushing the door closed slowly against Pope's cheer. "I'd like it if you stopped coming here. Make a note back at the coven."

Through the window in the door, Bradshaw saw Warren turn to go, but Pope stayed, staring for a few seconds.

Bradshaw was twelve years out of the Church and not going back. For a long time, a new set of missionaries had appeared every few months, cloaked in fresh optimism. Each time, Bradshaw's hunger to disappoint them had deepened, until he finally asked them to remove him from the Church rolls for good. To kick him out. It had taken months, but they finally sent him a letter of excommunication, revoking his baptismal blessings and eternal privileges as a member of the Church of Jesus Christ of Latter-day Saints. The letter read like a credit-card cancellation, and he and Cheryl had made much fun of it. "You're out!" she would say, and wrap her arms around his neck, and though he was glad he was out, too, her reaction made him defensive, and he would feel a germ of insult stick and grow. Now, staring at the place in the storm where the missionaries had vanished, he wished he'd asked what brought them back this time.

He heard the baby crying and went to check on him. He found Cheryl bouncing the boy gently, whispering, "And then the pig decided to become a happy pig and spread happiness into the world…"

"Who was it?" she whispered.

"Missionaries."

"You've got to be kidding," she said, bugging her eyes while she swayed and rubbed the baby's back.

"I'm not kidding."

Bradshaw leaned toward the boy and whispered, "Hello, Riley. Hello, Brother Bradshaw."

Cheryl pulled the boy away.

"Don't," she said. "That's not funny."

She was always serious now. Ever since the baby. Earnest. Riley was nine months old, and Bradshaw wondered what had happened to his partner in cynicism. They used to be in complete agreement about this if nothing else: Everything was such bullshit. Everything was so ridiculous. They had been bloodhounds for any trace of sentiment, any note of sincerity, upon which to pounce mockingly; after parties, they competed to do the best eviscerating impressions. New parents, all wide-eyed and self-absorbed, had been a specialty of Cheryl's. Such bullshit, people and their human mess. Now Bradshaw felt abandoned, adrift in his own head and swamped with hot-eyed exhaustion. The boy had started sleeping most of the night, usually waking just once, fussing and whimpering until Cheryl nursed him back to sleep. Bradshaw knew he had it easy by comparison, but still he felt flocked by trouble. Besieged. Once awakened, he would lie there for an hour or more, mind fixed on his current aggravation—an argument at work, something Cheryl had said, some spot of tension with the world. He would dream his constant dream of putting people in their place. Sometimes he lay on his side and watched the boy's head bob as he nursed, and Bradshaw would feel once more the pressure that had arrived with the child—a relentless sense that he was not up to this. That he was not made to be a father.

COMING HOME FROM WORK four days later, Bradshaw swung his car into the driveway, and the headlights washed over two spectral shapes in the grainy dusk. The missionaries. Pope had his hand wrapped around a rake shaft, talking to Warren, who was looking up and nodding. The snow had melted, and gluey brown leaves had been raked into a pile.

The open garage door spread a fan of warm light, but the house was dark. Cheryl and Riley were at her sister's. Bradshaw slammed his car door and only then did Pope look up, lifting his arm in an exaggerated wave, as though he were on a dock greeting a steamer.

"Brother Bradshaw!" he said. "Good evening."

Warren raised a hand briefly. He wore his embarrassment like a shawl.

Bradshaw stepped off the driveway onto the wet lawn, cold air like metal in his sinuses. The rake had been in the garage. They had gone into the garage.

"I bet you never thought we'd take you up on it," Pope said, smiling even as Bradshaw grabbed the rake handle and jerked. Pope held firm for a second, smile widening—in surprise or malevolence, Bradshaw couldn't tell—then let go, sending Bradshaw backward one step. Pope shrugged.

"Sorry," he said.

Warren laughed, snuffling behind his hand. Did he say something? Something to Pope? Bradshaw stared, seething. Breath crowded his lungs, and his vision tightened and blurred. Pope smiled patiently at Bradshaw, lips pressed hammily together. It was the smile of every man he had met in Church, the bishops and first counselors and stake presidents, the benevolent mask, the put-on solemnity, the utter falseness. It was the smile of the men who brought boxes of food when Bradshaw was a teenager and his father wasn't working, the canned meat and bricks of cheese. The men who prayed for his family. Bradshaw's father would disappear, leaving him and his mother to kneel with the men.

Setting the rake against his shoulder, Bradshaw ground the heels of his hands into his eyes. When he opened them, red spots expanded and danced across his vision. The missionaries faded, then clarified.

"Brother Bradshaw?" Pope said.

Bradshaw wanted to swing the rake at Pope's head. To watch his smug eyes pop as the tines sunk in. Why could he not just do it? He never could. Finally, he simply pointed toward the road, eyes averted, finger trembling. As they left, Pope said without looking back, "We'll be praying for you, Brother Bradshaw."

Bradshaw threw down the rake.

"Don't pray for me!" he shouted. "Don't you *dare* pray for me!"

He stopped when he saw his neighbor, Bud Swenson, standing at his mailbox, a handful of envelopes.

Later, after Cheryl returned, he sat on the floor with Riley, trying to get him interested in stacking wooden blocks. It was Tuesday of Thanksgiving week, and Cheryl was making pie crusts. She came in and watched them a moment, and when Bradshaw looked up, wooden block in hand, he was startled to find her on the verge of happy tears. It reminded him of the way his mother would get in church, swept up in the spirit.

"I still can't believe you want to do the whole Thanksgiving thing," Bradshaw said. "With a baby."

"I know," she said. "But I want to. I feel like we're finally a family."

"We are finally a family," he said. "But so what?"

WHEN THE BOY WAS BORN, Bradshaw kept waiting for it to happen. The flash of light. The surge of joy. Some brightness shining through the visible world. He had been so sure this would be it—the moment that he felt what everyone else seemed to feel, what his mother felt, what all the other Mormons felt, what people in other churches felt, what even people like Cheryl felt, people who were hostile to the very idea of religion: some spirit in the material. The thing behind the thing. Cheryl called it "an animating force."

"There has to be something, doesn't there?" she said. "When you really think about it. Something larger than us?"

Sometimes he thought she was right, and sometimes he thought she was wrong, and the fact that he could not decide had given him a sense that he was failing in a fundamental duty to believe. In something or nothing. He had always been that way—back as far as he could remember, his mind fixed on the yes or no of it, and always shifting. He recalled wondering, when he was baptized at age eight, why all these spiritual people needed a mime show like baptism. Instead of anything transcendent, he had felt awakened to the concrete moment—the water in the font, the thick wet of the baptismal garment.

As a teenager, at Church camp, he had watched as the boys and girls stood up at testimony meeting and swore they had faith in the Lord, that they had a testimony this was the true church. They wept and trembled, one after another, and soon he stood too and choked on his tears, swore he had been given a testimony. It was as though a bright beam of joy was pulsing from the heavens into the core of the Earth, threaded directly through him. But by that night, he felt it fading, and within days it was gone. He told himself that what had happened was not genuine, that he had simply been weak, swept up.

When Riley was born, the moment assaulted him in its earthbound reality—the blood and mucus under the bright lights of the delivery room, the boy's pinched eyes, magenta skin, clammy hair, and that cord, that bunched gray-red tube of matter and fluid. The moment arrived like an undeniable announcement—this is the one thing. His son struck him not as an angel or a spirit, but as an animal, a creature who would die without his care, a creature who would die, a creature bound to other creatures. Bradshaw pressed the scissors and the blades separated the boy from his mother.

Later, Cheryl told him she'd been overwhelmed by something she could not define. "Just some kind of... whatever," she said, and laughed. In the first days of it, when they would find themselves up at 3 a.m., waiting for Riley to stop gurgling in the bassinet, she would talk about it.

"Isn't it crazy?" she said, in a whisper of wonder. "It really is a miracle. It really is what people say."

She waited for him to answer. A pale parallelogram of summer moonlight lay over the closet door; he could smell cut grass outside, the cool of a sprinkler. What could he tell her? That he felt like he was being filled with life and drained of life all at once? That he had not imagined the consuming force of it? That he ached for the way he used to be filled with himself, only himself, all Bradshaw?

THE DAY AFTER THANKSGIVING, it snowed almost a foot. Everything rounded, muffled. Snow balanced in strips along fence tops and tree limbs; footsteps left deep wells across lawns. It snowed another five inches overnight, and the next day dawned bright and icy. That afternoon, Bradshaw shoveled the walk for the third time in two days. His neighbor Bud's German shepherd, Jake, a genial but bloodthirsty-looking dog, came over to be petted. He and Bud shouted pleasantries and shared weather statistics. Bradshaw heard footsteps squeaking and scrunching around the corner. Later he would think he had sensed the missionaries' presence before they appeared, trudging down the street since half the sidewalks were unshoveled.

Bradshaw took Jake by the collar, bent down and whispered in his ear, "Go get 'em, boy. Sic 'em, Jakie," and the dog braced. Bud called, "You're not telling him any of my secrets, are ya?" and laughed, and Bradshaw ignored him and watched the missionaries approach. They did not angle toward his walkway, but kept to the road, and as they drew closer Pope raised a hand and shouted, "Hello, Brother Bradshaw," and Bradshaw said, "Sic 'em, boy!" Jake shot off, barking ferociously, while Bud shouted at him to stop.

Pope scrambled back, slipping, but Warren stood in place. He held out one hand, palm down, and said, "Hey there. Good boy. Good boy. That's a good boy," in a soothing voice. The dog stopped a few feet from Warren and kept barking.

"Hey there, you're a good boy," Warren said.

He brought his other hand from his coat pocket and presented it, palm up. The dog stopped barking. His tail began to wag. He stepped toward the missionary and started to eat from his hand. Bradshaw stared. His stomach splashed like a boisterous sea. Warren patted the dog on the head, and the dog looked back at Bradshaw, tongue out, tail whipping the frigid air.

Bud called, "Come here, dammit," and glared at Bradshaw. The dog obeyed. Pope and Warren stood looking back and forth between Bradshaw and Bud, and when Bud shook his head and went toward his house, the missionaries turned and approached Bradshaw. He thought what he was feeling then—ribs like hot, heavy irons in his chest—was despair, true despair in the face of the grinding, unbeatable world.

"Missionaries always carry dog treats," Pope said, smiling once again.

Bradshaw said, "Look..." and Pope stepped to him, face bright with cold.

"May I ask you a favor, Brother Bradshaw? I know this sounds crazy, but could we possibly come into your home for a moment and warm up? That's all—just warm up? We're awfully cold right now, and my companion here is in worse shape than me."

Warren shivered, and his bright nose dripped. Bradshaw felt weakened by the demand. What kind of person was he, that he wanted so badly to say no?

"Okay," he said, turning and heading up the walk. Inside, they stood on the entry rug, in coats and hats, ringed by a dusting of snow.

"I'll be right back," Bradshaw said, and went to the baby's room. Cheryl was sitting by the rocker, reading a magazine while Riley napped. When Bradshaw told her what he'd done, she rolled her eyes and said, "It's your mess." He returned to the living room and saw the missionaries standing there, still bundled up. They seemed small. Young.

"Why don't you sit down for a second?" Bradshaw said.

Warren dragged a glove across his nose. Pope unzipped his coat and pulled off his hat. They unsheathed and sat down on his couch, and Bradshaw sat in a chair.

"Don't get any ideas," he said.

"Well," Pope said. "I wonder if I might ask you just one question."

Unbelievable. "You might," he said.

Cheryl had moved to the dining room. He could hear her clicking calculator keys, tearing off checks.

"I just wonder if you've ever read the Book of Mormon all the way through and prayed about it?" Pope said. "Just gave it one real chance."

The question shocked Bradshaw. He'd come to feel that it wasn't what Pope was up to after all. That he was here for something else. "I don't..." He couldn't figure out how to begin. "No, I haven't. I mean—you know what I think about when I think about the Church? The stupid seagulls." Bradshaw hadn't really thought about the seagulls in years. "How those bugs were eating all the pioneers' crops and great clouds of seagulls came and ate them up. Right? In Salt Lake? Saved everybody from starving? Divine intervention?"

"What do you think about it?" Pope asked.

"What a bunch of bullshit it is. I mean, birds eat bugs."

"I had some relatives there for that," Warren said. "Ancestors."

"Yeah? Okay. Whatever. Let's just say it's a nice story. A nice little *tale*."

Pope seemed confused. "Just keep an open mind, is all I'm saying."

"That'd be a bit too open for me," Bradshaw said, and now he was feeling better, kind of energized. "I mean, actually, that'd be way, way too open."

The gears in Pope's smile slipped. Bradshaw continued, "Really, guys, that book is no more an ancient record than I am the Duke of Scotland," and the air in his lungs felt good again. "Maybe *you'd* like to keep an open mind to a few things. The historical record, for instance..."

A gate unlocked inside him. The beasts trampled out.

"I mean, right there on the first page or two, you've got a guy named Sam. Sam!" he said. His voice felt harsh and spiny in his throat. He was thinking that he'd really start—really blast every story about Joseph Smith, about the "translation" of the Book of Mormon, about everything. Make the stupid fuckers see.

"Sam! Sam! Just some Central American dude, two thousand years ago, named Sam! Not Quetzalcoatl or some shit. Sam!" He couldn't stop saying it. Fury tightened his scalp, the sockets of his eyes.

A long wail came from the back bedroom. Bradshaw stopped and realized how loud he'd been. He looked at Warren gazing forlornly at his hands. Pope kept his eyes on Bradshaw, looking resigned and sad. Bradshaw heard Cheryl stand and walk to the nursery. Hard, angry steps. He sat hot-faced and trembling, embarrassment seeping in. The baby stopped crying, and still no one spoke.

Cheryl walked into the room, gently rocking the boy.

"I don't want you people in my house," she said, in her quiet-baby hush. "My husband can't seem to tell you that, but I'm telling you now. If you come back again, I'm going to call the police. I'll get a restraining order."

Warren said, "Yes, ma'am," and Pope's eyes bored into the floor. They rose and shuffled toward the door. Drew on their coats and hats. Warren stepped out, but Pope stopped and looked at Bradshaw.

"I just want to say, before I leave you alone," he whispered, "that I know the gospel is true. I know it. I know that it is true because God has told me it is true, and not because I'm special, or different than anyone else on this earth, but because He loves us all, all of us, all His children, and He will give us this knowledge if we ask Him for it. I promise you that, Brother Bradshaw. I swear it."

Pope, flushed and wet-eyed, ducked his head and left. Bradshaw felt an emotional swell that recalled that day when he had stood before the others at Church camp and wept. It was not that Pope was right and he was wrong, and not that Pope was wrong and he was right. It was that Pope had something he could not have, and he would spend his life not having it.

THE SNOW REFUSED TO STOP. Berms piled head high. Enormous icicles grew down from gutters to the ground. Bradshaw was shoveling the walk one night when he heard someone shout, "Hello!" He looked up and saw two shapes across the street, passing out of the street light and into the gray mist. One tall, one short. Both turned their shadowed faces to him as they passed.

The next night, dropping cans and newspapers into the recycling bin, he thought he saw a figure move behind a tree in his side yard. He walked toward it, stepping into calf-deep snow in his slippers. He thought he heard the soft crunch of a footstep.

"Pope!" he whispered harshly. "You better not let me find you out here."

Bradshaw's words billowed before him.

"I will make you wish you'd never been born."

Silence, but for the radical drumming of his heart.

"You're going to be in a world of hurt."

These were things Bradshaw's father used to say when he was angry, and they were things that Bradshaw had fantasized about saying to others, as his stronger self. His fantasy self.

"I swear to God I'll stomp a mudhole in your ass."

Bradshaw's father had only mentioned God when he was issuing a threat. His mom had dragged them all to church on Sundays, to the tan brick ward house on Main Street. Everyone could tell his Dad wasn't a part of it, just by the way he stared out windows or into walls. After his mom died and he lived with his father in a downtown apartment, they stopped going to church altogether. When the men from the ward came on Sundays to visit, his father wouldn't answer the door. They would sit inside, hold their breath, and wait for the footsteps to disappear down the hall.

"Pope," Bradshaw whispered, shivering, feet and legs soaked. "Pope."

Snowflakes began to fall. Bradshaw looked up into the purple sky, the glowing winter night. Snow plunged and swerved downward, and he felt drawn upward into a dark heaven. He was weightless. He would never stomp a mudhole in anyone's ass.

The next morning, before work, Bradshaw walked to the pine trees in the side yard—the huge, sixty-year-old tree and the littler pine tucked against it. The snow was sunken with footprints, drifted over by snow, crisscrossing, back and forth. He could not tell where they came from or where they were going.

RILEY WOKE THE NEXT DAY with a fever, cranky and wailing. Bradshaw tried to take his temperature under his arm, but he wouldn't stay still.

"Maybe we ought to try the rectal thermometer," Cheryl said.

"Maybe *you* ought to try the rectal thermometer," Bradshaw said. He put his hand on the baby's forehead. "He doesn't feel *that* hot."

By the time Bradshaw returned from work, the boy was blazing: 101, 102. He wouldn't take breast or bottle. His diaper had been dry for hours. He was radiant in Bradshaw's arms. Cheryl looked as if she hadn't left his room all day—still in her sweatpants and T-shirt, fretful and pale.

"This is getting worse, right?" Bradshaw said.

"I think so. I'm not sure."

Bradshaw cupped the boy's head in his palm. It felt like a stone on a riverbank, some noon in July. Riley wouldn't stop whimpering and fidgeting, rubbing his soft fingers around his face. Cheryl tried to give him a dropper full of pink Tylenol, but he spat it out.

"What did the doctor say?" Bradshaw asked.

"Come in if it gets worse."

"This is worse. I think it's worse."

"We should go. Shouldn't we go?"

Bradshaw drove slowly on the snow-packed roads, leaning forward with both hands on the wheel. About halfway there, three large snowflakes landed on the windshield and melted.

"It can't snow anymore," Cheryl said. "It can't."

At the hospital, the ER nurse said, "Oh dear, this little guy's dehydrated," and they hooked him up to an IV. The sight of the needle invading his son's arm, of the dry skin cracking his lower lip, made Bradshaw feel helpless—proof that he was being tasked beyond his capabilities. Cheryl hustled around the room, checking the diaper bag for wipes, watching Riley's skin color, rushing out to the nurses with questions. Bradshaw sat beside the boy, sliding crushed ice into his mouth. Soon, Riley was cooler and calmer, but the doctor wanted to keep him overnight, so Bradshaw left to get toothbrushes and underwear.

Outside, new snow was piling onto old. Cars stuck at stoplights, spinning as the lights went green. Bradshaw drove slowly along the busy arterial. When he got to his neighborhood, he built up as much speed as he could before turning onto the unplowed street, but he immediately bogged down. Halfway up the block, he spun to a stop and sat there, breathing loudly, mind hurtling—the boy would be okay, no thanks to him. But Riley's illness, his frailty and animal need, had sent an exact message: if the boy died—not now, he was not dying now, Bradshaw knew—Bradshaw would die as well. Not that he would kill himself, though he thought he would, but that he had become something else entirely, a new being who would only exist so long as his son existed. If the boy died, Bradshaw would become a ghost. He sat in his car as his breath fogged the windshield. He would never be free. He tried to slow his breathing and could not.

He climbed out, locked the car, and started walking the five blocks home. The storm blew sideways. Flakes clung to his eyelashes and nostrils. Trudging clumsily in his snow boots, he was exhausted by the time he reached his house, dark and unlit. He started up the sidewalk, and a voice came from the darkness. "Hey there, Brother Bradshaw."

Bradshaw stopped. He looked at his house and couldn't see Pope anywhere.

"Sorry to surprise you like this," the voice said.

It was coming from the edge of the front patio, from the two metal chairs they never used. Bradshaw stared, narrowed his eyes. He thought he saw a shape in one of the chairs. He took several slow steps toward it.

"Pope?"

"Who else?"

Now the shape seemed to be standing. He could hear Pope smiling. Bradshaw was glad he had returned. Furiously thrilled. He took another step, and noticed that someone had cleared the snow from the fake rock where they hid the spare key. The fake rock lay overturned, a bowl filling with snow.

"I need to come in, Brother Bradshaw."

"You're not coming in."

"I need to come in."

The shape and the voice seemed to separate.

"Where's your partner?"

"He's home. Sick," Pope scoffed.

"What are you doing out?"

"Knocking on doors." The shape hung before him, straight ahead on the walk, grainy, slowly growing into Pope in the weak light. "Doing the Lord's work. But I'm awfully cold now, Brother Bradshaw. I need to come in."

"You're not coming in."

Pope held up the spare key between the fingers of his glove.

"I'm coming in. You know it. You do. It's just another thing you're not letting yourself believe right now. But you know it. In your heart."

"Nobody knows shit with their heart, Pope. That's not what the heart does."

Pope sighed, a long weary breath that turned smoky in the air. "People are always telling me no, Brother Bradshaw. All day long. Do you have any idea how discouraging that is?"

He turned toward the door, and Bradshaw lunged, wrapping his arms around Pope's torso. It didn't feel like something he'd actually done—it didn't feel like anything he would ever do. He scrabbled for the key, but Pope twisted and fought. Hanging on from behind, Bradshaw drove him onto the snowy sidewalk, feeling his rib cage expand with every breath. Pope fought to his knees, and they lumbered and lurched, and Bradshaw found his right hand suddenly, accidentally, clamped over Pope's mouth, bony chin snug in his grip.

"Okay," Pope grunted into Brandshaw's hand, his body yielding. "All right."

Bradshaw's body wanted to do it. That was how he would always remember it—his body did it without him. His muscles twitched and fluttered with desire. His bones gathered and heaved backward. The sound was horrendous—a crack like a tree limb splitting—and Bradshaw felt it in his muscles and bones, in his own neck.

He sat back as Pope slumped onto his face, rear in the air like a sleeping toddler. Bradshaw breathed and breathed, watching each white cloud rise. Pope didn't move. Snow soaked through Bradshaw's pants. He stood. He noticed he didn't feel surprised. He hadn't expected this, but now that he was in the middle of it, it didn't feel unexpected.

"You're not coming in," Bradshaw whispered.

He leaned over and removed the key from Pope's glove, and used it to open the front door. He went in, took off his boots and coat, and began turning on lights. He walked the house, flipping every switch, every lamp, the bathroom lights, garage light, pouring on light. He stood in the blazing yellow of his front-room window and gazed at the dark shape in the snow. He raised a force field around his mind and kept everything outside of it—wife and child, mother and father, the idea that the sun would rise on him ever again. He thought: I could eat a whole chicken. Or a pizza. The snow fell and fell on Pope, and Bradshaw watched it and thought: I'm either damned or I'm not, but I am *starving*.

He went to the kitchen. He found ham and turkey and Irish farmhouse cheese in the fridge, and made a thick, chewy sandwich. Lots of mayonnaise. No vegetables. His mouth was dry, and he had a hard time choking down the first bite.

"Not coming in!" he said, spraying crumbs and bits of half-chewed meat.

It was a delicious sandwich. He took another bite, but it turned impossible in his parched mouth, and he spat it onto the counter, a fleshy lump. He'd have to clean this up before he called the police. "A *hell* of a sandwich!" he said. He was holding it in both hands, staring at the empty places he had bitten away. He walked toward the front of the house. He had a vision of himself welcoming the officers. His demeanor would be pitched perfectly. Just the way Pope would do it. It would be no time for smiling. Whatever he said would be believable.

BROADAX INC.

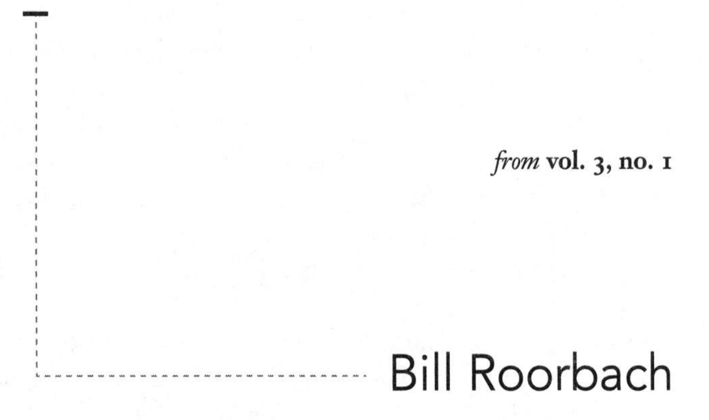

from **vol. 3, no. 1**

Bill Roorbach

MY OLD CHAMP AND PAL "Frederick" Duk Nuhkmongamong simply appeared at my office—first sign of trouble, no phone call. Marie allowed him past the reception desk because I guess he was so beautiful in that suit, so clearly belonged in the corporate suites. When I looked up from the telephone there he was, determined, but something else, too: diminished.

I stared at him bluntly, kept talking into the phone to one Ann Spray from Hartlee Commercial Properties. I was thinking how tender Ducky looked, how blue, and my stomach rose into my gorge with self-blame, but I was saying, "We can't pay that kind of footage for satellite warehousing, and I think your man must know this, no? You certainly know this, Ann." Harsh words gently delivered. And my friend did not crack his usual smile or make the usual word-mouthing fun of my business style. Still talking to Ann, admonishing her, still looking at Duk, I so calmly said, "Get back to me at nine thousand plus zeroes tops and we'll talk more."

Ann Spray's sprightly voice piped faceless: "How did it go with your mother?" and I hung up without an answer—let that stand as expression of emotion, and to hell with those who asked after dead parents in order to sugar their fuck-ups. Broadax Inc. did not need what Ann Spray had, always a pleasant position.

I thought a minute, jotted a note, only then looked to my friend. I said, "Ducky," fond as I could make it.

And he said, "Broadax."

We were the fellows who were roommates at Stanford, but twenty years older. I said, "One-nine they want, out in Bethel."

He said, "One-nine in *Bethel*? Har. They heard deep pockets."

"Why so grim?" Again, my stomach, normally steel, clenched. The guilt had gotten to me. To *me*, Mike Broadax, certified shark. They'd find license plates in my gut when they finally croaked me, whole propellers from ships, the skeletons of many a creature great and small, and *guilt*, whatever that looked like: slag, I pictured, great crusty lumps of formless, poisonous, weighty lead-smelter slag.

He looked away from me, first time since he walked in the door, looked back, and out with it: "Jilly and I have split."

"Oh, no, Ducky, no."

"It's a bad marriage, Ted, nothing to get sad about."

"I'm sorry, Ducky, I'm terribly sorry. And don't make small of it. This is terrible news! This is rotten news. I could cry! I am crying! It's...nuts." And it was nuts indeed, if he was initiating it: Jilly was brilliant and lovely and rich too, a predator herself, and from what I had seen, kind, devoted to causes, eager, hungry for life, intensely, um, sexual. A perfect wife as seen by the man who had nothing. I dried my eyes—they really had started in tears, though with that remark about crying I'd only been trying for a smile. "Nuhkmongamong, you idiot, I care about you! Have a seat—please, let's talk."

Duk did not sit, but leaned, leaned over my desk, and I saw he'd been crying too, that in fact he was all cried out: there was that dewy kind of redness at his eyes, his black, deep eyes. His tie that day was orange with the thinnest red diagonal stripes—no concession to sadness there—narrow knot pulled up so tight that his Hong Kong collar was a suicidal garrote cutting his thin neck.

"How to proceed?" he said businesslike.

"You're asking me?"

"You've been through it!"

Divorce, he meant. My own was six years old already, so once again I was the expert by default. "Ducky, brother, this is a different case. Every marriage is different. You want my advice? You go home and you two work it out, is my advice."

"If I could!" Ducky spouted, and lo, he was not cried out after all: here came the tears, a gushing geyser of the hot and salty. His hands flew to his face.

"Talk when you're ready," I said. I could just reach his elbow across the expanse of my beautiful new teak desk—all his weight leaned on that elbow, all the weight of all the love in the world, the veins of his forearms standing up blue. He was so thin. I leaned and reached and tapped his elbow affectionately. He said nothing.

I said, "Tell me..." Just soothing. I pictured Jilly, pictured her perfectly, and smelled her too, perfume, perspiration, so long had I wanted her. The fleeting, unkind, prepossessing, suddenly consuming thought came through my brain: Jilly Webster-Nuhkmongamong was available.

Jilly, she was a brain and generous and beautiful too, in her way, very tall with a kind of bow to her shoulders that came from making herself shorter for most of her life, and shorter yet for Ducky, who was five-five in thick soles. At my own six-foot-two I didn't look down on her, though perhaps she was not quite so tall as I. She was a sylph in earth tones, always in earth tones: dark browns, rusty reds, black sometimes, soft grays, all to offset her paleness, her unhidden freckles. She looked at my mouth when she talked to me, looked in my eyes when I replied. Her hair she dyed auburn, and it looked heavenly to me, lank and luminous; to get a Valentine's rhyme going, one word: *numinous*.

But I put all that out of my head. That's a shark who thinks like that, and not all of me was shark (but shark was the part that made Broadax Inc. tick). Okay, yes, there was a shark in me, swimming for Ducky; I could feel that sharp dorsal fin. But I was *for* Ducky that day, and not for me. Beautiful Ducky, the "Thai-stick" we used to call him in college, 120 pounds of imperfectly repressed fury, about as Thai as you or me (but then maybe you are Thai—my apologies), the only vestiges of the old culture after three generations American being his food sense (eleven kinds of basil growing in handsome glazed pots that covered his deck with view) and a kind of vague Buddhist outlook. Instead of stories of Jesus with loaves, the kind that are in my head, he had Gotama under the tree about to be enlightened, stories mostly serving the same purpose, reminders to kill the shark, or reign it in.

In college Ducky and I and our pals talked about this stuff deeply through drunken and sometimes drugged late nights, solemnly, thoroughly, with mutual respect for the faiths of our fathers, back when the Duk and I thought how different we two pod peas were. Even close as we remained all those years after graduation, I had never seen him cry before. This was serious.

Frederick Duk Nuhkmongamong met Jillian O'Reilly Webster during the course of an officers' retreat at Microsoft before that company was macro and before the whole industry leapt to giant money and, of course, before the whole industry got so limp (but Broadax Inc.—one didn't worry about Broadax Inc.—at Broadax Inc., we were sailing: our patents were deep essentials through broad swaths of the market; our sales base was broad in kind, from the hospitals to the military, from the entertainment industry to the universities; our top-performing products were indispensable, life or death to man and machine). Jilly, to get back to my point, with all her other talents, was awfully well-to-do: M-soft stock options, played timely. And the little consulting firm she started next served her well. Ducky had been less timely with his own options, but he was no pauper (prenup agreements: their money separate except for what the Duk told me they called their "grocery account," joint checking, six-figure groceries, I guess; I knew the balance because sharks at parties look through drawers): twin Jags in the drive, the works; what lacked for happiness in that marriage?

"Tell me," I said, patting that long, elegant hand.

My own divorce was no matter for tears: Myra wanted to get back to set design, wanted to do it home in New York, where set design would mean genuine theater work. And that was pretty much it. We liked each other fine, had a nice lunch after the court date that had sundered our marriage, went home and made love for two hours (effects of wine)—we'd never lost our lust for each other, a kind of proof of the divorce: it wasn't about your everyday death-of-sex issues, but about a lack of love between us. I don't remember being sad, though I must have been.

And Myra went back to New York. I had had two fairly wonderful (but in the end faulty) romantic connections since, no tears in parting, no lover at the moment of Ducky's visit, though in the weeks previous a couple of pleasing dates, and a particular and particularly painful make-out session, but more about all that shortly. I was forty-one and certainly successful, if not so gorgeous as a certain Thai-American roommate I once had. I was enjoying myself playing the field, deep center, as I pictured it, Yankee Stadium, the big time, seldom a hit my way, but still I was tense, my mitt oiled and ready, waiting to keep that one big home run of a love ball from going over my head.

But that was not the thing to tell Ducky. Ducky belonged with Jilly. I said, "What precipitated this? I mean, it's sudden, isn't it? Can you say?"

"Something I did."

I listened, I watched, I waited—this was painful for our boy, and I had never seen his brow knit so tight. Still, I was glad to detect it was not I who was at fault. It might easily have been yours truly and that one night with Jilly he'd come there thinking about. But she hadn't confessed, apparently. That one brief encounter with Jilly, nothing serious, ten minutes urgent tongue-kissing on a friend's balcony drunk, dinner-party aftermath, already a year past. And you'll blame me, blame my inner shark, but it was not only mine, Jilly's got one too—some fish, a killer whale, black and white and spouting, all mammal, plenty teeth, an eerie song one hears for miles. Oh, ho, wow, some kiss.

Duk stopped his crying, looked square at me: "Something serious."

I said, "Okay," keeping my face open, nonjudgmental, also unafraid. He had an affair, so what?

"Do you remember Monkey Six Internals?"

"That chip outfit? The 'biological chip' debacle?"

"I invested with them."
"Ugh."
"Lost all."
"And you didn't tell me?"
Ducky: "Ashamed."
"And, what, you didn't tell Jilly?"
"Worse."
"You told her?"

He narrowed his eyes, and I mean narrow: "No, no. Okay, dude. Here it is. I'll tell you what. Here we go, Broadax. I invested, got cocky, quit M-soft, as you recall, watched my money falcons ride the thermals, bro, put the works in Monkey Six, every cent I could leverage, from their IPO to the crash last month: a hundred and thirty-two dollars a share Thursday, the fifteenth, fifty-nine cents Monday late."

"Monkey Six was a shell game."

"Well, dude, we all know that now."

"Beware the Ides of March, Mr. Sticks." No smile. I could not get this man to smile. So serious: "Shit, Ducky. I sold Monkey Six in August at $150, and told you to follow. When did you stop listening to me?"

"I'm listening to you now."

"You're saying Jilly is going to leave you for that? No way."

"No no. She left me for this: I was overextended and needed big money very fast and couldn't ask her so I just went into her account and took it: five hundred thousand, first sweep, so easy, then the rest, total four million."

"You can't just *withdraw* that kind of money!"

"Full scam, Broadax. Suffice it to say, I pulled it off, her brokerage account to our joint account, simply—listen to this—imitating her voice on the phone," this last in a perfect Jilly voice, "and, you know, using her signature, number of other simple tricks, joking with Mitch Markham, you know, the loyal broker. Of course he did whatever she asked. But it was good money after bad, and within three weeks, gone."

"Gone!" I cried.

"Unforgivable," my man moaned.

"Stupid, too," I said. "Monkey Six!"

"Stupid is not the word. Criminal. Is the word."

Long pause. I took the time to absorb all my man had laid out for me. But it's easy to find the heart to help a genius of his caliber when you've got a company that needs his kind of brains badly. I got it all straight, planned it in my head, five minutes quiet, said, "Ducky, I can fix this. Here it is. We put you to work here. Obviously, this is not charity. We need you here at Broadax as much as ever, or more. I can preempt our international meat patrol with a call right now. Right this minute. You, sir, are our new programs manager. Title: Vice President. Plenty room to grow. Partner four years. Signing bonus: four million American dollars. Which will represent an advance on your yearly bonuses for three years hence, if recent payout is any indication. And we will disburse now. You leave here with a cashier's check. You show that to Jilly over dinner—in fact, you give her the check. And tell her exactly what went wrong—how *scared* you were. She'll know the feeling! You tell her you start here next week—and in the meantime, maybe the two of you snatch a little trip—jump over to Maui? Use my place?"

Appreciative tones, finally a smile: "Fuck, Broadax."

I buzzed Dot and she brought in the instruments and I wrote my old friend his advance-on-bonus right there, handed it over. He looked at the check a long time—small change here at Broadax—finally folded it, tucked it in his pocket. And gave a little bow, the likes of which I'd only seen him perform once, in the direction of his wizened father, at his wedding to Jilly. God, the gesture meant everything. My investment was sound. And here came Doug Blauveldt, Blondie we call him, and he and Duk shook hands a long time: Blauveldt was chief forest-meat safari man, director of personnel planning and development, that is, and knew his superstars by name. Doug left quickly at my nod, whence I dug through my top drawer (new desk, everything neatly arranged by Dot, thus impossible to find item one), tossed him the keys to the beachside condo, Maui. King bed. Old cognac. Housekeeper/cook (Leda Loa is her name, $36,500 annualized, pre-benefits, and worth every penny). Volcano in view. Another marriage saved.

But you can't leave love to chance, or to guys like Ducky, so

Saturday from home I called the condo, got my own voice, *beep*, said, "Mr. and Mrs. Schlebster-Dukmongamong, greetings, Broadax here," very cheerful, confident of the best, and sure enough the Duk picks up, jovial, full of good jokes.

"Yes, yes, boss Broadax! We are here! Life is good! Leda says Aloha. You are a lovely man, she says! Jilly says Aloha, Broadax. Your cook can sure cook! We haven't left the place yet!" And so on, many a warm phrase. The guy was back on his game, and I was glad to see it. In the background, Jilly giggling, shouting something out, and Ducky shushing her comically. "Kind of caught me in the middle of something, here, boss Broadax!"

"I'll let you go! Or come! Or whatever you're up to! And see you Wednesday. They're putting your office together right now! Tell Ms. Loa I will see her down there in two weeks' time, guests in tow."

All pleasantries, right to the click.

And so to the Broadax building to check on the physical-plant guys, people I seldom see. I'm glowing. Ducky is the best program developer in the USA, a security guru as well, and everyone knows it industry-wide, knows he'd been employed by M-soft preemptively—they didn't use him well, but no one else could have him. His hobby there was busting into every program they had running the place, and offering up groundbreaking cures, you know, fifteen minutes on a Friday after lunch and he'd be into the bowels of accounting, say, or flashing smiley faces on Big Bill's most private screens. At Broadax Inc., we'd been trying nine years to hire him, with offers far more garish than the new one.

I go on and on about the benefits to Duk and to the company. But the truth is, the hire was for me. How else assuage horrendous guilt? The Duk would have a teak desk, just like mine. He'd have the opposite corner office, my floor. His pay would never quite equal mine, but we would keep him nevertheless: that little bow he'd proffered said it all.

A SATURDAY STROLL amongst 'em. The pleasures of the single man: no one to inform, no one to call, just an aimless Saturday alone. Down to Santa Monica, maybe a latte, maybe a slow lunch with Puck, take a little walk down to the beach after... Springtime, hell, you might see someone you know. And it might be a woman. And of course I did: Jilly. Something was rotten in Hawaii.

THE LIES IN FRIENDSHIPS are generally small: *Can't make your party, sorry, I'm so sick. Can't take your dog, sorry, my houseman is allergic. Didn't kiss your wife ten minutes on the master-bedroom deck at Shelagh Lemoile's.* Well, come to think of it they can get pretty big, but tell me, are they really lies having gone untold? Yes? No? Not even to one another did Jilly and I ever mention the kissing, not in one conversation after, of which we had had ten thousand.

Jilly, Jilly. Jilly rushed up to me on the hot Santa Monica sidewalk, adither. Said, "Ducky's gone!" Said, "Have you seen Ducky?" Said, "He's been acting so *oddly*!"

There was nothing in her face of the woman who'd lost millions. After a hug, after some gentle reassurances from me that I'd just spoken to him, after yet another lie ("He's taking a little thinking time in Hawaii alone"), I said, "Have you checked your brokerage accounts lately? Talked to Mitch Markham? Been to the bank?"

Jilly is good-looking—did I say that? It's her self-possession, the centered being behind those green eyes. She's about to laugh at all times, and was about to laugh at that moment, looking into me, practically twinkling to see what was the joke. At thirty-five she could be ten years younger sometimes, ten years older other times, moment by moment shifting her looks like all great beauties. She's got the maturity. She's got the legs. She kicked me in the shin, sharply, ha-ha.

My reply was this sad face: no jokes here.

And on a beachside bench I finally convinced her to flip her phone and call the twenty-four-hour account access Markham is so proud of. She looked at me closely between poking the ten-dozen numbers she had to push, watched my mouth, a turn-on. Her mother's maiden name (which she was prompted to speak) was O'Reilly—I hadn't known this. The freckles are the Irish in her. I am in love with Jilly. I hadn't known this either, not truly, not as I knew it in that moment.

Real beauty, it doesn't fade in the face of bad news: her face dropped, yes, her mouth drooped, sure, her posture sagged, of course; a bejeweled hand went to her forehead in shock. But the thousand passersby to a man and to a woman turned their heads to see her: she looked an actress, movie star, countess, queen. The role here was tragic. She moaned back in her throat as if her legs were being kissed to the top, moaned with each piece of the electronic news: lots of small numbers where the big ones had been. Mitch Markham she found on the golf course (cell phones, phugh!). We shared the earpiece, heads together. Her fragrance! *Noa noa*!

Markham: "That's right, doll. Right. We left the seven accounts active, yes, as discussed. And as per your call the other day, we've drawn 'em each down to minimums, account transfer; yes, honey, as you requested, and I agreed, wise move to go real estate and munies right now. All the figures are on my desk. Is there a problem?"

Very cool, our Jilly: "Mitch, thank you. And yes, there is a problem. I will call you Monday to explain."

Four million bucks, her personal money, broken into seven chunks and fired over to their joint grocery account. ATM corner of Sepulveda and there's the rest of the news: no grocery money, ladies and gents, fifteen dollars only.

Bad Ducky!

Next call, of course, was to Hawaii.

Leda Loa rather sings when she talks, lovely deep voice, and it was she who picked up: "I drove him to the airport. His wife, she got off in town."

"Where was he going?"

"Malaysia, so he said."

"Malaysia."

"Via British Air. I have seen the tickets. Two weeks you, yes?"

"Two weeks me, Leda, yes."

She giggled. But not I: that check I'd written Ducky for four mil had joined another four mil and headed east. Weirdly, I felt some consolation in those facts—I didn't want Jilly to be alone in her loss.

And the two of us squatted on that bench a long time, pretty much the whole afternoon. Skaters who'd gone that way came back this. They all have eyes for Jilly—men, women, indefinites—all eyes on Jill.

ON A MORTGAGE THAT SIZE, they foreclose pretty well immediately. As a fellow *chondrichthyan*, of course, I understand their thinking: all those rows of teeth have to bite something quick. Broadax Inc. can absorb four million; Jilly Webster, private citizen, cannot. And the four million was just for starters. The Duk had ingeniously hidden three months of nonpayment, all their bills. Phones were dead. Power off. Furniture repossessed. Tow trucks came to hoist the Jags. A stout fellow from the supermarket, even, demanding a check.

No, we didn't call the cops; that desperate a move could await an explanation. And no, we didn't make prodigious or even simple efforts to find our man. Jilly didn't, for example, call his family. Imagine all the worry! I, for example, did not call all our mutual friends. At Broadax Inc., I simply told Doug Blauveldt to resume the executive search: our man had changed his mind. And I wrote a personal check to Accounting for four rather large ones—ouch—but otherwise it was going to be the law for Ducky, and no one wanted that, not yet.

Jilly's theory was that he would come back at crisis end, and she and I told each other this theory repeatedly in different forms, elegant each and every one. But the practical side of things—unstated—was how much she and I enjoyed being together. And we were together quite a bit after Jilly moved into my guest house. She got to work, operated her business from the kitchenette in there. Me, I quietly provided a few phones and computers and a certain amount of company, all the things she'd lost.

Sharks do fall in love. It isn't all just gnashing and splashing and arms coming off clean, bitten surfboards washing up on beaches. I took care of Jilly in her mourning. Multiple losses: Ducky, first of all, the actual missing person. Second of all, Ducky the nice guy. Dead. Third, her money. Phew, gone. Fourth, her idea of herself as unassailably savvy. This was one vulnerable lady sleeping just down the hill from me. I brought her a tray every morning, left it on the steps. I brought her a tray when I got home evenings—down by the guesthouse pool. She'd come out to greet me only slowly, often cried on my shoulder. I held her, that's all I could do. I listened.

Fifth loss, discovered late: her business had been sabotaged up and down the line, big to small and back again. The Duk, subtly hacking.

MY INVESTIGATOR, Jack Wax (this cannot be your real name, Wax, but I dig it), found that Mr. Nuhkmongamong did indeed embark on a British Air flight to Taipei. And that was the end of that. Not another clue further. Jilly figured he was in Bangkok—he has many a relative still living there. My own vote was London—just a hunch. I knew it to be the city Ducky loved most, a place he could actually speak the language, which he could not in Bangkok, ancestors or no. Jilly took to sunbathing naked, let our hugs linger friendly. No further kissing, however. She'd let me know when, or if, and I was content to wait.

Meanwhile, Broadax Inc. thrived. The new brainiac I put in the corner office was no Ducky, but he was worth the millions of his signing bonus immediately, surpassed all our expectations. Business was rocking, business was rolling. Our stock soared while all around us companies flailed. The world passed my desk, and I ripped off big bloody bites whenever I felt the urge, whenever I smelled life. Four lawsuits settled in our favor, one after the next. Trade barriers dropping in Asia, in Europe, in South America. A glowing segment on *60 Minutes*, listen to this: "The Honest CEO." True enough. Life was good.

Then Ted Brunk called up from accounting, asked for a face-to-face: one hundred fifty million was missing from the overseas fund. And then Kiki Minimizawa from customer relations: in a single month we had lost some eighty percent of our long-term accounts to a young British company that seemed to have copied our business plan exactly, and that had bid into our base with fatal preempts all up and down the line using information you could only call proprietary. I got on the phone for most of a horrendous afternoon. I heard this rumor and that rumor about Broadax, all lies. My fellow CEOs would not speak to me. Except Harvey Barnard back east at humble New England Graphics, that honest gentleman, who explained how he'd been wooed away, and told me all he'd heard about our product failures! We had had no product failures of any kind ever! Harvey pointed me to articles in the *Wall Street Journal*, the *New York Times*, *Crain's Business Week*, and the *Financial Times*, all in the previous two weeks. Why hadn't I seen any of these? Simple. The magazines had stopped coming to the office—every subscription in the place, gone missing.

"Hardly a rumor," Harvey said sympathetically. "And we felt to protect our softer flank we must go with your competition. Which is offering quite a value, I might add. My sympathy, Broadax." Said as one speaks to a shark.

I quizzed him and at length he gave me the answers I needed. Our new competition was Nuhkmongamong Ltd. of London, England.

MY GUESTHOUSE, just down the hill in that lovely canyon, was a neighbor's house till I bought it with an offer sufficient to send him packing. From my kitchen windows I could see when Jilly was by the pool, and as soon as she was each day, I dropped down to see her. That evening, of course, I was agitated. I brought her the usual drinks and dinner, whipped up admirably by Teddy Gonzales, my overpaid chef (formerly sous at Le Cirque). She was wearing her laptop and a frown of frustration, looking into its screen. I sat at her side, wearing my own frown, and a pair of sporty jams. Her side, by the way, had gotten considerably browner: all day in the sun.

Slowly, I said what I had planned to not say: "I fear Duk is behind some serious troubles at Broadax Inc." And went on to outline the subversion of our patents, the seduction of our client base, the careful placement of disinformation in the highest places. All of it quite likely the result of a supremely clever touch with the mouse and keyboard.

Jilly let her eyes roam to my mouth.

I said, "Let's speak directly. Did you tell Ducky about our balcony night?"

"I'm so happy you bring it up."

"Did you tell him?"

"No. Yes. But not exactly. I told him only because he knew. Apparently our dear hostess Shelagh observed us from an upstairs window—that was some kiss, Broadax—and felt *embarrassed* for

Duk. That's what Duk told me. And that's all I know. Information too long withheld, and I'm sorry."

"Duk's reaction?"

"He wept."

I pondered what had been withheld, sipped my vast martini. Shelagh Lemoile, cat-eyed sharkette, always with eyes for the Duk. Sunset glinted off the pool. Some kiss, Jilly had said. She watched my eyes. My best friend's wife. I said, "But surely that is not what precipitated all this."

Her eyes again found my mouth. "No. It was something worse. Let me show you." She rose like a vision, slid into the house naked, reappeared shortly, clad in one of my old silk robes (House of Weike Kwo, Singapore, my favorite tailors), in her tomboy's hands a thick letter, which she handed over.

She said, "This is a draft of an emotional letter to my sister, Kate, one of those letters you do not send. And if you do not send it, it might very well be in your sock drawer a month or two, or even nine weeks, and your husband might then find it and read it."

First line: *Dear Kate: I am in love with Mike Broadax.*

Jilly and I kissed, and then kissed some more, taking up where the party kiss had merely left off. We kissed and talked and rocked and rolled and before long Jilly was living in my house.

I DON'T HAVE TO SAY MUCH about the Broadax collapse. It's been the subject these last three weeks of every op-ed column and all the pusillanimous pundit palaver a man can stomach and even *Entertainment Tonight*. Competition from Europe is the official line—the president of the United States said it himself, in his address to Congress. Competition from Ducky, he should have mentioned. First our product, then our client base, then large numbers of our best people defecting, even Brunk, then Blauveldt, moving to London. Last our patents—all quite legally if unwisely sold to him, all traceable deals (these hard drives hold everything—every e-mail, every transaction—whether you've really written the e-mails or made the transactions or no). It's a brilliant, malevolent fiction. A fiction I can't counter, because every traceable link, every clue, every witness, says it is fact. Even my secretary, devoted Dot, seems to remember certain phone calls I never made. Dot is moving to London, by the way. She always wanted to head up a sub-corporation, apparently, and she loves Carnaby Street.

My personal financial collapse is another story.

The first sign was the Mayflower moving van at my guesthouse—all my belongings there removed under the eyes of the biggest sheriff's deputy I've ever seen. And then the lovely young couple I'd apparently sold the place to, moving in.

Jack Wax? Moved to London.

Next, Duk got my house. My legal team? Suddenly, a conflict of interest. "A new client," was all Buzz Dorfmann would say.

My retort: "London?"

"I'm not the least bit sorry, Broadax."

My personal checking account: frozen. My credit cards: maxed then cancelled. My cars, all four: leases terminated. My life insurance: never existed. Every last little souvenir I owned, sold, checks from eBay users around the world all countersigned by me, all deposited by me, all spent, apparently, all gone. Seventy-three bucks in quarters, dimes, and nickels from the jar in my empty garage got Jilly and me a night at a Super 8 Motel. This gave us an address to receive a wire of five thousand dollars from Jilly's sister, beloved Kate.

Have I mentioned the silver lining? The silver lining was Jilly and me. That Super 8 might have been the Casbah, for all the romance that therein bloomed. The two of us touching fingers and talking long by incandescent false-candle light at a chain called Fudpucker's that night—lovely.

Kate's gift of cash, without interception, would bring us to our final frontier. Ducky had won. I put in a call to Leda Loa. Coming as planned. I owned my Maui condo, my last bastion, free and clear, but Leda Loa didn't answer. A call to her home, and her sweet old mother just barked at me: Leda Loa had moved to London.

The hell with her. We'd cook for ourselves. But in Maui my condo was occupied. A gentlemanly fellow who worked in advertising. All the transfer papers were in perfect order. I'd sold the place. Made a good profit, too.

SO JILLY AND I ARE OUT on a hidden beach, property of a loyal old friend, a fellow whose name I can't reveal, but a man who's never once used a computer, let's put it that way. The goddess nymph princess and I are living in a shelter of driftwood. We lie together and watch the sunsets; our talk ranges widely; we read to each other; we make love all night. We surf by day. We help the local kids tie-dye T-shirts, take a cut of the impressive sales, which have responded to my marketing plan, enough cash for groceries, you know, and the occasional bottle of good gin. Jilly has taken the name Shaka. I'm Mr. Aloha. No more Broadax. No more Webster. We're that eccentric old surfin' couple with the deep tans and the easy laughs, grass skirts, floppy hats, Jimi Hendrix on the borrowed iPod, two sets of earbuds. You wouldn't recognize us—don't even try. There are coconuts here, and pineapples, and the endless beach, and we have each other and are madly in love. It's cost us some, but it's a hell of a good life, guilt-free at last.

I am a shark no more.

But I watch the waves for dark fins, even while I learn in joy to handle a short board through the tubes: you never know. And Jilly, my own, her belly big and round as a full moon, watches too.

Duk, we're sorry, we apologize, we bow to you, good-bye.

AT THE CULTURAL EPHEMERA ASSOCIATION NATIONAL CONFERENCE

from vol. 7, no. 1

Robert Olen Butler

BILL

In those first few moments I have to confront my name. The moderator introduces me to her as "William" and she has eyes the color of blue ice and I can't remember the last time I cared about my name, though for some years, as a young man, I did. But now I care once again. I shake her hand, and her eyes seem restless upon me, but we are turning to our places and we sit behind our name placards. Two other scholars of the Cultural Ephemera Association separate us at the table, and before us are blank legal pads, an untouched pitcher of ice water and four glasses, a few dozen sleepy-eyed scholars in Naugahyde hotel chairs. Everyone went drinking last night, deconstructing the texts and designs of the pulpboard beer coasters, by the end laughing crazily over obscenities only they could see. I sat apart. She was not with us. I did not know she existed. No. I knew her name. I'd read a paper or two of hers about Cadbury chocolate cards as artifacts of British colonialism. But I did not fully understand how she existed in a body until her extraordinary eyes were told to see me as "William." What are my choices? My mother called me Willy from the start and I carried it through grade school. In London or Liverpool a willy is a penis. Will? A confrontation with the ephemera of a life left after you're bound for worms and dust. Bill, of course. It's what I settled on long ago. A bird's beak. A demand for money. But I accepted that it was me. Not William, because that name has always felt too formal, passionless, disenfranchised from a body. I accepted Bill with the wish to keep some informality about myself, hoping that it registered as personal warmth, though I am William to her from the start, and when I meet her I am indeed William, having lived in my body and my senses as all of us do but in some deep way never having lived in my body at all, never having truly touched anyone. On the morning I meet her I am William.

CLEO

I am a grown woman. Why do I still argue in my head with my mother? At the oddest times. Perhaps not so odd, because the man whose hand I am shaking when I've already put on my scholarly game face, already prepared myself to say some enlightening things about the Cadbury *Titanic*, this man has my eyes. But I am not a narcissist gazing into the forest pool. I have always thought I had a thing for dark-eyed men. Gallics and Slavs and certain Brits. I see that preference now as just another compromise. For this man has eyes nearly the blue of the Gulf when Daddy took me troll fishing off Orange Beach. I see this color in my own eyes sometimes, when I'm feeling good about myself. When I've spent enough time with my own thoughts—which Philip, which my husband Philip, with his dear but distracted literalist heart, can never share, ever—when I've followed in my mind where I dare go only alone and I look in the mirror and it is a certain time of day and the sunlight is coming through the bathroom window and I can see my eyes and I feel I can be alone with this part of me, at that moment it feels okay to be alone with it, but I shake this man's hand on the second morning of the conference and I see his eyes and they are my eyes and they are not my eyes, they are his, and I realize I've been lying to myself, and I sit down and I am glad I'm not presenting first because I find myself arguing with my mother, which is foolish and I never said this to her in life, I never said this before she died, but in my mind, this morning that I meet him, as I reach to the water pitcher to pour myself some water as I wait to read my paper, I say it to mother: Why the hell didn't you just go all the way, why didn't you name me Cleopatra? I would have embraced that name and it would have embraced me. I would never have compromised in my life. I would never have been attenuated to Cleo and I would have waited for a man who could be with me fully.

BILL

She speaks in her paper of the scrim of history, of the ironies of popular culture, of new evidence that it was upon the tenth anniversary of its incorporation after seventy-five years as a private company that Cadbury created this card of what the world anticipated to be the greatest ship ever built, it being known among scholars that it was the only card of the ship issued before it sank, but the specific year of its release not being known. She makes a persuasive case that it appeared in Bournville cocoa tins in 1909, soon after the ship's keel was first laid down. And she speaks to me afterward as we stand at the back of the dais until we are the only two people in the room, speaks of the feelings she could not put into the paper, she speaks to me of how a child opened the tin of cocoa and how the doomed vessel sailed bow-forward through brilliant lithography and a choppy sea into the bright consciousness of this child, and she speaks to me of how the child carefully put the card away in his innocence, at age nine or ten, and how three years later, in puberty, just coming into his life force, his sexuality, he hears the terrible news and holds that card again, alone in his room, with trembling hands, and he imagines death. In the doomed brightness of this chocolate card, he confronts the mystery of death for the first time. She speaks of how the seemingly incidental artifacts of popular culture can play crucial roles in our lives, can imprint themselves on us forever. And she touches my arm at this and her voice trembles and I can feel her passion. Even about this. Especially about this. And I know I am falling in love with her. Already I know. "Cleo," I say. And I hear myself and I try to correct myself: "Doctor—" She cuts me off. "You can call me Cleo," she says. "Cleo," I say, "I understand." "I know," she says. And I touch her hand that is still upon my arm.

CLEO

He spoke of two things I myself might well be speaking of—an early feminist and Shakespeare—and I am impressed with him. He has a ringing voice and he does not hold it back from these hungover, mostly male scholars. He veritably performs the story of Anna Elizabeth Dickinson, who played Hamlet in Boston and New York in 1882, and who was thus portrayed that year in a lithographed advertising card. A stock card, reproduced over and over throughout the country by milliners and grocers and shoe retailers and patent medicine vendors to advertise themselves. He spoke of the wild ridicule of the artwork—Anna's face made long and mannish, her thighs made thin and her calves made fat beneath her short petticoat breeches, a long claw of a forefinger laid almost pickingly against her nose—and he admires her, I can hear that. I am even a little jealous before his passion for Anna Dickinson, now almost unknown but a teenage wonder during the Civil War, a national orator for abolition, at twenty-one addressing Congress and President Lincoln himself, called the Joan of Arc of the Union cause, and at twenty-six a famous lecturer taking up women's rights—famed for her eloquence and passion and unsuppressed anger at injustice—and at thirty cast aside by a society not ready for her beloved cause, and at thirty-four a playwright and actress portraying another strong woman, Anne Boleyn, but reviled by the press she had castigated as a lecturer, and at forty playing Hamlet to unbridled cultural savagery. But on her advertising card she is given to say, "To be or not to be. That is the question." And this man understands. On this morning, in a hotel conference room in New York City, to a few dozen scholars who are creatures only of their minds, he gives voice to a woman's complex feeling: how Anna Dickinson suffered the public ridicule but embraced

Hamlet's soliloquy and made it her own and made it the central question for all women. To be or not to be? Fully be. So I talk to this man. We talk together and I talk too much, I talk about what was in my heart before he presented his paper, not what is beating in it now. But I have this much sense. At the end I say to him, "William," and he stops me and he says, "Bill," and I pause, and I say, "May I call you William?" and he pauses, and he says, "If you wish to," and I say, "I love him," and though there is no syntactic reason for either of our reactions, his eyes widen just a little and I feel the heat come to my face, and quickly I say, "Shakespeare. William Shakespeare. I love him." He laughs. And I say, "William, shall we have a drink tonight away from the academics?"

The man bought a glass of lemonade. He said, "I have a problem. Maybe one of you girls can help me." He'd driven up in his car and parked at a reckless angle to the curb, like the boys at school who refused to hang their coats on the hooks provided at the back of the classroom and let them fall to the floor in arrogant puddles. The man said his problem was that he needed to change his clothes. He gestured to Sheila with a wrinkled paper bag that she assumed was filled with his new outfit. He had a job interview, he said. A very important job interview.

"But I need someone to guard the door," he said.

"Why don't you change in your car?" Trudy said.

"That wouldn't be very private," the man said. "It might be embarrassing."

Sheila's body understood first, and then her brain followed, knowledge spreading out like a stain. She could tell by the penitent silence of the younger girls that they could tell something was wrong too. Still, no one screamed "Stranger, danger!" the way they had been taught.

"Just around the corner," he said. "There's a little garden shed, but the door doesn't lock. Anyone could come in, and that would be embarrassing, wouldn't it?" The way he repeated the word made Sheila believe that embarrassment was somehow tangled up in pleasure.

"We can't help you," Trudy said. She was fourteen.

"Really?" he said. "Not even you?" He looked directly at Sheila.

Sheila was twelve. She wore a halter top and she liked the way the bumps of her new breasts felt against the nylon. The man's eyes searched her face, but she did not look away. She felt a curious ambivalence about his wrinkled paper bag, and the fact that he wanted to do something bad to her. What was "bad"? she wondered. How bad did a thing have to be before it was something you would never get over for the rest of your life? Two boys rode up on bikes. They asked how much for the cookies. Trudy said you couldn't buy cookies without lemonade, and the boys began to argue with her. When the boys didn't leave, the man got into his car and drove away. The little girls burst into giggles, and Trudy told the boys what had happened, exaggerating for effect. Sheila felt the way she did when she took a corner too quickly on her bike and an oncoming car swerved to avoid her; the sip of breath, the way she could see her life and her death at the very same moment. She put her arms across her chest to hold herself.

"What's wrong with you?" Trudy said.

"I'm cold."

"It's a hundred million degrees out here." The attention of the boys had unleashed Trudy's haughty condescension. She told everyone to pack up the stand. "Right away," she said, like their mother.

Sheila and Trudy walked home, carrying the plastic container half full of lemonade and an unopened bag of cookies. Sheila felt as if everyone were watching her—the lady kneeling by her flower bed, the kids across the street playing Chinese jump rope, even God. She was sure He was watching because something important had happened, some small shift that had a ripple effect. Suddenly, she felt beautiful and much older than she had been ten minutes earlier. She was certain of it. How silly Maggie and Jeannie looked to her, dragging the folding table and chairs across the lawn toward their house. How alive she felt, walking beside her older sister, the summer air touching her back like a warm hand.

"Don't tell," Trudy hissed, "or they'll never let us do anything ever again."

Sheila agreed to keep silent. She would never tell her parents that for the first time she had been taken seriously.

SHEILA WAS THINKING about that long-ago afternoon right before her dog Patsy tried to kill herself. Sheila and Patsy were making their way through a development about a half hour from Sheila and Colin's house downtown. The residential area had burst into full-fledged existence the previous year. These shingle-roofed homes, meant to evoke a cleaner, less cumbersome version of the past, were so newly constructed that their pale decks had not yet weathered to an earthen brown. Sheila had chosen this inconvenient location because it was outside the city ordinance and she could walk Patsy without a leash, and because the development came complete with an instantly mature and bucolic woods and a level, litigation-proof pathway. Sheila had undergone bypass surgery four months earlier, a shock at age thirty-seven, and although she was otherwise healthy and her doctors assured her that she could live a "normal life," she had grown wary. Assumptions that the earth would be there to meet her foot when she put it down, or that her body would remain upright without her expressly willing it to, were no longer certain, and she found herself hesitating more than she used to, as though to give the world a chance to announce its true intentions. Sheila had been a springboard diver in high school, and occasionally she dreamed of diving, not of meeting the water, but of the seconds before, when she was suspended and gloriously weightless, when the possibility of disaster was unimaginable. When she woke, looking automatically at Colin, big and comfortably thick beside her in their bed, she wondered at the transparency of dreams.

The path hugged a ravine, and she and Patsy trotted to the edge of the embankment to look down at the stream below. The water moved sullenly; only the light coming through the trees and glancing off the stream's surface indicated the direction of the current. Sheila inhaled the moist, spoiled odor of the late fall and waited as it mixed with memory, creating a pleasing sorrow for irretrievable things. Patsy sniffed too, but only because that was her nature. Patsy was overweight—more barrel than dog—and Sheila had to suffer the condemnation of neighbors who would stop to inform her that her dog was fat and then list the medical conditions that would befall Patsy as a result of Sheila's negligence. A childless couple living in a neighborhood of families presented a troubling puzzle. People assumed Sheila must have been careless to have gotten into this situation, and that she needed their help.

Why did Patsy jump? There was no rustle in the bushes to alert the dog to a skunk or gopher, no distant bark to set her hair on end. There was no food below emitting its siren scent—Sheila knew this because she slid down the embankment on her backside to rescue Patsy and did not see a castoff hamburger wrapper or even an apple core.

Sheila carried the forty-pound, bristle-furred mutt to her car and drove to the veterinarian's office. While the doctor operated, Sheila sat in the waiting room, paging through limp pet magazines, inhaling the ammonia scent of urine mixed with disinfectant. A steady parade of sick animals and solicitous owners came in and out of the office. Sheila knew she should coo at the pets or inquire after their maladies but she was worried about Patsy. Two hours later, the vet appeared from the surgery and informed Sheila that Patsy had broken her two back legs and cracked a rib, but that she would recover fully to her old dog self in four to six months, give or take a limp.

"Old dog self?" Sheila said.

"You know," the doctor said, smiling a beat too late, as though she had to remind herself to do it. "Happy, bouncing."

When she got back home, Sheila phoned Colin at his office. "Patsy tried to kill herself."

"What?" Colin said, adjusting his voice. It was hard for him to be in two places at once. He worked as an investigator for a law firm, and was used to people shutting doors in his face and threatening to call the police. This created a tentative quality to his daily demeanor, as if he were speaking while walking quickly away. He had been about to leave Sheila for a woman in Seattle when Sheila discovered the problem with her heart.

"She jumped off a cliff," Sheila said.

"You mean she fell?"

"She leaped, Colin. She just leaped!" When she said the words, she felt something open up inside her.

"I don't understand," Colin said carefully. "Is she okay?"

"I guess it's a matter of how you define *okay*," Sheila said.

Colin was silent for a moment. "Can we talk about this later?" he said, finally.

"Of course," she said. Ever since he had told her about his affair and she'd had her surgery, they had tacitly agreed to inhabit a postponed space between "now" and "then," when discussions would be had and decisions made. Their marriage felt like the waiting room at the vet's office—everyone trapped in an expectant tense.

WHEN SHEILA WAS YOUNG, her mother told her not to go looking for trouble, but that didn't seem to be good advice. How else would you find it? She envied the boys she knew for whom trouble came in the form of discrete activities. You could steal a car. You could get someone pregnant. You could become a small-time drug dealer in your neighborhood and be able to go to all the best concerts. Boy trouble produced a lot of noise and fuss and trips to the police station. Sheila didn't really want to drink her parents' liquor or break into a stranger's house and rearrange the pictures on the walls. These journeys to peril were round-trips; you always ended up the same person you had been before. Girl trouble, on the other hand, was transformative. You could be driven home by a father after a babysitting gig and let him touch your breasts. You could have a fight with your boyfriend and get out of his car on a lonely road and be picked up by a stranger. You could have sex with a boy in his dorm room while his roommates walked in and out.

Colin had shown up at her door five years earlier to take down a statement regarding the lawsuit one of her colleagues had brought against the school district. The teacher's name was Frank Gibbons, and he had been fired midsemester after he had left hydrochloric acid out on the lab table overnight. This was his third offense. Colin was collecting information, he said, because the district had to be very careful when they terminated a teacher, especially if that teacher were a minority.

"Frank is white," she said.

"He has a false leg."

"I didn't know that," Sheila said, intrigued. "Was he in the war?"

"I'm not at liberty to disclose more information," Colin said.

Colin's tall and muscled body was squeezed into an ill-fitting suit, which made him appear awkward. Sheila answered his questions, which weren't interesting enough: How long had she known Mr. Gibbons? Did she have any particular dealings with Mr. Gibbons? Had any students ever spoken to her about Mr. Gibbons in her capacity as guidance counselor? He didn't ask whether or not she thought Frank Gibbons suffered from Asperger's, or if he ate the same exact lunch every day—a green apple quartered and a crustless tuna fish sandwich. Colin didn't ask whether she thought he had nefarious intentions when he left the acid lying on the table, knowing that Vanessa LaConte, the remote but brilliant junior with skin the color of espresso beans, would be coming in early the next morning to work on her advanced placement lab. In fact, the interview was over within a few minutes. Colin clicked his pen and handed her his card.

"What should I do with this?" she said.

"In case there is anything else you can think of," Colin said, stiffly. "And, well, you know, it's policy."

"Policy?"

"To identify myself."

Three months later, he arrived again at her door. "They settled the case," he said.

"In favor of?"

"The school district."

"So, he didn't have a leg to stand on, so to speak."

"It was a farm tractor accident."

There was something unsettlingly straightforward about Colin. He was like a toy robot that hits a wall over and over again because all it knows how to do is go forward. She was thirty-two and was attracted to wily and insinuating men. One had stolen a purse from a street vendor and given it to her as a present. Another asked her to wash herself before sex. She would learn that Colin was not good at innuendo and that he was easily hurt by sarcasm, but by that time, she had already fallen in love.

"YOU BROKE MY HEART," she said to Colin through the oxygen mask as the paramedics carried her out of the restaurant where their meal had been interrupted by her sense that an elephant had stepped on her chest. Colin ran alongside the stretcher, clutching her purse, which looked comically small in his big ex-quarterback hands. She wished she hadn't made the joke, because now it would be another thing between them that was misunderstood, like monogamy. At dinner, he'd told her of his affair with a woman he had known in college. They had reconnected on the Internet, he'd said, shaking his head as if he had been kidnapped by the wonder of technology. The woman was divorced with two kids. Sheila asked to see a picture of the children.

Colin hesitated. "It's over," he said. "I'm not going to see her anymore."

But suddenly her request felt crucial. It was the only concrete thing she could think of to do or say, the only way to gain some purchase on this new unsteady terrain of her life. Unhappily, he reached across the table to show her a picture he'd taken on his cell phone during one of his secret trips to Washington. The children were adorable, with hair so blond you could see sunlight reflected on the tops of their heads. Sheila could imagine Colin's lover taking the picture, her smile upsetting the camera so that the image was off-kilter. In Sheila's job at the high school, she sometimes used felt boards and generic family member cutouts to help the kids access their feelings. You could arrange the pieces any way you wanted. The students thought the game was childish but that was the point. As she gazed at the photo on the phone, Sheila began to feel strange, as if all the cells of her body were performing a square dance and were changing partners.

"I don't understand what's happening to me," she said, as she grabbed her left breast.

AFTER COLIN FINISHED WORK, he and Sheila drove to the veterinarian's office to visit Patsy. The dog wore splints on her hind legs, and lay inert in her cage. Colin started to cry.

"Oh shit," he said. "I'm sorry."

"It's normal," the vet said.

"She just looks so helpless," Colin said, smearing his nose with the sleeve of his shirt.

"You love your dog," the vet said, her hand finding her throat and dandling the necklace there. Sheila checked to see whether Colin noticed this gestural flirtation, but he was staring mournfully at Patsy.

He was still upset on the drive home. "Dogs don't commit suicide," he said. "You're a guidance counselor. Didn't you study stuff like this?"

"I work in a school, not the zoo."

"Animals are . . . they just want food. They want to live. It's evolution!" He said this with anguish, as if he had come to the limit of what he could understand. Sheila imagined how flummoxed he must have felt to find himself in a situation of having a mistress with two children who wanted him to take their smiling pictures.

"We give Patsy her food," she said. "She doesn't have to think about hunting and gathering. Her survival is assured."

"So?"

"She's got time on her hands. She thinks about what her purpose is in life. She comes up empty."

"I don't know, Sheila," Colin said, doubtfully.

She felt such great affection for the limit of his emotional opacity, even as she knew how she had been hurt by it.

She looked over at him thoughtfully. "I know you don't," she said.

SHE HAD NEVER GIVEN MUCH CONSIDERATION to her heart until someone had reached inside her and touched it. After the operation, the doctor explained to her that three of her arteries had been 80 percent blocked; it was astonishing that she wasn't already dead. She listened woozily as Colin asked questions about her recovery and prognosis. He wrote down all the answers, asking the doctor to repeat certain phrases, the way he did when he was conducting an investigation. The doctor was young, and Sheila could sense that he was growing nervous in the face of Colin's precision. She wanted to tell the doctor that Colin was an adulterer in order to mitigate Colin's threat, but she couldn't make her mouth work.

"Can she still have kids?" Colin said, shyly.

"Let's see how she does," the doctor said, and left the room.

Why had he asked that question? Was he seeking some kind of justification? A doctor's note like the ones the kids forged in school to get out of PE? But she knew Colin was not capable of such cruelty, and that he was asking for her sake, because he knew that a child was something she wanted, even though, together, they had not yet managed it.

Colin was constant during her recovery. Sometimes she expressed dismay, her discomfort and bedridden boredom compelling her to pick at the scab of his infidelity. She brought up moral relativism, which she knew was unkind. She remembered when Trudy had taken it upon herself to teach Sheila vocabulary as if three-syllable words were the armor Sheila needed to get by in the world. "Quixotic!" Trudy would scream and Sheila would have three seconds to give a definition. Colin withstood Sheila's petulance with calm, implacable smiles, something she imagined he'd learned from his job. His size came in handy, as she needed to be carried up and down the stairs of their house until she was strong enough to do so on her own. He brought her food and washed her hair. They sat in bed together night after night and watched infomercials. He traced his hand down the vertical scar that bisected her torso and, two months after the surgery, he made love to her carefully. They did not talk about the woman in Seattle. The tension of the unspoken caused Sheila and Colin to become familiar to one another in a new way, as if they were prisoners of war, sharing a cell and a meager bowl of rice, listening for the footfalls that might seal their fates. When she began dating Colin, she announced to him that if he ever cheated on her, she would leave. But it turned out this was not true. Hurt was not such an obvious thing, and happiness was still more obscure. Her marriage had become perilous and strange, and she felt as she had as a younger woman, when her roommates passed through the room where she and her boyfriend made love. Colin's adultery exposed her desire, turned it into something both pornographic and banal, private and essential.

FOR THE FIRST TWO WEEKS after Patsy's surgery, the dog could not move. Still, she tried, starting at the hysterical yips of the neighborhood dogs greeting passing trucks or the sound of the mailbox squeaking open and closed, her instinct trumping the pain of her broken body. Patsy could do nothing for herself, and Sheila had to lift her and carry her outside to do her business. The process was awkward and messy, but Sheila didn't mind. In the afternoons, when she came home from the school, she sat on the floor next to the dog bed and stared into Patsy's large, wet eyes, wondering what had drawn Patsy toward nothingness.

By the third week, Sheila resumed working full-time. On Monday, she sat in her school office across her desk from Morton Washburn. He was a long, angular boy who wore his hair across one eye like a slash of black felt pen marking a grammatical error. Having shed the previous year's gothic persona complete with black fingernails and white-powdered face, he now affected a prep-school style completely out of place in his inner-city high school—deck shoes and square black-framed glasses, collared shirts peeking up above sherbet-colored crewneck sweaters. The burden of his name was so great that he had to work with extra ingenuity in order to turn it from blight into irony. Sheila noted that he insisted on being called Morton rather than Morty, an affectation she thought shrewd. Morton came to speak to her nearly once a week. He was doing well in school and had not gotten into any trouble. He came from an intact home and his parents always showed up for conferences and signed his report cards. He never had much to say at their sessions, but Sheila felt he was working his way up to telling her he was gay. There were times when she wanted to give him a nudge so that they could get on with it, but instead she sat patiently each week while he tried to manufacture problems that needed her attention. This week, he was having a failure of imagination and they stared across her desk at one another in silence.

"My dog tried to kill herself," she said, finally.

"But why?" he asked. "Was she sad?"

"Define your terms," she said.

Morton sucked in a breath of air. Sheila saw the spark that students got when they matched what they knew to what was being demanded of them and found themselves equal to it. "Despondent, rueful, sorrowful."

"Someone's been studying for his SATs," she said.

He shrugged off an embarrassed smile. "Are you sure she didn't just fall?"

"No. It was intentional. I was there."

"God," Morton said. "Poor baby."

"Do you ever think of hurting yourself, Morton?" she asked. She was supposed to ask such questions when a student expressed anxiety or depression in order to estimate the element of risk. If a student didn't want to discuss such things with her directly, there was a computerized phone intake they could access. A recorded voice asked: Are you taking any drugs? Press 1 for "yes," 2 for "no." Have you considered suicide? Press 1 for "yes," 2 for "no."

"No," Morton said, wearily, as if even that option would not solve things for him. She believed him. It was the ones who proclaimed the impossibility of such an idea whom she worried about.

"Anything else you want to tell me today?" she asked.

"Not really. I feel a lot better, though. I'm glad your dog is okay."

She started to question his assertion but stopped herself. Morton was hesitantly searching for a single answer to the complicated question of himself. Perhaps it would frighten him to know that it was possible to be okay and not okay at the same time, that a thing—a dog, say, or yearning—could exist only alongside the possibility of its absence.

"I like your colors," she said, waving generally at his shirt and sweater as they both stood.

"I just can't wear what everybody else wears," he said, looking down at his chest with anguish.

"It's hard to be a style icon," she said.

"Thank you," he said, relieved.

IN FEBRUARY, winter settled in decisively. The afternoon sun was low, and the lights in the houses on the street shone with a kind of menace, as if to say that warmth was locked away. Sheila and Colin unloaded grocery bags from the car while Patsy gamboled in the hedges by the side of the driveway. Sheila watched as her husband hoisted two bags and settled them into his arms like twins. She thought about the man at the lemonade stand, about the secret hidden inside his wrinkled bag. She realized that he could not have had interview clothes in the bag because they would have been wrinkled too. She had not thought of that when she was younger. She had not fully understood the danger of his desire. She stared at Colin.

"Oh, my God," she said.

"What?" Colin said. "Are you okay?"

"You're going to hurt me, aren't you? You're going to leave."

Colin looked pained. "I love her. I'm sorry."

His clarity rendered her speechless. How could she have known that the bad thing she would never recover from would be love?

THE VET WAS RIGHT. Patsy returned to her normal self. Bouncing and happy. Her hair had grown back in the places where she'd been shaved for the surgery. Sheila took her for a long walk, along the steady path of the same development they'd gone to that autumn day. Now the two of them benefited from the smoothness of paved walkways, the gentle ups and downs, Patsy with her gimpy leg, Sheila with her heart. It was April now, but there had been a spring snow the night before. The sun splashed on the white so that Sheila had to avert her watering eyes. She walked Patsy to the embankment and watched the stream below, which moved quickly, hastened by the snowmelt. Patsy put her nose to the ground to sniff at the tough, determined growth that poked through the winter-hardened crust of earth. Sheila had not put Patsy on a leash; she was not worried the dog would jump. Patsy had already taken her leap.

Earlier that day during school, Sheila had seen Morton in the hallway. He was talking to Vanessa LaConte. Vanessa carried the flesh of her late childhood with her into adolescence just in case, as though she had overpacked, not knowing what she would need. Sheila remembered her ridiculous fantasy about Vanessa discovering the beaker full of acid. All she wanted now was for the girl to emerge from her childhood unscathed, for no one to hurt her, or even try. She was pleased to see her talking to Morton. But when he leaned down to kiss her on the mouth, Sheila had to stop herself from calling out "No! No!" as if they had stepped into the path of a bullet. She walked past them, careful not to embarrass them by acknowledging that she had seen them or that she knew Morton in any particular way. And did she know him? She had been certain he would not want to kiss girls. But maybe she was wrong. Or maybe she would eventually be right. She turned a corner feeling suddenly happy, her heart full of a radiant possibility. There was so much time between now and eventually. There was so much trouble yet to come.

HORSE PEOPLE

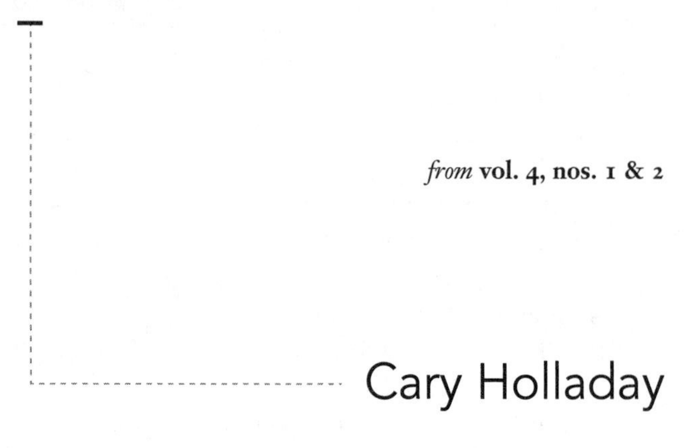

from **vol. 4, nos. 1 & 2**

Cary Holladay

BARRETT FENTON BELIEVED his father really did love all his sons the same. By October 1927, the oldest, John, was eighteen, and the youngest, Dudley, was two and a half. Barrett was next to last, almost eight. One Sunday, when church and dinner were over, Barrett was retrieving a book he'd left on the porch when his father started for the stable.

His father said, "Want to go riding with me?"

Barrett knew he was lucky, being out there at the right time. They were going to fetch a cook, his father said.

They already had a cook. "What about Nehemiah?" Barrett asked.

"Time for Nehemiah to go on home," Barrett's father said. "Retire."

Barrett could hardly imagine the kitchen without Nehemiah stoking the coal stove and the woodstove, snacking on biscuit dough, and sharpening knives. Nehemiah was old, but he still seemed fine. "Why is it time?" Barrett said. "Is he going to die?"

"My guess is Nehemiah'll be around a good many years, but your mother wants to hire somebody younger. We'll pay Nehemiah every month, same as if he still worked for us. There's a young man named Philip who'll be our new cook. His father is a carpenter, but he's sick," Barrett's father said. "I asked the doctor to go see him."

Barrett knew his father, Richard Fenton, was an important man, a judge for the Orange County Juvenile and Domestic Court. People sometimes came to the house to seek his help outside court. Barrett's father would sit with them on the porch, talking, and they'd leave with a lighter step. They'd tell Barrett, "Your father's a good man, a fair man."

His mother was not as fair. She had favorites among the boys, usually Alex and Miles, the second and fifth ones. These days it was Dudley, the youngest, because he was sick with scarlet fever. At the moment, Barrett knew, his mother was writing letters. She spent a great deal of time on correspondence with relatives, friends, and business associates. Barrett's Aunt Iris was reading to the other boys. Barrett was supposed to be with them. He was on the porch only because he'd dawdled when getting his geography book.

"I've spoken to your mother already," his father said, "and Iris."

Barrett set his book on the swing, and off they went.

It would be the first time Barrett had ridden since getting over scarlet fever himself. His father would ride Hurricane, a charcoal mare. Barrett had taken a long time to name his pony. It seemed to him that the best names were taken by his mother's horses—Card Party, Florian, Arrow, and She Will. At last he'd settled on Skedaddle, a word his father liked.

Blood from the sire, beauty from the dam, Barrett's mother often said. Horses were what she loved. Barrett knew his father didn't feel the same passion for them, though Hurricane was a great favorite of his. He'd tell Barrett's mother to watch out for horse people. Barrett didn't understand. Weren't his mother and father horse people too? Their property, known as Fairfield, was a horse farm. They were foxhunters. They were on the board of directors of the horse show. His mother didn't trust people anyway.

Barrett's father saddled up Hurricane and the pony, and off they went.

It was a blue-skied day, warm for October. "Beauteous," Barrett's father said, leaning his head back and letting Hurricane carry him along a grass trail within the pasture.

Usually, on weekends, Barrett's oldest brothers—John, Alex, and Gordon—were home from college or boarding school. They'd go hunting. It was a fine thing on a fall day, to know his brothers would be coming back at suppertime with rabbits or quail they'd shot. Because Barrett had been sick, and Dudley still was, the older ones had to stay at school. Barrett had heard his mother on the telephone, her voice stern, which meant she was almost crying.

Very briefly—and not within Barrett's memory—Barrett had a different younger brother, a child born between him and Dudley. "A beautiful baby who died in his crib," his father told him once. "Don't ask your mother about him." Barrett wished he could remember that baby.

Barrett rode beside his father. Above them, buzzards wheeled so slowly; Barrett realized how patient they were, as if they weren't hungry for whatever dead critter they were eyeing. Patience was something his Aunt Iris talked about, and the preacher, yet Barrett didn't think they meant the buzzards' kind. Barrett's stomach clenched at the sight of them. He worried about his mother, worried she would fall from her horse when she was away from home, and that only buzzards would find her. Daily she rode, usually by herself.

"Beauteous," Barrett's father said again, and if Barrett hadn't known different, he'd have thought his father was a happy man. There was somebody named Ben Burleigh who was causing bad feelings between Barrett's parents. Barrett didn't know exactly what was happening. The unhappy feeling, though, was a fact, like the buzzards, something sinister that was close and distant at the same time. Ben Burleigh was a horse person too. Sometimes when Barrett did lessons with Aunt Iris, he would realize that his mother was not at home, and he knew, somehow, that she'd gone to see that man. "Your mother's friend, Ben Burleigh," Aunt Iris dared to say once, darting a look at Barrett. Much as Barrett loved Aunt Iris, he thought she shouldn't have said that to him. The comment felt like a poke in the eye.

The sun was getting hot. Barrett and his father stopped at a creek for the horses to drink. After a while, making their way up a hillside, they reached a barn Barrett had seen only a few times before. The barn was old, with boards spaced widely so that light came through the walls. Its open bay allowed horses to shelter in its central aisle.

Along with the Thoroughbreds that Barrett's mother and father raised, a special horse lived in the surrounding field, a red horse with a coal-black mane. Ben Burleigh had given the animal to Barrett's mother. The horse appeared, as if he knew Barrett was thinking about him. He whipped along the crest of the hill, and when he was close, he kicked up his heels and raced away. Hurricane jerked at her bridle. Barrett's father said a quiet word to soothe her.

The red horse never let other horses get near him, Barrett noticed, never formed friendships the way the others did, grazing together or just standing side by side. He was the most beautiful animal Barrett had ever seen. Barrett's father never mentioned him. Barrett could almost believe, around his father, that the fiery figure was something he had only imagined.

Barrett's father led the way into the barn. Even in the dimness, Barrett saw hoofprints in the packed red-clay floor. How fine it must be to take cover there in the dark or during a storm. His father unlatched a door at the rear of the barn, and they rode through it into a brushy field. No horses lived back there.

Barrett recalled the purpose of their trip. Soon, Nehemiah would leave, and a new person would be there instead. He didn't think Nehemiah would miss them. Around Barrett's mother, Nehemiah spoke softly, but his jaw was tight. For Barrett's father, he had a quick smile but kept his eyes cast down. Nehemiah's ancestors, who'd been slaves, were buried along the fences in the field, Barrett's father said. That was the old way, he said, pointing to the rail. The ground was soft underneath, easy to dig.

They reached a wall made of rocks, with a gate in the middle. They passed through it. "This is where we leave our land,"

Barrett's father said. They entered deep woods. All around them, bugs made a glistening sound. The black walnuts were already bare; they lost their leaves first. Other trees were still green, or just turning. There was a tall tulip poplar, Barrett's favorite kind. He loved persimmons too, with their sweet fruit on the ground like a picnic.

Barrett was worn out. Scarlet fever had kept him in bed for days and made the grown-ups ban his brothers from his room, but Dudley caught it anyway and was even sicker than Barrett had been. The doctor came every day to see Dudley. The doctor still asked Barrett how he felt, holding a stethoscope against Barrett's chest and telling him to eat eggs and go to bed early.

A cabin came into view, a welcome sight.

And what was that happy sound, like a party? The cabin door swung open, and people spilled out of it, a big colored family with several children, greeting them.

An old woman said, "Mr. Fenton, that boy..." and she doubled over, laughing.

A younger woman explained, "Philip got a pet chicken. Emmy."

A girl about Barrett's age said, "We put the chicken down the chimney, to clean it." She made flapping motions with her arms.

"Well, let's take a look," Barrett's father said, swinging out of the saddle and holding out a hand to help Barrett climb down from Skedaddle. For a second Barrett's legs buckled, but his father didn't seem to notice. Barrett's father said, "Meet my son—Barrett."

The family said Barrett favored his father, and Barrett was pleased. The girl and the two women led them into the cabin.

In the middle of the floor sat a boy clutching a grimy white hen. Feathers littered the hearth. The cabin had some plain furniture, Barrett saw, and windows, though some panes were cracked. Barrett smelled something savory. The old woman offered fried squirrel. Barrett ate a piece: delicious. They offered coffee too, but it was so bitter, Barrett couldn't drink it. One of the children brought a dipper of water. Barrett did drink that.

The laughter had died down like leaves settling on the ground after a breeze. The boy bent his head over his crossed arms as if protecting the chicken. Barrett saw that the boy was older than he had thought at first, almost a man.

"Philip didn't like what we did," the old woman said, "using Emmy that way."

Philip, the young man, raised his head, a grin flickering over his lips. "She did right well," he said.

Barrett's father looked around and asked, "How is Robert? Was the doctor here?"

"Here he is," the old woman said, gesturing to a pile of bedding in a corner. Barrett realized that the old woman was probably Robert's mother, and Philip was Robert's son.

The other woman spoke up. Barrett guessed she was Robert's wife and Philip's mother. "He was bit by a spider, the bad kind," she said. "That's what the doctor said."

Barrett's father made his way to the corner. The women lifted the covers from the man's legs. Barrett glimpsed a bare, bloated knee with a craterlike sore in the middle. A scary, rotten smell reached Barrett's nose.

"Robert, can you stand up? Can you walk?" Barrett's father asked.

"No," the man said, his voice hoarse, his pupils glittering, and Barrett remembered how hot and dry his own eyes had felt when he was sick.

"Did the doctor leave this?" Barrett's father said, picking up a jar of medicine.

"It don't seem to help," said Robert.

Barrett's father said to Robert's wife, "Put him in the wagon tomorrow morning and bring him to the road. I'll be waiting in the car, about eight o'clock. I'll take him to the hospital."

She nodded.

Robert said, "Philip goes back with y'all, Mr. Fenton. He knows that."

Barrett's father said, "Philip, does that sound all right to you?"

Philip agreed. Philip's mother ran outside and tore something off a clothesline. His other shirt, she said. Philip kept the white chicken in his arms, and Barrett realized the chicken would go with them. Philip's grandmother tied up the chicken's feet with string. "So Emmy can't fly away," she said.

Barrett's father put Barrett on Hurricane with him, and Philip rode Skedaddle, holding the chicken in one arm. His long legs almost trailed the ground. The younger children followed at a distance through the woods. Barrett kept looking back until they were gone.

NEHEMIAH TRAINED PHILIP for a few days, and then Nehemiah was gone. Philip was born to cook, Barrett's mother declared. He learned how to fix roasts, game, vegetables, and sweets. Breads too, batter bread and rolls. Barrett's mother had cookbooks, and Nehemiah used to look up recipes, but Philip couldn't read, Barrett realized.

Philip slept out in the stable, in the tack room. He and the stable boy shared a coal stove for heat, a flush toilet, and a sink with a single tap. Early every morning, Philip let himself into the house through the back porch. Every night, he let himself out and made his way back to the stable. Barrett sometimes heard the soft sweep of the door. Philip had every other weekend off, and he would go home to his family. Barrett pictured him walking through the woods. It had taken a long time to reach the cabin on horseback. How long would it take to walk?

Philip never married. There was a man who visited him, a black man older than he was, who would come over in a mule-drawn cart, and he and Philip would go off together in the part of the afternoon when Barrett's mother was napping or riding. Barrett's brothers said bad words about Philip and his friend, and Barrett said them too, trying out the slurs. There were questions Barrett wanted to ask, but he didn't know how. Philip and his visitor went clattering off in the cart, and where they went and what they did were mysteries to Barrett, despite his brothers' jokes. When Philip returned, he never looked or acted any different. He'd be humming as he washed dishes.

Philip stayed slim. His face had a reddish tint, like Nehemiah's. Barrett would have sworn Philip was Nehemiah's son or grandson, but his father said no, they were from different families. Barrett admired the way his father could keep entire Orange County genealogies in his head. He knew the names and kinships from all the years people came up onto his porch and asked for advice. He loved them, Barrett realized, as if having seven sons only made it easier for him to love the people of the entire county.

BARRETT AND HIS BROTHERS GREW UP and went to war, all seven, deployed to the Pacific or to Europe. Even the oldest brothers went. John, at thirty-two, was divorced and had no children, and Alex, thirty, was married and had a son born while he was overseas. They kept in touch through letters and the prized occasional visit home. Barrett saved the letters his parents wrote during his tour, about sausage-making and new foals. Aunt Iris wrote too. Barrett's father had a heart attack, Aunt Iris said, and the doctor insisted he rest. Philip helped him up and down the steps. A photograph Aunt Iris sent surprised Barrett: a tired old farm couple squinted into the sun, their shoulders sagging. Where were the vigorous, dashing parents of his childhood? On the deck of his merchant marine ship, in the brilliant oceanic light, Barrett held the picture close. Nearsightedness and flat feet had ended his time in the army, but he liked the merchant marine better, because he traveled more. He bought a small portable motorcycle, and on shore leave in Italy, Belgium, and Poland he explored the cities and the countryside, often with some pretty local girl to guide him.

With great good fortune, Barrett and all his brothers survived the war. Barrett had been home for only two weeks when his father had the second heart attack, which killed him. And then it seemed to Barrett that although his own life picked up its pace, his mother's and Philip's continued almost unchanged. Philip worked for Barrett's mother during her long widowhood, fixing three meals a day, and party food when she wanted to entertain. Barrett and his brothers, married now, with careers—Barrett was a civil engineer—gave Philip extra money when they were home. They were afraid their mother wasn't keeping up with his pay. Aunt Iris died, and Barrett had the feeling his mother didn't miss her, though Philip did. His face looked heavy and sorrowful, and suddenly, his hair was gray.

Whenever Barrett's brothers' wives tried to chat with Philip, he was pleasant with them. He knew which one was married to which son, and which children belonged to whom. But he wasn't much for conversation, as Barrett explained to his wife. Pamela was shy and gentle. She grew up in Williamsburg, the daughter of a doctor who died about the same time as Barrett's own father did. Barrett was glad Pamela didn't badger Philip the way the louder, wilder wives did, teasing him and drinking whiskey in the kitchen. Barrett sensed Philip would have preferred to be left alone to do his work, and imagined he was grateful to Pamela for the respectful distance she kept. Besides, Pamela didn't enjoy the other wives very much. "Show-offs," she complained to Barrett. "There's a lot of one-upmanship. Women are worse than men, that way."

For decades, Philip appeared in holiday photographs, wearing a white jacket, serving at the dining room table. Barrett was the first Fenton to get a Polaroid camera. It pleased him that his brothers got so excited, wanting Polaroids too. He told Pamela, "It's the only thing I've ever had that they didn't."

"And me," Pamela said.

"And you," said Barrett.

Finally, Barrett's mother, nearing ninety, pensioned Philip off like she'd done with Nehemiah. "He cried," she told Barrett on the phone. "He didn't want to go home." Barrett and Pamela were living up North by then, in Connecticut, with three daughters. His mother was scared of somebody dying at her house, she admitted, afraid of authorities coming. It was one of the few fears Barrett ever knew her to have.

"He went on home," she said, and Barrett pictured the cabin deep in the woods. The darkness and remoteness came back to him. What condition was it in, he wondered, and what had become of Philip's family? Was the cabin deserted, with branches poking through the windows, or was it shipshape, with somebody baking bread to welcome Philip home?

"I think it's a mistake to let him go, Mother," Barrett said. "It's not too late to change your mind. Ask him to come back."

His mother grew angry and hung up the phone. She hated to be contradicted. She was never easy to get along with, Barrett fumed to Pamela, and was only getting worse with age.

Barrett had trouble remembering the names of the cooks and companions that followed. None stayed for long. Philip didn't live more than a year after he retired. The news traveled the circuit of Barrett and the brothers. Barrett felt his mother's own time was coming to an end. His brothers and their wives asked, How long can she go on?

She died in August 1976, aged ninety-three.

One of the seven sons, Gordon, had died in '58, at forty-four, but he'd lived hard, drinking and gambling. Their mother willed her property equally to the others. Barrett borrowed money and bought out his brothers' portions. It was what he wanted more than anything, to own Fairfield and live there again, though he would have to work hard to pay it off. He knew he could do it. His three daughters were grown, finishing college and making their lives elsewhere.

Pamela objected. She didn't want so much debt or such a big house. She wanted nothing to do with farming. They quarreled sharply, and Barrett felt their marriage wobbling toward divorce. At last Pamela relented, but she extracted from him two promises: they would not raise horses, and they, or at least she, "wouldn't have to go to funerals all the time."

Barrett was surprised she didn't make more demands. He agreed readily to her terms. His boyhood friends were starting to die, and funerals always upset him, to the point where he could have wept at a stranger's. He would go to those that mattered most, but he'd go alone. As for horses—he'd never felt about them the way his mother did, so he suggested to Pamela that they rent out the barns and pastures, and the horses that lived there would belong to other people. That was fine with Pamela, and they packed their belongings and moved.

Barrett easily found horse people to rent the barn and the fields, and Pamela occasionally strolled out to chat with them. But when Barrett suggested they invite their tenants in for coffee, she'd say, "The four-legged ones would be okay, but not the two-legged ones."

Barrett laughed, though he sometimes wished Pamela were more sociable. He had told her how his father warned his mother about horse people, and she repeated the admonition so often that for Barrett it wore a little thin. Through the family grapevine, Pamela had learned of the affair between his mother and Ben Burleigh. She marveled, "With all those children, how did she have time?" Barrett tried to divert her: "Aw, it was so long ago." Pamela mused, "How much was physical, do you think? Or was it more of an emotional involvement?" and Barrett would change the subject. Didn't she understand it was hurtful, even now?

When Barrett's brothers brought their wives back to the old place, Pamela served simple meals and adeptly discouraged overnight visits. Barrett's brothers lived out their span of days, and some grew old and older still. Barrett outlived them all. He was the last one.

HALFWAY HOME, that October day in 1927, Emmy broke free from Philip's grasp. She shook the binding from her feet and flew up into a pine. Philip cried out, lunging from the saddle. As the white hen settled in the bough, with the sun streaming behind her, Barrett realized it was late in the day. In the woods around Philip's cabin it might already be dark.

"Well, look at that," Barrett's father said. He took off his hat and waved it toward Emmy's perch, but the chicken stayed where she was.

Philip slid off the pony and ran toward the tree. He angled his thin body into the limbs, but he fell, tearing his pant leg, and his face showed fear. Barrett felt suddenly as if he and his father had kidnapped Philip. What he was seeing was homesickness and sorrow. Emmy was still in sight, but it would be hard to get her back.

Barrett's father dismounted, went to the base of the tree, and called, "Birdy, birdy, come on down."

"I'll get her," Barrett said and eased his legs over the saddle. Sixteen hands high, Hurricane was. Barrett fell, knocking the wind out of his lungs, but he stood up again.

The tree was so tall that he thought of Jack and the Beanstalk. Up and up he climbed. Sap stuck to his hands. He was hungry and thirsty. At home, his mother and brothers and Aunt Iris might have already eaten supper. Above him, the chicken was a rustling white blur. Despite being tired, Barrett knew he was well again, that the doctor was satisfied when he listened to his heart. Barrett's thoughts moved back and forth. A spider bite could lame a man, even kill him. How could he have forgotten about Philip's father, the man in the corner, for even a little while? What if his father forgot about the man? No, his father would be waiting on the road in the morning as he'd promised. Yet maybe that was too long to wait.

The chicken sailed out of the tree.

She flew higher than Barrett knew a chicken could go, to the very top of the pine, where she disappeared. Barrett balanced himself and looked down. It was the highest he'd ever been. His father looked up, and their eyes met. His father's face was serious and attentive, the way it was when he sat on the porch with people who were troubled about legal matters. Most other men would be laughing about Philip and Emmy, laughing so hard their shoulders would shake. Other men would tell the story at the table and laugh all over again, but not his father.

Barrett himself would tell this story, he realized, though he didn't know what words he would use. And who would listen? Dudley would, and Aunt Iris. And Barrett felt there were future people he would tell, people waiting for him when he was grown.

For an instant, while his father's gray eyes held his, Barrett saw right through his father's life. His father must be feeling old. He was in his middle fifties, yet he had been a boy once, bareheaded and free. You were young for a while, Barrett saw, and then, if you lived, youth was gone. He had a chill, and he couldn't tell if it were a last wave of sickness or something else. One day, his father would be gone, and his mother, and his brothers.

Philip kept his hand over his mouth, staring up at the tree. At last, he sobbed. The sound carried in the still, chilly air.

"Come on down, Barrett," his father said. Barrett did, and they got back on the horses.

"I'll come back and look for her," Barrett told Philip.

He did. For days after that, Barrett and his brothers packed their pockets with dried corn, took Philip with them, and hiked back into the field. There was never any sign of Emmy.

LATE IN LIFE, when Barrett was so old that people saw him as a person from another time, he lived alone in the house where he'd grown up. Pamela had died, and their daughters and grandchildren lived in other places. Still there were beauteous days at Fairfield, with warm afternoons and nights crisp as apples. Barrett loved coming back to his wide porch after a game of golf, a meeting of his grief support group, or a date with a girlfriend. He gave parties, and afterward he loved the silence. It held so much. No brothers hunted in the fields, no Fentons but himself clambered up the steps, but the stillness was cheerful. He had a long run of good days, good years, doing things just the way he wanted.

One Thanksgiving, when his daughters visited with their families, the memory of that day in 1927 came back to him. His daughters had known Philip as their grandmother's cook, when they were children. Barrett began, "My father took me with him when he went to get Philip. That family lived way far back in the woods."

He paused, and his oldest daughter said sharply, "Daddy, you're too thin. Here, have some more cake."

"I don't want any more," he said, but she pushed another slice onto his plate.

The middle girl, the fidgety one, bit her lip, but she was paying attention. Of the three, she was the most likely to ask about his early life. The youngest one's phone rang, and she glided away. Outside, Barrett's grandsons shouted and threw a Frisbee.

Barrett's train of thought deserted him. "It's getting hard for me to hang a story together," he said, lifting his hands as if trying to pack the story between them, feeling how impossible it was to tell the truth of an event, to know the truth of another person's life. His mother's, for instance: she was a mystery, yet the older he grew, the more his father seemed a mystery, putting up with Ben Burleigh. Why hadn't he sought a divorce? Maybe he thought it would be too painful for his sons.

And what had happened to the red horse with the black mane? Plain as day, Barrett saw his mother struggling to mount the animal. The horse propped, sticking out his front legs and lowering his head, so she slid right down his neck. That enraged her. Was he sold? Was he buried in the red clay somewhere on Fairfield's two hundred acres? And Ben Burleigh: he fell off his horse during a hunt, dead. Barrett's mother, a widow by then, grieved so hard, she took to her bed.

Barrett's daughters cleared the table, and he went into the living room and sat in his favorite chair, feeling tired, the meal he'd eaten settling heavily in his stomach. A grandson burst into the room, waving a skinned palm. Then they gathered around Barrett, daughters, sons-in-law, and grandchildren.

The middle daughter said, "Daddy, finish telling about Philip."

Barrett took a breath and found it was there after all, in his mind: the taste of fried squirrel, the big family, and in a corner of the cabin, Philip's father, Robert, so desperately sick.

Barrett said, "His father wanted Philip to have the job," and then he was silent. His daughters exchanged glances. He saw that. The long ride to the cabin and back, on the horses—he wanted to describe that journey, but he found himself leaping ahead. "When we got back, Dudley ran out to meet us. He'd been sick with that bad thing." *Scarlet fever* was on the tip of his tongue. "He was a whole lot better," he said, "almost well again."

His daughters nodded. Dudley, their favorite uncle, had died the previous year.

Barrett said, "Father picked Dudley up and swung him around, just laughing."

His father's laughter was a deep, wonderful *Ho-ho!* Barrett's mother said, "See, the roses are back in his cheeks," and she hugged Dudley. She hugged Barrett too, and he thought, It'll be all right now. He hoped the hug meant Ben Burleigh would go away. Nehemiah brought out a cold supper for Barrett and his father. Then Nehemiah took Philip back into the kitchen and fed him too. By then it was dark outside, and the house felt warm and safe.

Amazing, to reach back eighty years and find all that. His parents' happiness had delighted him; he felt it all over again. But back at the cabin, back at the cabin: something tugged at Barrett.

"And then what, Daddy?" asked the youngest daughter, tucking her phone into her pocket. Barrett felt the sadness on his face before he knew the reason for it. His daughter asked, "Did something bad happen?"

"His father," he said.

"Whose father?" rattled his oldest daughter, and Barrett shook his head, searching through her impatience to find quiet again.

"Philip's father," the middle daughter murmured. "Just let him talk at his own pace."

Yes: it was Philip's father, Robert, who filled Barrett's mind. Barrett was struck with concern, a useless emotion now that so much time had passed. Hadn't he thought even once of Robert in all these years? He felt as worried as if Robert were still waiting in that cabin with his ruined leg and bright, dry eyes.

Barrett's daughters gazed at him expectantly. He wanted to finish the story, but he didn't know if he could.

There'd been talk of the hospital, of poisonous spiders, of the fact that lying on a cold floor wouldn't help a man get better. Barrett remembered that, but he couldn't remember if Philip's father had lived or died.

the way the other fellows hunch lower, bringing their heels up to the fire—he'll circle all the way back to the beginning of his story again, starting with how he had left this camp—a couple of years back—and hiked several miles to a street, lined with old maples, that on first impression had seemed very much like the one he'd grown up on, although he wasn't sure because years of drifting on the road had worn the details from his memory, so many miles behind him in the form of bad drink and that mind-numbing case of lockjaw he claims he had in Pittsburgh. (The antitoxin, he explained, had been administered just in time, saving him from the worst of it. A kind flophouse doctor named Williams had tended to his wound, cleaning it out and wrapping it nicely, giving him a bottle of muscle pills.) He hiked into town—the first time—to stumble upon a house that held a resemblance to whatever was left in his memory: a farmhouse with weatherworn clapboard. A side garden with rosebushes and, back beyond a fence, a vegetable patch with pole beans. Not just the same house—he had explained—but the same sweet smell emanating from the garden where far back beyond a few willow trees a brook ran, burbling and so on and so forth. He went on too long about the brook and one of the men (who exactly, I can't recall) said, I wish you still had that case of lockjaw. (That was the night he was christened Lockjaw Kid.) He stood out in the road and absorbed the scene and felt an overwhelming sense that he was home; a sense so powerful it held him fast and—in his words—made him fearful that he'd find it too much to his liking if he went up to beg a meal. So he went back down to the camp with an empty belly and decided to leave well enough alone until, months later, coming through these parts again after a stint of work in Chicago (Lockjaw couched his life story in the idea of employment, using it as a tool of sorts to get his point across. Whereas the rest of us had long ago given up talking of labor in any form, unless it was to say something along the lines of: Worked myself so hard I'll never work again; or, I'd work if I could find a suitable form of employment that didn't involve work) he decided to hike the six miles into town to take another look, not sure what he was searching for because by that time the initial visit—he said last time he told the story—had become only a vague memory, burned away by drink and travel;

aforesaid confession itself attesting to a hole in his story about having worked in Chicago and giving away the fact that he had, more likely, hung on and headed all the way out to the coast for the winter, whiling his time in the warmth, plucking the proverbial fruit directly from the trees and so on and so forth. We didn't give a shit. That part of his story had simply given us a chance to give him a hard time, saying, You were out in California if you were anywhere, you dumb shit. Not anywhere near Chicago looking for work. You couldn't handle Chicago winters. Only work you would've found in Chicago would've been meat work. You couldn't handle meat work. You're not strong enough to lug meat. Meat would do you in, and so on and so forth. Whatever the case, he said, shrugging us off, going on to explain how he hiked the six miles up to town again and came to the strangely familiar house again: smell of the brook. (You smelled the brook the first time you went up poking around, you dumb moron, Lefty said. And he said, Let me qualify and say not just the smell but the exact way it came from—well, how shall I put this? The smell of clear, clean brook water—potable as all hell—filtered through wild myrtle and jimsonweed and the like came to me from a precise point in my past, some exact place, so to speak.) He stood outside the house again, gathering his courage for a knock at the back door, preparing a story for the lady who would appear, most likely in an apron, looking down with wary eyes at one more vagrant coming through to beg a meal. I had a whopper ready, he said, and then he paused to let us ponder our own boilerplate beg-tales of woe. Haven't eaten in a week & will work for food was the basic boilerplate, with maybe the following flourish: I suffered cancer of the blood (bone, liver, stomach, take your pick) and survived and have been looking for orchard work (blueberry, apple) but it's the off-season so I'm hungry, ma'am. That sort of thing. Of course his version included lockjaw. Hello, ma'am, I'm sorry to bother you but I'm looking for a meal & some work. (Again, always the meal & work formula. That was the covenant that had to be sealed because most surely the man of the house would show up, expecting as much.) He moved his mouth strangely and tightened his jaw. I suffered from a case of lockjaw back in Pittsburgh, he told the lady. I lost my mill job on account of it, he added. Then he drove home the particulars—he assured us—going into not only Pittsburgh itself (all that heavy industry), but also saying he had worked at Homestead, pouring hot steel, and then even deeper (maybe this was later, at the table with the entire family, he added quickly, sensing our disbelief) to explain that once a blast furnace was cooked up, it ran for months and you couldn't stop to think because the work was so hard and relentless, pouring ladles and so on and so forth. Then he gave her one or two genuine tears, because if Lockjaw had one talent it was the ability to cry on command. (He would say: I'm going to cry for you, boys, and then, one at a time, thick tears would dangle on the edges of his eyelids, hang there, and roll slowly down his cheeks. Oft times he'd just come back to the fire, sit, rub his hands together, and start the tears. You'll rust up tight, Lockjaw, one of the men would inevitably say.) In any case, the lady of the house—she was young with a breadbasket face, all cheekbones and delicate eyes—looked down at him (he stayed two steps down. Another technique: always look as short and stubby and nonthreatening as possible) and saw the tears and beckoned him with a gentle wave of her hand, bringing him into the kitchen, which was warm with the smell of baking bread. (Jesus, our stomachs twitched when he told this part. To think of it. The warmth of the stove and the smell of the baking! We were chewing stones! That's how hungry we were. Bark & weeds.) So there he was in the kitchen, watching the lady as she opened the stove and leaned over to poke a toothpick into a cake, pulling it out and holding it up, looking at it the way you'd examine a gemstone while all the time keeping an eye on him, nodding softly as he described—again—the way it felt to lose what you thought of as permanent employment after learning all the ropes, becoming one of the best steel pourers—not sure what the lingo was, but making it up nicely—able to pour from a ladle to a dipper to a thimble. (He'd gotten those terms from his old man. They were called thimbles, much to the amusement of the outside world. His father had done millwork in Pittsburgh. Came home stinking of taconite. He spoke of his father the way we all spoke of our old men, casually, zeroing in as much as possible on particular faults—hard drinking, a heavy hand. The old man hit like a heavyweight, quick and hard, his fist out of the blue. The old man had one up on Dempsey. You'd turn around to a fist in your face. A big ham-fisted old brute bastard. Worked like a mule and came home to the bottle. That sort of thing.) In any case, he popped a few more tears for the lady and accepted her offer of a cup of tea. At this point, he stared at the campfire and licked his lips and said, I knew the place, you see. The kitchen had a familiar feel, what with the same rooster clock over the stove that I remembered as a boy. Then he tapered off again into silence and we knew he was digging for details. Any case, no matter, he said. At that point I was busy laying out my story, pleading my case. (We understood that if he had let up talking he might have opened up a place for speculation on the part of the homeowner. The lady of the house might—if you stopped talking, or said something off the mark—turn away and begin thinking in a general way about hoboes: the scum of the world, leaving behind civility not because of some personal anguish but rather out of a desire—*wanderlust* would be the word that came to her mind—to let one minute simply vanish behind another. You had to spin out a yarn and keep spinning until the food was in your belly and you were out the door. The story had to be just right and had to begin at your point of origin, building honestly out of a few facts of your life, maybe not the place of birth exactly but somewhere you knew so well you could draw details in a persuasive, natural way. You drew *not* from your own down-and-out-of-luck story, because your own down-and-out-of-luck story would only sound sad-sack and tawdry, but rather from an amalgamation of other tales you'd heard: a girlfriend who'd gone sour, a bad turn of luck in the grain market, a gambling debt to a Chicago bootlegger. Then you had to weave your needs into your story carefully, placing them in the proper perspective to the bad luck so that it would seem frank & honest & clean-hearted. Too much of one thing—the desire to eat a certain dish, say, goulash, or a hankering for a specific vegetable, say, lima beans—and your words would sound tainted and you'd be reduced to what you really were: a man with no exact destination trying to dupe a woman into thinking you had some kind of forward vision. A man with no plans whatsoever trying as best he could—at that particular moment—to sound like a man who knew, at least to some degree, where he might be heading in relation to his point of origin. To

that he had been given medical care in Pittsburgh (an injection of antitoxin by a kindly charity doctor; the wound cleaned out and bandaged; a bottle of muscle pills to boot) and had found himself wandering off before the cure set in, only to collapse several hundred miles away on the rods at Stateline junction, giving all the details—about the rods, the way the tower worked—and keeping the tone even and believable until the entire table was wide-eyed for a moment, with the exception of the man of the house who, it turned out, had done a stint as a brakeman on the Nickleplate, worked his way up to conductor, and then used his earnings to put himself through the University of Chicago Law School. The man of the house began asking questions, casually at first, not in a lawyerly voice but in a fatherly tone, one after another, each one more specific, until he did have a lawyerly tone that said, unspoken: Once you've eaten you pack yourself up and ship out of town before I call the sheriff on you. Go back to your wanderlust and stop taking advantage of hardworking folks. Right then, Lockjaw thought he was safe and sound. Dinner & the boot. Cast off with a full belly, as simple as that. But the lawyerly voice continued—Lockjaw went into this in great detail, spelling out how it had shifted from leisurely cross-examination questions—You sure you fell across a rod hard enough to bend it? You sure now you saved the day exactly as you're saying, son? To tighter, more exact questions: Where you say you're from? What kind of work you say you did in Pittsburgh? Did you say you poured from a ladle into a thimble, or from a ladle into a scoop? You said interlocking mechanism? You sure those things aren't fail-safe? You said an eastbound and a westbound approach on the same line? (At this point, most of the men around the fire knew how the story would turn. They understood the way in which such questions pushed a man into a corner. Each answer nudged against the last. Each answer depended on a casualness, an ease and quickness of response, that began to give way to a tension in the air until the man of the house felt his suspicions confirmed in the way the answers came between bites, because you'd be eating in haste, making sure your belly was as full up as fast as possible, chewing and turning to the lady, and, as a last ditch, making mention of a beloved mother who cooked food almost, but not quite, nearly, but not exactly, as good. These are the best biscuits I've ever had, and that's factoring in the fact that I'm so hungry. Even if I wasn't this hungry, I'd find these the best biscuits I've had in my entire life.)

WHEN LOCKJAW TOLD THIS PART of the story, the men by the fire nodded with appreciation because he was spinning it all out nicely, building it up, playing it out as much as he could, heading toward the inevitable chase-off. One way or another the man of the house would cast him off his property. He'd stiffen and adjust his shirt collar, clearing his throat, taking his time, finding the proper primness. A stance had to be found in which casting off the hobo would appear—to the lady of the house—to be not an act of unkindness but one of justice. Otherwise he'd have an evening of bitterness. When the man turned to God—as expected—after the cross-examination about work, employment, and the train incident—Lockjaw felt his full belly pushing against his shirt—a man could eat only so much on such a hungry gut, of course—and had the cup to his mouth when the question was broached, in general terms, about his relationship to Christ. Have you taken Christ? the man said, holding his hands down beside his plate. Have you taken Christ as your Holy Savior and Redeemer? (I knew it. Fuck, I knew it, the men around the fire muttered. Could've set a clock to know that was coming. Can't go nowhere without being asked that one.) At that point, the man of the house listened keenly, not so much to the answer—because he'd never expect to get anything but a yes from a hobo wanting grub—but to the quickness of the response, the pace with which Lockjaw had said, Yes, sir, I took Christ back in Hammond, Indiana, without pausing one minute to consider the width and breadth of his beloved Lord, as would a normal God-fearing soul, saved by Christ but still unable to believe his good grace and luck. (Gotta pause and make like you're thinking it out, Lefty muttered. Gotta let them see you think. If they don't see you thinking, you ain't thinking.) Lockjaw had given his answer just a fraction of a second too quickly, and in doing so had given his host a chance to recognize—in that lack of space between the proposed question and the given answer—the flimsiness of his belief. Here Lockjaw petered off a bit, lost track of his train of thought, and slugged good and hard from the bottle in his hand, lifting it high, tossing his head back and then popping the neck from his lips and shaking his head hard while looking off into the trees as if he'd find out there, in the dark weeds, a man in white robes with a kind face and a bearded chin with his arms raised in blessing. Fuck, he said. All the man of the house saw was a goddamn hungry tramp trying to scare up some grub. We faced off while his wife prattled away about the weather, or some sort of thing, giving her husband a look that said: Be nice, don't throw him out until he's had a slice of my pie. But the man of the house ignored her and kept his eyes on mine until he could see right into them, Lockjaw said, pausing to stare harder into the woods and to give us time enough to consider—as we warmed our feet—that it was all a part of the boilerplate: The man of the house's gaze would be long & sad & deep & lonely & full of the anguish of his position in the world, upstanding & fine & good & dandy & dusted off, no matter what he did for a living, farming or ranching or foreclosing on farms, doctoring or lawyering—no matter how much dust he had on him during his work he'd be clean & spiffy with a starched collar & watch chain & cufflinks & lean, smooth, small fingers no good for anything, really, except sorting through papers or pulling a trigger when the time came. A little dainty trigger finger itching to use an old Winchester tucked upstairs under the bed, hazy with lint but with a bullet in the chamber ready for such a moment: cocky young hobo comes in to beg a meal and wins over the little wife only to sit at the table with utter disrespect, offering up cockamamy stories that make the son go wide-eyed and turn the heart.

AS LOCKJAW DESCRIBED THE STARE-DOWN with the man of the house, his voice became softer, and he said, The man of the house excused himself for a moment. He begged my pardon and went clomping up the stairs, and I told the lady I probably should be going but she told me about her pie, said she wanted me to have a bite of it before I left, and I told her maybe I'd have to pass on the pie, and we went together to the kitchen, he said while we leaned in intently and listened to him because the story had taken a turn we hadn't expected. For the sake of decorum, most of us would've stayed at the table until the gun appeared. Most of us too hungry. (At least I think this is why we let him simply close his story down. He shut it down and began to weep. He cried in a sniffy, real sort of way, gasping for breath, cinching his face up tight into his open palms, rubbing them up into his grief again and again. He was faking it, Hank said later. He was pulling out his usual trump card. He had me up until that point. Then his story fell apart.) None of us said a word as night closed over us and the fire went dead and we slept as much as we could, waking to stare up into the cold, flinty sky, pondering the meal he had eaten—the green beans waxy and steaming, the mashed potatoes dripping fresh butter, and of course the pork, thick and dripping with juice, waiting to be cut into and lifted to the mouth of our dreams. Then the train came the next day and we went off into another round of wander—west through Gary, through the yards, holding on, not getting off, sticking together for the most part, heading to the coast for the winter and then east again until we found ourselves at the same junction a year later, the same trees and double switch and cross-tracks where the line came down out of Michigan and linked up with the Chicago track, and once again, as if for the first time, Lockjaw said he recognized the place and then, slowly, bit by bit, he remembered the last visit and said he was going back, heading up through the verge with his thumbs hooked in his pockets, turning once to say he'd try to bring us back a bit of pie. By golly, she said she'd put the pie on the sill for me, he said. She told me anytime I wanted to come back, she'd have it waiting for me. If you remember what I told you, I was running out the door with the gun behind me when she called it out to me, he added, turning one last time before he disappeared from sight. (Forgot all about that foolishness, Hank said. Guess he's home again, Lefty said. And we all had a big, overripe belly laugh at the kid's expense, going on for a few minutes with the gibes, because in Lincoln and in Carson and Mill City and from one shitting crop town to the next he had come back from whatever meal he had scrounged up with the same kind of feeling. He seemed to have an instinct for finding a lady willing to give in to his stories.) By the time he came back the jokes were dead and our hunger was acute. Like I said before, he had the pie on his face and a plate in his hand and he's already talking, speaking through the crumbs and directly to our hunger, starting in on it again, and when he comes to the smell of the brook, we interrupt only to make sure he doesn't go back over the story from the beginning again, sparking him with occasional barbs, holding back the snide comments but in doing so knowing—in that heart of hearts—that we'll make up for our kindness by leaving him behind the next morning, letting him sleep the sleep of the pie, just a snoring mound up in the weeds.

THE BLUE TREE

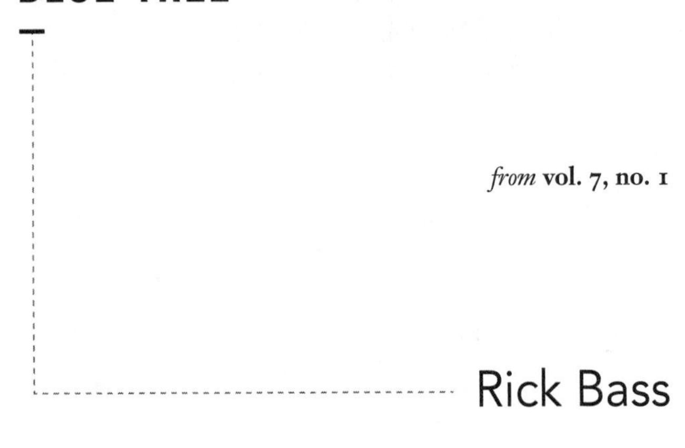

from **vol. 7, no. 1**

Rick Bass

IT'S THE AFTERNOON of the day before Christmas Eve, and still there is no tree. Somehow the week has just slipped away. It's taken them forever to get packed and ready for the trip to their cabin in the woods, but finally Wilson has issued the proclamation to his wife and daughters that it's time to relax and start enjoying the holidays, damn it. After twenty years, he's lost his job as a road-construction engineer, and though he knows, intellectually, that he's foolish to be brooding on it at a time of year when his priorities should be reordered, he can't help it, he's still a little tense. Belinda's not working, she's been focusing on being at home as much as possible while their girls, Stephanie and Lucy, are young. Wilson never thought he would be out of work. He thought work always existed, like air. You breathed, you worked.

It's a tendency of his: the more imperfect things become, the more he wants them to be otherwise. In most years by now they would have already been at the cabin for their weeklong time away from town, work, everything. Wilson and the girls would've gone into the woods together to cut down their tree, an annual ritual he started the Christmas after Stephanie was born, with her bundled and huddled against his chest in a papoose. But this year they'll have to get their tree *tonight*, as soon as they make it to the cabin, Wilson has told them, in order to spend Christmas Eve day decorating it, and settling in: cooking, hanging their stockings, shoveling snow, sledding. Coming back home with their toboggans in the fast blue dusk to the delicious odors of the holiday—ginger, cardamom, cinnamon, peppermint—with the fragrant tree in their living room, adorned with its familiar ornaments, each one recalling for them a certain story, and lit with the colorful lights that remind them of the luxury of even a little electricity, here so far back in the woods, gotten from the little battery-and-solar-panel system that Wilson takes such pride in having designed.

The big family feast, a lovely candlelit dinner in their warm home, just the four of them, with the snow coming down outside—the elegant dessert, a chocolate chess pie or flaky rhubarb—and then the reading aloud of "The Night Before Christmas" (never mind that Stephanie, eleven, no longer believes, and Lucy, eight, is hovering on the edge; this may be her last year even for partial belief: and all the sweeter, Wilson thinks, for that going-awayness), until at last the opening of one gift from beneath the tree.

Stoking the woodstove up to a fire then, before going upstairs to their beds. Leaving on the table by the hearth the half cup of milk in the ancient Santa mug, and the paper plate heaped with cookies, the carrots and celery stalks for the reindeer.

There's a second tree at the cabin, actually, one which they don't really count or think of as a Christmas tree. It's a big spruce out in the yard, perfectly formed and living. Years ago Wilson climbed it and laced lights all the way up, alternating blue and white to the distant top. He engineered the string with enough slack so that as the tree grew there would be room for the lights to grow with the tree—and all he had to do was add another string at the bottom every few years.

From the house he laid an underground pipe going out into the yard, to where the tree stood some hundred feet away, at the bottom of the long driveway descending from the main road, and threaded a series of extension cords through the pipe, so that when he flipped a switch on the porch, they could watch the yard tree—one of many there in the forest—leap into instant, brilliant life, sizzling with color in the darkness. That image is as stimulating to Wilson in the gray-blue creep of early dusk as it is at inky, starry midnight, or with snow falling so heavily that the bright lights appear gauzy and more distant than they really are: as if they are some farther destination he has been seeking for a long time.

BY THE TIME THEY NEAR THEIR CABIN—with each passing mile taking them farther into a snowier and more silent country, with entire mountains shrouded in the season's new snow, and every tree likewise caped with white, and the river along which the little road travels all but frozen over, nothing more than a thin dark thread of icy current coursing through it—it is almost dusk, nearly always dusk down in these blue valleys, with the only visible sunlight the orange alpenglow that gilds the serrated ridges of the highest peaks, while far below, all else remains in deep shadow.

They churn their way down the long driveway, winding back at last to the snow-clad cabin. They spend half an hour unloading. Wilson gets a fire going in the woodstove; the cabin itself stretches and groans as it begins to warm. Belinda begins preparing an early dinner. The girls have rented movies to watch on the VCR—there is no television reception, no satellite dish, no anything, save forest and each other—and casually, cautiously, Belinda asks Wilson if he's planning on waiting until the early morning to get the tree.

It is the kind of question which married couples of twenty or thirty years or longer pose to each other—the suggestion that tries only faintly to masquerade as a query, the old "So were you planning on cleaning out the garage on Saturday or Sunday?" gambit.

But, for Wilson, *tomorrow* is out of the question. Even if they arose before dawn and struck out after the tree at first light, it would be out of the question, for it would mar the wholeness and fullness of the last day-before. That's just not the way they do it and Belinda knows it. Wilson wants, has always wanted, the whole day, soft and easy, with the tree already in place. He doesn't think he's asking for too much.

"It has to be tonight," he tells her. "It'll be easy. I marked it out ahead of time. It's just a little ways up Turner Creek. We'll go in, whack it, and come back out. Piece of cake."

"Turner Creek?" she says. "Down past where they've stopped plowing the road?"

"The cat hunters have been cruising it. It'll be passable."

"The cat hunters drive *tanks*," Belinda says. "We drive a Subaru. Don't go out tonight. Sure as anything, you'll get stuck. If you're set on getting stuck, wait to do it in the daylight." She sees him shaking his head, though, and knows how he is about traditions. He's never once not had the tree put up with the girls by the morning of Christmas Eve, and he's not going to let this year be an exception. "At least take the old truck."

"Truck's too loud," Wilson says. "I don't want to smell the exhaust coming through the floorboard. Don't worry, if the snow's too deep, I'll turn around," Wilson says, when he sees that Belinda isn't persuaded. "I won't get stuck." He throws his hands up. Can't she see there's no choice? He would love nothing more, this first night back at their cabin, than to stay home and tuck in by the fire. But soon there will no longer be any space left for delay and flexibility; at some near point it must all begin to go according to plan.

With only minor grumblings, the girls dress for the quick trip. Lucy starts to walk outside in her sandals, but Wilson reminds her to always wear boots in the winter, in case there's car trouble and they have to walk.

"Or in case you get stuck," Belinda says. Wilson looks at her, tucks the thermos of hot chocolate under his arm, and grabs a Christmas CD as he and the girls head out the door. On the porch he flips the switch for the yard tree, and they are rewarded with the quick blue-and-white blaze, made elegant by the screen of lightly falling snow that has just begun.

They set off like hunters on an adventure. They drive slowly up their narrow driveway, the snow mesmerizing in the headlights. At the top of the drive they turn northward, ascending the long ridge to the point where the county snowplow stopped grading after Thanksgiving. It's a dark road that is hemmed in by evergreens, a narrow corridor through the cold forest, with a lane of stars piercing the blackness above them. In the forest there are numerous deer, elk, bears, coyotes, wolves, and lions. It's the favorite haunt of the lion hunters, who cruise it once or twice a week in their huge trucks, with their dogs kenneled and whining in the back, until they find fresh lion tracks across the road. At that point, they loose their hounds and follow them down farther into the woods, the hounds' bays echoing throughout the forest. The hunters are not allowed to kill the lions, can only chase them with the hounds, but the lions don't know that. It's a good system, one which keeps the lion hunters out of the smoky bars during the long miserable snowy blue twilight of the winters, and which keeps the lions somewhat respectful, even fearful, of people.

After a couple of miles, they come upon the little mound that demarcates the place where the snowplow has stopped plowing for the year. Wilson drives over and through the still-modest snowdrift.

They are into deeper snow now, with the twin ruts of the lion hunters' path the only guide: but it's passable, as long as Wilson keeps the sled of his car straddling the deep snow between the ruts. Soon, though, the new snow beneath them is brushing and scraping against the tinny undercarriage, the floor flexing and warbling against their feet. Immediately the girls protest, urging Wilson to turn around and go back before they get stuck, but it's too late, their counsel has barely been spoken before the car begins to slip and spin, and then, almost gracefully—as if it were a goal Wilson had long been seeking to accomplish—they are stuck.

He puts the car in reverse and tries to back into his old tracks, then tries to front-wheel muscle his way a little farther forward, but there is nothing, only ice-spin, the studded tires useless. With each revolution they merely compress the wet snow further into a dense and intractable cast of ice.

Wilson tells the girls not to fret, he'll see what he can do, and gets out to investigate—surely a little digging will be able to clear a lane out—though in the backseat, a thermonuclear response, a bona fide chemical reaction, is building in Stephanie, who is (quite justifiably, Wilson thinks) already launching into "Why didn't you listen to Mom?"

Lucy, in the front seat, is thus positioned to defend Wilson, and so the girls go at it, jawing back and forth in the darkness, the crystalline stillness, while outside the car, kneeling in the snow with a penlight, Wilson examines the maw that has gripped the car.

The car rocks with the girls' argument as they shift and flounce—Lucy advises her older sister to just grow up and deal with it—and yet Wilson does not panic, thinks instead what a good learning experience this will be once he scrapes a trough for the front wheels, steers back into the lion hunters' ruts, and they continue merrily on their way. Life in the north woods.

Except it does not quite work out that way. The problem is that even after Wilson has excavated, with his hands and his feet, a shallow trench, the instant his tires bite into new snow, the friction transforms the wetness into slick ice. The car has become an ice-making machine, a perfect arrangement of temperature, humidity, dew point, and snow depth—even the temperature of his *tires* is perfect for this phenomenon—and Wilson realizes, with an unpleasant jolt, that they're screwed. That indeed Belinda was right: that she was in fact perfectly fucking correct.

Nevertheless he paws and kicks at the snow some more, gets back in, spins the tires some more, creating more ice—the car is swaddled now in a cradle of ice, and could easily remain here until next May—and although Stephanie does not know how to drive, Wilson explains to her how to let out the clutch while pressing down on the accelerator. He and Lucy get out and push from behind while Stephanie tries to power the car out.

This effort yields nothing but more ice and a burning clutch, the acrid odor of which seems now to permeate their clothes, their hair, and the forest itself, as well as all the snow and ice around them.

Wilson looks up at the stars and considers his two options: to simply walk home, which is only three miles distant—less than an hour's walk—or to dig out, to grunt and heave, not like an engineer, but a barbarian. The air is raw and damp, and Wilson does not want to go through the usual north-woods ordeal of crawling down into the ice and raising the car up on its spindly hydraulic lift—a toy jack—shoving dead branches under the one lifted tire, before lowering the car and moving the jack to each of the other three wheels, in turn, to do the same thing, and then driving forward just far enough to get ice-spun stuck again, whereupon he would have to return to the woods, scrounge around some more, and start all over again.

And thus the night would proceed, melting into midnight—the girls would squabble for a couple of hours while he slogged around beneath the low belly of the car, drenched and shivering, numb and blue-fingered—until finally they had driven forward enough to be able to reverse course and turn around for home, back to the starting point, where things had first begun to go wrong.

There would be less humiliation in digging themselves out, rather than walking home, but without hesitation Wilson chooses what's best for the girls. He does not want their day-before-the-day-before memory to be one of ice-bound entrapment in the car and excruciating boredom, and so he chooses the long walk in the darkness over the interminable Big Dig.

In any event, they will return treeless. What is it about this year? he wonders. Why is everything he touches turning to failure?

They have one faint flashlight to share among the three of them. Wilson casts it on the car one final time before they abandon it, and the translucent ice field of its own making, which surrounds it, glints silver, reminding Wilson of the hue of a web-trapped housefly wrapped in spun silk. Then they turn and set off down the road wordlessly, into the darkness: united, Wilson thinks, in their little adventure.

That dream of unity, of Christmastime family togetherness, lasts all of five seconds. It turns out that although Lucy did change out of her sandals before leaving the house, she merely replaced them with her old black vinyl cowboy boots, and did not even take time to put on socks: believing her father when he said the tree was within easy walking distance, and yet not believing, or heeding, him when he spoke of the possibility that everything might not go their way.

Not only are the vinyl boots brittle-cold against the snow, offering little more protection than a pair of plastic bags, but they have slick-bottomed soles, so that each of Lucy's steps forward in that strange snow yields half a sliding step backward. Wilson watches her struggle, sees the problem instantly, but doesn't fuss at her; on the contrary, a sweetness floods him—that she should still be so trusting of the world, unaware of the way it rebels against almost all of mankind's planning. It's the sort of thing a little girl would do, and while he knows he will enjoy and take pride in the young women they will soon become, he is not in the least ready to say good-bye to the days of girlhood, and thus is comforted by Lucy's choice in footwear. A cowgirl, a ballerina, a fairy princess. Soon she will have to grow up—as Stephanie is doing so rapidly—but there's still time. She reads *Charlotte's Web*, maybe believes in Santa Claus—is willing to entertain, or negotiate, the idea of loopholes, special dispensations, possibilities.

As Lucy falls back, Stephanie stalks ahead of them, muttering that Wilson "should have listened to Mom." This doesn't rile Wilson; on any given day she could just as easily be haranguing Belinda with "Why can't you be like Dad?" When she gets off scale in her fury, it's best just to let her wind down—and then be there when she eventually drifts back into orbit through the brute gravity of the family structure, with his yearning at its nuclear core.

Is it this way? He has no idea, only hope. Maybe there is no centrifugal force to urge his daughters', or his family's, return. Perhaps there is no orbit, but instead only haste, acceleration, and flight. Even here on this snowy lane through the dark woods he feels stretched and stressed, wanting to rein in Stephanie a bit—she's getting farther ahead of them with each furious stride—while wanting to urge Lucy, a step behind him, to stay closer.

There is a reason this is the road the cat hunters cruise; it's where the most deer are, which also means it's where the lions wander. Wilson has no doubt that the lions are out there, back in the dark forest—that there are lions within the sound of their voices, lions catching their scent. Lions which might even be watching them through the trees, observing the faint trace of their flashlight, the weave of it bobbing slowly down the road. What was he thinking? Wilson wonders now. What the fuck was he thinking? It's just a tree.

Lucy is crying silently, stalking and stomping as well: hating her cowboy boots but too stubborn to acknowledge it. Wilson offers to carry her on his back, but she rejects this out of hand. "I'm not a little girl, you know," she says, and Wilson can see she's frustrated that her older sister, so much more physically capable, is leaving them behind. Were they alone, Lucy might consent to Wilson carrying her, but pride has intervened now, pride and misery.

Wilson calls ahead to Stephanie, warns her of the lions and tells her to stay closer.

"Yeah, right," Stephanie says. "Like you'd be any help. You're five foot *two*."

She's robbing Wilson of six inches, but it's a touchy subject with her this year; she's playing basketball and has had it explained to her that she's done most of the growing she's going to do. Nonetheless, she slows a bit, allows the strung-out procession of Wilson and Lucy to draw nearer.

Lucy is shivering even as she walks, and she allows Wilson to give her his jacket. All he has now is a T-shirt. They travel a little farther, and Stephanie, lamenting how cold her hands are getting, permits Wilson to stop and take his socks off, so that she can turn them inside out for mittens. He pulls his boots back on over his bare feet, hopping in the snow as he does so, and they continue on.

From time to time Stephanie stops, perhaps with lions on her mind, and tries to see behind them, which of course causes Lucy to stop too and peer behind her with great concern. Their little flashlight, one of those windup self-generating models, is so puny. For purposes of security, Lucy's carrying it, winding it from time to time. When she does so, the dull glow flickers, flares a bit more brightly, like a candle guttering, and the more nervous she becomes, the faster she winds the little plastic handle, which creates a whirring sound, making the flashlight seem like part toy and yet partly also the thing that is carrying them forward.

They ascend a long hill, the switchback that looks down on the dark forest below, and Stephanie, still slightly ahead, stops and holds her hands out, then takes a step backward. "What's that?" she says. Either there is true fear in her voice, or she's pretending, in order to terrify her sister. Neither Wilson nor Lucy can tell which it is. To Wilson it sounds like the real thing, while it seems to Lucy to sound like something Stephanie is saying out of meanness, or something Lucy hopes, in this instance, is being said out of meanness: and she yells, "Stephanie, cut it out!"

"Shut up!" Stephanie shouts, and takes two more steps back toward them.

Wilson grips Lucy by the hand and moves two steps up, so that the three of them are closer together than they've been all night—and now Wilson hears it, something quiet moving across the snow on the hill below them: not a deer, the sound of which he knows well, but something different. An electrical prickling discharges a chill along his skin, and the hair on his neck and arms stands up.

He squints into the darkness, takes the toy light from Lucy and shines it ahead of them, but sees nothing in its weak beam, only sparkling snow-glint—and he speaks firmly into the darkness, saying, "Go on now, we're coming through here."

He does not say "Go on, lion," as he does not want to verify the girls' terror. "It was probably just a deer," he tells them—but they can hear the lie in his voice, and they draw closer to him.

Lucy's grip on his hand is like that of a blacksmith's upon the hammer, and she is crying. It's unlike her to cry at all, and Wilson can't tell if she's frightened or angry—angry at him or perhaps at her sister, as if believing Stephanie has somehow conjured the lion in order to scare her.

They hear the soft soundprints upon the snow again, closer, and Wilson tucks the girls in even tighter. He's prepared to receive any charge. He speaks again to the darkness—"It's just us, go on now"—and when there is no response, he's emboldened, and shouts into the night, and the girls shriek.

He thinks he can hear the lion breathing. Wilson snarls, and a bottomless quiet follows, and it seems to him—perhaps to all of them—that the lion is tensing, reconsidering. Something in the air is different.

Wilson tells the girls, "Okay, let's get going."

They know the road home from here, and now that they've crested the little summit, it's downhill all the way; they walk quickly, with Lucy still slipping in her vinyl boots—she deigns to hold on to Wilson's arm now, whenever it gets too icy. She's stopped crying, though Wilson can see that some of the tears are frozen in her lashes.

Stephanie's still furious—the closer they get to the top of their driveway, the farther ahead of them she pulls, though not quite as far as before—and at one point when she grouses back to him about how cold it is, Wilson says, exultantly, "I like the cold air, the frost-blushed cheeks. It reminds us we are alive!" He's parodying himself, baiting her, but she does not take it, only mutters, and then—again, whether out of sheer devilment, or true fear, he cannot tell—she slows and looks behind them, so that once more Lucy spins too, wanting to see what has drawn her sister's attention.

"Stop it," Lucy hisses, to which Stephanie responds, "Make me!"

"I *will*," Lucy says.

"How?" challenges Stephanie—and once more Wilson scrambles to hold the atom together, calling out his warning, "Girls, stop it," even as he's thinking, *Stop, or what? I'll make you walk home?* "Please," he says to them, "please."

They reach the top of their long driveway, and it is all the girls can do to keep from breaking into a run: they've attained the safety of the castle gates. They're coming down the home stretch now. Soon the windows of their cabin will come into view, the yellow light tattered at first through the trees, but then reassembling into full, buttery squares. They'll see the luminous thread of smoke rising from the chimney, almost silver against the sky and its stars.

Wilson wonders what the girls will remember. Is it possible they'll remember only the good—the adventure—as if Stephanie were never cruel, Lucy never fearful, as if he, Wilson, had never made a mistake, never been obstinate or in any other way imperfect?

He is already adapting, plotting, redesigning: attempting, as ever, to get back out ahead of the flow of time. After the girls are warmed up and settled, he and Belinda—if he can convince her—will go back out in the old truck and attach a chain to the Subaru and tug it out. He'll take the snow shovel, as he may have to do some digging. He'll continue on then for the tree. It may be two o'clock before he returns with it, but it'll be there on the porch in the morning, ready and waiting for them. They'll bring it inside. It will be fragrant and perfect, and they will begin decorating it, Christmas Eve morning, right on schedule.

And just as Wilson is devising this solution to their problem, and just as the girls begin to hurry even faster, with Lucy having drawn alongside her sister despite the challenge of the boots, the first thing that comes into view is not their yellow-lit cabin, but the blue-lit tree, astounding and otherworldly in its brilliance, isolate in the deep darkness.

The tree is even more amazing for the fact that it is wreathed in snow, the blue lights encased by ice. The lights do not burn with individual twinklings, but instead emit a great blue glow, like a lighthouse: something they never expected to see in their own yard. The tiny heat from each bulb has melted the snow, which has then refrozen, so that the giant tree is ice-clad and shimmers and pulses with that beautiful blue glow.

The girls stop and stare at it without speaking, for two full breaths, three breaths, their hearts pounding from their run down the driveway. And Wilson stands there with them, behind them—their three breaths rising in a great unifying cloud—and looks at the thing they are looking at.

Its blueness is perfect. Only black night surrounds it. This is all he wants. This is enough. Five seconds, six seconds, seven seconds, eight: they stand there catching their breath, gazing at this special thing, and then Stephanie hurries on down the hill and past the tree, to the cabin, eager to tattle on Wilson, and Lucy comes along just as fast behind her, eager to defend him.

And though Wilson knows he cannot make his memory be their memory, he lingers a moment longer, staring at the glowing blue tree—but already the moment is dissolving, and in nothing but darkness after the long walk, with his daughters no longer next to him, the sight quickly diminishes, it is just a pretty blue tree in the dark forest; and Wilson, too, hurries down to the cabin, and the moment, hoping it has not already moved on. This is what it feels like to be perfect, he thinks.

With each step, he savors it, knowing it won't always be this way. But it is now. More so than he could ever have designed.

A BIRTH IN THE WOODS

HE HAD BEEN WARNED that there would be blood.

Caleb's mother had told him in their daily lessons, "No one is actually hurt. Blood doesn't necessarily mean pain." She showed him a drawing of a baby floating in space, connected to the placenta. "The baby may be bloody when it comes out, but it isn't bleeding. We'll wash him off, wash the sheets and towels, and you won't even remember it." Since his parents had decided that Caleb, six years old, would assist with the birth, he found an unending list of questions for his mother to consider. When he asked if there had been a lot of blood when he was born, his mother shook her head. "You were easy," she said. "You were so easy."

His father whittled a block of wood into a duck for the unborn baby before he took his penknife and dug it into the tip of his thumb. When the blood rose to the surface of the skin and trickled down his father's hand, Caleb looked away, nauseated. His father swung him around, softly, and held up the sliced thumb. "It's just blood," he said. "It gets out sometimes and that's not the worst thing in the world." Caleb held out his hand, and his father made a quick slice into the boy's own thumb. When the blood bubbled up, Caleb and his father laughed. "Blood's nothing to worry about," his father said, and Caleb felt safe, another lesson learned. His father regarded the half-whittled duck, now streaked with brown-red blood, and threw it into the woods surrounding their cabin, the expanse of trees so dense for miles in every direction that it seemed to Caleb that no one else in the world existed. "Don't show your mother what we've done," his father said, and Caleb nodded. He wondered how long he would have to wait until he could retrieve the duck for himself.

THIS WAS HOW CALEB WAS TAUGHT, by what was around, the things closest to him, which did not include other children or adults. When the potatoes had come into harvest, his mother had shown him how to use one to power a clock. She did not explain the principle behind this, seemed bored in fact by the particulars, and was intent only on showing Caleb the strangeness of the world. She sliced worms in half, and they watched for weeks as one of the halves grew into a new worm.

"Does this work with people?" he asked.

"No, never," she said quickly.

"Sometimes, actually," retorted his father, who then smiled, pleased to have the chance to make trouble.

"That's not true," said his mother, and then thought about it for a few seconds. "No," she said again, assured of her answer.

Caleb placed his finger on the worm and watched the animal bend and curl from his touch.

He was learning to read, slowly, without much progress, though his mother seemed pleased. "The Browning Method of Typographical Comprehension and Reading," she would proudly say as she held the pamphlet for Caleb to see. She would show him a letter from the deck of flash cards; they were up to *L* in the alphabet, a ninety-degree angle, a thumb and index finger extended. Once he had the letter, he was given a book, something random from a garage sale or one of her old college texts. He was to search the book for that single letter and circle it each time it appeared. He would scan the lines of each page for the shape of the letter, the space it occupied within a word. He had noticed how an *E* looked slightly different next to a *C* than it did to a *D*, the open mouth of the *C* inviting the *E* closer, while the *D* bowed out, pushing the *E* into the next letter. She never showed him a word, never touched a line of letters and made the sound of their joining. "When will I be able to read, though?" he would ask her, his hands smeared with ink. "Soon enough," she would say. He did not believe her, but he had no choice. He needed her to tell him the things he would know.

NOW THERE WAS THE BABY INVOLVED, about to arrive. His mother's stomach was huge. The unmistakable bulge seemed to suggest that she was growing shorter each week. Her belly was a thing she always cradled with both hands while she walked, as if she were afraid of injuring something with it instead of the other way around. She would weigh herself and then laugh, stepping off the scale as the arrow zipped back to zero, before Caleb could read the weight.

"You didn't tell me your weight," he complained, but she would walk away, giggling.

"It's broken," she would say. "It's certainly not working correctly."

One night, when the baby shifted and pressed against his mother's spine, she cried out and then instantly tried to pretend that she had been singing a song.

"Maybe we could go to the doctor," his father said. "Just a little preliminary visit."

"The baby is going to be big," she said. "Why pay a doctor to solve that mystery for us?"

When his father mentioned the hospital a second time, his mother frowned. "We decided, Felix. We decided that we would make a world apart from the world. We can't give up on that every single time things seem difficult."

Caleb put his hand on her stomach and felt the baby kick twice, his mother wincing each time.

When she had first explained to Caleb about the baby, the fact of it, she had sat down beside him on the floor and swept the math sticks, individually carved blocks the length and width of a finger which he used to add and subtract, out of the way. "We're going to put math on hold for a while," she said. "For the next few months, we'll focus on science. Biology. Caleb?" He had picked up one of the math sticks and was rubbing his thumb across the smooth grain of the wood, but he put it back down. She smiled. He was learning. "We're going to have another baby," she said. "You're going to be a brother."

"What?" he said, still trying to understand.

"A baby. A little boy or girl."

"When?" he asked.

"Soon," she said. "Six or seven months."

"Why?" he asked.

"Because your father and I thought we would all be happier with another person in the house, someone else to be a part of our family."

"Where?" he asked, moving along the questions he had been taught to ask when he did not know exactly what was happening.

"Right here," his mother answered. "Right here in the house."

SHE HAD WORKED to teach him the how of this baby, but it was difficult. She used hand gestures, stick figure drawings, biological terms like *ovaries* and *sperm*. Caleb still did not understand, though he nodded sometimes just to make her happy.

"I know," she said. "It doesn't make a lot of sense, does it?" He nodded. "I think maybe I know a way to help you understand exactly what happens," she said. "A way to learn."

Later that night, he could hear his parents as they argued in their room.

"No," his father said as he tried to keep his voice from rising. "Jenny, I am not going to do that."

"He wants to understand, Felix. He wants to know how it works."

"There are things he can learn from us and there are things he can learn on his own. We can't teach him everything."

"We can," she said. "You just don't want to."

"I guess not," he said, and then they were quiet.

Caleb got out of his bed and crawled to his parents' room. He looked through the open crack of the door. His mother rested her head on his father's chest, and he stroked her hair. "You're a good teacher," he told her. "He'll understand eventually."

"I am a good teacher," she said, softly.

The next morning, Caleb's mother told him that she had talked to his father last night and they had realized that they weren't entirely sure themselves how a baby came to be. "In some ways," she said, "it's a mystery, and mysteries can be just as wonderful as knowing."

IT WAS EVENING. Snow fell heavily in the mountains and ice formed and then shattered, scraping along the tin roof of the house. His father had gone to the shed to collect wood for the stove. Even inside the cabin, Caleb could see his own breath. His mother breathed in short, rapid bursts and the dense air hovered around her. "It's close," she said, "it's nearly time."

He was prepared for the baby. His mother wanted him to be near in order to observe what was happening, to be a part of the procedure.

"We're all making this baby," she said. "Each one of us is doing our part."

While his father brought wood into the house and fed it into the stove, and his mother held the baby inside her and timed her contractions as the spasms shot across the surface of her face, Caleb placed new batteries in the flashlight and tested the brightness. He would hold the flashlight steady and direct the light toward the place where the baby would come, to help his father see the head when it emerged. He threw the light into the corners of the room and stared at the wide spot of light and how it illuminated the walls, the wood beams that his father had placed together to make the house. He swung the flashlight around on himself and stared directly into the light until his mother called out for him to focus on his work. He turned toward her figure, but all he could see was the leftover imprint of light, pure brightness, and it took several seconds before he could make out his mother, heavy with the baby and watching him.

While she sat on the sofa with her legs pulled up to her chest, his father laid a plastic sheet over the mattress, then one of the fresh bedsheets.

"The same thing," his mother panted, "do it over."

"I did all this the last time and the boy came out fine," his father said. He placed another plastic sheet over the bed, followed by the final bedsheet. Caleb watched him and forgot his own work, which was to tape two copies of *The Guinness Book of World Records* together and place them in a sack. They had told him several times that the books were to keep his mother's hips raised, an important task. He carefully edged the newly made book—taped together, unable to be opened and read—into the sack, trying hard not to rip the paper. His work did not seem nearly as interesting as the sheets, the bed, the place where everything would happen.

"Why do you need two plastic sheets?" Caleb asked. Neither parent answered, focused on their own concerns. Blood, he thought. It had to be blood.

"It's happening," his mother said calmly, her breathing unaltered. A puddle of liquid collected on the floor and seeped between the slats of the wood, and his father ran over with a clean linen nightgown for her to change into. "Look away, Caleb," his father shouted, but his mother laughed. "It doesn't matter. It's going to happen soon, Caleb," she said as she slipped out of her nightgown and held her arms over her head. Though he had seen her naked before, Caleb turned and looked at the wall, embarrassed about the water that had pooled at her feet. "Once the membrane ruptures," she continued, "something irreversible has occurred. You'll see. The baby will be here soon."

THE WOODSTOVE WAS BURNING full now. The windows fogged over, and somewhere deep in the woods, trees began to snap in half. The room was filled with empty plastic bags, bowls, and pillows. Cotton towels, steaming and sterilized, had been pulled from the oven, and smelled faintly of smoke. Next to the bed, the nightstand was covered with gauze and sanitary pads, everything a perfect, brilliant white. Caleb rubbed a hole in the fog on a window, stared out into the darkness at the expanse of ice and snow, and turned back to the sheeted bed, empty and white.

On the edge of a wooden chair hung the still-wet nightgown. He noticed the reddish coloration that dotted it. His mother had told him about it. She had called it "bloody show," but she had said she would tell him when it happened and she hadn't. He was about to ask her about it when his father called for his help in moving his mother. She seemed calm, but her hands were shaking. Caleb wanted the baby to come.

He held his mother's left hand while his father stood on her right side and helped her to the bed. Without any apparent effort, his father lifted her into his arms and gently placed her on the bed. Her belly wobbled and she turned onto her side to face Caleb, who again placed his hand inside hers. "Soon," she said, and grimaced as she squeezed his hand.

Though they had insisted that he would help deliver the baby, his parents kept sending Caleb farther away from the bed to do various tasks. He went to the upstairs closet for a heating pad, though the house was already sweltering and dry with the heat from the fire. His father would hand him a pillow and send him into another room to shake the dust off. When his mother complained of the heat, he took a plastic bag and stepped into the cold outside. His boots crunched the ice. With a wooden spoon, he broke up the snow and scooped it into the open bag before he finally twisted it shut. When he came back inside, he heard his father say, "I just don't like this weather, all this ice." He stopped talking when he saw Caleb, who held the already-melting snow in his hands. "Bring it over here, son," he said. His mother's face was red and splotchy from the heat and the waiting, and Caleb hurried to the bed and placed the bag against her forehead.

"That feels nice," she said. She turned from Caleb and said to his father, "See? The snow helps."

His father sent him back outside for more. Each time he returned, his mother looked more and more exhausted. Her face was wrinkled with confusion.

"It's taking too long," she said as she rolled softly from side to side.

There were already seven bags of now-melted snow on the floor of the room, but his father asked him to go outside again. The bags reminded him of the time his father had returned from town with a plastic bag that held two goldfish and how quickly, almost instantly, when they were placed in the waiting fishbowl, they had died. Caleb thought that moving them out of the bag had killed them but his parents assured him this was not true.

His mother moaned in pain, and his father pushed him toward the door. He was beginning to trust the word of his parents less and less with each minute that passed without the baby's arrival. His hands were numb but he plunged them into the snow again.

Back in the house, the heat stung his face. His mother struggled to sit up, but the weight of her belly dragged her back down. His father wiped the sweat from her face and arms with a washcloth. A contraction traveled through her body and she screamed, the sound strangled and broken but loud. His parents continued to shift and reposition themselves, unable to settle into the thing that was happening. He had been so easy and now they were making something difficult and it was hard for Caleb not to be angry with his parents. The snow melted and spilled out of the bag, but he did not put it down. He was unsure how to proceed, and he could only wait until his parents told him what was next.

His mother relaxed for a moment, the time between contractions. In the brief space of calm, both of his parents finally noticed his presence, and their faces became unlined and assured.

"Come closer," his mother said, and Caleb placed the bag of melted snow on the floor and went to her. He wanted to touch her stomach, but he couldn't do it, did not want to cause her any more discomfort. "It's hard right now, but it will get easier," she said, and Caleb only nodded, afraid to speak.

His father went to the kitchen and returned with a jar of honey. "You need this," he said to her as he unscrewed the jar, "for your strength." Caleb reached out his hand for the jar, wanting to help. He took the wooden wand from inside the jar, sticky on his fingers, and drizzled honey onto his mother's tongue. She smiled and then nodded for more. He did this three times, until she held up her hand. "It's coming," she said. "We need to get ready." She grabbed the bedsheet in both hands, waiting for the contractions, and Caleb wanted to run back outside, into the cold and quiet and darkness, but he stayed beside his mother and waited for the baby to come.

She screamed again, though Caleb could not hear the sound, only a humming as he stared at his mother's open mouth and closed eyes. He could hear only the tree limbs as they crashed to the ground, the fire in the stove, the sound of his heartbeat. She screamed yet again and squeezed his hand tightly. The tips of his fingers all met at the same point, and the pain in his hand opened his ears to the sound of his mother, who now whimpered as the next contraction came.

"Okay," his father said, and crouched between her legs. "We're getting close. Stay calm."

Caleb remembered the flashlight, which was at the foot of the bed. "I need to hold the flashlight," he told his father, who again looked surprised to find him in the room.

"No," his father said, "you stay with your mother, hold her hand, give her honey and water. I don't want you over here." His mother nodded, squeezed his hand again, though her eyes were still closed.

"But the flashlight," Caleb whined, unwilling to give up his job.

His father grabbed the flashlight and dragged an end table close to the bed. He turned on the flashlight and directed it toward Caleb's mother. "See?" his father said. "This will work fine," and Caleb instantly felt unnecessary; he was ashamed that his job could be performed by a table, that he was not going to learn anything from this.

IT WAS STILL SNOWING OUTSIDE and filling up the space around the house until they were the only people left on earth, three of them crowded together, the fourth still to come. The air was hot and used up, ragged. His mother was breathing strangely now. The air left her body only to be sucked quickly back in, over and over. Her belly was stretched tight, to the point that the skin seemed to vibrate. Caleb was simply a hand to be held, a presence, as his mother never opened her eyes, only breathed and pushed and screamed when it became too much. It felt like seconds, though an hour had passed. Time was mixed up in the repetition of the actions, the darkness and snow outside, the fire in the house, the baby.

It was coming now, no stopping it. His father called for her to push and his mother tried, her hand barely able to squeeze Caleb's any longer. "Something's wrong," she kept saying, but his father seemed not to hear her, only ever asking her to keep pushing, to breathe, to bring this baby into the world. He shouted again for her to push, and she screamed back at him as the pain shook her, and Caleb held on. His body pulled farther and farther away from his hand and deeper into his heart, and he held his breath until he could not last any longer and had to take another huge gulp of air. He closed his eyes and even when his father said, "Here it comes, one more time," he did not open them. Even when his mother screamed with such force that her voice gave out. Even when his father whispered, "Oh, good Lord," and the baby made its first sound, howling itself into existence, Caleb remained shut off from the things around him.

When Caleb did open his eyes, the baby was still howling, its tiny lungs powering its body, as if sound were what kept it alive, and all he saw was what he had been told to expect. On the sheets, on his father's hands and shirt, on the baby, or what he thought was the baby. Blood.

His mother was now quiet. The baby overpowered all the other sounds in the room. As Caleb listened more closely, the sound alternated between a high-pitched and insistent howl and a low, rumbling moan. His mother let go of Caleb's hand, and though he tried to hold on, eventually he let her go. His father moved quickly. He cut the cord, and a thin line of blood spurted across his face. He put the placenta in a bowl, where the mass seemed to move like a beating heart. The baby was now on a pillow on the floor, and it wriggled and barked, its body bluish-red. Caleb stayed near his mother. Though her breathing was regular again, her skin was pale, and his father shouted for him to help.

Caleb didn't move but then his father shouted again, "Goddamn it, Caleb, hand me the towels. Goddamn you." Caleb lifted the stack of towels from the table and brought them to his father. On this side of the bed, he could fully see the blood on the sheets as it spread farther and farther out. At the sight of it, so much, Caleb felt dizzy. He got lighter, and then threw up on himself, clear and tasteless. His father didn't seem to notice and kept working. He pressed the towel against Caleb's mother, and a small red blot appeared on the clean white fabric and then, so painstakingly slow that it seemed a trick of the eye, grew larger. His father said, "Goddamn it, goddamn it," the words quick like a succession of sneezes.

Caleb's mother finally spoke, hoarse and raspy words forced out of her body. "I want my baby." The baby still screamed, the reason for all of this, now forgotten on the floor, the blood all they could focus on. His mother squeezed her legs together to hold the towel in place and Caleb's father lifted the baby. He gasped as he held it in the light and then said, "Something's wrong, isn't it? The baby, this isn't right."

Caleb watched the new thing, large and substantial in his father's hands. It was a baby, but it was covered all over in dark black hair, which was slicked with blood and mucus. It had a long, bear-like snout and its fingers were mashed together into useless claws. It growled, and its furry hands reached up toward the ceiling and batted at his father's face. Caleb realized now that it was not his brother, not a baby, but an animal, a creature, something wild. It was something inside their house that should not be there.

His mother continued to motion for the baby, and his father, dazed, disconnected from what he was holding, placed it on her chest. She held on to it, stroking its face. "My baby," she said. "It's my baby."

"Jenny," his father said, his voice now quiet but anxious with what he had to say. "It won't stop. I can't make it stop."

She touched his father's face, kissed him. "It will be okay. This is our baby, Felix. We have our baby."

"We have to take you to a hospital. Something's wrong. The baby needs a doctor too; there's something wrong with him."

His mother kept yawning, her eyelids heavy. "We can't go. We're here—we have to stay here."

"Jenny."

"Go find help."

His father went back to the foot of the bed and removed the towel, which was now heavy with blood, and threw it to the floor. "Jenny," he said again, crying now, pleading with her. With the baby still resting on her chest, she fell into a half sleep. The baby tried to wriggle out of her grasp, but she held on to him.

His father pressed a new towel tight against her. Caleb stared at the bloody towel, twisted and curled on the floor. His mother was dying, he now realized; the baby had brought something else with it, slow and painful.

"I'm taking you to a hospital," his father said finally. As he walked toward her, he tripped over the towel, and it uncoiled, showing slashes of white cotton patterned against the blood. He moved to pick her up, but she moaned in pain.

"No," she panted. "Don't do that. I don't think I can move, Felix."

His father touched her forehead, which left a streak of blood. It looked like a lowercase *j* to Caleb, sweeping over and up with a dot, before it mixed with the sweat on her forehead and became nothing, only blood. "I'll be back as soon as I can," he said. She nodded, closed her eyes, and nuzzled the baby.

Caleb's father threw on his jacket and took the flashlight from the table. His hands shook so hard that the beam of light jittered across the room before he finally turned it off. Caleb was afraid of him, of the look on his face, but he did not want to be left in the house. "Can I come with you?" he asked, but again his father did not seem to hear him. Caleb pulled at the arm of his jacket. "What about me?" he asked.

"You watch over them," his father said, and now tears were spilling down both cheeks. "Keep them safe."

HIS FATHER STARTED THE TRUCK, and the engine clacked and then hummed with power. He rolled down the window and told Caleb, "I'll be right back. I'll come back with help, and we'll fix this and we'll all be okay." But he was still crying and Caleb could hardly listen anyway. "Okay?" his father repeated. Caleb nodded and the truck backed out of the driveway, onto the road that led to town, which was nearly obscured by the snow. Ice crunched underneath the wheels, and the truck crept at such a slow pace that it seemed like it might be going in reverse.

Caleb went back inside and leaned against the window, afraid to go back to his mother and the baby. He felt the possibility of his father's never returning move down his spine—that he would drive into town and keep going into the next town and the next, until home and the new baby, the strange thing he'd made, were only a memory.

The truck slid down the road and made the first curve. There was the sharp sound of the brakes tapping on and off, and the headlights were steady on the road in front of it. Caleb rubbed the fog from the window and watched as the car headed into the next curve, nearly out of view, and then he heard the brakes dig in, and the wheels skidded across the ice. Too fast, it seemed, still going, around the bend and disappearing from view, the lights gone, the brakes still squealing, and then, for one brief second, silence, the snow falling. Then a crash, loud and jarring, and the sound of metal twisting, the world giving up its shape.

Caleb ran beneath the dinner table and hid himself under a white sheet. His mother called out for him, but he didn't answer, could not bear to go to her. "Caleb?" she asked again, her voice so soft. "I'm sorry, honey. I didn't know it would be like this." The baby started again. Its cries were now empty of anger or confusion, merely a noise to fill the house. He could hardly hear his mother, but he refused to move from under the table. Instead he strained his ears to the sound of her. "Take care of him, Caleb. This is your brother and I want you to be a good brother and make sure he's safe. I need you to watch over him until your father comes back. Will you do that, Caleb?"

He didn't answer, pulled the sheet tighter around him.

She was crying now. "Caleb? I'm so sorry."

He waited for her to speak again but there was only silence, interrupted by the occasional sound of the baby's whimpers and cries. Caleb closed his eyes and pretended to be asleep, waited for her to come to him, to lift the sheet off and carry him to bed. With every minute that passed, he grew more tired, lulled by the nearly imperceptible sound of snow freezing, turning into ice.

The fire had all but burned itself away, and the house was growing cold. Caleb did not want to move. He willed his body to stop shaking, but the cold was getting inside of him. When he finally stirred, pushing one of the chairs out of the way as he crawled from under the table, the baby heard the sound and gave a small cry and then stopped, as if waiting for a reply. Caleb walked to the stack of wood and removed a piece. The weight was heavy in his tired arms. He opened the door to the stove and slid the piece into the waning fire, watched the wood slowly ignite around the edges and hold the flame. As he warmed his hands, he looked toward the bed, where his mother was still and quiet. He moved a step closer and saw the baby shivering under its soft coat of black fur; it had fallen from his mother's hands onto the bed and had pulled its limbs tightly against itself.

When Caleb touched his mother, he knew that she was dead. He could not explain the feeling except to understand that his mother's arm felt lifeless, that nothing was left to move through it. He quickly pulled his hand away and stared at her calm face. He took a washcloth and wiped the streak of blood from her forehead. While the baby softly moaned and kicked in its sleep, Caleb cleaned each of his mother's fingers, scrubbing the nails until they were spotless. He kissed her cheek and his lips tingled until he looked down at the baby, the only other thing alive in the house.

He poked at the baby, trying to jab it awake. The fur on its head was soft, but the hair on its body was like steel wool, rough and bristly and flecked with blood. The baby finally stirred and immediately began howling, its mouth a perfect O, though Caleb was not yet up to that letter in the alphabet. To him, the mouth was a circle, around and around and around, with nothing but a sound coming out. The sound echoed through the house and hung in the fire-warmed air. This thing had killed his mother. It had come in the dead of night and left his mother hollowed out and empty.

Caleb placed his open palm over the mouth of the baby. He pinched the baby's snoutish nose closed with his thumb and forefinger. The muffled sound traveled through his arm, thrummed against his elbow. He could feel the anger inside the baby and he clamped down harder as he felt its lungs shrink with the effort to fight back. He could end it right now, could snuff the baby in mid-scream and hide it in the woods. Perhaps it wasn't meant to live long, was strangely twisted up inside and could not last on its own. Its breath stumbled and sputtered against the closed door of Caleb's hand. A few seconds more.

But he couldn't continue. He didn't want the baby and what it had created, but he could not take the easy steps to end it; he remembered his mother's plea for him to protect his brother. He took his hand from its mouth and the baby sucked in air, pulled the world into its lungs. The scream returned; the baby's claws curled up in rage. Caleb lifted the baby into his arms and pulled the heavy weight close to his chest. He sat on the floor and held his brother in his arms, allowed him to fight and scream and scratch the air until he had tired himself out. Caleb took the honey from the night-stand and removed the wand from the jar. The baby sucked on the end like a pacifier, his first food in the world. When it was gone, Caleb pried the wand loose. The baby had a small tooth, mal-formed and gray, on the top left side of his mouth. Caleb touched it with his finger and found the edge surprisingly sharp. The baby clamped down and Caleb removed his finger just in time. He dipped the wand into the honey again and fed the baby this way for the next few minutes; after each feeding, he would wipe the sticky excess from his brother's mouth to keep him clean. The baby was his brother and they were alone in what was left of the night, pitch-black and cold except for the tiny space their bodies occupied. Caleb reached into his pocket and produced the duck his father had whittled, with its dark blood. He placed it between the baby's paws and the baby twitched as he sniffed the blood that had soaked the duck before he was ever born. The object seemed to further calm him, and Caleb continued to steady the duck as it constantly threatened to slip out of the baby's grasp. As if teach-ing him a lesson, Caleb softly quacked and then shook the duck so gently that it would not frighten his brother. "Duck," Caleb said, though the word sounded as if it were from a language that had died out hundreds of years ago. He knew it meant absolutely nothing to anyone but him.

The baby curled against Caleb's shirt and squirmed to find com-fort, unable to sleep. His body left a damp, bloody imprint on the fabric. Caleb would watch over him.

When the front door opened the next day and the morning sun spilled into the room, there was Caleb, stained with blood, and the newborn baby, finally asleep in Caleb's arms, all that was left of the day before.

ABUNDANCE

from **vol. 7, no. 2**

Lauren Groff

THE BOY! Light boy, last boy, boy of Oscar's last dark days, boy in whom the man had begun to reveal himself in lip fuzz, in sharpness at the jaw. Simon had fallen asleep miles ago and his breath bloomed and shriveled on the passenger window; his elegant, bitten fingers curled on his lap. Oscar longed to enfold them in his old-man own. But: impossible. To cover such young flesh with Oscar's cloy would take nerve he no longer possessed. He contented himself with driving down the tunnel of wet maples, the music murmuring low.

What appalling form, Oscar thought, to fall asleep to Mahler. He envied Simon his first taste of such beauty, tried not to resent this waste of an hour.

The tunnel of trees petered out. The clouds sat heavy on the road. When Oscar pulled around a curve, the sun split the seams of the day. The world, from darkness, flared. Oscar's half-dead heart in his half-dead chest annealed, sounded a minor note, broke.

OSCAR HAD RISEN BEFORE DAWN, as ever, in his family's drafty saltbox above the sea. Pity he wouldn't be around to see the house tumble over the cliff as it would in a decade; he envisioned the chute as a fat old lady diving, her tiny hands cocked as if in prayer above her head.

His housekeeper, Agatha, had ever been the gorgon at the gate. When he announced how very sick he was, she in her furious loyalty announced no visitors; but even she couldn't keep them away. Oscar was beloved. The house had been infested with guests. Now it was Susan and her boy who had shown up unannounced a few days ago, both extenuated from divorce. She, his almost daughter, his family by love not blood, had suddenly turned middle-aged, her mouth gone bitter. In his sleeplessness, he'd seen the car snaking up the road in the sideways rain of midnight; he prepared himself; and he was there with blankets in his arms when at last they stood bedraggled on his doorstep. While the boy had carried the luggage upstairs, Susan had marched to the bookcase, taken down her father Henry's novel, and hidden it in the secretary. She wouldn't meet Oscar's eye. The house now prepared for her son, she found herself able to break down; and did, everywhere, wetly.

And so, since their arrival, Oscar's solitary dawns had taken on even more import. He crept through the house feeling his weakness, over the dark garden eroding even as the cliff wore away. Down the stone steps by feel. He no longer knew if he loved his morning bathe in the wildly churning sea or loathed it; bore it the way he bore so many other unpleasant facts about himself. It was spartan, the salt sear on the wounds of his feet and legs, the cleansing chill to the marrow. If he only let go of the barnacled rock, the ocean would float him gently away.

Not yet, no. He climbed out. He put his fleece pajamas back on, shuddering: life still had worth if there were such comforts as skin-warmed fleece. He slowly regained the lawn. Every inch was haunted by himself at various ages. Here at twenty, one arm thrown around Henry's shoulders, staggering drunk. Here at fifty, tall and strong, his lascivious, goaty years. Here at four, the small watchful son of parents who loved their venom more than their child. He waved at his past lives tiredly and gained the enclosed porch even as the sun flushed shining pheasants over the windows.

What's this? A strange noise; and only when he listened did the sound separate into music. Chopin. Nocturnes. Through the glass he saw the boy, Simon, his raw wrists and ankles poking from his pajamas, his hair cowlicked into feathers at the crown. Curious. Oscar had forgotten he possessed a piano. It had been buried for so many years in Agatha's geraniums. The boy played so softly Oscar knew it was an intimate affair, hands delicate and caressing, lip caught between his teeth.

And Simon, who had been to Oscar heretofore uninteresting on the monthly visits each summer, first a shrieking polyp of his mother, then a plain infant, at last a boring boy, had, in a breath, transformed. The hands, the long throat, the maidenly flush, the golden hair. Here was Henry; restored.

Oscar leaned against the door until his legs stopped shaking. He waited until there was a break in the music, and came inside. The room was green with the smell of geranium. The boy startled and reddened. He scowled murderously away.

I didn't know you played the piano, Oscar said. You're very good.

I don't, the boy said. Taught myself.

Chopin? Oscar said. Impossible.

The boy shrugged and played the air over the keyboard with his left hand. It's all the music we had. I don't know. It blocked out the fighting.

Aha. Oscar sat at the breakfast table and probed, but the boy was a disappointment. Brahms, Beethoven, Wagner, never heard of them, Mozart, yes, but he couldn't hum one refrain. The child was even, maybe, addlepated: believed some kind of radio band was the best group ever to write music. Simon didn't really like classical. It was for old men who smelled like joint cream. This, with mischief; and Oscar, an old man who smelled like profuse ointments, smiled.

They heard Agatha before they saw her, thundering down the hallway with the breakfast trolley. Oscar distanced himself back in his chair and waited. She muttered to herself and slammed the platters of food down, waited until the boy began shoveling the mess into his mouth, left. Oscar's stomach growled but he contented himself with black coffee, one boiled egg. He had to starve himself to live even this feeble life.

Now in the doorway, Susan, looming. She was bleary in the same nightgown as yesterday, as ethereal as her horse face allowed.

Baby, she murmured, kissing the part of Simon's hair. Oscar, she said, kissing him on the cheek as well. She sat and gazed at Oscar. You shouldn't be swimming, she said. You're a skeleton. You'll get pneumonia. It's insane.

I know, said Oscar. But one can't help what one loves.

Susan's face clamped down and Oscar saw again the girl she'd been, just after Henry had died. Her mother busy butterflying about in France, tiny Susan had been sent to Oscar for her summers. She had been a savage child, biting and picking at herself until she bled; but he had known how to soothe wounded children. Chocolates on the nightstand, hot water bottles tucked like warm puppies into her arms when he sent her upstairs to bed. Every night he had waited until she was firmly asleep, her damp face placid in the wedge of light from the hall, before he allowed the parties downstairs to begin.

The boy had stopped eating, was watching his mother. She pulled herself together and said, I'm going back to bed. She took her coffee with her.

Mater prima donna, Oscar said, smiling.

Yeah, the boy said. She gets a divorce and acts like *she's* the one dying. The boy looked shocked, as if someone else had spoken.

Not everybody is as tough as we are, Oscar said lightly. The boy had already gobbled down the heap of food; this hunger, too, was Henry's.

Agatha pounded in again to remove the plates. The boy who had blossomed under Oscar's eye became remote once more, and he wanted to tell the boy not to be afraid of anybody, that if only one looked carefully enough, one would see that all people are bewildered, that everyone has been wounded, even great Agatha of the ages.

An overwhelm, the urge to implant in that young brain all that he knew. But there was so little time left to them. And he had only now *seen* the boy. Such a terrible shame.

The idea hatched all at once, miraculous, into the day.

He waited until Agatha was gone, and whispered, Go pack. A road trip. I will show you what real music is. Just three days. Let me make some calls.

The boy at first was startled, then beamed, an imp. At last in the pale morning, he shone.

SUCH BLINDNESS. It came over Oscar suddenly, goggles glassed with vertigo. He slowed to a crawl, and kept the car straight by feeling the wheels on the shoulder and centerline. He closed one eye and it was a little better. The landscape spread and mounded into hills. Cows philosophized in the fields. Susan would be getting up now for her lunch and would find the letter on the Chippendale game table in the hall. Couched in terms of quiet, peace, recovery for a broken heart, the trip wouldn't immediately make her think of kidnapping. She would hear a quiet house, the sea below endlessly returning in waves of calm.

But when Oscar had stood before Agatha in his beautiful ancient suit fitted to his slender twenty-year-old frame—joy! he was thin enough to wear it again!—and told her that they were off, the old housekeeper's face had pinched in suspicion. She had cleaned up after him his whole life. She had been around, gnomelike even when he was born, her hands already chapped with scrubbing. She had seen him go off with dewy others, on earlier, other road trips. Agatha knew all. Like a terrible eye in the heavens, she saw. She loved, even so.

He drove, picturing her where she was right now, where she always was when she punished him: sitting on his mother's fauteuil, watching deafening soap operas and dipping Ritz crackers into Oscar's carefully hoarded cans of foie gras, which she called liver paste, the silly philistine. Ah, well. She was welcome to everything. Minus the half destined for Susan, it was all Agatha's when he was gone. Hers would be a rich widowhood, if of the spirit.

Now he saw from afar the very late lilacs marking the drive, a purple so blatant it seemed artificial. The tires on the gravel woke the boy. He rubbed his face and, lionlike, yawned. Vivi stood in the doorway of her stone cottage, the dancer in her spine but the skin gone witchy. Her clothes were layers and shades of blue. Her loose white hair flicked in the wind. She had once had a mattress on the floor of a Village walkup with churned and filthy sheets, teacups porcupined with cigarette stubs. Vivi of the angel face, viper heart.

When Oscar stood from the car, she advanced, saying, What the *fuck* are you up to, O.? but then she caught sight of his wasted frame and went watery. She advanced anew, kissed him. A sob in her throat as she murmured, So it's true. You're sick.

Dying, he said. Practically moribund. May I introduce Simon?

Vivi looked at the boy down her long nose and said, Why, it's Henry himself. Henry reborn. The very picture, down to the cheeks. She was angry, but touched Simon's face with a gentle hand.

He is Henry's grandson, Oscar said.

No wonder you like him so, she said, meaning the worst.

Don't be a hag, Oscar said.

She held his eye and Oscar held hers, and between them Simon carried the bags into the warmth.

THEY HAD TIME for a swift supper: poached lake trout in dill sauce, roasted fingerlings from her garden, cold local wine. Oscar heard the boy getting ready in the room next to Oscar's own, but his heart sank when the child came shyly down the stairs. He wore wrinkled khakis, the blue school blazer already too small one month into the summer.

God, Vivi said. There's the first difference. Henry was always impeccable.

It's all I have, Simon said, ashamed, and Oscar said, It doesn't matter.

No, it doesn't, Vivi said. He'd be beautiful even if he were naked, and she laughed her cigarette smoke past Oscar's ear.

How angry she'd always been, banshee her animating genius. Even during those two long years when he had tried so very hard for her, she'd been angry. Somehow she'd known. Their very last argument, he'd said, But I've done nothing. I've hurt nobody. Wants aren't sins, Vivi.

She had shouted, They are. They are! *Fetal* sins. And she threw a stool through a window and walked out and he didn't see her for ten years until she showed up abruptly at the house on the cliff one summer in their midthirties, mysteriously his friend again.

Tonight, furious Vivi drove to the opera house out in the fields. There was a faint smell of manure on the wind. She had to disappear for a few minutes in her function as artistic director, and Oscar and Simon found their seats in the throng. They sat quietly together watching the sides of the barnlike building silently slide shut against the twilight. Just before the conductor came out to applause, Vivi dropped into her seat, and nestled her old bony knee against his own.

Two children dressed in white climbed a ladder to the stage. They played in the darkness before the black curtain, the boy chasing the girl, catching at her skirts. The music slowly swelled, overripe Cherubini. At Oscar's side, Simon leaned forward and Oscar lost the opera entirely, watching the music breaking against him, filling him, watching the music move across the clay of the boy's lovely, lovely face.

THE PAIN WAS WORST in the night. The ants crawled under the skin, the throat constricted with thirst. Thank God for the catheter; before it, the fight between prostate and bladder was severe. By now, however, the pills had stopped lulling him to sleep. Oscar's doctor down in the village had refused to prescribe stronger ones.

You fool, he had said a month before. You can choose to kill yourself, but I'm not going to help you. The doctor, too, had loved Oscar. He'd been a soft boy whose melancholy Oscar had recognized for what it was, and now was a sweetly sad middle-aged man with a graying beard. There had been a summer of tennis on Oscar's grass courts, the white clothes turned transparent after their cool-down swims. Oscar had paid for his college, then medical school. The least Oscar would expect in return was understanding, but the doctor refused understanding, wouldn't countenance that Oscar hadn't made a choice, really. Oscar had run out of insulin and simply hadn't gotten more. He was tired, in the end, of needles.

No more tiny pricks for me! Oscar had laughed, and the doctor had kicked over the medical waste can, spilling its gauze.

The frogs chirruped in Vivi's pond, the owls answered in threat. Oscar lay beset in Vivi's chill white guest bed and thought of the boy in the room next door, the clear skin that was also Henry's skin, his hunger also Henry's, the same octaves-spanning hands. He imagined the boy's long slow breath in the dark, his sleep-spiced breath.

The door opened. Oscar froze. And the faded smell of Vivi entered, and Vivi's body climbed into the bed behind Oscar and she fitted her thin body to his and she held on to his shaking bones.

INTO THE MORNING they drove and the boy's patience began to tatter and he asked, bluntly, for a stop to all the music talk. Oscar was dismayed. He had only gotten to the diatonic scale. What would you like to talk about? he asked, but the boy only grunted. Oscar thought of the last time he'd seen Simon's parents together, a visit the summer before. The father had leaned on the legs of his wrought-iron chair and shredded one of Oscar's lilies to confetti that blew on the sea-wind all across his garden. There was already the other woman, Oscar understood; Simon's father was already beyond them. The boy, still a child, had spent the whole time watching the seabirds pinned in place above the cliffs by the wind, the early moon that rose behind them.

You want to talk about the divorce? asked Oscar, but Simon turned his head away and said, No. He lifted his marvelous fingers to his mouth, but Oscar gently took them away. Do you want to talk about how your mother was as a little girl? After her dad died?

No, the boy said. Yes. Tell me about Henry.

A swift siphoning of breath, but Oscar recovered. He said, What do you want to know?

I mean, the boy said. My great-grandfather was your gardener. You were rich. But you became friends.

I'm not rich, Oscar said, but this was untrue. In shadowy bank vaults, the gold bars his parents left him had mounted one another with mineral ponderousness and fucked great litters of nuggets into the world. Growing his money was all he'd ever been good at; he'd dilettanted through his forties. After Henry, there'd been painting, Vivi, a halfhearted stint as impresario. And then he'd retired to the cliff house year-round and the party had come to him.

Yes you are, the boy said. I go to school with rich kids and they always say they're not. Your friendship must have been wonky. Like, unbalanced.

It wasn't, Oscar said. He beat me up the first time we met. That balanced it.

The swift smile over the boy's face: something submerged there. Boys at school with their effortlessness, the teases Simon had gotten for being middle-class and disheveled. Henry wore the same look when he deflated Oscar; Henry could deflate him so easily.

Oscar explained. He had been seven, Henry the same. Lifetimes ago. Unseasonably warm, the day, the shoots of his mother's sunflowers worming from the ground; the family had just arrived from the city, his mother was fretting over the mouse droppings in the drawers. The new gardener had brought his son and Oscar had been irritated, it was his place, he wouldn't share the petrel nests with another boy, the low-tide grotto shining with kelp below the cliff. He had sulked off under the apple tree, and when the gardener kneeled to weed, he had presented Oscar with an irresistible target. He, who had never hurt anyone, had found the rotten windfall under his hand, had thrown. Out of nowhere, Henry had fallen on him in a moment (flushing, cussing Henry), put Oscar's tooth through his lip before Henry's father meandered over and separated them. When the bleeding stopped, Oscar showed Henry the steps down to the bathing rock. He could still see Henry, princely, descending.

My mom never said how her father died, Simon said. It's, like, the world's biggest secret.

Oh, darling boy, Oscar said. It's the old stupid story. Suicide. A noose and note and all that.

The road spooling beyond.

You know what they say, Oscar said, trying for brightness. There's no life after suicide.

I'm sorry, Simon said quietly, and Oscar wiped his eyes.

No, he said. It's mostly a happy story. We were inseparable. My parents gave up and sent him to school with me, you know. Your school, he ate it up, then Yale. We went on a trip like this when we graduated, camping in a tent all across America, fishing for our breakfast. When we returned, Henry said he was getting married to your grandmother. Diana. Somehow he had met her while I hadn't been paying attention. And then he wrote a novel. And then at twenty-four he died. Far too young. A half century ago, if you can believe it.

I read the book, Simon said slowly.

Oscar waited for the inevitable, his heart lifting, at last, but the boy had entirely missed the point. He said, Was Oriane really like my grandmother?

Oscar thought of Henry's wife Diana, small, plump, mousy, social-climbing. He thought of the novel's Oriane, dark, tall, rich, tempestuous. Well. A little, he said.

The boy thought for a mile then said, It's a very bad book, isn't it.

It has a certain interest for some, Oscar said.

He felt the boy looking at him until his loyalty deflated. It's terrible, he admitted. But Henry would have written classics, had he lived. First books are rarely good.

You still miss him, Simon said. He sounded surprised. As if, Oscar thought, a mere fifty years could be enough compensation for anything so deeply lost. He wanted to slap the boy back. Instead, he let it go.

THE DAY APPEARED HUMID, as if the buildings, trees, people of New York were only visible through a muslin scrim. He had lost sense of his body somewhere over the Tappan Zee Bridge and tremblingly brought the car to rest at the old hotel he had known, the one his family loved. He had arranged a stay with friends, but they were on the other edge of the park, and he, simply, could not: the hotel would have to do. How strange it was to be here again. Life as pentimento: scratch a little and there he is, decanting jet-lagged from an airport taxi, feeling that long-ago winter's Alps still cold in his bones. Scratch deeper, and here he is trailing his mother in kneesocks, face set against tears, carrying an intricate birdcage with a frantic blue budgerigar inside it. He had named it after Agatha, he remembered; further, the bird had mysteriously died a week later, its tiny blue tongue protruding from its open beak.

From the car to the hotel gusting cold—such lovely doormen they've always had, this world so cheap with youth!—there was a bad dark moment. But the boy's shoulder was now under his hand and the receptionist's face was floating in the darkness behind the desk and there were key cards in his hand and they were moving through potted palms. Elevator sliding shut, and there they were, old man, young boy, reflected a hundred times in the walls of mirrors, and he fixated on the smallest of the boys he could see until the doors opened again.

You're breathing really fast, a voice said.

And then Oscar was lying down on a bed, and there was business near his shoes. They were coming off. Oscar bellowed, No! because he understood that the boy would see the swelling, the terrible bursting boils on his legs, the padding drenched in pus, and the boy backed away, still an innocent, his hands in the air. Water, Oscar panted, and the boy brought him water, and he gestured toward the coffee maker, and the boy brought the whole thing over, coffee packs and maker and basket of creamers and sugar. Oscar fumbled with a tiny white pack of sugar with fingers made of wood, and the boy poured it in his mouth. When Oscar could at last focus, he found the boy ruddy, blinking.

Give me a few minutes, Oscar said. The boy said, No.

Give an old man his dignity, Simon, Oscar said. Twenty minutes. It's not much to ask.

The boy wavered. At last, he said, Fine. But I'm bringing the key with me and I'll be back in twenty minutes, exactly.

Dear boy, Oscar murmured, but the child was already gone.

HE WOKE TO A TONGUE like desiccated sponge. He drank water, ate a handful of walnuts from his chest pocket. When he could, he crept to the bathroom and cleaned himself up, changed the catheter bag, showered, changed. Aftershave for the old peacock. A yellow silken kerchief for the breast pocket. His heart went pell-mell in his chest.

The boy edged into the room, cell phone in hand, and nearly went boneless with relief when he saw Oscar alive, sitting on the bed, waiting.

Oscar looked at the cell phone until the boy said, Oh. My mom made me take it.

Oscar said, She knew we were leaving?

What he meant was, he supposed, And she let you come?

Simon smiled and for the first time there was something knowing in the soft pink face. Oscar disliked it very much. She trusts you, Simon said.

You are kind, Oscar said.

He was an absurd old man. He was ridiculous. He knew all this, but still it stung.

He stood. I have a gift, he said. Come.

THERE WAS NO SMELL so divine as this, leather and musk and something chill and freshly bloodied, like a hunt bag after a quail shoot, grass, twilight, autumn. Oscar had read in a Maupassant story once about a cologne charmingly called New Mown Hay. He sat with his head back upon the chaise and felt aggrieved that he'd never had such a scent made for himself.

The boy came out of the dressing room, shy, pinned. How luxurious it all was, the feeling of being the still point at the heart of a flurry of hands. Philippe emerged, glowering. He had burst into tears when he saw Oscar frail in the doorway, but now was making up for it by being formal and severe.

I regret, Philippe had said when he looked at the boy this way and that way in the triptych mirror, that his first true suit is not bespoke.

It is the best we can do in the time we have, Oscar said.

Which is not much, Philippe said, as if to himself.

No, said Oscar. And, fearing a repeat of waterworks, said, Tonight we go to the symphony.

Ah! said Philippe and added three shirts and a pair of cuff links to Simon's pile.

They would look at valises while the Peruvian tailor in the back of Philippe's did his work: Oscar had decided the boy's flimsy nylon duffel would not do. The store was a block away, still within question for Oscar, though his leg bones had been replaced with columns of warm wax. Out again in the thick hot day. Unbearable. He blinked to clear the clouds from his eyes, but all was gauze. He took the boy's arm, and they walked slowly, carefully.

Through the mist, two figures, crossing the intersection. Oscar lost his breath. Swinging down the street, laughing, seventeen, fair and dark, tanned from the summer; the plane trees threw fistfuls of shadows and light on them as they moved. It was Henry and he. Here, now! Oscar felt his dry cheek; he thought he must be dead.

But Simon was calling to the boys; the others, well bred, paused. Hey, Sim, good to see you, they were saying, and Oscar slowly understood that these were not ghosts but actual boys, ones who went to school with Simon, that they were smacking fists, and there was a bright look on Simon's face, his pleasure unmistakable that these popular boys knew his name. Oh, child, Oscar thought, heart panging. What Oscar could teach him: the art of aloofness, the art of being sought.

Now, of course, the familiar disappointment of closeness, the boys far from Henry and Oscar's younger selves. The Henry was sporty but stolid, his complexion bad. The Oscar was neither as tall nor as bull-shouldered nor—forgive him his vanity!—nearly as beautiful as the real Oscar had once been. Simon, explaining why they were in the city, and Oscar's famous last name in his mouth was an obvious preen . . . my grandfather, he was saying. Getting a new suit for me. The boys looking upon Simon with new respect; names had weight for such creatures.

Oscar felt ill. Grandfather? Horrors. How far from grandfather, if he'd been healthy, the boy would never know. And the air between the boys shifted slightly in Simon's favor and the other two shook Oscar's hand as gently as if it were a hurt bird. Simon was pink and humming with happiness when, at last, the others went on their way.

IN THE HOTEL AGAIN, he sat on the edge of the bed. There was no sap in him. He was unable to change the dressings on his legs. He hoped the smell would not rise through the soap and aftershave. Such shame, when all his life he'd been so fastidious.

He was a man turning to sugar. His flesh, if tasted, would be sickening, sweet.

He panted to tie his shoes, nearly swooned back onto the floor.

When he sat up, he could feel it, dark and patient on the bed behind him. Dense and cold. He froze, feeling its breath on the small hairs of his neck. He could not hold out for long.

Deliverance in the beautiful boy, knocking on the door, calling out in his clear voice, and in the presence of such life, the thing heaved backward. A golden rope, the boy, he propelled Oscar up, over the endless stretch of carpet to the door, swung it open, pulled Oscar, man of spun floss, out into the dim-lit hall.

THE CITY UNSPOOLED past the taxi's window, twilight slowly swallowing it all. He had walked these streets. He had loved these people with their ridiculous sweat stains, with their terrible hair. Oscar? said a voice near his ear and Oscar turned, startled, to see the boy biting his fingernails, to see the fine tiny hairs of his earlobes lit in the dying sun. He had forgotten Simon. The boy, pitying, dropped his fingers from his mouth and took Oscar's hand in his own.

SOMEWHERE OVER THE CARROT SOUP Oscar went reckless. It was so very delicious and he was so very tired of starving. Besides, the luscious jewel-box apartment, the Shostakovich, hid old friends fat Hans and ascetic Bob, made such greed seem permissible. He finished the bowl, downed his wine.

Hans and Bob stopped their storytelling about the old bad days in Key West, and watched each rising spoonful with alarm. But the boy, who couldn't understand, grinned.

He loves the soup, Simon said. I haven't seen him eating more than a few bites of anything for days. This is amazing. Put some meat back on your bones.

On to the next course! Oscar shouted and, already drunk, poured himself another glass. The roasted duck, scaled with orange slices, was hoisted to the table. Pierced, it billowed steam. There was crème fraîche in the sunchokes, onion tartine. Oscar fell to.

O., stop. You can't, said Hans. But Bob, cold and dry as ever, said, Let him be. He is an adult. He is allowed to make his own decisions.

Oscar smiled and filled his mouth again.

Hans moaned, hid his eyes. But I don't have to be an accessory. I don't have to witness.

The boy began to look worried. Witness what? he said. What's happening?

Only an old man's last remaining pleasure, said Oscar. It'd be a cruelty to deny it to me.

No one ever has denied you a thing, you tragic old asshole, said Bob. Apparently, no one ever will.

That, my friend, is only *mostly* true, Oscar said.

OSCAR'S BREATHING. It was loud, louder than the orchestra warming up with its hivelike strings. He could barely remember the car over. It was a flash. Now the faces in the dark were turned in annoyance toward him, like fish in murky ponds.

The boy was pale. He and Hans and Bob were in the aisle, whispering, girding themselves for action. Oscar eked to the other aisle. They didn't notice. He went up, through the doors. Down, the banister silky under his hand; farewell, old friend, you have given me pleasure. In a step, he went from light to dark. A blast of wind. He tottered into the first cab he could find. There, he collapsed. He laughed, panting; the others would be looking for him. He thought of Hans running roly-poly into the restrooms, peering under the stalls. The boy saucer-eyed in the entryway, scanning the stairs in panic. Let them look. The cabbie's eyes dark on him in the mirror.

The doorman had to carry him inside. What extraordinary muscles he had. Oscar wanted to say something but nothing could be said; he closed his eyes against the repeated refrain of his sick face in the elevator mirrors. *No doctor. Need rest only*, he got across, and was at last alone. The room was dark, he could not feel a light switch from where he lay. It was either the bed or the floor. It mattered not at all.

It was a failure. The trip. And tomorrow, they were to go to the ballet. Terrible shame. Couldn't even make it three sad days. Well, the boy would remain a simpleton. There were worse fates.

Poor Susan. He saw her pulling Henry's novel off the shelf, hiding it, hiding her eyes from him. After all this time; to discover that she had always known. Agatha would be weeping if she were watching now. Vivi would kick him in the ribs. Oh, he regretted.

Enough of that. Of this.

He believed in nothing, not even darkness after this was over, because darkness implied eyes. Comfort implied pain, and that wouldn't be, either. He had been lucky. He had once been loved.

From the shadows, Henry. Boy Henry, scabby, cold-fingered.

The day turned and brightened until it was blue, the sea playing catch with balls of sunlight, wave to wave. The black grotto made blacker by the sun outside, Oscar blind, the feel of Henry's breath warm and tingling across his cheek. And the side of the tent filled with light and leaf-shadow, breathing in the wind, Henry's soft whistle as he set the kettle on the campfire and the smell of smoke, and under Oscar's hand the body-warmth still in Henry's bedroll. At the diner in the black night, Oscar bleary, watching three pies go down, the waitress, plain and laughing at thin Henry's terrible hunger. The landscape of America scrolling past Henry's face, his breath clouding and retracting on the window. In the fisherman's bar, dank and smoky, Henry carefully unlooking at Oscar, studying beerfoam instead, Henry whose cheeks still bore the summer sun; Henry was getting married, to a woman, a Smith girl. Softly, *O., I'm sorry, I have to* try, *I have to*, and Oscar's emptiness, his submitting. When the wall between them had been firm, Henry came to him again, sliding a book into his hands. Oscar reading himself into a woman in Henry's words, a well-lusted woman, at that. He laughed at such prurience. Such hurt.

How, even now, it could hurt.

The nothing rises in terrible silence. The world is behind him. At some point, not too far from now, there could be no more.

THE TRAITOR OF ZION

from vol. 6, no. 1

Ben Stroud

THEY HAD BECOME something of a fascination of mine: communes cut out of the interior, new societies where all were equal and either Jesus or Liberty reigned. Some days, after reading an account of a blind prophetess leading her followers to Illinois, or of a mill town where all shared labor and wealth equally, I yearned to give up my life and join them. I felt as if we lived in a hurtling age. It seemed all humanity stood on a precipice, that in the distance, beyond the coal smoke and the tangle of telegraph wires, could be spied a shining metropolis where men would be re-formed. But I spent my days stuck in my father's shop—at twenty-three I was his peer in making the fiddles and other cheap instruments we sold to travelers embarking from the docks—and my nights in drink with friends. I need only walk the streets of my Baltimore, pass a slave carrying bricks on his crooked back or a rheumy-eyed sailor, ruined by the sea, begging alms and ale, to feel the rottenness in my soul. Men could not be changed, and I, one among millions, would never make it to any dream city.

Even so, the yearning never left me. One night, during yet another of my regular debauches, I rose without a word and left my friends in a steaming oyster house. I had seen notices in the paper of a Hebronite meeting. Their leader and revelator, Josiah Kershaw, was touring the East to summon new followers to the city he was raising on Peaine Island, a wilderness in the far northern reaches of Lake Michigan. All week the papers had mocked Kershaw. To them he was a gross fabricator, the great paradise he promised a myth, the prophecies on which he claimed his authority pure forgeries. But I was intrigued. His talk of harmony, of plain lives lived according to rule, stirred my hopes. I had passed the last weeks in a violent melancholy, pining for a woman who didn't know me, a ship captain's young wife. Increasingly I had seen my future, bound by an invisible chain to the worktable just like my father. And so, unsteady on my feet after five whiskeys, I searched for the inn where the meeting was to be held. By the time I found it my heart beat heavily in my chest and sweat dripped from my skin. My nerves were electric with anticipation.

Eyes turned to look at me when I stumbled into the room. The meeting was already underway. At the front a graybeard clutched a Bible and kept his eyes shut as he recited a prayer. I sat in the back and gripped my knees to keep from swaying. The graybeard droned on. People yawned and scratched their noses. After fifteen more minutes of this—the prayer was unending!—I could barely master myself. I was an imbecile. There was nothing for me here. I glanced at the door, but before I could rouse the courage to get back up, the graybeard sat and another man stood.

"Those who walk in the way of the Lord will receive His blessings," he shouted, and with those words and that marshal's voice I was seized. My drunkenness lifted from me. My eyes steadied, my mind ceased to yaw, my limbs stiffened with sober life. I recognized Kershaw from the newspaper illustrations. He was tall and spare, with a trimmed auburn beard and a high forehead seemingly shaped for the guarding of truths. His eyes glittered as if catching the wonders of his heavenly Guide. He paced before us, and something in him called to me. Without knowing why, I hungered for his blessing.

Five years earlier, he told us, he had been a coal shoveler in Chautauqua County. There, one black night, angels of the Lord bearing heavenly candles had shown themselves to him and revealed a golden scroll hidden in a cave. On this scroll he found descriptions of Peaine Island. The Lord had chosen it as the site for a holy city, a place where men would live in harmony under new laws and seek pleasure in labor, purity in distance from all the corruptions of the East. Already the city was begun. Kershaw had registered it as Port Hebron, after the ancient city of refuge, but when it reached its ordained population of 144,000 it would take its true name of Zion. Then ambassadors from all the world's nations would wait upon him and his followers, Kershaw told us, and Jesus would descend to take His golden throne. I felt the island rise inside me: the pines, the clear water, the small bay, the city shining like a diadem in the lake. The Lord was speaking.

The next morning, as I departed, my father damned me for a fool. He stood as I packed my set of Italian tools and forms and enough cured maple and ebony for a dozen violins. At last he called me cruel for abandoning him and refused to give me his hand in farewell. Ever since my mother died I had been his sole companion, though it had been a companionship passed in silence. His words pained me—I had always been a dutiful son, always done as he asked—but I had heard the call.

I TRAVELED BY RAIL to Buffalo and there waited a week for the steamer that took me up the lakes. I spent my days on board watching the shore, which grew wilder once we left Lake Erie and passed Detroit. The stands of birch and pine along Huron seemed unending. Isolated wisps of smoke, from a cabin or a camp of loggers, signaled the only life.

When at last we put in at the Mackinac settlement, surely one of the remotest in our Union, the sailors shoved their way into the pine-board bars that lined the harbor beneath the fort. Such places repulsed me now, and I and my fellow Hebronites—we'd soon found each other on the ship—walked along the beach and talked of our new lives on Peaine Island. It was on this walk that I saw my first whiskey trader. He sat on a shop porch, wrapped in furs. His cheeks were dirt-stained, his eyes as smoldering coals. He watched me and the other Hebronites as we strolled past, and his look made me shiver. Soon I would learn of the hatred the traders felt for us, but as yet I was ignorant. I tried to shake the look from me as I walked to the boat. The next morning the steamer left Mackinac, passed through the Straits, and called a little past noon at Port Hebron.

It was late September. Already a thousand Hebronites had settled the island, and the chosen city was a trim cluster of cabins and cottages spread along the back of the bay. Directly after we stepped onto the dock we were taken to the Temple and brought one by one before the Council of Elders. To them we professed our faith in the Lord and His Revelator, Josiah Kershaw. Our covenant recorded, the elders gave us our tasks. There was no demand for instruments, so I was sent to a stout, red-cheeked cooper named Pickle. I was his only worker. He gave me a corner of his cabin for my quarters and allowed me to hang my violin in the window, in the small hope of attracting customers for my own trade. My first night on the island he told me his story. A widower, he'd left five grown children behind after hearing Josiah's call in Toledo. He'd been taking part in a Presbyterian synod on hymnals, he said, and had never before thought to stray from his church until, stuck in a crowd on the courthouse lawn, he listened to Josiah tell of a perfect city in the lakes where the Lord spoke and men lived as one.

OVER THE NEXT WEEKS I found Peaine Island just as I had hoped. Our lives were ordered, all were cared for, and each day had its purpose. Sabbaths were set aside for Temple services and rest. After worship I would play my violin or walk into the island's deep wood. Seventh days, to which all men were subject, were given to the building of the kingdom: mine often found me engaged in road clearing, preparing boulevards for the throngs of newcomers Josiah prophesied. And the other five days were given to our own labor. Within a week Pickle had me trained in all the minor points of splitting and planing barrel staves. In the mornings I rose to work, rested only for lunch, and in the evenings I sat at Pickle's table, listening as he read from the Bible and *The Book of Truths*—the volume, printed by Josiah, that contained his first revelations and the rules by which we lived. By the light of a single candle we took our supper, corncakes and molasses with the occasional helping of bacon or ham.

The only break in our routine came when we made sorties against the whiskey traders. Every capable man on the island drilled with the militia on two of his seventh days, and we drew lots to decide who would be called on each week in the event of a sortie. I had learned about the whiskey traders soon after my arrival. They had lived on the island before Josiah and the first Hebronites came to take possession, and had kept a store by the bay, sold whiskey to the Indians in breach of the law, and idled away their days in corruption and filth. Josiah drove them out. Their souls were broken, he said. They were nothing more than the tarred stains of what we had left behind, ungoverned men who shut their eyes to the light of the Lord. Now they lived in nomad camps on the islands that surrounded our own, moving between those and the Manitous to the south or Mackinac and the Charlevoix coast to the east. Josiah had consecrated what was once theirs; he had cleansed their cabins and trapping grounds of their sin and given their land and possessions to his first followers to serve the Lord's purpose. Ever since, the whiskey traders, in their blindness, burned for vengeance. Some nights they came across the lake to steal chickens or a pig, and some nights we sought them out in their camps and put an ax through their whiskey barrels. In this way an uneasy peace was kept.

Under Pickle's roof I earned a simple happiness through daily toil and praisegiving. Winter came swiftly. Deep snows covered the island, ice locked the lake. Finally the spring. I had found what I had sought and eagerly looked forward to the Day of the 144,000. Then, Josiah told us, all people would be judged and the world would be shaped anew. I trembled at the thought—I prayed for my father and my former companions, that they might be prepared. But I awaited the day with fervor.

So might my life have continued, so might that day have come, had I never known Dorothea.

*

PICKLE'S WORK YARD FRONTED on Josiah Street, offering a view of the shops along the harbor, and it was there I first saw her. I was leaned against my ax in rest, and she was stopped in the street to gather up the lengths of patterned fabric that had come loose from her bundle. When she glanced back, her eyes caught mine. That was enough.

This, of course, could not really have been the first time I had seen Dorothea Bainbridge. She came to town once a week with her mother, and so must have walked past me before. No doubt my eyes had chanced upon her in the Temple as well. But only with that met glance did she wake my slumbering heart. I felt a fool. How had I not recognized her earlier, how had I not understood sooner that she was to be the sole repository of my love? To make up for my belated revelation I embarked on a careful study of her person whenever she passed. I discovered that her cheeks dimpled when she smiled, that she most often wore her hair in two looping braids, that she wrote poems about fairies and angels (this when I picked up a scrap of paper she'd left in her pew in the Temple). I suffered when she giggled—wishing I was the one making her laugh—and delighted when she frowned, imagining myself her comforter.

I burned with the very thought of her.

My various secret pinings in Baltimore were nothing to this. I was plunged in turmoil, so much so that Pickle worried for my soul and offered to redouble his prayers. Occasionally Dorothea glanced at me, but always I was too shy to introduce myself. Then in late spring, as I was leaning once again on my ax and watching her walk past the work yard on her way to Teague's store, a breeze came up the bay and whisked her bonnet off her head. I ran to it and snatched the bonnet before it could land in a pile of night soil. "William Ames, violin maker," I said, and, bowing, presented the bonnet to her. I pointed back toward the window in Pickle's cabin: "My shop." I did not add that it occupied only a corner of the cabin, and that this corner also served as my home.

Dorothea settled the bonnet on her head and tucked in first one raven braid, then the other. With each movement she made I ached.

"I'm here every day, and I'd be glad to play for you," I said.

She gave no answer, and I was about to let her walk away when I thought again of what Josiah had said the night of my conversion, that the blessed were those who seized the gifts the Lord put before them.

"May I call on you?" I said, forcing out the words.

She had already gone a few steps, but at that she stopped. "I thank you for my bonnet, Mr. Ames, but my father doesn't allow callers."

"I'll plead with him," I said.

"That wouldn't be any use."

"I'll wait by your farm, then. I can walk you to town or to the Temple. If you don't want me, just send me off." At this her face colored. I had gone too far. "I apologize," I said. "I did not mean—"

"Come next Wednesday," she said quickly, her voice pitched at a whisper: her mother had emerged from Teague's and was calling her. "I make no promises. My father might not let you in." Then she ran to her mother, and the two of them walked up the street until they disappeared around the other side of the bathhouse.

I COULD NOT BELIEVE my fortune. I had been bold, and the Lord had blessed me. On the agreed-upon Wednesday I left Pickle's work yard an hour early and walked to the Bainbridge farm.

Since my meeting with Dorothea I had spent my spare moments carving hands. With the clearest blocks of scrap pine I could find, I sat by my lamp each evening and whittled. I planned to present the best of the lot to Dorothea and had worked out what I would say. "Might I exchange this rude carving, which I have gripped so delicately all week, for its truer, purer model?" The sixth hand came as near to perfect as I could get. I clutched it by its fingers now as I walked, warming it with my flesh.

The Bainbridge farm lay in the remoter, southern quarter of the island, beyond the village of New Nazareth. I found the cabin at the end of a track that led first through a birch wood and then into a clearing planted with potatoes. As I walked I had assured myself of victory, but now that I approached the Bainbridge cabin

I grew nervous. What if Dorothea's father refused me? I considered methods for clandestine courtship. Secret meetings, a hollowed tree for depositing notes.

These imaginings proved unnecessary: though he received me coldly, Bainbridge let me in.

"Mr. Ames," he said upon opening the door. He led me to the cabin's crude parlor, where Dorothea sat working on a stocking. A paperboard screen and blankets slung over strings were all that divided the cabin into rooms. On the walls hung a few newspaper illustrations of Mexican scenes, from the recent war. A glass hutch filled with dull china stood across from the door, and the rest of the furniture took the form of trunks, save for the chairs gathered around the hearth. I was offered the one next to Dorothea while Bainbridge sat across from us, beside his wife. Dorothea glanced up, then returned to her stocking, and Bainbridge stared at the two of us while his wife poked at the fire. Every attempt I made at a pleasantry—on the weather, on the last Sabbath's sermon—was met with a "hmph" by Bainbridge and silence by Dorothea and her mother.

This continued for some time, and I despaired. Was my love to founder so quickly? Then Bainbridge rose to visit the privy, and, at a nod from her mother, Dorothea spoke. "I'm glad you came," she said, putting down the stocking and grinning up at me. "I was worried you wouldn't."

"I had to." With that I offered her the wooden hand and made my speech. Her cheeks reddened, and she took the hand and gave me hers in return. Dorothea's mother had focused her eyes on the small fire and was pretending to ignore us. I wondered then if she had argued for me. For a full five minutes I clutched Dorothea's hand. She pulled it away only when the scrape of the back door announced her father's return.

Once a week, all through the rest of May and into June, I called on Dorothea. Each of my visits followed the same pattern. We would sit in silence as her father watched us, me with my hands folded, Dorothea working on a stocking. Then, once Bainbridge absented himself, her mother would turn away, pretending to contemplate some particular coal, and I would present my gift—another hand, so that I might hold both, and after that a piece of polished burl I called her cheek, which I gave Dorothea in exchange for a kiss of its original. In those rare free minutes we would talk of our days or play teasing games with one another. Once she read me a poem, and another time she made me keep silent while she searched my face. The moment I left her I ached as if fevered, and with each visit it seemed our souls were being knit together.

At our sixth meeting, though, I found her altered.

As before, she worked on a stocking while her father sat with us, but when he left, rather than wake into the girl I had come to know, she stared into her lap. Her mother, sitting across from us as always, ignored the fire and twisted a handkerchief in her fingers.

"Dory," I said. But she didn't look up. "Dory, what is it?"

Then came the scraping of the back door—her father returning sooner than usual. In a moment he was standing over me and telling me it was time to leave.

"I hope you got to say your good-byes," he said once we were outside. "That's the last of your calls, Mr. Ames."

"I don't understand," I said. "My intentions are honorable." I wondered if this was what concerned him. "I hope to marry Dorothea."

"I won't permit it," he said.

His flat refusal surprised me. I stood there more flabbergasted than hurt.

"Sir," I said, "there must be something I can do."

"Nothing," he said.

"But, Mr. Bainbridge," I protested, "surely—"

"You'll get my permission the day you're raised to the Order!" he shouted, and his face grew fiery. He meant to say I had no hope. The Order of Maccabaeus was the highest honor ordained by Josiah. It had as yet no members. I could not understand Bainbridge's stubbornness, and to distract my sick heart—for with each passing moment hurt pumped in—I spent my long walk home cursing him and his arrogance.

IT WAS SOME WEEKS AFTER that last meeting with Dorothea—lost weeks, despairing weeks—that Josiah summoned everyone to the Temple. For four days he had kept himself shut in the

Chamber of the Most Holy. While I had been courting Dorothea doubts had been spreading across the island. According to *The Book of Truths*, with the passing of spring we were to have left the Years of Preparation and entered the Years of Manifestation. By now thousands were supposed to be arriving each week. Instead there had been only a trickle of new converts. And where were the promised wonders, the signs of the New Age? Why hadn't angels appeared on Mount Nebo, or fire broken the sky to devour the homes and stores of those sliding into apostasy? Some were saying our faith had fallen short, that we need only trust more in the Lord. Others whispered that Josiah and the elders were in secret taking new wives, like the Mormons of Utah, and the Lord was displeased. Still others, couching their words in the claim that they were merely repeating what they'd heard, accused Josiah of fooling us all with humbuggery. The doubts could no longer be ignored, and at the most recent Sabbath Josiah had announced he was going into the Chamber of the Most Holy to beseech the Lord to show him where we had erred. Each day I had prayed for him. My faith had never wavered.

As I entered the Temple that day, my eyes sought Dorothea and soon found her raven braids peeking from beneath her bonnet. She sat with her father and mother near the front. In the last weeks I had felt as if part of me had sickened and died. There was little more than a cool emptiness left within my chest. Pickle had been solicitous, warning me of destruction and praying I'd return to reason and moderation. Now if I saw Dorothea it was only from a distance, here in the Temple or when she came to town with her mother to Teague's store or with her father during his visits to Josiah. It was rumored Bainbridge was being considered for eldership. Always she would bow her head rather than meet my eyes. I still had not learned the reason for the breaking of our courtship, and the letter I had left for her at Teague's went unanswered. I tried to keep from looking at her, to stare at the rafters or out the windows, but it was impossible. With her back to me I could study her without consequence: her shawl-wrapped shoulders, her bare neck, her bonneted head. Was she happy?

Once everyone was settled, Josiah stepped through the door at the front of the sanctuary, bowed his head as he walked through the Arch of the Blood, and mounted the pulpit. He looked out over us, and an even deeper quiet fell upon the pews.

"There has been confusion and uncertainty," he began, his voice calm. "I've shared it myself. We have come to the site of Zion, we have begun building the city, and yet we look around us and wonder, Where are the multitudes? Last night, the fourth night of my vigil, the Lord put me into a deep sleep, then took me up and showed me a vision of our island. I saw Port Hebron, I saw the forest and the farms, I saw the lake around us, wide as a sea." Now his voice began to rise. His hands gripped the pulpit's sides. His eyes flashed. "The Lord made me to look at the lake and, lo, fire appeared on the horizon, blazing toward our shores. The Lord said, 'This unholy fire you must quench.' Then the fire fell away, and in the middle of the island a pit opened and out of the pit came a cloud of pestilence. The Lord showed me the pestilence spreading among us. It killed everybody it touched. The Lord's voice said, 'This unholy plague you must cure.' I said to the Lord, 'The fire I understand, the traders who circle our island. But the plague? The plague I do not understand.' "

Josiah gazed at the assembly room's ceiling and stretched out his arms, as if still in dialogue with the heavens. " 'There is a sickness among you,' He said. 'I will not send My Son to reign over the impure.' 'But what is this sickness, and how am I to cure it?' I asked. 'You will not see it, you will not know it, you will not cure it, but I will send a Judge who will do these things,' He said. 'You must make ready for him. You must build him a house, a seat from which he can spy out your pestilence.' The Lord then showed me how we are to build this house, and I have spent all morning setting down His instructions here." Josiah waved a paper scribbled with notes. "We begin work tomorrow. Praise be to the Lord."

Hunched over the pulpit, sweating, exhausted, he awaited our response. The room remained silent. Perhaps the doubters were considering whether the vision quelled their anxieties, the accusers of humbuggery assessing its authenticity. But after only a few seconds we answered in unison, each of us shouting the words Josiah had taught us: "Glory and thanks to the Lord for His guiding hand!"

*

A FEW NIGHTS LATER I was in my corner of Pickle's cabin, playing my violin, when Elder Williamson came to the door. It was past ten—darkness had finally fallen—and Pickle was readying himself for sleep. Elder Williamson told me to get my rifle. Some whiskey traders had come from Mackinac and set fire to Elder Hunt's cabin. They'd not yet been so bold, and even though the cabin was saved Josiah had ordered a sortie to chase them; since the vision he'd demanded more vigilance. After Elder Williamson left I splashed my face with water. My previous weeks on sortie duty had been quiet and I felt unprepared. Bidding Pickle good night, I took my rifle and went to the dock. The others had already begun the prayer. Josiah was there, placing his hand on each one's forehead. I raced up and he put his hand to mine.

We paired into canoes; I was matched with a man named Spofford. I didn't know him well. He'd arrived at the island after me and worked in one of the logging camps. Josiah had elected to lead us himself, and at his orders we paddled out of the bay toward the near islands to the east, the likeliest place we'd find the whiskey traders. Above us a thick spangle of stars cast a faint light on the water. As Josiah had instructed, we took care with our paddles, guarding against every needless splash.

Halfway to Garden Island we spied a rocking lantern. I had heard stories of ghosts on the lake, and I started, but Spofford reached a hand back to quiet me, then, following Josiah, steered us toward the light. As we drew nearer, I saw it was only an Indian in his canoe, night fishing. Josiah gave him a present of smoked beef and a small sack of cornmeal, and the Indian told us that he'd seen the whiskey traders pass three hours earlier, heading toward the notch bay on Garden Island's western point. We paddled in that direction and soon made out the glimmer of the traders' fire on the shore, heard their shouts echo across the lake.

"I'd say they're a few sheets," Spofford whispered back to me. We went past the notch, to a narrow spit of land just to the east, and pulled our canoes up the beach. Once we were in the wood, Josiah gave his instructions. Elder Williamson would lead four men through the trees to a position behind the whiskey traders' camp while the others crept along the sands. We were only to give the traders a scare, Josiah warned us, but enough of a scare to show them we were prepared to fight. After Elder Williamson's party took a five-minute start, the rest of us set out along the shore with Josiah.

The traders had bivouacked at the tree line, their camp not fifty feet from the water, and as we took our positions along the lake's edge I counted them. There were six circled around the fire, and they passed a jug while one among them, a blond-bearded man wrapped in furs and skins, bellowed a story about killing a bear. They didn't see us. The fire was too bright in their eyes, their attentions too occupied by the story.

I looked to Josiah, who was holding up his hand. He dropped it and let out an animal screech. At that Spofford raced off to set fire to the traders' canoes and the rest of us shot our rifles into the air and hooted like crazed owls. From the darkness of the wood Williamson and his men echoed us.

The whiskey traders leapt up at the tumult. They reeled and stumbled drunkenly as they looked about in terror.

"Who's there?" one of them called, aiming his rifle at one blackness after another.

"Damned God-squawkers!" another shouted as he sat back down and applied himself to the jug.

"We didn't mean for it to burn," pleaded a third, and knelt in the sand.

We stood in our places and kept up our hooting. Behind us the lake, black and calm, lapped at the shore. Down the beach the traders' canoes were in full blaze.

We were about to return to our own canoes when the trader who'd been telling the story bolted toward us with a shout of "Goddamn it!" We were not prepared for such a turn, and nobody moved to stop him. By luck he came right at Josiah and tackled him. "Got one of you now!" the trader shouted. Josiah lay struggling on the sand, pinned beneath the trader's knees. Something glittered in the starlight. A knife. My stomach lurched. Without thinking I rushed at the trader and swung the butt of my rifle into his temple. I pushed him off and gave my hand to Josiah, who took it, rose, and whistled for the sortie's end. The remaining whiskey traders fled into the trees with their gear. Only after the last had gone did I return to Josiah's attacker. I shook the man, but he didn't stir. I felt him. Already his body was cooling.

As the others circled Josiah, I stayed beside the trader's body. His face revealed that he was my own age. On his chest lay a necklace of animal teeth, among which was a silver locket. I opened it and a loop of fiery hair fell onto my palm. Bound in its tight circlet, it had the feel of some new metal. I imagined a faraway sitting room, then a darkly lit brothel of the sort I and my companions in Baltimore had always been too timid to enter. What woman had been in possession of the trader's heart? My own clenched quickly with the thought of Dorothea. I replaced the hair and snapped the locket shut. Blood now seeped from the side of the trader's head and had begun to soak the sand.

I was overcome. I thought of the trader's family, of the red-haired woman, and imagined all the better ways I could have stopped him, the ways I could have saved Josiah without killing. I was a sinner, a brute.

Meanwhile, as I watched over the trader's body, the others talked. As of yet there had been no bloodshed between us and the whiskey traders. If anyone learned of what had happened, Josiah warned, there would be more killing. Elder Williamson asked what should be done, and Josiah related his plan. The other traders had only seen their fellow disappear onto the beach and could be certain of nothing. We would take the body to the canoes and dispose of it in the lake. The true account of the night could never be disclosed: when asked, we would say the trader who had attacked Josiah fled into the wood, after his fellows. Once this was agreed to, Josiah called me over and made me swear a vow of secrecy with the others.

I did not carry the body. That I was spared. But I helped gather rocks. We filled the trader's pockets with the heaviest of them and lashed more to his feet, then put him in a canoe with Spofford and Big John Biggs. Josiah took Spofford's place in my canoe—I trembled when I saw him come near—and as soon as we'd paddled a quarter mile out, he ordered us to stop. Spofford and Biggs pitched the body over. The moon had risen, and it lit the trader's face as he sank beneath the lake. His cheeks and forehead flashed pale, and then his body turned. The last I saw of him was his hands. Unbound, they floated above his hair, reaching toward me, it seemed, until the darkness finally swallowed them and he was taken by the deep.

We paddled on. I tried to distract my mind from the image of the trader's mute face, from the terrible seeping wound. I could not. As we neared Port Hebron I began to understand the full ramification of what I'd done. Damnation would be upon me. I would be forever locked out of the celestial kingdom. I assumed Josiah had taken Spofford's place in the canoe to tell me just this. But, as if knowing my inner struggle, at that very moment he told me to ease my mind. "You raised your hand to save me," he said as we came past Apostle's Point, "not to take that man's life. He forfeited it. The punishment falls on his soul." He paused, and then he said, "Because of what you've done, I'm raising you to the Order."

I ceased paddling.

"The Order?" I asked. I stared at Josiah's back and waited for him to tell me I had misheard.

"Yes, the Order," he said. "You'll be the first."

I was struck by the pure shock of the honor. The Order! Then, with a jolt, I remembered. My mind thrilled with visions of Dorothea. I saw her, waiting for me in her father's cabin. Bainbridge's thundered words the night of my last visit resounded in my head. I had him. One of the greatest sins, according to *The Book of Truths*, was to break an oath. He couldn't refuse me now.

Once we returned to Port Hebron, the others, tired from the sortie, drifted back to their cabins and cottages with a few mumbled salutations. But I couldn't rest. I rushed across the island to the Bainbridge farm and arrived just as dawn broke. I didn't pause to knock but stepped into the cabin and went straight to Dorothea, who stood at the fire boiling oats. "William!" she said. "You can't be here. My father."

Just then Bainbridge emerged from behind one of the hanging blankets, risen to take his breakfast. "Mr. Ames," he said when he saw me, his voice cold as the gray ice that had covered the island's roads and paths all through winter, so many forgotten months ago.

"Remember your oath, Mr. Bainbridge," I burst out.

He drew his face into a blank of confusion.

"The night you forbade me to court Dorothea, you said you would allow me to propose to her the day I was raised to the Order."

"A figure of conver—"

"You made an oath, Mr. Bainbridge, an oath and a bargain. I have fulfilled my end. This night I was raised to the Order. Now you must let me offer myself to Dorothea."

Dorothea looked to her father. "Is it true?" she asked.

Bainbridge ignored her. Hoping, I imagine, to trap me in a lie, he asked how I'd accomplished such a feat. I told him the version of the story I and the others had sworn to, then added that he could ask Josiah himself if he doubted me. Bainbridge groaned and sat. He put his hand to his forehead and seemed to be deliberating. "Very well," he finally said.

I knelt at Dorothea's feet, and before I could pose the question or even wonder what she might say, she nodded. Her pale cheeks blushed and her dark eyes filled with tears. How strangely the Lord had worked to unite us! Her father stormed out of the cabin, but I was too delighted to pay him any mind. I took hold of Dorothea's hand and kissed it, saying now that it was truly mine I would never let it go.

AS WE CROSSED THE SPINE OF JULY, high summer reached the island. Side-wheelers began putting in each day, taking on the cordwood we sold them for the run east through the Straits or south to Chicago, and fishing boats arrived in our waters to pack their holds with trout and sturgeon. With the demand on barrels I had few hours free from Pickle's work yard, but those few I spent with Dorothea. Now that we were betrothed we were allowed to walk together. Her father absented himself whenever I appeared, and Dorothea and I strolled along the edge of the potato field and sketched our lives, I telling her how someday I would open my violin shop, she telling me how she longed to sail the lakes, to have a boat and explore the wild coasts. In our fantasies we built our house, we named our children, we stood at the rising of the kingdom. Our thoughts were littered with promise. She would close her eyes as we talked and curl her mouth into a grin, resting her cheek on my shoulder. Afterward she would lead me into the wood and let me put my lips to hers, let me touch her cheek and hold her in my arms. My fingertips trembled against her flesh, and I felt again what I had felt the night of my conversion: the island growing within me, the future coming as it should.

Most of my visits passed like this, but on occasion Dorothea would be caught in a dark study. Once I found her sitting in her small flower garden with her arms tight around her skirts, clutching her folded legs to her chest, staring off above the birches. Rather than jump up when she heard me approach, as she usually did, she refused even to turn.

"Dory."

No answer.

I sat beside her, asked about the garden, tried any number of ways to gain her attention until at last she seemed to rise back to herself. She presented me with a smile, and asked if we could go for a walk. Then we strolled and talked as usual, though she ignored my inquiries about the state in which I had found her.

It was after one of these appearances of her shadow—for that is how I called it to myself—that I was asked to Josiah's home. His cottage, the finest on the island, sat apart from town, to the north, and was surrounded by a picket fence and flanked by two six-pounder cannons. Despite being raised to the Order, I'd never been asked to the cottage before, and had spoken to Josiah only a few times since the night of the sortie—mostly in the Temple, where, as the Order's sole member, I performed my one duty, standing guard in a velvet tunic beneath the Arch of the Blood while Josiah prayed.

When I arrived, Josiah's wife, Celia, showed me into his office and brought us glasses of honeyed milk. She was a gray-faced woman five years his senior and rarely left the cottage. It was said, under breath, that the money from her first husband's estate had laid the foundation for our colony. Josiah was at work, writing. Uncertain what to do with myself, I sipped from my glass and looked about the room. Behind Josiah hung a map of the island showing Port Hebron as Zion—the completed Temple, the grid of streets stretching across the island to house the 144,000—and below the map stood shelves of plant specimens, which, I'd heard,

Josiah regularly sent to a professor at Union College. The study's window faced onto the harbor, and mounted on its sill was a brass telescope, pointed toward the open lake beyond the bay. The harbor had grown yet busier in the last weeks. Soon, Josiah had told us, the federal gunboat that patrolled the upper lakes was to put in. He was expected to go down and greet her captain.

My eyes had made it as far as a snake coiled in a jar—it sat on the floor, directly beneath the telescope—when the scratching of Josiah's nib stopped and he looked up and said, without preface, "I've learned you are to be married to Dorothea Bainbridge. Is this true?"

I was a trifle surprised, but lost no time in answering. "It is."

"I take an interest in all my charges," he said, "and you especially. I owe you my life."

Josiah drank from his honeyed milk, then proceeded to study me with his gaze. I grew nervous. His eyes pierced mine. The pages of my soul lay open before him. He was testing me somehow, though I wasn't sure why.

When I thought I could stand this gaze no longer, he rose and gave me his holy blessing. "In *The Book of Truths* it is written that a man must not become too attached to the things of this world," he said as he walked me to the door. With that, our meeting was ended, and I left his house as confused over the visit's purpose as when I had entered.

MY NEXT SEVENTH DAY I was assigned to work on the Judge's House, which was being built, as commanded in Josiah's revelation, atop the low slope of Mount Nebo, the island's highest point. The house's plans called for a long five-roomed cottage with a high tower at one end. From the top the Judge, whom Josiah told us to expect daily, would be able to see over the treetops. I enjoyed working on the Judge's House. It was only a mile from the Bainbridge farm, and at the end of the day I would walk there and spend the entire evening with Dorothea.

I was helping a pig farmer named Morris nail planks to the floor of the cottage's porch when Josiah came riding up on his dappled gray. He spoke to our foreman, a man named Pearson, then clicked his tongue and spurred his horse down the southern path, toward New Nazareth. Not long after that we ran out of nails. It was too late in the day to fetch more from Port Hebron, so Pearson gathered us together, gave a prayer of thanksgiving for our labor, and let us go early. The others started their walk back to town, but I set off toward the Bainbridge farm.

I would be an hour early, and I delighted myself with thoughts of Dorothea's surprise. Perhaps I would find her in the garden, weeding away the clover, or in the cabin, tending a stew over the fire. I would sneak behind her, wrap her in my arms, and whisper in her ear.

By the time I reached the Bainbridge farm a fine rain was falling. I paused to pick some dandelions, then took the track through the birch wood and into the potato field. When I came to the clearing, I stopped. Josiah's dapple stood outside the cabin, head down, nibbling at grass. My skin prickled. I thought of Dorothea's shadow and the meeting with Josiah, and a sick chill shuddered through me. I tried to calm myself, to quell the fumbling realization. I recalled Bainbridge's rumored candidacy for eldership, told myself Josiah had come simply to consult with him. But then the cabin door opened, and Josiah walked out. Dorothea stood behind him. Her braids were undone, her dress loose.

My reason gave way like a shattered pane. Josiah and Dorothea hadn't yet seen me, and I made to run to the cabin. Before I could, I was grabbed from behind. It was Bainbridge. He put his hand over my mouth and held me down hidden in the brush while Josiah rode away.

"It was revelation," he whispered into my ear. "It was revelation. I tried to run you off."

As soon as Josiah was gone, Bainbridge let me go. I pushed myself from him, then turned to look at him.

"She's his," Bainbridge said. He shook his head and covered his eyes with his palm. I'd never imagined he could be so abject. "That's why I sent you off. The Lord chose her as one of Josiah's royal concubines, like King David had. He told me we must keep it secret. Then you, with that damned oath. I begged him for a release, to let you marry Dorothea, but he said you can't stop revelation."

I left Bainbridge and went straight to the cabin. Dorothea had gone back inside and I found her at the table. She was staring at the wall, her face drawn into a familiar absence. I called her name, but she didn't turn. Her mother sat beside her, holding her hand and stroking her hair.

I had entered intending to shout, but my heart shivered and the words wouldn't come.

TWO WEEKS LATER the federal gunboat *Superior* was spotted on the horizon. It was now September, a year since my arrival. Summer had begun to ease itself from the lake. Save for one night, I hadn't ventured farther than Pickle's work yard. I had skipped the Sabbath services, I had stayed at home on my seventh day. After discovering the truth, I contemplated returning to Baltimore. My father would welcome me back to his shop, and I could take up my old life again. I packed my things into a single bag, counted and recounted the dollars I had left: enough for passage to Detroit. But my rage boiled and wouldn't let me leave. At night, in his corner of the cabin, Pickle mumbled his prayers on my behalf.

Already two ships had put in, the Chicago steamer *Lady of the Lakes* and a fisherman called *Sutton's Fancy*, but the sighting of the *Superior*, with her promise of uniformed sailors, a troop of marines, and a band of fife and drum, caused a stir. Hebronites and passengers from the *Lady of the Lakes*, who'd come ashore while she took on wood for her engines, crowded the docks to watch as the gunboat came past Apostle's Point. I went down to the water, too, but kept back from the others. Stacks of cordwood lined the shore in rows, and from just beyond the end of these I could see the entire breadth of the bay. The sun shone brightly, turning the waves to diamonds, bleaching the sky of its blue. On the docks some of the men held children on their shoulders and waved their hats in salute. Gentile women giggled and pointed at the boat from beneath their parasols. Their pink ribbons and white summer dresses gleamed.

The tableau of cheerfulness was too much. I looked away, and that's when I saw the whiskey traders. Two of them stood among the cordwood stacks. They were got up in broadcloth suits and had trimmed their beards, but I recognized the wildness in them, recognized the slouch that bespoke discomfort with civilized clothes, the brute dullness in their eyes that came from their animal life of sin. Unlike everyone else, they were turned away from the boat and looking toward town, their hands in their pockets.

The one night I had strayed from Pickle's cabin, it had been to go to them. I had taken a canoe and paddled across to the near islands until I saw the glow of one of their camps. They took me captive once they spotted me, held a knife to my throat, pushed me down against the sand. Their eyes glinted in the firelight as they leaned over me. I had not tried to hide, and they asked me what I was playing at. When I told them I had killed their fellow, one of them called for rope. I shouted that I sorrowed for it now. It wasn't a lie, the dead trader's face haunted my dreams. And I said that I regretted having let Josiah live. Curses fell from the hollows of their mouths. Bits of elkhorn hung from the one who brought the rope. They pulled me to the water, made to push me under, but I kept shouting. I told them about the press of the late-summer traffic and the commotion of the federal ship's arrival. There they would have their chance, I said. At that, they released me, and I slipped into Pickle's cabin just before dawn. He stirred when I entered, but didn't wake.

Now I watched the whiskey traders among the cordwood stacks. From Josiah's house one of the six-pounders fired a salute. I turned in time to see him step from his front door. He was to come down to the dock to receive the gunboat's captain in a short ceremony. Following the cannon's salute, the *Superior*'s band struck up a military air. As she came into harbor, the melody carried over the chuffing of her engine and the slap of her side paddle wheel. The men on the pier hurrahed.

The path from Josiah's house to the dock would lead him past me, and he appeared in good spirits as he approached, whistling and nodding, in his freshly brushed coat. A few yards beyond me he would be caught between the whiskey traders and the cordwood. His life would be in their hands. But now, again, it was in mine. I could step forward, could reach out to stop him and save our paradise, broken as it was. Or I could remain still and let it be taken.

A buffet of wind whipped up from the lake. There was a splash, a shout, laughter—someone on the dock had dived into the water.

It was easy. Josiah hadn't yet noticed me. I let him pass, then turned away. I didn't care to watch.

I HEARD THE FIRST SHOT when I was halfway to Pickle's cabin, then three more. By the last the gunboat's band had ceased playing. A lone scream cut through the stilled crowd, then the air itself seemed to breathe before erupting into a confused, wailing din that spread up from the docks. Someone had lifted Josiah's body and called now for help. Several of my brothers ran past me, on their way to the water. Celia's blanched face emerged from the cottage amid the clamor. I recalled Josiah's telescope and wondered if she had been watching through it.

Pickle came in after dark, hours later. I had last seen him standing on the dock, cheering the *Superior*. Now his boots were caked with mud, his clothes damp with sweat and pricked with burrs. When he saw me in my corner, from which I hadn't shifted since noon, he took a little step back. "I thought you were with the others."

I shook my head.

"We chased those dogs across the island, but they got to their canoe. They're with their fellows. Can't you hear them?"

I'd not noticed the sound before, but now I could make out the whiskey traders' hoots and curses echoing over the water. Pickle sat on his bed, head bowed. Then he convulsed, and I realized he was weeping. I glanced away, at his calendar covered with *x*'s, at my violin hanging in the window, at the lampglasses black with soot. He had been good to me, and I had cut him from the kingdom.

THE FEDERAL GUNBOAT DEPARTED, the captain having claimed this was none of his affair. The other ships left soon after, and the elders shut themselves in the Temple. Some of the brethren had already abandoned their cabins and made camp on the dock to await the next steamer. By morning the news had reached across the island: God's judgment.

Overnight the sky had turned gray. Thick clouds pressed low against the lake, and cold seeped through the cracks in the cabin's walls. I ignored the breakfast Pickle made, put on my black coat, and walked to the Bainbridge farm, where I found Dorothea's father lifting their trunks onto a borrowed wagon. He saw me, but refused to meet my eye. Dorothea's mother was in the yard, boiling their clothes. She pointed to the clothesline. Dorothea was there, hanging sheets.

I waited for her to turn, but she ignored me. When the last sheet was hung she began adjusting the first, careful not to come near where I stood. Her manner made me anxious, but at the same time I became angry. Something promised me was being withheld.

"You're free," I said. "We can marry."

"After what you saw? After everything?" she said. She showed me her face and it was twisted in anguish. "It's too late."

"It's not," I said. "I promise, I'll forget everything." I took her, held her in my arms. "Meet me tonight at the Judge's House," I said. "Will you?" Only when she nodded did I let her go.

All through the first hours of night I paced the timber skeleton of the Judge's House. I imagined Dorothea waiting for her father to fall asleep, or writing a long letter to her mother. But as the night grew longer, I began to fear the worst. Finally I went back to the farm. It was empty, and at the sight a dizziness rippled up from my feet. I raced to Port Hebron and arrived an hour after dawn, in time to see a steamer leaving the bay. I searched among the dock camp that now spread along the shore, but Dorothea wasn't there. After questioning a few acquaintances, I ran into Spofford, who told me he'd seen the Bainbridges board the boat. I looked out over the water and felt the bruises of my heart turn black.

I returned to Pickle's cabin. When Pickle came in he told me that two of the elders had fled the island, taking the sacred books and the treasury with them, and that Celia had shut herself in the cottage; Josiah's body lay spread on the dining table, and she refused to let him be buried. I stayed at the window. At night the whiskey traders returned to the bay in their canoes. Their shouting stirred me like a summons.

A day later another steamer put in. Pickle gathered his belongings into two carpetbags. He offered to pay my passage, but I told him I wasn't leaving.

He stood in the doorway. "It's all gone," he said.

I told him my decision had been made, and when he asked what I meant, I got up, took my violin from the window, offered it to him, and bid him go.

FOR A WEEK LONGER, as the island cleared, I stayed in the cabin. I did not shave, nor did I visit the bathhouse, which was shut up now, anyway. I ate our last stores of food—hungrily, greedily, as if both nursing the wound within and feeding the fever that spread through my veins. At the end of the week I opened the door and stepped outside. By now the streets were empty. The whiskey traders had remained in their camps, and silence had descended, encasing every building in Port Hebron in a thin glass shell. The few noises were the sharper for it: a rodent scurrying from the sight of me, the crackle of a fire burning unchecked. Even the scent of the air was changed, carrying nothing but a tinge of smoke. In this strange, vacant quiet I felt my new beard. I searched abandoned cabins and wrapped myself in the furs and hides left behind. I bent to the ground and darkened my cheeks with mud. Then, at last, I went down to the water and yelled for my new brothers to come.

NOTES ON CONTRIBUTORS

STEVE ALMOND is the author of the story collections *God Bless America*, *The Evil B.B. Chow*, and *My Life in Heavy Metal*; the novel *Which Brings Me to You* (with Julianna Baggott); and the nonfiction books *Rock and Roll Will Save Your Life*, *(Not That You Asked)*, and *Candyfreak*. His stories have appeared in *Playboy*, *Zoetrope: All-Story*, and *Ploughshares*, among other magazines, and have been reprinted in *The Best American Short Stories* and *The Pushcart Prize*. He lives outside Boston.

RICK BASS is the author of thirty-one books, including the novel *All the Land to Hold Us*. He lives in the Yaak Valley of northwest Montana, where he is a board member of the Yaak Valley Forest Council and Round River Conservation Studies.

KAREN E. BENDER is the author of the novels *Like Normal People* and *A Town of Empty Rooms*; a story collection, *Refund*, will be published in 2015 by Counterpoint Press. Her stories have appeared in the *New Yorker*, *Granta*, *Narrative*, *Ploughshares*, *Zoetrope: All-Story*, *Harvard Review*, and other magazines, and have been reprinted in *The Best American Short Stories*, *The Best American Mystery Stories*, *New Stories from the South*, and twice in *The Pushcart Prize* series. She has had two stories read as part of *Selected Shorts* on NPR and won grants from the National Endowment for the Arts and the Rona Jaffe Foundation. Visit her at karenebender.com.

KEVIN BROCKMEIER is the author of seven books of fiction, among them the novels *The Brief History of the Dead* and *The Illumination*. His eighth book, *A Few Seconds of Radiant Filmstrip: A Memoir of Seventh Grade*, is forthcoming in 2014. His work has been translated into seventeen languages. He lives in Little Rock, Arkansas, where he was raised.

ROBERT OLEN BUTLER has published fourteen novels and six volumes of short fiction, one of which, *A Good Scent from a Strange Mountain*, won the 1993 Pulitzer Prize for fiction. His latest novel is *The Star of Istanbul*. He teaches creative writing at Florida State University. He collects paper ephemera.

GEORGE MAKANA CLARK is the author of a novel, *The Raw Man*, and a story collection, *The Small Bees' Honey*. His work has appeared in *The O. Henry Prize Stories*, *The Granta Book of the African Short Story*, *Tin House*, *Zoetrope: All-Story*, *Glimmer Train*, *Transition*, the *Georgia Review*, *Witness*, the *Southern Review*, *Black Warrior Review*, and elsewhere. Clark was awarded a National Endowment of the Arts Fellowship and named a finalist for the Caine Prize for African Writing. He teaches fiction writing and African literature at the University of Wisconsin–Milwaukee.

BROCK CLARKE is the author of five books of fiction, most recently the novels *Exley* and *An Arsonist's Guide to Writers' Homes in New England*. Clarke's stories and essays have appeared in, among other places, the *New York Times Magazine*, the *Boston Globe*, the *Virginia Quarterly Review*, *One Story*, the *Believer*, the *Georgia Review*, *New England Review*, and the *Southern Review*, and in the anthologies *The Pushcart Prize* and *New Stories from the South*, as well as on NPR's *Selected Shorts*. Clarke's sixth book, the novel *The Happiest People in the World*, will be published in 2014. He lives in Portland, Maine, and teaches creative writing at Bowdoin College.

BEN FOUNTAIN is the author of a novel, *Billy Lynn's Long Halftime Walk*, which received the National Book Critics Circle Award and the Los Angeles Times Book Prize, and was a finalist for the National Book Award. His story collection, *Brief Encounters with Che Guevara*, received the PEN/Hemingway Award and the Barnes & Noble Discover Award for Fiction.

LAUREN GROFF is the author of *Arcadia*, a New York Times Notable Book and finalist for the Los Angeles Times Book Prize in fiction; *The Monsters of Templeton*; and *Delicate Edible Birds*, a story collection. Her fiction has appeared in *The Pushcart Prize* and *The PEN/O. Henry Prize Stories*, as well as in the *New Yorker*, the *Atlantic Monthly*, *One Story*, *Tin House*, *Ploughshares*, and twice in *The Best American Short Stories*.

CARY HOLLADAY grew up in Virginia. Her seven volumes of fiction include *Horse People: Stories* and *The Deer in the Mirror*. Her work has appeared in *The O. Henry Prize Stories*, and she received a fellowship from the National Endowment for the Arts. She teaches at the University of Memphis.

REBECCA MAKKAI is the author of two novels, *The Hundred-Year House* and *The Borrower*, a *Booklist* top ten debut, an Indie Next pick, an *O, The Oprah Magazine* selection, and one of *Chicago Magazine*'s choices for best fiction of 2011. Her short fiction was chosen for *The Best American Short Stories* in 2008, 2009, 2010, and 2011, and has been featured in *The Best American Nonrequired Reading*, *New Stories from the Midwest*, *Best New Fantasy*, and several college literature textbooks. Her stories appear in *Harper's*, *Tin House*, *Ploughshares*, and *New England Review*, and on public radio's *This American Life* and *Selected Shorts*. She teaches at Lake Forest College, StoryStudio Chicago, and Sierra Nevada College. Visit her at rebeccamakkai.com.

MIHA MAZZINI lives in Ljubljana, Slovenia. He is the author of twenty-seven published books, translated into nine languages, as well as the screenwriter of two award-winning feature films and the writer-director of five short films. His novel *Guarding Hanna* was recently re-released by North Atlantic Books. "That Winter," his first published story in the United States, also appeared in *The Pushcart Prize*. Visit him at mihamazzini.com.

DAVID MEANS is the author of *The Secret Goldfish*, *The Spot*, and *Assorted Fire Events*, which won the Los Angeles Times Book Prize in fiction and was a finalist for the National Book Critics Circle Award. His work has appeared in the *New Yorker*, *Harper's*, *Zoetrope: All-Story*, *McSweeney's*, *The Best American Short Stories*, and *The Best American Mysteries*. He lives in Nyack, New York, and teaches at Vassar College.

DANIEL OROZCO is the author of *Orientation and Other Stories*. He is the recipient of a National Endowment for the Arts fellowship and a Whiting Writers Award. He teaches in the creative writing program at the University of Idaho.

EDITH PEARLMAN is the recipient of the PEN/Malamud Award for excellence in the art of short fiction. Her new and selected story collection, *Binocular Vision*, won the National Book Critics Circle Award, the Harold U. Ribalow Prize, the Julia Ward Howe Prize, and the Edward Lewis Wallant Award, and was named Foreword Book of the Year and a finalist for the National Book Award, the Los Angeles Times Book Prize, and The Story Prize. She is the author of three previous story collections, *Vaquita*, *Love Among the Greats*, and *How to Fall*, and her stories have been reprinted in *The Best American Short Stories*, *The O. Henry Prize Stories*, *New Stories from the South*, and *The Pushcart Prize*. New stories appear in *Harvard Review* and the *Antioch Review*. She lives in Brookline, Massachusetts.

BENJAMIN PERCY is the author of two novels, *Red Moon* and *The Wilding*, as well as two books of short stories, *Refresh, Refresh* and *The Language of Elk*. He is a contributing editor at *Esquire*.

RON RASH is the author of the 2009 PEN/Faulkner finalist and *New York Times* best-selling novel *Serena*, in addition to four other prize-winning novels, *The Cove*, *One Foot in Eden*, *Saints at the River*, and *The World Made Straight*; three collections of poems; and five collections of stories, among them *Burning Bright*, which won the 2010 Frank O'Connor International Short Story Award. His work has appeared twice in the *The O. Henry Prize Stories*. He teaches at Western Carolina University.

BILL ROORBACH's newest novel is *Life Among Giants*. His next, to be released in 2014, is *Storm of the Century*. His short fiction has appeared in *Harper's*, the *Atlantic*, *Playboy*, and lots more places, such as on NPR's *Selected Shorts*. He was a cake judge on Food Network, but only once. Visit him at billroorbach.com.

MAGGIE SHIPSTEAD is a graduate of the Iowa Writers' Workshop and a former Stegner fellow at Stanford. Her first novel, *Seating Arrangements*, won the Dylan Thomas Prize and the Art Seidenbaum Award for First Fiction as part of the Los Angeles Times Book Prizes.

MARISA SILVER is the author, most recently, of the novel *Mary Coin*, a *New York Times* bestseller. She is also the author of two previous novels, *No Direction Home* and *The God of War*, which was a finalist for the Los Angeles Times Book Prize for fiction. Her first collection of short stories, *Babe in Paradise*, was named a New York Times Notable Book and was a Los Angeles Times Best Book of 2001. When her second collection, *Alone With You*, was published, the *New York Times* called her "one of California's most celebrated contemporary writers." Silver made her fiction debut in the *New Yorker* when she was featured in that magazine's first "Debut Fiction" issue. Her stories have been included in *The Best American Short Stories* and *The PEN/O. Henry Prize Stories*, as well as other anthologies.

STEPHANIE SOILEAU is a lecturer at Stanford University, where she was also a Truman Capote Fellow in the Wallace Stegner Fellowship Program. Her fiction has appeared in *Glimmer Train*, *Tin House*, *Gulf Coast*, *StoryQuarterly*, and *Nimrod*, and has been reprinted in three volumes of *New Stories from the South*.

BEN STROUD is the author of *Byzantium: Stories*. His fiction has appeared in *Harper's*, *One Story*, *Electric Literature*, *The Best American Mystery Stories*, and *New Stories from the South*, among other places. Originally from Texas, he currently lives in Ohio.

ANDREW TONKOVICH edits *Santa Monica Review* and hosts *Bibliocracy Radio* on KPFK in Southern California. Recent work appears in *Faultline*, the *Rattling Wall*, *Green Mountains Review*, and the *Los Angeles Review of Books*. He blogs about literary Orange County for *OC Weekly*. "Falling" appeared in *The Best American Nonrequired Reading 2013*.

SHAWN VESTAL is the author of *Godforsaken Idaho*, a collection of short stories. A newspaper columnist and graduate of Eastern Washington University's MFA program, he lives in Spokane, Washington, with his wife and son.

BRAD WATSON is the author of *Last Days of the Dog-Men*, *The Heaven of Mercury*, and *Aliens in the Prime of Their Lives*, in which "Alamo Plaza" appeared. The collection was awarded the Mississippi Institute of Arts and Letters Award and short-listed for the PEN/Faulkner Award for Fiction. Recently Watson received the Arts and Letters Award from the American Academy of Arts and Letters. He lives in Laramie, Wyoming, and teaches in the University of Wyoming MFA program in creative writing.

DOUGLAS WATSON is the author of a book of stories, *The Era of Not Quite*, and a novel, *A Moody Fellow Finds Love and Then Dies*. He lives in New York City.

KEVIN WILSON is the author of a novel, *The Family Fang*, and a story collection, *Tunneling to the Center of the Earth*, which received the Shirley Jackson Award. He lives in Sewanee, Tennessee, and is an assistant professor at The University of the South.

ACKNOWLEDGMENTS

"Hagar's Sons" from *God Bless America* by Steve Almond. Copyright © 2011 by Steve Almond. Originally published in *Ecotone* in 2008, vol. 4, nos. 1 & 2. Reprinted by permission of Lookout Books.

"The Blue Tree," copyright © 2012 by Rick Bass. Originally published in *Ecotone* vol. 7, no. 1.

"Candidate," copyright © 2007 by Karen E. Bender. Originally published in *Ecotone* vol. 2, no. 2, and reprinted in *New Stories from the South 2008: The Year's Best* (Algonquin Books).

"The Year of Silence" from *The View from the Seventh Layer* (Pantheon Books). Copyright © 2008 by Kevin Brockmeier. Originally published in *Ecotone* in 2007, vol. 3, no. 1, and reprinted in *The Best American Short Stories 2008* (Houghton Mifflin Harcourt). Reprinted by permission of Kevin Brockmeier.

"At the Cultural Ephemera Association National Conference," copyright © 2012 by Robert Olen Butler. Originally published in *Ecotone* vol. 7, no. 1.

"The Wreckers," copyright © 2009 by George Makana Clark. Originally published in *Ecotone* vol. 5, no. 1.

"Our Pointy Boots," copyright © 2008 by Brock Clarke. Originally published in *Ecotone* vol. 4, nos. 1 & 2, and reprinted in *The Pushcart Prize XXXIV: Best of the Small Presses* (Pushcart Press).

"Abundance," copyright © 2012 by Lauren Groff. Originally published in *Ecotone* vol. 7, no. 2. Reprinted by permission of Lauren Groff.

"Horse People" from *Horse People: Stories* (Louisiana State University Press). Copyright © 2013 by Cary Holladay. Originally published in *Ecotone* in 2008, vol. 4, nos. 1 & 2, and reprinted in *New Stories from the South 2009: The Year's Best* (Algonquin Books). Reprinted by permission of Cary Holladay.

"The Way You Hold Your Knife," copyright © 2011 by Rebecca Makkai. Originally published in *Ecotone* vol. 6, no. 2. Reprinted by permission of Rebecca Makkai.

"That Winter," copyright © 2010 by Miha Mazzini. Originally published in *Ecotone* vol. 5, no. 2, and reprinted in *The Pushcart Prize XXXVI: Best of the Small Presses* (Pushcart Press).

"The Junction" from *The Spot* by David Means. Copyright © 2010 by David Means. Originally published in *Ecotone* in 2010, vol. 5, no. 2, and reprinted in *The PEN/O. Henry Prize Stories 2011* (Random House). Reprinted by permission of Faber & Faber, Inc., an affiliate of Farrar, Straus & Giroux, LLC.

"Only Connect" from *Orientation and Other Stories* by Daniel Orozco. Copyright © 2011 by Daniel Orozco. Originally published in *Ecotone* in 2008, vol. 4, nos. 1 & 2. Reprinted by permission of Faber & Faber, Inc., an affiliate of Farrar, Straus & Giroux, LLC.

"What the Ax Forgets the Tree Remembers," copyright © 2012 by Edith Pearlman. Originally published in *Ecotone* vol. 8, no. 1.

"The Tree," copyright © 2009 by Benjamin Percy. Originally published in *Ecotone* vol. 5, no. 1.

"Burning Bright" from *Burning Bright: Stories* by Ron Rash (Ecco). Copyright © 2010 by Ron Rash. Originally published in *Ecotone* in 2008, vol. 4, nos. 1 & 2.

"Broadax Inc.," copyright © 2007 by Bill Roorbach. Originally published in *Ecotone* vol. 3, no. 1.

"Something Like the Resurrection," copyright © 2012 by Maggie Shipstead. Originally published in *Ecotone* vol. 7, no. 2.

"Leap" from *Alone With You* by Marisa Silver (Simon & Schuster). Copyright © 2010 by Marisa Silver. Originally published in *Ecotone* in 2010, vol. 5, no. 2.

"The Ranger Queen of Sulphur," copyright © 2011 by Stephanie Soileau. Originally published in *Ecotone* vol. 6, no. 2.

"The Traitor of Zion" from *Byzantium: Stories* by Ben Stroud (Graywolf Press). Copyright © 2013 by Ben Stroud. Originally published in *Ecotone* in 2010, vol. 6, no. 1.

"Falling," copyright © 2012 by Andrew Tonkovich. Originally published in *Ecotone* vol. 8, no. 1, and reprinted in *The Best American Nonrequired Reading 2013* (Houghton Mifflin Harcourt).

"Winter Elders" from *Godforsaken Idaho* by Shawn Vestal. Copyright © 2013 by Shawn Vestal. Published by Little A/New Harvest. All rights reserved. Originally published in *Ecotone* in 2013, vol. 8, no. 2.

"Alamo Plaza" from *Aliens in the Prime of Their Lives: Stories* by Brad Watson. Copyright © 2010 by Brad Watson. Used by permission of W. W. Norton & Company, Inc. Originally published in *Ecotone* in 2010, vol. 5, no. 2, and reprinted in *The PEN/O. Henry Prize Stories 2011* (Random House).

"New Animal" from *The Era of Not Quite*. Copyright © 2012 by Douglas Watson. Reprinted with the permission of The Permissions Company, Inc., on behalf of BOA Editions, Ltd., boaeditions.org. Originally published in *Ecotone* in 2012, vol. 8, no. 1.

"A Birth in the Woods," copyright © 2011 by Kevin Wilson. Originally published in *Ecotone* vol. 6, no. 2, and reprinted in *The PEN/O. Henry Prize Stories 2012* (Random House).

The Kierkegaard quotations in "New Animal" are taken from the 1849 essay "The Sickness Unto Death: A Christian Psychological Exposition for Upbuilding and Awakening," in *The Essential Kierkegaard*, edited by Howard V. Hong and Edna H. Hong (Princeton University Press, 2000), page 352.

Ecotone founding editor David Gessner and publisher Emily Louise Smith would like to thank the following current and former editors for their discerning taste and thoughtful stewardship of the fiction section over our first decade of publication:

Mike J. Bull, Nicola Derobertis-Theye, Ben George, Nina de Gramont, Kimi Faxon Hemingway, Lukis Kauffman, Anna Lena Phillips, Sumanth Prabhaker, Meg Reid, Rachel Richardson, Nick Roberts, Beth Staples, and Heather Wilson.